The Story of Our Life

Shari Low lives in Glasgow and writes
a weekly opinion column and Book Club
page for a well-known newspaper. She is
married to a very laid-back guy and has two
athletic teenage sons, who think she's fairly
embarrassing, except when they need a lift.

The Story of Our Life

Shari Low

a

First published as an ebook by Aria, an imprint of Head of Zeus, in 2016

First published in print in the UK by Aria in 2017

9 7 5 3 1 2 4 6 8

A catalogue record for this book is available from
the British Library.

ISBN (PBO): 9781786692450
ISBN (E): 9781784978242

Typeset by Adrian McLaughlin

Printed and bound in Great Britain by
CPI Group (UK) Ltd, Croydon CRO 4YY

Head of Zeus Ltd
First Floor East
5–8 Hardwick Street
London EC1R 4RG

WWW.HEADOFZEUS.COM

To J, C & B,
Everything Always.

And to Rosina B. Hill,
My wonderful Godmother,
Who has given me a lifetime of love...

I

Spring 2016

At the Church

Fifteen years ago, I walked up the same church aisle.

Back then, the first person I saw was Annie, my gloriously indomitable grandmother, in dramatic purple and a hat that resembled a frisbee, disguising her tears because she was born of a stoic generation that was disdainful about crying in public.

Next to my grandmother were my parents. My father, resplendent in his best morning suit and golfing tan, no doubt keen to get the formalities over with so he could squeeze in nine holes in before dinner. Meanwhile, the woman who gave birth to me was preening, loving the attention being mother of the bride brought her, while breezily overlooking the fact that she'd shown no interest whatsoever in her daughter's wedding. When I called her to tell her we'd set a date, she'd said, 'Oh right, Shauna. Let me write that down so I don't forget it. I think we were planning to be in Spain that weekend. I'll check my diary.' Still, she'd made it. My gain was the Marbella Golf Club's loss.

In the rows behind the star attractions, a sea of smiles beamed at us as we walked down the aisle. Steps behind me were my best friends, Lulu and Rosie, in matching pastel elegance. Was it okay to call them 'best friends' at our age? Did that belong back in the days of teenage territorialism? Okay, so my 'closest' friends, their grins masking hangovers that were crying out for a dark room and a box set of *Grey's Anatomy*.

Rosie, a hopeless romantic, had been on board with the wedding from the start, but Lulu had been resistant, listing all the reasons I should wait and keep my options open. I was only twenty-four. My catering company was growing and would demand lots of attention. I was an independent woman with a flat, a job I loved, a bank account that was (just) in the black. And besides, a piece of paper didn't matter to a relationship. Marriage was an outdated institution. Married women inevitably dumped their friends in favour of nights in, pandering to their men while gaining five pounds a month and neglecting their roots – hair, not ancestry.

Not for the first time, I ignored her.

And the reason was there in front of me. Colm. My gorgeous Colm. Standing there at the altar, in a suit that fitted him to perfection, showing not a trace of nerves. His expression radiated enjoyment, like this was a party he'd been looking forward to for ages and now he was thrilled it was starting.

I was too.

I wanted to dance towards him, sashay and pirouette into his arms, skip straight to the kissing and cheering part.

I saw flowers, and light and love. I saw promise. Commitment. Belonging. Delight. Contentment. Lust. Excitement. The realization of dreams. An incredible future.

I saw happy ever after. Until forever.

But that was then. Before everything happened. Before time, like a well-worn yet inevitable cliché, took its toll. Before my heart was broken. Before one of those closest friends betrayed me. Before my husband slept with another woman.

Before death.

Fifteen years ago, I walked up the aisle in white.

This time, I'm wearing black.

2

2001

When Shauna Met Colm...

If he had been ten minutes later we'd never have met.

The bar was getting too crowded and too loud, with the sound of smug, boorish after-work suits trying to outdo each other.

'Nailed six million, mate. The yen played a fucking blinder for me this week.'

'Not bad. Keep it up and you'll get to play with us in the big boy pool. My margin on pharmaceuticals this week is buying me a Porsche,' his buddy gloated, his repetitive nose-rubbing suggesting he'd been celebrating with pharmaceuticals of a different kind.

Their chronic wankery didn't detract from the fact that I loved this bar. The classic white colonial frontage sat on the bank of the Thames, supporting the huge wooden deck that overlooked the water and Richmond Bridge, only yards away to the left. Even on a chilly October evening, as we stood outside, getting jostled by the masses, there was something of a fifties romance about it.

We'd come here for celebration drinks with Vincent, a mate from college, who had decided to start up a corporate catering service on the other side of the city. He was now deep in conversation with a five foot ten Cindy Crawford lookalike who was eyeing him with such lust I expected her to unhinge her jaw and swallow him whole at any moment. Vincent had that effect on women. Except me. The dark-haired, chiselled jaw, brooding hunk thing wasn't my type so I found it amusing to watch as he... yep, there it was. Cindy reached up and kissed him, then he gave me a wave, blew me a kiss and the two of them disappeared out the door.

Not a bad idea. It was time to go home.

It had been a long week. My feet hurt. I'd had three hours sleep thanks to a delightfully wealthy Battersea housewife who'd booked me to prepare a banquet breakfast for a fundraiser, ignoring the fact that if they'd just gone for bacon butties the recipients of the charity would have been a few hundred pounds better off. Not that I was complaining. The wealthy-housewife market had been a fantastic source of income in the two years since I'd launched the company. When I say 'company', I mean me. And a van. My only other assets were boundless optimism, enthusiasm, and a small but growing customer base, so I was thankful for the work, even if it did mean that the aroma of eggs Benedict and smoked salmon blinis had followed me around all day like a sinister yet appetizing stalker.

The following morning, I had a children's party for thirty

twelve-year-olds in Balham and those chicken goujons weren't going to prepare themselves.

My bed was calling me until Lulu, in typical fashion, changed my plans.

'Shauna, I'll be five minutes. Cover for me if Dan arrives,' Lulu hissed, before punctuating the request with a kiss on the cheek that definitely constituted coercion, possibly even conspiracy, with an added twist of emotional blackmail.

Every guy in the bar watched her as she wiggled her way past them. Captivating. Mesmerizing. I was probably the only one who noticed that she was actually following a tall, gym-formed Australian she'd been subtly flirting with across the bar all night.

A mental image of my bed faded. In Lulu's world, five minutes could mean thirty, or longer. She'd once left me holding her drink while she popped out of a bar for a cigarette with a ski instructor, and called me the next day from Gstaad.

'Bloody outrageous!' I added to the list of descriptive terms for the Jessica Rabbit redhead who was heading to the back of the restaurant.

'Who's outrageous?' Rosie asked, breaking off from the conversation she'd been having for the last fifteen minutes with Paul, the mature student. This was the third time she'd invited him to join us for a drink, and there was a spark there, but he was a very measured, analytical academic who was studying geology, or psychology, or zoology, or one of the ologies, so the spark was taking a long time to ignite into anything more than deep discussions about... actually, I had no idea what they were talking about.

6

'Our friend,' I whispered, smiling as I gestured to the departing wiggle. 'Remind me to kill her at some point. I promise I'll make it painless.'

'I'd help dispose of the body but I'm a bit preoccupied,' she replied, making sure Paul was out of earshot. I hoped he was good enough for her.

If ever there was an illustration of how there was no equality or fairness in the distribution of confidence and self-assurance, my friends were it. Lulu killed at life, at fun, at demanding attention and getting it. She took risks, and she grabbed what she wanted. Rosie, on the other hand, the eternal people-pleaser, quirky, with a huge heart, lived in hope of love and adoration finding her.

The restaurant was filling up now, the noise level increasing as Toploader finished 'Dancing In The Moonlight' and handed over to Kylie who was, for some inexplicable reason, 'Spinning Around'.

'Bugger, there's Dan,' Rosie whispered, urgently.

Of course it was. Because, hey, the Gods of Reckless Friends loved this kind of shit. I should have left already, made the escape sooner, before the devastatingly handsome boyfriend of my darling friend was strolling towards me, while aforementioned darling friend was outside, undoubtedly doing something immoral, possibly illegal, definitely wild, with a tattooed Australian. Instead, I was about to give a performance that would win me an Oscar for 'Best Liar In A Friendship Situation'.

'Hey girls,' he greeted us, with a kiss on each cheek. I'd always thought that Dan Channing was one of those enigmas, people who looked like they were something other than what they actually were. He looked like a square-jawed, impossibly handsome male model or an actor. Or at the very least, one of those firemen who strips naked with a strategically positioned hose in a Christmas calendar. But no, he was in sales of something I wasn't exactly sure about. Car parts? Mechanical supplies? Anyway, he managed a sales team that travelled around garages flogging some vital component of a vehicular nature.

'Where's Lulu?' was of course his first question.

'In the ladies',' I replied. 'She might be a while. Think the cystitis is playing up.'

A mischievous lie but I couldn't resist laying the seeds for a discussion that would make Lulu squirm. It was less than she deserved for putting me on the spot. My grin was quickly accompanied by a scarlet flush of the face, as he stepped to the side to reveal the curious gaze of green eyes of a tall, cute guy standing right behind him. 'Guys, this is Colm. Colm, meet Rosie, Paul, and the one that's talking about cystitis is Shauna.'

Ah, a resounding moment of dignity, one which Colm took in his stride by reaching out to shake my hand, saying, 'Pleased to meet you. And just to get it out of the way, I have never suffered from cystitis.'

Yes, those were the first words the love of my life ever spoke to me. It wasn't exactly Mills & Boon, but that didn't matter. I've no idea whether it was the soft Irish accent, the rapid humour, or the way he smiled the most open smile I'd ever seen, but right there and then I decided he was mine.

3

2015

Shauna and Life Before Everything Changed...

We were a few minutes away from Lulu and Dan's house and he still hadn't asked me. Maybe he wouldn't. I'd noticed that lately it was sometimes just taken for granted, a raised eyebrow of question in my direction when he opened the first beer. Invariably, I'd nod, almost imperceptibly, using fourteen-years-married coupledom telepathy to convey my agreement. Okay, you drink, and I'll drive home. I didn't mind, but sometimes it would be nice to be asked.

'You okay?' Colm asked, taking one hand off the wheel to put it on mine.

'I'm fine, just tired. Been a long week.'

A definite understatement, yet I bit my tongue, determined not to do that thing where I listed all the tasks I'd carried out that week and pointed out that he was probably oblivious to them all. You know the one... 'I worked six ten-hour days, took our daughter to school every day, ferried her to five after-school clubs, did two lots of baking for school functions, cleaned the house, organized flowers for your mother's birthday, booked the car in for a service, spent hours researching a holiday that meets the needs of everyone in the family, cleaned the house from top to bottom, organized a sitter for tonight, cooked a meal in advance and left it ready for the sitter and our daughter to eat later, then rushed upstairs and got ready in five minutes, throwing on the first decent thing I could find, and slapping on a quick make-up job in the car, so YES, IT'S SUNDAY NIGHT AND I AM BLOODY KNACKERED.'

Instead I just turned my attention back to staying awake while letting his touch soothe me out of 'harassed working mother and wife mode' and into me mode. Just Shauna. If I really tried, I might even summon up sociable Shauna, and enjoy our first night out in ages.

I felt myself responding to him, stroking my thumb against his palm, as I glanced at him and realized he looked tired too.

'I think it's time to have the chat again,' I told him amiably, as I leaned my head back against the cream leather headrest, a motion that took my ponytail to a whole new level of messiness. With a bit of luck it would at least camouflage the fact that highlights for my dark blonde hair were long overdue.

Colm nodded. 'The one where we say we have a crap work/life balance and we need to redress it?'

'Yep, that's the one.'

How often? Once a month? More? Probably as often as

work allowed – and that was the problem. We'd slipped into 'work to live' instead of 'live to work'. We had to sort it out. Definitely. And we would. When we had a spare five minutes to breathe. I mentally added it to the to-do list. Defrost fridge. Arrange new school uniforms. Address roots. Have life-defining conversation with husband.

We pulled into the drive and I grabbed the bottle of Prosecco and huge tub of eighties retro sweets – Lulu and Dan's respective favourites – then headed up the path. Lulu and Dan's home had a façade that belonged on a Christmas card. Left to them by Dan's grandparents, the four-storey, red-brick Georgian house overlooking Richmond Green had the beautiful white panelled windows that were typical of the era. The stairs up to the front door were bordered by wrought iron, and ivy wound its way around the red gloss door. Lulu and Dan lived on the ground floor and basement, with the upper levels split into two more apartments, which they rented out to give them a healthy monthly income. Dan had been meticulous in retaining as many of the original features as possible, so it still had the original tile floors, high ceilings and ornate cornicing. It was gorgeous, which made Lulu's ongoing mission to persuade Dan to sell up and move to a modern, eye-wateringly expensive, high-tech shoebox down at the river so much more perplexing.

Exhaling, I slapped on a smile and shook off my fugue just as the door was answered by a giggling Lulu.

'Come in, come in! Hey gorgeous, how are you?' That was directed at Colm, not me, but it did make me laugh. Lulu, the irrepressible flirt, had barely changed in personality or looks in the two decades I'd known her. Eternally wild and reckless, she still had the long flowing red hair, the ridiculously curvy shape, the wide eyes that were designed for mischief and her alabaster skin was almost unlined despite the fact that, let's face it, forty was on the horizon, ready to ambush us.

'I suppose you're not bad either,' she offered, when she prised herself away and hugged me next.

'I could kill you with one squeeze,' I told her in my best serial killer tone.

'Please do, it'll save me from Dan,' she countered. I was probably the only person who would pick it up, but it was there, the undertone of truth beneath the jocular barb. Oh God, not again.

'Hey, we're matching!' she observed, pointing to my black jumpsuit, with the crossover front, cinched waist, and mildly protruding shoulder pads, a style match to her red version of the same look. Gotta love cyclical fashion trends. If the eighties were wrong, I didn't want to be right.

'Jesus, we look like a Nolans tribute act,' I told her truthfully. 'If either of us could hold a tune, there could be a new career option here.'

'Fuck it, I need a new job. Make it happen and I'll mime,' she retorted. There it was again. Lulu had worked with Dan for the last six years, ever since he and Colm had gone out on their own and set up their management and training consultancy. In the early days, Lulu did the books, typed up the invoices and generally took care of everything that needed to happen to let Dan and Colm go out there and earn. That was then. Now the business was a bit more established, with a steady income, she'd taken the first opportunity to reduce her workload. With no mortgage and no kids, and a firm belief that there was more to life than slogging in an office during her prime years (her words, not mine), she cut back to a couple of days a week doing the paperwork and spent the others in a function she called 'networking and raising the company profile'. Others would call it 'shopping and doing lunch'. The reality was that it left Lulu with far too much time on her hands – a dangerous situation for someone with the attention span of a fairground fish. When it came to Lulu, too much time led to boredom, which led to a need for excitement, which led to trouble, usually for either her bank balance or her marriage. Or both.

We headed through to the open-plan kitchen and dining area at the back of the house, which had been extended to add a lounge area too. It was the only room that was thoroughly modern, with its white walls, cream travertine floor and glass doors that spanned the whole of the back wall, letting the solar lights of the garden create little spheres of gold that looked like floating stars.

The others were already sitting round the dining table. Rosie was the first to welcome us. 'Hello lovelies,' she said, her beaming smile as wide as the large goblet of red wine she held aloft in greeting. I'd always thought Rosie was the personification of a Betty Boop cartoon, with her short black pixie cut, her huge blue eyes, and eyelashes that could sweep floors. Not much over five feet, she celebrated her curviness in fifties-style clothes that made her stand out for all the right reasons. Tonight she was in a white low-cut top, with red polka dots that matched the scarlet of her lips, with a co-ordinating scarf tied around her neck.

In my standard colour palate of funereal black, I suddenly

felt resoundingly bland compared to my technicolor friends. More stuff for my to-do list. Must wear colour. Must take longer than five minutes to apply make-up.

I did the rounds of hello's – Rosie first, then her boyfriend, Jack, a life coach who sat somewhere between hipster trendy and those guys who wore man buns and carried yoga mats. They'd met in Rosie's café, and despite the fact that he could be a little studious and earnest, we were all hoping for Rosie's sake that this one was a keeper. Six months in, the easy vibe that flicked between them suggested that he could be. However, we'd been here before so we weren't buying hats just yet.

After hugging Dan, I slid into the empty seat next to him. Over at the marble island, Colm flipped open a bottle of beer. Ah, there it was, as predicted – the raised eyebrow of enquiry.

'Honey, what would you like to drink?' Colm asked.

'Vodka, straight,' I answered, and watched as a momentary flicker of surprise was replaced by a grin.

'Or maybe I'll just stick with water,' I said, smiling. In truth, I didn't really mind. Beth had ballet in the morning and a crowd of five-year-olds wasn't something I wanted to negotiate with a hangover.

Next to me, Dan immediately lifted a large jug from the centre of the table and poured iced water into the wine glass in front of me.

'You didn't bring Beth?' Rosie asked, with a hint of disappointment.

There were many things I adored about my friends, and one of them was that they treated Beth as a communal child, not a hindrance or an irritant to spoil their sophisticated chat. (Not that we ever actually had any sophisticated chat, but that was beside the point.) So many of these dinners ended with Rosie on the floor with Beth, doing a jigsaw or channelling Little Mix on the karaoke, the two of them laughing helplessly. Jack, whose sole experience with children extended to informing Kensington mothers that their family life was encroaching on their opportunities for meditation and growth, didn't ever give a hint that he minded his evening being interrupted by an impromptu game of rounders in the garden. Even Lulu and Dan, who had no plans to add to their family, loved having Beth around, mostly, I suspect, because they got all the fun but didn't have to deal with the responsibilities.

'Cinema and sleepover with one of her classmates,' I answered, before the bang of the oven door diverted our attention to Lulu. 'Something smells great,' I told her.

'Lasagne, garlic bread, salad,' she replied. 'I'm not winning any prizes for originality over here.'

I loved the fact that it clearly didn't bother her in the least. Tonight, like all our gatherings, was about chat and catching up. The food was way down the priority list, and given that I'd spent a long week cooking for other people, I was just happy that it wasn't me over there using a cheese grater to slice cucumber into a bowl of leaves.

Colm joined us at the table and immediately turned to Dan. 'How'd you get on with the Bracal Tech pitch prep today?'

'Hey, hey, hey! No work talk at the table please!' I interjected. It was the one overriding rule, set down about a year after the guys first went into business together. 'Lulu has salad tongs and she's not afraid to use them,' I added, gesturing to Lu, who stood one hand on hip, raised tongs in the other.

Whilst the others were laughing, it took me a moment to realize that, beside me, Dan was uncharacteristically straight-faced.

His demeanour didn't change too much throughout dinner. On the surface, the conversations were as convivial as ever but I sensed an undertone. I decided not to question it. Nothing good could come of probing.

Instead, I had a couple of chunks of garlic bread and let the company of my closest friends shake off the lethargy that had been seeping into my bones earlier.

Colm looked like it was having the same effect on him. The dark shadows under his sea-green eyes were still there, but his crooked grin and the remains of a garden tan saved the day. Right now he was telling some story about a buff, Lycra-clad guy in the gym who'd hit on him the week before, and the others found it hugely amusing that he'd been so concerned about hurting the guy's feelings that he'd let him down gently then taken him for a coffee. That was Colm. The dark brown hair might now be flecked with grey, and there may be a few grooves on his face that weren't there fourteen years ago, but he was still the loveliest, funniest guy I'd ever known.

Next to me, it was obvious that Dan still wasn't feeling the same happy effects of the gathering. In my peripheral vision, I could see his jaw was clenched now, his knuckles pale as they squeezed his glass. A quick glance from Rosie told me she'd noticed too. It wasn't like him. Sure, he could be impatient and was sometimes easily riled, but in this environment, surrounded by friends, he would usually be chilled out and regaling us with stories of his week.

Rosie had obviously decided to steer the conversation to a topic that would cheer him up. 'So, guys,' she said breezily, directing the conversation at Lulu and Dan, 'I was thinking, we should do something for your wedding anniversary next month.'

In a perfectly executed act of dark comic timing, Lulu, who was clearing the table, picked that moment to drop the salad bowl, laying a carpet of withered, leftover rocket across the floor tiles.

'Fuck,' she blurted.

I jumped up to help her clear it up, but ended up doing it myself as she'd already moved back to the centre island and was decanting several inches of red wine into her glass, her sociable joviality suddenly replaced by a silence and barely supressed irritation.

'Let's wait and see if we make it that long, shall we?' Dan replied tersely, removing any semblance of forced joviality from the group.

Oh God. I suddenly wished Beth was here to divert us all with an innocent game. I spy with my little eye, something beginning with an excruciating silence and a murderous glare-off between Lu and Dan.

Eventually, Lulu was the first to blink.

'You really want to do this now?' she asked, her exasperation tempered with something that sounded like defiance. It was classic Lulu. When under attack, go on the offensive. When irritated, scared or just bloody fed up, steam right through those feelings with a forceful blend of rebellion and boldness, then hope for the best.

'Might as well,' Dan shrugged, meeting her gaze. 'Do you want to go phone your boyfriend first and ask his permission?'

Suddenly my weariness had returned and I could see it settling on Colm and Rosie too. Jack was too new to the group to understand the dynamics and history of this situation.

Actually, I was a founding member and struggled to understand it too. Throughout their entire relationship Lulu and Dan had adhered to their own set of rules and they were written in a language that no one else understood. However, even when they were in one of their frequent rocky patches, they generally kept things convivial when we were together as a group, so whatever was going on now was obviously serious. One thing I absolutely did know for sure was that the worst thing we could do was intervene. I really wished I wasn't driving. A cocktail would have been much appreciated right about now.

Lulu took a gulp of wine then set it down on the worktop with the slow, definite movement of someone who was trying desperately to stay in control.

She barely skipped a beat before she spoke. 'I'm not sure of the number. Perhaps your girlfriend might look it up for me?'

'If it salves your conscience to think that, you go ahead,' Dan retorted, his voice low with anger. 'But we both know this one is on you. Why don't you tell our friends about the afternoons at the Richmond Hotel?'

'You bastard,' Lulu hissed. 'You had me followed?'

'Didn't need to. You used your credit card.'

'For personal training sessions! And I can't believe you checked my card. How low can you go?' Lulu retorted.

'Not as low as you, it would seem. I checked. You're not a client there. So go on, come up with as many excuses and explanations as you want… or you could save us all the trouble and be honest. Admit it. You did it again. Who is it this time? The guy who works in the gym? The local estate agent? Or are you going for a variety and spreading it around?'

My previous resolve to stay out of it crumbled in the face of Dan's fury and the sure knowledge that I had to try to cut this off before it got out of control.

'Dan, don't,' I cautioned gently. I wasn't taking sides, but I couldn't let this escalate because I instinctively knew it wasn't heading to any kind of happy place. I had no clue as to Dan's culpability in whatever battle they were having, but I recognized Lulu's expression. It was the same combination of guilt and determination not to cry that she'd shown in every sticky moment in her life, especially when the problem was of her own doing.

Rosie was watching it all, mouth agape. Colm was rubbing his temples with his fingers. And Jack was studying the empty plate in front of him with intent fascination.

'Look, we should go,' Colm said. 'It's getting late and my head is banging.' He didn't add, 'And I can't do this again,' but I knew that was what he was thinking. How many times had we been through this? Three? Four?

Lulu and Dan had the most tempestuous relationship

I'd ever known. Her relentless need to flirt and hedonistic tendencies had been a constant source of discord in the early days, but it was her need for thrills that would surely break them. There had been two affairs that I knew of on her side, one on Dan's. They were a couple who needed constant drama, constant excitement, to survive. I couldn't comprehend it when they were dating and I couldn't comprehend it now, but I knew the best way to deal with it was to bail out until they'd sorted it out themselves. Taking sides would be a fatal friendship mistake, because when they made up – which they had done on every previous occasion – you didn't want to be the one who'd bad-mouthed the other.

Rosie was already on her feet. She was no pushover, but she hated confrontation, avoided disharmony at all costs and, like me, knew that this was all going to get messy and the best thing to do when Lulu was escalating to battle stations was to evacuate the area. 'I think so too. Jack?' She didn't need to ask twice.

Jack was on his feet and already heading for the door, waving as he went. 'Er, thanks for dinner. It was lovely.'

I winced in pity for him. Clearly he was in the 99.9 per cent of the population who would find this deeply uncomfortable.

Dan sat staring morosely at the table, while Lulu followed us out, handing over our coats from the vintage stand at the door.

I slipped mine on. 'You okay? Why don't you come stay at our house tonight?' Guilty or innocent, at fault or not, I wanted to give her a way out of tonight's shitstorm.

She shook her head. 'Not tonight, but I might take you up

on it tomorrow night. I'm leaving him, Shauna. I can't do this any more.'

Droplets of tears gathered on her lower lids and she blinked them away. To be honest, I didn't take her vow particularly seriously. The number of times she'd threatened to leave him over the last fifteen years stretched to double figures.

I gave her a hug. 'Let's talk about it tomorrow. If you change your mind about staying, come over any time during the night. Just use your key and crash in the spare room.'

Her squeeze was cutting off oxygen to my windpipe.

'Thanks babe.'

Beside me, Colm still hadn't said anything, and he remained silent as he headed out the door and back to the car. Only when I'd switched on the engine did he finally speak. I wished he hadn't.

'I don't know how you can stand by her when she does this. Come on, Shauna, she's a nightmare.'

'Hey, Dan did it too.'

'Only after he'd put up with her humiliating him for years. Not the same.'

'How isn't it? You can't judge her, Colm. You don't know the dynamics of their marriage and what makes it work. Or not,' I finished ruefully.

'Maybe not, but I know enough to be bloody sick of the way she treats him. Dan works damn hard to give her a great life. Why can't that be enough for her?'

I sighed and leaned back against the headrest as I steered on to George Street, heading towards Richmond Bridge. Brilliant. My friend was allegedly having an affair, yet it was Colm and I who were now fighting.

It didn't help that Lu was the one person who could press Colm's easy-going, live and let live buttons. In the years since that first night at the bar in Richmond Bridge, they'd developed a relationship that had almost a sibling dynamic. They loved each other, but Colm didn't shy away from calling her out or standing his ground with her. When she was wrong, he was direct and honest with her, even when she didn't want to hear it. When she was right, he'd be the first person to step in to help or back her up. She drove him crazy, yet two minutes later they'd be buckled in mutual hilarity at some inside joke.

But hilarity was in short supply tonight.

In my peripheral vision I could see that he had his eyes squeezed shut, and he was rubbing the bridge of his nose.

'Are you okay?' I asked, more to break the atmosphere of conflict than anything else. I wasn't big on confrontation avoidance, but tonight I was so damn tired I was making an exception.

'Thumping head,' he said, surprising me. I'd thought it was just an excuse to leave when he'd mentioned it earlier.

'I've got some paracetamol in my bag,' I told him, gesturing to the handbag in his footwell.

I thought he was leaning down towards it, but then realized that his hand had veered over towards the radio and was twisting the volume dial. It wasn't on, so his actions had no effect.

'What are you doing?' I asked, puzzled.

'Trying to switch this damn thing off.'

'Colm, it's not on.'

'So what's the noise?'

Was this a joke that I wasn't getting?

'What noise?'

He sat back in the seat. 'You can't hear that?'

'What?'

'It's like... I don't know. Radio interference. Like a crackling sound.'

I'd have blamed the alcohol, but I knew he'd only had a couple of beers. And not only was the radio off, but there was no other noise to be heard. Had to be a joke.

'Okay, skip to the punchline,' I told him lightly, grateful that he wanted to add a bit of levity and salvage the mood of the night.

'Shauna, I swear I'm not kidding around. You honestly can't hear anything?'

'No.' I pulled up at a set of traffic lights on red, and turned to him to see a mask of confusion and uncertainty. This no longer felt like much of a joke.

'This is so weird,' he said quietly.

'Has it happened before?' I asked.

'Couple of times. Think it used to happen to my mum, though. Migraines.'

'Yeah, migraines can have all kinds of weird symptoms,' I said. 'Couple of painkillers and a good night's sleep and you'll be fine.'

The lights turned to green and I pulled away, trying to ignore the creeping unease that was infiltrating my nerve endings.

I should have paid attention.

4

2001

When Colm Met Shauna...

Crash. Bang. Holy crap.

I'm not one for romantic words or any of that kind of nonsense, but I'm fairly sure that was a fair account of the stuff that was going on in my head the first time I saw her.

Dan had dragged me out for a pint, to – as he said – stop me being the kind of prick who got pissed on a Friday night and ended up shagging the girl I'd just broken up with. Or the wife I'd been married to for six years.

I appreciated his point, but I had no worries on that score. Jess and I had finalized our divorce a month before and I had no intention of going back there. None at all.

In fact, if there was a stray band of celibate monks roaming the streets of London that night there was a fair chance I'd be up for joining, as long as they had beer on tap, a pool table and a subscription to Sky Sports.

Still, Dan was the guy on the sales team who was always up for a laugh, always the life and soul of the party, and right now I could do with a bit of nonsense. I was divorced, not dead.

I'd envisaged a night in the city centre; maybe hit a couple of clubs. Did people even say 'hit' a club any more? My grasp of trendy vernacular was slim, since I'd settled for married life in a Victorian terrace in the not-as-posh end of Notting Hill. Jesus, just past mid-twenties and I was already out of touch. Probably just best settle for a few pints and keep my mouth shut if anyone under twenty-five was in hearing distance.

Anyway, seemed that Dan had a different idea of a night on the town, dragging me way out to Richmond, because his latest girlfriend was out there. Brilliant. First night out in years and I was going to play third wheel to a work colleague and a woman he described as '100 per cent babe'. Again, Jesus. I'd already decided that if she was twenty-two and took the piss out of my dated chat, I was bailing and heading home.

My mind changed the minute I saw Shauna. I don't go for all of that 'love at first sight' rubbish, but there was something about the combination of the messy blonde hair, the cute freckles and the completely contagious smile that made me want to just stand there, staring like a lemon. It was a special person that could open a discussion with cystitis and still come over as adorable.

There was some kind of row between Dan and his girlfriend, Lulu, but to be honest, it didn't matter to us. Shauna and I started talking and ended up being the last two people still standing, huddled together so tightly that we didn't care that the temperatures had dipped to bollock-shrinking cold. No uncomfortable silences. No awkward comments that betrayed the fact this was the first time I'd chatted up a girl in years. I don't even remember anyone else leaving.

When the bar staff got fed up of sweeping around us, we finally left, and I walked her home, over Richmond Bridge, to her flat a few streets away on the Twickenham side. She invited me in, making shushing gestures so that we wouldn't wake her flatmate, and then, with cups of coffee in our hands, we headed to the tiny concrete balcony off her kitchen.

This was all new. The girl, being in someone's flat, and sure, I was pretty much out of my depth, but I figured if I could just keep her talking there was less of a chance she'd toss me out or – worse – fall asleep in my scintillating company.

'So you've never been married?' I asked her, really hoping the answer was no – and not just because I wanted to check that some bloke wasn't going to storm in and lamp me at any moment. I'd never been much of a fighter.

She shook her head, making even more wavy blonde curls collapse out of her hair. 'I was engaged,' she admitted, almost sheepishly. 'We broke up a year ago.'

'Am I allowed to ask why, or is that too forward?'

Her laugh was low and raspy after a night of shouting to each other to be heard over the riot of sound in the pub. 'You're sitting on my balcony in the middle of the night. I think we can take "too forward" off the table.' She took another sip of her coffee. 'It just didn't work out. Realized

I'm a bit of a commitment-phobe. The thought of the whole "one person forever" thing makes me uneasy. I change my mind about the wallpaper in the hall every six months. Clearly I have long-term-commitment issues.'

She was smiling, but even at my non-perceptive best, I could see there was a chink of sadness in her smile.

'What about you?' she asked.

Ouch. I'd led the way straight into that one. Twenty-seven and already one failed marriage under my belt. Wasn't the best reference, was it?

She mistook my hesitation for something else and looked searchingly at my left hand. 'Oh shit, tell me you're not married. I should probably have checked that before I asked you back here.'

I shook my head. 'Nope, not married.'

'Oh thank God.'

The sensible part of me was demanding that I leave it at that. I could fill in more details later, when we knew each other better. Start slow. Take it easy. Not too much too soon. Unfortunately, the sensible part of me wasn't having much of an influence on what was actually coming out of my mouth.

'But I was. I'm divorced. It was all finalized a month ago.'

She was silent for a few seconds and I mentally gave myself a good boot in the defrosted bollocks. Score zero for honesty. She was bound to want shot of me now. Who needed the hassle of being the person who picked up the pieces after a divorce?

I made one last bid for clarification. 'Look, I know that's not long ago, but I'm not an emotional disaster. The divorce was definitely for the best.'

That was true.

'And there are absolutely no regrets, and it wasn't a messy break-up.'

That wasn't true, but hey, cut a guy a break.

'So...'

I braced myself for 'it's been nice meeting you and show yourself out'.

'...Are you sworn off marriage for life?'

Oh God, here we go again. Truth or not? Truth or not?

'Pretty much,' I admitted. Truth.

She looked over and her blue eyes met mine as she laughed. 'Then I think we'll get on great.'

I wasn't sure what had just happened but I wasn't on my way out the door so I was going with it. She disappeared into the kitchen and came back out with a coffee pot and refilled our mugs. Right, no more revelations. Everything else could wait until I'd succeeded in not fucking up, and she'd agreed to see me again.

I changed the subject. 'So what made you start your own business?'

She shrugged. 'Just wanted to run my own life. It's a kind of loose ten-year plan – slog to build up the business now, so that I can bring in other people to run it if I suddenly wake up one morning and decide to travel, or have a family, or maybe join a cult. You know, the usual stuff. I don't ever want to be dependent on someone else or end up being one of those women who are totally exhausted because they're juggling high-pressure jobs, long hours and kids.'

Alarm bells rang. This girl was way too smart and sorted for me. I'd never met someone with a life plan. I had to get one of those, but in the meantime, I pulled every amusing story out of my past and hoped I could distract her from my lack of focus and depth with nonsense. It seemed to work. I've no idea how much longer it was when she gestured skywards.

'First plane of the day. I love watching them come in. Like shooting stars coming to land.'

I looked up to see soundless flashing orange lights crossing the sky and realized we were underneath the flight path for Heathrow. Against the backdrop of the sun coming up, and if you ignored the sight of all the bins on the ground below, this felt like the perfect place to be.

After being with the same person for years, I was way out of practice with this stuff, but I was pretty sure this was one of those moments in which I could do what I'd been wanting to do all night.

I bottled out and went for clarification first. 'So I really want to lean over and kiss you and I'm just checking that would be okay with you?'

'Did your wife divorce you for lack of romance?' Shauna asked, eyebrow raised, cheeky smile on her face.

'Nope, it was because she was intimidated by my stunning good looks,' I joked back

'Ah, I can see why that would be a problem.' Her expression was completely deadpan, which had the opposite effect on me and I creased up laughing, only stopping when I realized that she was on her feet. She took a couple of steps towards me, then twisted and sat on my knee, before leaning down and kissing me. That answered my question, then.

I'd love to say it was the most romantic moment of my

life. It absolutely could have been – if the rickety wooden chair beneath us hadn't chosen that very moment to commit chair suicide, and crumble to the ground, taking us with it.

We'd already ascertained that I wasn't gifted in the areas of romance or suave moves. But as we lay there, laughing while waiting for the pain receptors to deliver the bad news, I couldn't help thinking that there was no way any of those hundreds of people flying above us had ever had a moment as brilliant as this.

5
2015

Shauna and the Self-diagnosis

'So have you heard from her today?' Rosie asked, her voice echoing from the depths of my fridge. Before I could answer she emerged clutching a strawberry yoghurt, then headed to the cutlery drawer for a spoon. Today she was wearing a forties-style pink tea-dress, with a short red cardigan and navy kitten heels. It should have been all wrong and yet it looked great – a very glam contrast to my old jeans, grey gym T-shirt, bare feet look of zero grooming.

'No, nothing. I called but she didn't pick up and I texted her a couple of times but no reply. She doesn't make it easy for herself, does she?'

'Never,' Rosie agreed. 'She'd be great at providing storylines for soap operas though.'

'You're right. Do you think Dan has an evil twin he can produce at short notice?'

On the surface of it, it probably seemed like we were

being unkindly blasé about our best friend's marital woes, but in our defence, we'd been here so many times before we were probably just slightly inured to the situation.

'So how's the romance of the year coming along then?' I asked, while folding the pile of towels I'd just dragged out of the washing machine.

'If I say it's great, do you think I'll jinx it?' Rosie asked.

'Definitely not.' Or at least I hoped not. I was cautiously optimistic and hopeful that Jack would prove to be the guy Rosie had been waiting for, the one she would settle down with, who'd give her everything she deserved.

'In that case, it's great. Like, strangely so. I keep waiting for the hitch. You know, the "I've got a criminal record" convo, or the "I'm only going out with you so that I can scam your bank account and leave you destitute" one. I've seen them all on *Jeremy Kyle*.'

'Rosie, Jack's a life coach from Kew. I've never seen *Jeremy Kyle*, but I've watched every episode of *CSI* and I can tell you life coaches from Kew are not the usual demographic for serial killers and scammers,' I said over the top of a huge navy bath sheet. 'Since when did you become cynical and jaded?' I paused in a moment of realization. 'That should be Lu and I's nickname. Cynical and Jaded.'

Rosie laughed. 'Years of defeat have worn me down. It's a battlefield out there. Anyway, like I say, Jack has passed all the tests so far. Own hair, own teeth, a real job.'

I took her checklist a little further. 'No porn addiction or previous restraining orders? And did you google him and check there are no images of his penis anywhere online?'

'I did. No penis pictures. And he's lasted six months so

far, so he's obviously not just after random hook-ups. With all that and a pulse and no plans to take off in the near future, he's practically perfect.'

It was great to see her so happy. I was a big believer that no woman needed a man to define who she was. A few of my friends were single by choice and loving the lifestyle and freedom that gave them, but Rosie wasn't one of them. She would never take the easy way out and settle with the wrong man, but she definitely wanted to meet someone who would stick around. She'd had a rough run of luck. Over the last two decades there had been many relationships, each one self-destructing around the twenty-four-month mark. The two-year curse, she called it. There was Mark, who decided to go off trekking in South China to find himself. Zak, the roadie, who'd got a job as a tour manager for a band and had never been seen again. Jason and Colin, who both called it a day because they weren't ready to commit. And who was that guy she was seeing when I met Colm? It took me a moment. Paul. Yep, that was it. He moved north to work in a zoo and Rosie had decided he loved wildlife more than he loved her. She always chose guys who were, like her, a little bohemian, then was surprised when they went off and did something... well, *bohemian*.

Touch wood, Jack, the life coach, seemed like he might have staying power. Even if Colm claimed it was a whole load of 'psychobabble crap', and he did give me a slightly creepy feeling that he was analysing me and planning a schedule of improvements every time we spoke.

Rosie had met Jack when he popped into her café for morning coffee. After a decade of temping and saving her cash while she tried to decide what she wanted to do with her life, she'd finally stumbled on a tiny café that was closing down just off Chiswick High Road. In an inspired moment of spontaneity, she'd rented it, before going on to refurbish and reopen it as a forties retro café called Doris's Day. It was all doilies, big-band music and tables that looked like they belonged in your granny's front room, and while it was never going to make her a fortune, it was doing well and she loved it. If things worked out with Jack, then her life would be pretty close to perfect and I'd be thrilled for her – just as long as she still found time to come sit here in my kitchen and discuss life's joys and stresses. And Lulu.

The banging of the door announced a new arrival and, checking the clock, I realized it was too early for Colm. He was over in Canary Wharf running a training course for a software company today and I didn't expect him home before 6 p.m.

My money was on Lulu, but it was Dan who walked in the kitchen door, accompanied by a fairly large holdall. This couldn't be good.

He opened with a rueful, 'Hi.'

Beth chose that moment to pop her head through from the dining room, her huge messy mass of blonde curls appearing a couple of seconds before the rest of her. 'Uncle Dan!' she bellowed, running towards him and jumping just in time for him to catch her and swing her round. Colm aside, Dan was her very favourite man.

I waited until she was back on the floor. 'Right, honey, off and finish your dinner, then it's bath time.'

'I'm getting to eat my dinner next door!' she announced

to Dan, like it was a proper achievement. Which, in her world, it was. I usually insisted we all ate at the table but had decided that censoring the conversation with Rosie would be too difficult after last night's events. At five, Beth was probably too young to learn the words, 'affair', 'infidelity' and 'betrayal', so her favourite sausage and spinach pasta while watching *Frozen* won – or saved – the day, especially now that her favourite uncle had wandered in with the weight of the world on his shoulders.

She beetled back off humming 'Let It Go', the song from the movie that she chirped on a repetitive loop all day long.

There was a highly pregnant, slightly uncomfortable pause before I gestured to Dan's huge bag. 'Is Lulu in there?'

He at least managed to muster something approaching a smile as he sat down across from Rosie at the table. There were lines of weariness etched into his handsome face. I wanted to help. I may have known Lulu for longer, but my loyalties were split, because I loved Dan too. I automatically poured him a coffee from the pot that was permanently brewing on my kitchen worktop. My whole adult life had been conducted to the aroma of medium roast.

'I was tempted, but no. Look, I know it's an imposition but...'

'It's fine. You can stay. You don't need to ask.' Over the years he'd crashed here many times after fights and fall-outs. I decided not to acknowledge that this time felt a lot more serious.

A few of his lines eased as relief took over. 'Thanks, Shauna. We can't even be in the same bloody house together. It's done this time. I'm seeing the lawyers on Friday.'

Rosie leaned over and rested her hand on his. 'Are you sure? Maybe it's a mistake, or a...'

She stopped, realizing how ridiculous that sounded. We all knew it was highly unlikely that it was a mistake. This was Lu we were talking about. It wasn't her first adulterous rodeo.

'Thanks Rosie, but you know how it is.'

We did. That's what made it so sad and bloody infuriating. What do you do when it's your closest friend that's in the wrong? And how many times over the last thirty-odd years had I been torn between wanting to hug her and kill her? Too many to count.

I took a key off the tiny gold hook next to the back door and handed it to him. 'Here's the key for the flat. There's fresh bedding in the cupboard. If you need anything just shout,' I told him.

'Flat' was probably an optimistic term. Colm had converted the garage into a man cave, with a sofa bed, TV, tiny kitchen area and bathroom. 'Studio' was probably a better term. I preferred 'claustrophobic demonstration of sexist maledom'. Over the years, Dan and Lulu had stayed there many times after dinners or parties, but for now it could be Dan's home. Hopefully it wouldn't be long before they sorted this out and he was home again.

Rosie got up and lifted her cherry-red satchel from its dangling position on the back of the chair. 'I need to head off. I'm meeting Jack at seven o'clock and there's some serious grooming to be done. Dan, if you need anything just call me. And if you get kicked out of here, there's always my couch.'

Her efforts to inject some levity into the conversation almost made the whole situation sadder. God, poor Dan.

He got up at the same time, kissed me on the cheek and headed back out the door, key for the flat in hand. I made a mental note to pop in on him later and see how he was doing... after I'd put the laundry away, poured a coffee, had a snuggle with Beth, bathed her, made Colm and I's dinner, and planned the schedule for a lunch I was catering the following day for a baby reveal party. Seriously. This woman was inviting fifty of her closest friends round to reveal that she was pregnant with her third baby. As with her previous two children, in twelve weeks' time, there would be a 'gender reveal' party. Then a baby shower. Then a christening. Yes, she was definitely milking the experience for maximum attention and gifts, but hey, it made her a fantastic client.

'Hi m'darlin, how's you?' I'd been so deep in contemplation of Mrs Tower's announcement that I hadn't heard Colm come in.

'Fed up with laundry, tired, short-tempered, sore back, overworked and irritated,' I replied, smiling to dilute the moan.

'Ah. I was just looking for "fine",' he said, grinning, as he put his hands around my waist and kissed me on the neck. After all these years I wasn't sure if it was romantic, shallow or ridiculous that the minute his arms went around me the day got just a little bit better.

'Daddy!' Beth screeched, throwing herself at us to join the embrace. Our daughter didn't do subtlety or patience. 'Uncle Dan is here!'

'Where?' Colm replied, puzzled, before opening the fridge. 'Is he in here?'

Beth shrieked with laughter.

'Nope,' Colm went on, bending over to look under the table. 'Down here?'

'No!' Beth giggled.

'Ah, then he must be in here,' he said, opening the oven.

'He's in the garage!' Beth announced triumphantly, delighted to be a credible source of information.

His eyes met mine in a questioning glance.

'He's come to visit for a little while,' I told him in my best child-friendly, all's well, run along, nothing to worry about, tone.

He got the hint, sweeping Beth up and throwing her over his shoulder, then marching her back next door. I felt a huge pang of gratitude that, no matter what, he always had time for his girl. He was never too tired for her, never too busy to listen to what she had to say. There was no doubt he was Fun Dad, the soft touch who couldn't say no, while I was the one who handled all the practicalities. No surprise there then. But much as it sometimes needled, there was nothing I loved more than seeing them laughing together.

Over the next couple of hours, I ticked off everything on my list, right up to the point where our dinner was on the table. There was silence from upstairs, so I guessed Colm had finished with his storytelling and was now probably asleep next to his daughter on her bright blue sleigh bed. Her choice. She was in a militant, anti-pink, tomboy phase.

I trudged upstairs, and popped my head in the door to her bedroom. She was sound asleep, upside down, covers thrown to one side. I decided to rearrange her later when she'd had time to get into a deeper slumber.

Colm wasn't in our bedroom, so I headed to the smallest room, which doubled as a study. There he was, staring intently at the screen. That was unusual. He rarely worked from home, didn't have Facebook or Twitter or any of the other social network websites that sucked up time.

'Babe, dinner's ready,' I told him.

'Okay,' he answered automatically, his focus not leaving the screen.

The fact that he was engrossed piqued my interest and I moved closer to see what he was staring at with such intent. It took a few seconds to work out that it was one of those medical self-diagnosis sites.

'What are you doing?'

He shrugged. 'Och, I know these things are rubbish but I was just curious. Hang on, I'm almost done.'

I scanned the list of questions he'd already completed, starting with 'Headaches?' He'd ticked that one, and several of the others down the list. I had time to read a couple of them. 'Audio distortions.' I knew about those. 'Vision disturbances.' I had no idea what that meant. Other than the weird sound stuff and the headaches, he'd never mentioned any other symptoms. I still wasn't too concerned though. Didn't migraines often come with flashing lights or strange zig-zaggy lines?

He was at the last one and ticked 'no' in the box after 'weight-gain', then pressed 'enter'.

'I can't believe you're doing this,' I told him. Colm researching anything online was very unusual. 'It'll probably tell you that you're pregnant. Or a hypochondriac.' I wasn't buying into this at all. Hadn't I read a dozen articles that talked about how these websites were wildly inaccurate? Apparently, people were going in droves to the doctors after self-diagnosing life-changing illnesses on the internet. There was a name for it. I racked my brain. Cyberchondria. Yep, that was it.

He pulled me down on to his knee. 'I know, but it's this or the doctor and I don't have time for the doctor. I'm a busy and very important man.'

I was still laughing when the computer pinged and the results came up on the screen.

Most likely cause? Number one – migraines. As predicted by Doctor Colm, and seconded by my extensive medical expertise gathered from watching *Casualty* on a Saturday night. There was a whole list of other possible causes detailed below it – everything from concussion to head wound, to brain tumour. I could see why these sites had been accused of scaremongering.

'Aw, not pregnant. Are you gutted?' I asked him with mock sympathy. 'My name is Colm O'Flynn and I'm a cyberchondriac,' I told him, kissing him between words. 'Come on. Let's get dinner and then go make sure Dan isn't lying in the man cave with a tub of ice cream singing Shania Twain break-up songs.'

'Hang on, just want to do one thing…'

With his free hand, he used the mouse to flick back to the previous page.

'I noticed my jeans are feeling a bit tight on me,' he said, as he changed his answer to the 'weight-gain' question. Tick.

'That's because you haven't been out running this week,' I said, standing and pulling him upwards. 'Come on, you've a heartbroken pal to attend to.'

He was already on his feet when there was another ping from the screen.

The results had changed slightly.

Number one on the diagnosis probability scale?

Brain tumour.

I stared at it for a second, long enough for a chain reaction that went something like 'oh for goodness sake, how bloody ridiculous' to 'it couldn't be, could it?' Closely followed by a tiny niggle of fear and doubt, then a swing to 'of course not, but let's get it checked out anyway and get the problem sorted.'

The next day, I called the surgery and made an appointment for him to see the doctor.

6

2001

Shauna and Colm's Third Date

'You've shaved your legs. That's an admission of filthy intentions right there,' Lulu's cackles made the red wine in her glass slosh from side to side. She was lying on my bed in my tiny Twickenham apartment armed with vino, chocolate and a forthright opinion on my attire. 'So what's this, date four?'

'Three,' I corrected her. 'We met last Friday, went out for a drink on Sunday, and then tonight.'

'And you haven't shagged him yet?' she asked sceptically.

I fired back with amused sarcasm. 'I thought I'd wait until I know things like... ooh, his favourite colour. His star sign. Maybe even his surname.'

'Dan told me that it's O'Flynn. Now get on with it.'

I tossed a hairbrush in her direction and she artfully ducked to avoid it.

'You're beyond shallow.'

'I know,' she agreed.

After a quick rummage in my 'best undies' drawer, I pulled out a black bra and matching knickers. Lulu responded with a knowing nod as I pulled them on, then shimmied into my favourite black crêpe shift dress.

'Stop that. I'm not sleeping with him tonight. I'd rather get to know him, and that way, if the sex isn't great, I'll still know there's something to work on.' It was true. I was no prude – I couldn't be, with Lulu as a friend – but casual sex had never been my thing.

She threw a square of chocolate up and caught it in her mouth. 'That's ridiculous. If the sex isn't mind-blowing you change your phone number and if you see him in the street you pretend you don't know him.'

I zipped up my black suede knee-high boots, then added chunky silver jewellery.

I had a horrible feeling there was a grain of personal experience in her theory, but there was no time to ask as she pushed herself up on the bed so she could give me the head-to-toe scan.

'Passable,' she declared. 'But it could be a bit tighter and there could be a bit more cleavage.'

'In that case it's perfect,' I countered, earning a glare of disapproval that made me smile. She was absolutely incorrigible.

I'd been planning on taking the train, but at the last minute hailed a cab instead, deciding that I'd had a long week and if twenty quid saved me from a train, a Tube and a walk at the other end in these heels in the rain, it was worth it.

I was halfway there when my mobile rang. Annie. 'Hi

Gran,' I answered, smiling. It was impossible not to. Annie was my favourite woman on earth. I spoke to her most days and I'd like to say it was for her wisdom and profound philosophies in life, but the truth was that she delighted in being thoroughly irresponsible. She was the woman who had told me to punch a playground bully at school, then gave the teacher a piece of her mind when I got detention for it. She'd taught me to cook, to change a plug, and how to make a decent pina colada. She also threatened my first boyfriend with kneecapping if he ever hurt me or let his hand wander under my jumper. I never saw him again.

'I phoned your house first,' she opened, her Scottish accent still detectable even after decades in London. 'And Lu tells me your dress should be tighter and show more cleavage. Dear God, you'll be single forever.' Her woeful tone made her words even funnier, especially because they were coming from a woman who resolutely refused to even entertain the idea of a relationship. Widowed over twenty years before, she regularly declared herself an 'independent woman who had no desire to wash a pair of men's socks ever again.'

'Now have you given Lulu the address so that if you don't come home we can storm the building?'

'I have.'

'Right then. Better to be safe than sorry. Have a lovely time though. I'm fairly sure it won't be a situation that'll end up on *Crimewatch*. Right, I'm off to bingo. Love you, lass.'

'Love you too, Gran.'

As I closed my flip phone, I realized the taxi was coming to a halt.

Colm's house was in Notting Hill. Not the gorgeous, multi-million quid, Julia Roberts and Hugh Grant Notting Hill, but the slightly less salubrious Portobello Road side. Still nice, but the old homes had been divided into flats that – unlike the posh bit – came with a monthly rent that was less than the price of a Ferrari.

The cab dropped me off outside a red-painted front gate, which matched the red door of the Victorian terrace house Colm shared with two other guys. As I walked up the path I realized I was grinning. If there was a manual for playing it cool, I really needed to read it. For the first time ever, my stomach contained a full swarm of butterflies and, either I was about to suffer some kind of cardiac ailment, or my heart was thudding out of my chest from pure excitement. I had absolutely no idea that I had an inner love-struck teenager, but now that she had somehow surfaced at the age of twenty-four, I gave her a stern talking-to and grounded her for the rest of the night.

How ridiculous was this? Lenny and I had been a couple for two years, and nothing had made me feel like this: not meeting him, not our first kiss, not when he suggested we move in together, and not even when he went down on one sunburned knee on a romantic first night in Zante, presented a beautiful sapphire and silver ring and asked me to marry him.

And yet, here I was, fighting my way through an Amazon of overgrown rhododendrons to see a guy I'd met only twice in my life, and I was close to requiring resuscitation. I feared that if we ever did get to the sex stage, I was going to need a medivac team on standby.

The door opened before I even reached it, and there he was, languidly leaning against the door frame in jeans, a black T-shirt and bare feet. 'Okay, so I know I'm supposed to be all cool and wait until you actually ring the door-bell, but...'

I didn't let him finish. In a spontaneous action that came with zero warning and zero control, I stepped forward and kissed him, a long, slow, incredible snog that I only cut short when I realized that all my physical symptoms – the butterflies, the excitement, the beating heart – had given way to a weakness of the legs that could leave me, buttocks-first, in the rhododendrons.

Laughing, he gently tugged me inside by the lapels of my coat, kicked the door shut with his foot and we took up where we left off, this time pressed against the wall in his hallway.

My hands found their way into his hair, his slipped around my neck, and we kissed and touched and breathed together, until a bang from the other side of the door finally broke the spell of the moment.

'Hi,' he said, his breath still hot on my face.

'Hi,' I answered.

'That noise was my flatmate, Doug. Can't fecking do anything without causing a riot.'

'I bet your neighbours love you,' I teased.

'Oh they do. They've only called the police twice this week.'

In a moment of perfect comic timing, the door opened and out walked an unusually tall guy wearing a full police uniform.

'Right, I'm off,' he announced, before sticking out his hand. 'Doug.'

'Shauna,' I replied.

'Ah, thank God you're here. He's been checking the window every ten seconds for the last hour.' So it wasn't just me then. That thought made me like him even more.

'Just when I couldn't get any less cooler,' Colm interjected, feigning desolation.

PC Doug made a swift exit and, taking my hand, Colm led me into an open-plan space that was a stark contrast to the Victorian exterior. The distressed wooden floors went from the lounge area at the front to the open-plan kitchen at the back. It was undeniably a guys' space. Not because there were lad mags or Y-fronts on the floor (there were neither) but because one wall was punctuated only by a huge TV and three full-size men's racing bikes, the latter dangling from metal brackets.

'Those are Jamie's, the other flatmate,' Colm answered my unasked question. 'He's a mad cyclist. Does it for fun, even when beer and football are offered as an alternative. I don't get it.'

Slipping behind the wooden breakfast bar, he pulled two glasses from one of the black gloss units. The butterflies had subsided, leaving me with just a tingle of pure happiness. I liked this. The flat. The friend. The guy. The smile.

'Shall we have a drink before we go out? Wine or beer?' he asked.

'A beer would be great. Bottle is fine.'

'God, you're perfect.'

'I know.'

After taking two bottles from the fridge, opening them and handing one over, he pulled a wooden stool out from under the worktop. I did the same.

'Since I'm already clearly uncool, is it okay if I tell you that I'm glad you're here?'

'Absolutely. I'm pretty glad I'm here too. In a cool way, though.'

'Obviously.'

There was a momentary silence and I saw that a tiny frown line had appeared between his eyebrows. I had a sudden feeling of impending doom.

'Look, I was going to tell you this later, but I need to just do it now because I'm fairly shite at keeping secrets...' he blurted.

Oh bugger. Here it was. He was getting back with his ex. He'd never left. He was a serial killer. He didn't want a relationship. He was leaving the country.

The butterflies returned and this time they were on a sinister attack.

'I have children. Two boys. Twins. Davie and Joe. They're four. And I should have told you sooner but I....' He stopped and was looking at me searchingly. 'I didn't know if it would make a difference, and I didn't want to find out if it did.'

I took another gulp of the beer. Out of all the things I'd expected him to say, announcing he had twins didn't make the top hundred. Twins. Kids.

A tidal wave of relief flooded through me. Okay, he wasn't a serial killer and he wasn't leaving the country. We could work with this.

I realized that he was still looking anxious and waiting for a response.

'Why didn't you tell me before?' I was calm. Curious. Let's face it, it wasn't insignificant news and he'd had plenty of chances to impart this on date one or two.

He shrugged, embarrassed. 'Honestly? I've met a couple of women who were horrified by the thought of spending every second weekend with two crazy energetic kids. But they're great boys, they really are. I mean, they have their moments. Joe put my shoes down the toilet last week.' The way he smiled when he said it told me that he thought it was more amusing than naughty. His gaze was directly matching mine now. 'I just wanted to get to know you better before I scared you off.'

'Okay.'

Another pause. He was first to break it.

'So are you? Scared off?'

The truth? If anyone had told me a week before that I'd be feeling like a love-struck teenager over a bloke with two kids, I'd have been highly doubtful. I knew how hard it was to come into a ready-made family. One of Rosie's ex's had children and it had been one long negotiation, with plans regularly getting changed by an ex-wife who still controlled his actions, and by default, Rosie's too. They'd booked holidays, only for them to be cancelled at the last minute because the children were suddenly coming to stay. A huge chunk of his salary went on maintenance payments. Rosie had spent her birthday alone because one of the kids was sick. And the things that made him a great dad made him a difficult boyfriend. Rosie had given up after six months, and I didn't blame her. In all honesty, it wasn't something I was ready to jump in to. That whole commitment-phobia thing? Applied to children too. Because if it didn't work out with the dad, then there were little hearts at stake too and I wasn't ready for that kind of responsibility. So, no. Going into a relationship that was already complicated? A week ago I'd have said I'd have avoided it if I could. Now, though, I couldn't. I suddenly had a vision of two mini-Colms, with curly hair, big blue twinkly eyes and mouths that were quick to smile. Two kids? If he came as a package deal, then bring it on.

'I think I can handle it,' I told him with total surety.

His eyes widened as his facial features rearranged from worry to delight.

'Really? Are you sure? Because I'd totally understand. I know it's a lot.'

'I'm absolutely sure. I think... I think it's great.' And weirdly, that wasn't even a sugarcoated truth.

His shoulders visibly lifted with relief. Then the bottle went down and he leaned over the breakfast bar and took my chin in his hand, before kissing me with cold beer lips. The sensation made me shudder with an emotion I couldn't identify. It was more than happy. Beyond excited. Overjoyed. Totally and utterly lost in the moment and in whatever this effect was that he had on me.

Did I mention turned on? Absolutely, definitely and utterly turned on.

He was completely off his stool now, and without breaking the lip seal, he'd managed to work his way around to my side of the counter.

If it was a movie, he'd sweep everything off the worktop with one dramatic flourish of his hand before effortlessly lifting me up and laying me across the granite surface. Fortunately for the two beer bottles, the bottle opener, the Post-it pad, the sandwich toaster and his spinal column, he didn't. Instead, he pulled me up to a standing position as his hands found my neck again, then my hair, then my face, tracing a line down each cheek in the slowest, sexiest movement.

'I think you're incredible,' he said softly, ending the declaration with another kiss.

'Thank you. I try,' I said, but there was no disguising the fact that my voice was thick with something more than a flippant joke. Our hips pressed together and I could feel the heat as I slipped my arms under his T-shirt and gently stroked his lower back, making him groan.

Without even being fully cognizant of what I was doing, I pushed his T-shirt higher, until he broke off to pull it over his head. His shoulders were wide, but not over-muscled, his torso lean and clearly no stranger to a sit-up.

He leaned down to kiss me again. 'Are you sure?'

I knew what he was asking. My hand on the buckle of the belt of his jeans, flicking the leather loose, gave him the answer, but I confirmed it just in case there was any dubiety. 'Absolutely,' I murmured.

There was another involuntary groan as his lips met mine again, before his hand reached around and peeled the zip down on my dress, letting it fall to the floor. I said a silent prayer of thanks for the shaved legs and the matching underwear. Perhaps my subliminal intentions had been on the Lulu side of raunchy after all.

Now he lifted me up and sat on the edge of the worktop, as his head nestled into my neck. More kisses, this time working a trail down from my ear, to my throat, along one shoulder and then the other, before crossing my clavicle and moving towards the lace of my bra.

I felt a movement in the middle of my spine and suddenly my bra popped open. As he leaned back to remove it, I saw that he was laughing again.

'I swear to God I've never managed that first time before!' he told me. Kiss. Then another.

'Yeah, sure. Tell the truth. You were up all night practising.'

I didn't hear his answer because he was kissing me again.

This was intoxicating, sexy, funny… perfect.

Suddenly, I had a flash of anxiety as I heard Lulu's words replaying in my mind.

So this was it. I was about to find out if I'd have to change my number and cross the road when I saw him coming. And I really, really hoped not.

7

2015

Shauna and the Truth About Lulu

'Are you okay? You seem a little... distracted. Is anything wrong?' Rosie asked, as we stopped the car.

'You mean, apart from the fact that we're about to stage some kind of messed up intervention on our friend?' I asked wearily, as I turned off the ignition.

'Yeah, apart from that,' Rosie answered, with a weak smile.

I could see she was dreading this, probably even more than I was. Lulu and Dan were now a couple of weeks into their separation, and on the one hand, their marriage problems were none of our business. On the other hand, Dan had called me in a panic – just as I was serving up a retirement lunch that consisted of a seafood buffet for thirty, in honour of the fact that the banking chief was giving it all up to go sailing round the Caribbean with a childhood sweetheart he'd reconnected with on Facebook – to tell me that Lulu had gone berserk because he'd been to see the lawyer that morning.

She'd made an unannounced visit to the office to pick up some petty cash, checked his online diary and realized he wasn't there because he had a twelve o'clock with Macalister & Johnston Solicitors. It didn't go down well. According to Dan, on his return to work, he was greeted with a furious Lulu, a screaming match had ensued and she'd screeched off with the warning that she was going to take him for everything he had.

He'd immediately mobilized the equivalent of a friendship SWAT team to his former marital residence in the hope of calming her down and checking she was okay. He didn't dare go himself in case he ended up being one of those chalk outlines on the floor in an episode of *CSI*.

I'd left the lunch as soon as I could, called in on Rosie at the café, coerced her into joining me, and we'd headed straight over to Lulu's house.

'Is she in?' Rosie asked, stretching to see if Lulu's red BMW was parked anywhere on the street.

I gestured up ahead. 'There's her car, so I'm guessing she is. Do you want her to be out?'

'Absolutely,' Rosie answered honestly. 'I'm not designed for conflict. I'm designed for muffins. And kittens. And reruns of *Calamity Jane*.'

My mobile phone rang and I considered ignoring it until Dan's name flashed up.

Bugger. 'Hey…'

'Are you there yet? Is she okay?'

'We've just arrived outside the house and the car's here.'

'Oh thank God. I had visions of her crashing and it would have been on my conscience forever. I'm sorry to involve you in all this, Shauna, but you're the only one she has ever listened to.'

'It's fine.' It really wasn't. His obvious concern made me second-guess his earlier move. 'Dan, it's none of my business... But does this mean you're not going ahead with the divorce?'

There was a moment of silent deliberation at his end, then, 'I'm still divorcing her.' Very definite. Then immediately, 'I don't know.' Less certain. So there was hope.

'Dan, maybe this will give her the shake-up she needs, snap her to her senses. If she agrees to talk, will you at least hear what she has to say?' I was floundering, but I had to try. 'I'm sure she'll want to.' I desperately injected some confidence into my voice and hoped he bought it. In reality, I had no idea what Lulu wanted. She hadn't returned my calls or any other attempts to contact her this week, other than a couple of vague texts promising to 'talk when ready' and saying she 'just needed space to think'.

She was clearly still in Soap Dialogue Central.

'Look, I'll call you later and let you know how this goes,' I promised Dan.

'Thanks Shauna. I owe you.' Yes, he did.

I disconnected the call and checked my watch again. I didn't have time for this. I really didn't. I had to collect Beth at four o'clock and it was already close to three. I fired off a text to Colm, asking him to do it. His reply was immediate.

Can't. Doc apt at 4.

Bugger, how could I have forgotten? I really was a crap wife sometimes. I rested my forehead on the steering wheel.

'Are you sure you're okay?' Rosie asked again.

I nodded without lifting my head. 'Yep, just haven't had time to eat today so I'm hungry and tired.' I didn't add, 'And pissed off being in a SWAT team', but I admit I was thinking it. Sleep. I just needed to sleep. The four hours I'd managed last night, between catering a birthday party in Ham and getting up at 5 a.m. to get started on today's lunch, just weren't cutting it.

'Right, I've got forty-five minutes before I need to go pick up Beth. So... In, out, persuade Lulu to try to save her marriage,' I said, in the manner of a general going into battle. I just wished it didn't feel like a suicide mission.

'I'm right behind you,' she said, her apprehension muffled by the noise of her car door slamming. Obviously we weren't using stealth as a tactic.

First there, I rang the doorbell and waited a few moments. No answer. Damn. I rang again. Still no answer. My internal profanity continued, now edged with panic. Why wasn't she answering the door? Oh bugger, was she okay? Was she drunk? Had she fallen? I chided myself for being ridiculous. She must be in the bath. No, Lulu hated baths. The shower. Yep, that was it.

'What shall we do?' Rosie asked.

I was trying to work out how to get round the back of the terrace when the door finally opened and there was Lulu, in a cream cashmere dressing gown, her hair still wet. So I'd been right about the shower.

'We just came over to check on you, make sure you're okay.'

Her chin jutted up defiantly. 'I'm fine. Why wouldn't I be? Just because that dick wants a divorce?'

And there it was again. Lulu's inherent character idiosyncrasy – no matter how you're feeling, meet attack with attack. It had taken me years to realize that underneath that shell of pure venom, she was sometimes scared, sometimes hurt, sometimes confused. But vulnerability wasn't in her DNA – not when she could come out fighting. If ever someone was a product of her childhood, it was Lulu. But that conversation was for another day.

'Yep, that. And because you're not returning your calls. Anyway I really need to pee and yours was the closest house.'

It was a ploy, I admit it. I'd been standing on the doorstep too long and it was starting to rain. It was clear she wasn't inviting us in and I hadn't come here just to be fobbed off by Lulu in battle mode.

Yet still, she hesitated.

'Lulu, I need to use the loo,' I repeated. Reluctantly, she stood to one side to let us in. I passed her and headed for the cloakroom toilet, washed my hands to make my alibi credible, then headed through to the kitchen, where she and Rosie were already sitting at the table. Without asking, I started making a pot of coffee. It was normal practice, with all of us treating each other's homes like our own, yet I saw Lulu flinch. Why? The only explanation was that she was upset that I'd let Dan stay at our house and was taking it personally. It wouldn't be out of character for her to see it as a betrayal.

As I flicked the coffee machine on, I decided to go for bold openness.

'Are you pissed off that Dan is bunking at our house?'

She shrugged. 'No. Why would I be? At least it means he's not here.'

On one level that made sense, but I wasn't convinced. Something was off about the way she was acting.

'Come on, Lu, enough.'

Her only response was an eye roll.

'So is it the architect? The one you met when you were planning the extension?' I asked, continuing the policy of upfront confrontation.

Rosie's eyes widened and I realized this was news to her. Sometimes that happened. The unfortunate dynamic of having three in a friendship group was that occasionally you forgot to fill the third person in on a one-to-one discussion. I only knew about him because I'd come by one day when he was here with a set of blueprints and sensed a connection between them that went further than casual flirting. I'd asked, Lulu had denied it, we both knew she was lying, I chose not to press the issue. However, that was before her husband was living in my converted garage and pulling me out of work situations to handle his emergencies. Did I sound unsympathetic? I wasn't. Truly. I just had enough on my plate, and besides, with Lulu, straight talking and avoidance of niceties were the best way to go.

'The architect?' Rosie asked quietly.

Lulu had the decency to look slightly embarrassed as her gaze moved to the table in front of us. Avoiding eye contact. Another admission on the totem pole of guilt.

Bugger, not again.

'We've been having a… thing.'

Rosie groaned. I felt my teeth clench. Why? Why did she do this? Of course, I already knew the answer.

'Don't judge me.' She was looking straight at me, head held high, eyes blazing with defiance.

I raised my hands in a shrugging gesture. 'I'm not. But how many times, Lu? You promised him after the last time…'

I didn't need to finish the sentence as we all knew the story. She'd been out with a guy she'd met on an IT training seminar. She'd gone on behalf of Dan and Colm's company to learn a new accounting system and had ended up 'getting close' (her words, not mine) to one of the guys on the course, a finance officer for a blue-chip corp. It had blown over, but not before Dan had stumbled across an email trail planning a weekend in a country house hotel in Yorkshire. Lulu cancelled, swearing it hadn't gone beyond flirting. Everyone chose to believe she was telling the truth, despite the fact that it wasn't her first indiscretion and we all knew it wouldn't be the last. Enabling her irresponsible behaviour had become second nature to us all. Perhaps, now that Dan was no longer going to tolerate her antics, it was time for that to stop.

'He's no angel either,' she replied sullenly.

This was an argument I wasn't going to win and I didn't have the stomach or the time to try, yet I heard myself saying, 'Lu, I think he'll go through with the divorce this time. You're pushing him to it. Is that really what you want?'

I honestly wasn't sure that it was. Pushing him, testing him, neglecting him, treating him terribly – all absolute certainties. But leaving him with no choice but to end their marriage? I wasn't convinced.

A shade of uncertainty clouded her face, but before she could speak, a noise jolted us all. A floorboard. A creak. Directly above us.

Slowly, with a depressed, furious knowing on my part, I turned to meet her gaze.

'He's here?' I asked calmly. 'Upstairs.' So that's why she'd taken so long to answer the door.

She shrugged. 'What does it matter, Shauna? Dan's divorcing me anyway.'

I don't have a violent bone in my body, but somewhere deep in my core, her petulant nonchalance made me want to slap her. Time to leave.

'You know what, Lu? Knock yourself out. Do what you like. We love you and we'll be here to pick up the pieces, but for the record, you're making a mistake. You know what this does, Lu.'

She knew. She'd grown up with a mother and father who'd blazed a trail from affair to affair, leaving carnage in their wake that had affected all of us. So yes, she knew.

Upstairs, more creaking of the floorboards, then a door closing. I knew the layout of the house well enough to surmise he'd gone into the shower.

'I think we should go,' I said to Rosie, who nodded, then reached over and put her hand on Lulu's arm.

'What Shauna said about loving you… you know we do,' she said gently. 'And so does Dan. Even if you don't always make it easy.'

Lulu didn't answer. Not a word. No eye contact. Not even a 'goodbye' as we headed out of the door.

Back in the car, I could see that Rosie was on the verge of

tears. 'Don't worry,' I told her, as gently as I could. 'They'll work it out. They always do.' I had no idea if that was the case but I was trying to cheer Rosie up. It didn't work.

'I'm not so sure this time. You know, I just don't understand it.' Anger was now seeping into her sadness. 'They have everything. Fucking everything. They love each other. We all know that. But they're both so bloody stubborn and stuck in this pattern of destructive power plays.'

I took one hand off the steering wheel and found hers, squeezing it tightly. 'I know, honey, but maybe that's just it. They're stuck. They're hurting each other. Something has to change.'

I didn't say the obvious, that perhaps divorce would be the best solution for them, didn't want to upset her any more. Besides, much as I knew that might be true, I didn't want to give up on them yet either.

'Get you with the psychological lingo…' I teased, trying to distract her from her despair. 'What's with the "destructive power plays"? Jack the life coach is clearly rubbing off on you.'

That made her smile, so I added a little more positivity.

'I'll talk to Dan when I get home,' I offered. 'We'll try to help them, I promise.'

I dropped her back at the café and then sped over to collect Beth from her after-school choir practice. Five years old and she'd already decided she wanted to be Taylor Swift. God help us. Annie said the desire to perform came from her. Three vodkas and soda and she would belt out every one of the Carpenters' greatest hits. It was a gift that clearly skipped a couple of generations before it landed on Beth.

My little songbird filled the car with happy chatter all the way home and I finally felt the strain in my muscles easing. When had it become normal to be so tightly wound up every day in life? The conversation with Colm on the way to Lulu and Dan's house last week came back into my mind. We so needed to have that work/life balance discussion.

I'd just dumped my bags on the kitchen table and sent Beth up to change when Colm came in the back door behind me. It was one of the strange aspects of our semi-detached house – just a couple of streets away from the flat I'd lived in when Colm and I met – we had a perfectly good front door but no one except the postman ever used it. Instead, we all used the back door that led through the utility and into the kitchen.

'Hi m'darling,' he greeted me, before landing a kiss on my lips and tossing his jacket over the back of one of the kitchen chairs.

'You look tired,' I told him, flicking the coffee machine on as I spoke. 'How did you get on at the docs?'

'Definitely migraines,' he said. 'Gave me these.' He held up a paper bag with the local chemist's logo on the front. 'Painkillers and beta blockers. Apparently the beta blockers can help prevent them and the painkillers can ease them, so between the two, they should hopefully sort it out.'

Of course they would. I was glad I'd made the appointment and it was good to hear the doctor confirming that it wasn't a serious ailment. I chided myself for letting that bloody internet site freak me out. Of course it was nothing sinister. Since when had I been one to overreact? I blamed over-work. And sleep deprivation. And the stress of keeping us solvent. Perhaps this was the wake-up call we needed. An ironic turn of phrase given the fact that my 5 a.m. alarm was part of the problem. However, this was definitely a big bloody red flag signalling that we had to make adjustments to the way we were living our lives.

I slipped into the chair across from him. 'Babe, something has to change.'

'Aaah, *that* conversation,' he retorted, feigning horror.

'Babe, it has to. We're killing ourselves with work and stress and I've no idea how it came to this.'

He responded by pointing out the obvious. 'Because we made the decision that we'd both be self-employed. Look, it'll get better.'

'How long have we been saying that?'

'But it will. I'm on the verge of landing that ongoing training contact with Bracal Tech, and when that happens, we'll have guaranteed income for five years. I'll be travelling less, won't have to do as much sales development and pitching for stuff all over the country, and the revenue will allow you to ease back on your side of things. It's just about to come good, sweetheart. All this will be worth it, I promise. We just need a few more months and we'll be out of the woods.'

A few more months and we'll be out of the woods. If ever there was a phrase that summed up our lives, that was it.

It wasn't that I didn't love my job, because I did. The business had surpassed expectations over the last decade, growing year by year, and making enough of a profit to allow Colm to decide to start up the company with Dan. They were doing well now too, but not enough to catch up on the lean years of building, when mine was the only salary paying the bills and the mortgage. Our credit card balances were huge, and I was fairly sure our collective overdraft gave our bank manager nightmares. We'd even considered selling the house, but thanks to those tossers in the banking industry who'd caused the crash, it was in negative equity. As a result, there had been nothing else to do but work our way out of this. I had a vague memory of my younger self, so sure and determined, telling Colm when I met him that setting up my own business had been part of a master plan to get the work/life balance right. If the gods were listening they must have been having a good laugh at the naivety of my youth. The last few years had given me no choice. It was work or lose everything, so – whether it was what I wanted or not – there was no point complaining.

Besides, Colm was right about the progress. As always, his confidence was contagious, one of his many traits that I adored. We were on our way to balancing the books, with half the start-up debt already gone. Just a few more months. Then, as a family, we'd be back in the world of solvency, allowing me to take on some permanent help instead of the temp staff I brought in on a job-by-job basis.

I'd no longer be living on five hours sleep a night, so I could shrug off the zombie tiredness and snatch back that elusive life quality called 'free time'. I'd be a happier, more chilled out wife and mum.

Colm would thrive on the success of his company and the migraines would hopefully stop. I'd feel less guilty that I wasn't spending enough time with Beth, or arranging exciting stuff for Davie and Joe. The twins were nineteen now, and the days of fixed access were long gone, but they still stayed over at least once a week. We were hugely thankful that they still wanted to hang out with us.

We might even start taking holidays again, or going on weekend breaks just for fun. The five of us could head to the cinema on a Saturday afternoon, then spend the rest of the day playing football in the park. We might even get one of those date nights we'd been threatening to have since the beginning of time. I'd finally, finally, get to have that life I'd always wanted – fulfilled at work, happy marriage, time to enjoy my family and the husband I loved.

When was the last time I'd told him that I adored him? We'd slipped so far down a narrow tunnel of going through the motions, of ploughing through obstacles to reach an end game, that we'd stopped taking time just to be together.

'I love you, you know that?' I told him.

'Och, you're only human,' he replied, his grin wide and cheeky. I didn't see that face enough. I missed it.

For the first time in weeks, I leaned over and properly kissed him, slowly, tenderly, until the blissful effect of touching him worked its way around my body, awaking senses and sensations that had long since been battered to death by the combination of stress and sleep deprivation.

We'd be fine. We were almost there. A few more months.

'Yukkkkk! You're kissing!' Beth exclaimed from the doorway she now filled with wild curls and outrage.

Her precociousness transformed the romance of the moment into a cacophony of giggles.

'Yes, we are,' Colm confirmed, in mock seriousness. 'You should really consider a career as a detective.'

'No way! I'm going to be a singer,' Beth shot back, before wandering off into the lounge while belting out the chorus of 'Let It Go'. Again.

'We really need to teach her a new song,' Colm joked.

'Yes, we do. Before I let go of my sanity.'

'How long have we got until the boys arrive?' he asked.

'About an hour.' The boys lived in Regent's Park with their mum, Jess, and stepdad, Steve, who were always happy to work with us in getting them to and fro between their homes. As co-parents went, we'd always had an amiable relationship and kept it friendly for the sake of the boys, who pretty much came and went as it suited them. They were both in their first year at King's College London and it preyed on both our minds that they were another step closer to leaving home and building their own lives, and we'd never get this time back with them, so we encouraged them to come as often as they could.

'Excellent. Now, where were we?'

I didn't answer, preferring to show him instead. I was once again kissing my husband and feeling so good, until he suddenly stopped, pulled away.

I opened my eyes to see his brow furrowed in confusion.

'What's up?'

'I don't know – it's the weirdest thing. I can see you perfectly, but the peripheral vision on my right side keeps… disappearing. If I hadn't been at the doctor's today, this would be completely freaking me out,' he added, making my stomach twist just a little.

'He said it's definitely migraines though?' I asked, unable to hide a tinge of uncertainty.

His frown was making me uneasy. Colm underplayed everything. He was the least hysterical, least dramatic person I'd ever known. 'Och, it'll be fine. It'll all work out,' was his stock reply to any problems. 'We'll worry about it when it actually happens,' was his frequent counter when I raised any possibility of future issues.

Now, he was saying neither. Instead, his complexion had turned a deathly shade of pale and no glib platitudes were forthcoming from a mouth that was pursed with worry or pain or something.

He picked up the chemist's bag from the worktop and emptied it out on the table, before opening the packet of beta blockers and popping two from the foil.

'Definitely. I'm sure I just need to get these down me and I'll be fine. The doc said there's nothing to worry about and a few weeks on these and I'll see a difference. I'll be fine.'

Of course he would. After all, we were almost out of the woods.

8

2001

Shauna and Colm's
Four-Week Anniversary

The banging of the bedroom door against the wall woke me and I groaned, then managed to prise open one eye to check out the source of the disturbance. It was standing right in front of me.

'Happy anniversary!' Colm announced proudly, as he stood there, in his boxer shorts holding a huge wooden tray. When he put it down on the bed, I saw there were two glasses of fresh orange juice, both of which had been over-filled and were dripping down the sides, two bananas, a tub of Ben & Jerry's ice cream and the pièce de résistance, a large pancake with a candle in the middle.

'What are you talking about, you crazy person?' I murmured, glad my vocal cords were working because most of the rest of my motor skills seemed to be refusing to wake up. How long had I been asleep? It felt like one hour, but according to the clock at the side of Colm's bed, it had been four. I rolled over on one side, my groaning body feeling like I'd run a marathon. Not that I knew what that actually felt like, but I was pretty sure it would come with the same aching legs and stiff muscles. Again, I had no personal frame of reference, but I was fairly sure that several hours of incredible sex was far more enjoyable than a marathon too.

Turns out I hadn't had to change my number or cross the road when I saw him coming after all. God, it was so good. So, so good. And everything else about our time together over the last month had been pretty fantastic too, including this morning's decision to wake me up with a pancake.

I pushed myself up to a sitting position, reached down, grabbed the white vest I'd been wearing last night and pulled it on. I made it a general policy not to eat breakfast with my boobs on show. 'What anniversary?'

'Four weeks today,' he replied, like it should have been obvious.

I slipped my arms around his neck and kissed him. 'That is pathetically over-sentimental and romantic.'

'You're absolutely right. I'll probably be drummed out of the manhood. To be honest, I only remembered because Doug told me last night on his way out to work. He does a four-week shift pattern and he remembered it was his first night shift last month that I met you. I don't want you suing me under some trade descriptions act, so I'll confess now that I'm usually shite at stuff like this.'

It was clear that admitting his failings didn't trouble him. Actually, I'd learned that nothing much troubled him at all. Other than our time at work, we'd been pretty much inseparable, alternating between spending the nights at my flat and his.

I felt strangely at home in his bedroom, but it was a fairly safe bet that he wouldn't win any awards for interior design. If I threw a white cotton pillow in any direction it would hit something that had been bought in IKEA.

Thankfully, other than a slight lacking in the soft furnishings imagination department, I hadn't detected any underlying character flaws so far. No controlling behaviour, no temper, no distasteful personal habits, other than a fondness for eating cheesy Wotsits in bed.

I took a spoon and dipped into the ice cream. Caramel. My favourite. 'What time are we picking up the boys?'

'Noon.' He took a bite of the banana. 'Nervous?'

'Not really. I suppose I'm more apprehensive about meeting your ex.'

'Och, don't worry about that,' he said, as he flipped his legs on to the bed and pushed up so he was sitting beside me. 'Jess moved on a long time ago.'

'So what's your relationship with her like now?' I probably should have pondered this subject and asked this question before now, but I'd been otherwise occupied by emotional and orgasmic bliss.

He shrugged. 'It's fine. There are no hard feelings. We'd been together since college. Way too young. She just wanted a different life. The fact that I'm living with *Men Behaving Badly* and she's now dating a guy who bought her a Porsche as a birthday present says it all. She's happy. Feck, I might shag him too for a Porsche.'

Only a month in and I'd sussed that this was how he

dealt with most things. He was a curious blend of humour, impulsiveness, deflection and decency, with a large slice of 'fuck it, why not.' He claimed his whole family back in Blackrock, near Dublin, was exactly the same. I already knew that one day I hoped to find out for myself. Wow, I was actually thinking about meeting his family. Clearly my inner commitment-phobe was currently having a lie-down in a dark room.

Thankfully, he hadn't mentioned any such longing to meet my family. That could only be a good thing.

'What's up?' he asked.

'Nothing, why?'

'You shuddered. Are you cold?'

'Nope.' Close call. I changed the subject. There was nothing that could spoil a perfect morning more than talking about my family. I knew a thing or two about deflection too. 'So what's the plan for today?' I asked.

'I thought I'd make up a huge picnic and we could take it to Regent's Park.'

'Really?'

'Nope, I'm lying. Not about the park bit, but, Christ, I brought you a pancake and a banana for breakfast. Do I strike you as the kind of guy who owns a picnic basket?'

Ice cream midway to mouth, I decided this was worth giving up the opportunity to cater for forty ten-year-olds at a birthday party in Hampton Wick. It had been a last-minute call and I never, ever refused business, but this time I made an exception and referred the client on to my old college pal Vincent. His business was doing great and we occasionally passed clients over to each other if we were double-booked. He didn't normally operate out of the city but he'd made an exception for me this time. I was so glad he had. A night with Colm definitely trumped chicken goujons and hot dogs. Although my bottom line wouldn't thank me if it became a habit.

I noticed Colm was staring at me. 'What?'

'That ice cream is dripping on the sheets I washed in honour of your visit. You're in some kind of ninja trance there.'

'Sorry I was thinking about work.'

'Good to know I'm keeping you interested here,' he joked. 'Right, I'm about to pull my best moves, so pay attention.'

I've no idea what happened to my spoon, but it was cast aside as he kissed me, a long, delicious snog that I'd have been happy to prolong for the rest of the day.

When hunger and the thought of melting ice cream got the better of us, he released me, and pulled the tray into the newly formed space between us.

'So are you definitely sure about today, about me meeting Davie and Joe?' I asked, hoping he hadn't changed his mind.

'Absolutely. They'll love you.'

I really hoped he had a contingency plan in case they didn't. According to Lulu, I just had to be bold, otherwise, 'They'll smell the fear and then you'll be toast,' she'd warned me. I was fairly sure she hadn't been quoting verbatim from a 'dealing with children' manual.

I should have researched this. Studied the best way to approach it. Sought advice. But then, when I wasn't turning down jobs to spend time with my new boyfriend, I regularly catered for large parties of small children, and I hadn't broken or lost one yet. In fact, they mostly seemed to quite like me. That had to go for something. Even if I took into account the fact that I was usually plying them with cake.

A niggling thought popped into my head and I immediately pushed it away. It came back. I resisted for a few moments, then succumbed to curiosity.

'Have you ever introduced anyone to them before? I mean, like a girlfriend?'

It blurted forth from my mouth. What was I thinking? I'd never pegged myself as particularly jealous before now.

As far as relationships went, when I was engaged to Lenny I never grilled him on where he was going, where he'd been or who he'd been with. I was pretty laid-back. I trusted him.

But this wasn't about trust. This was something more, and I had no idea where it was coming from. Great. I was coming over as needy and suspicious. I'd be dumped before I got my Big Mac and fries.

He turned to look at me. 'At least a dozen. One a week. I had them lined up, all dying to date me and take on a father-of-two so they could spend alternate weekends in the screaming hell of an indoor play centre.'

There was an involuntary eye roll from my side of the discussion, before he lifted my chin and kissed me softly.

'Never,' he said, uncharacteristically serious. 'You know Jess and I were separated for two years, but we were only divorced a month when I met you. Honestly, they're great little guys and they'll be cool about it.'

'Are you sure it'll be okay? What if this isn't the right time for them?'

I sounded like I was having doubts, but I wasn't. I was

sure about this, about him, about meeting the boys, about all of it. I just wanted to know that he was too.

'It's the right time. Besides, they have to meet you now.'

The fact that I'd just chomped down on my banana delayed my bewildered response. 'Why?'

He rolled over towards me, sending the ice cream flying off the bed, stopping when he was up on one elbow, his face only inches from mine.

'Because I love you. I know that sounds crazy after four weeks, but to be honest, I could have told you on the first night I met you. If this terrifies you and you feel the need to call law enforcement, I think Doug just got home, so he'll be in the kitchen.'

For all the joking around, his voice, his expression, his eyes, all told me that he meant every word. And I could see that, despite his surety, there was a question there. Without thinking, I reached over and ran my finger down his nose, then rested the tip on his bottom lip.

'You know, this should be terrifying. Or at least grounds for a restraining order. But you're only saying exactly what I've been feeling too. I... love you back.' I did. It was crazy, and wild, and if anyone had predicted this I'd have told them they were crazy. And I couldn't believe he felt the same. 'Even though you don't have a Porsche.'

He grinned as my hand slipped into his hair, then leaned towards me and kissed me slowly, tenderly, before pausing, pulling back, looking at me again.

'Shauna Williams – you know we're getting married don't you?'

It was so matter-of-fact, so blasé, that my first instinct

was that he was joking again. My second instinct told me he wasn't. My third told me he was right. My fourth was that I agreed with him. And every reaction was sweetened with the thought that I couldn't wait to tell Annie. She'd be blowing the dust off her best hat before I'd finished the story.

And she'd tell me to trust my instincts.

Into my mind popped the memory of our first date, of talking about how neither of us saw marriage in our future. Now, four weeks later, I knew, with absolute certainty, that it was. Nothing had ever felt more right than this moment.

'Yes,' I answered in the same casual tone as his question. I didn't even find it strange that I wasn't feeling even a tiny twang of doubt.

'Great,' he told me, his grin making his eyes crease up at the corners. 'I'm thinking next week. Are you free?'

'Absolutely. But do we have to wait that long?'

9
2015

Colm and Dan Make the Pitch

'How do you think it went?' Dan asked, looking about as nervous as I'd seen him in the decade or so we'd worked together.

'Grand. Honestly, mate, I think it's ours.'

His shoulders went down a bit and he pulled his tie loose with one hand, then picked up the bottle of Bud I'd placed on the kitchen table in front of him with the other. 'God, I hope so. It would really take the pressure off.'

I wasn't arguing. The Bracal Tech contract would transform us from a young company that had to fight for every bit of business we got, to a secure organization with guaranteed work and income for the next few years. It would take the pressure off. Reduce the hours. Give us a bit of a life back.

'Although…' Dan continued, 'would be fucking typical.

Winning a big contract just as Lu buggers off with some other bloke. I'd be as well just buying them first-class holidays to Barbados.'

It was meant to be a joke, but he spat it out with real anger. I didn't blame him. She'd delivered a mighty boot in his bollocks, and what made it even worse was that she didn't seem to give a toss.

But hey, it was his business, not mine.

He needed something to go right, though, so it mattered even more that we got the contract that we needed to secure our future. The three hours we'd spent that afternoon in Bracal Tech had felt positive. We'd made the presentation, a comprehensive five-year training schedule that encompassed their entire workforce and every area of their business – inductions, standards, ongoing performance evaluation and targets.

If we didn't get it we'd survive, but this was the difference between just getting by and really consolidating the company.

It had to come in. For all our sakes. Most of the time, I tried to shrug off stress but I was pretty sure that's what the headaches were about. Shauna and I had been slogging it out for years, and I hated seeing her killing herself to help keep us solvent. And it wasn't just her job. I didn't kid myself that she was also the one doing the graft with Beth, taking care of the house, sorting everything else out so I could concentrate on work. I had no idea how she did it, but that was Shauna. Always on top of stuff. She could cope with bloody anything.

That didn't stop the guilt on my part though.

Sometimes I wondered if it was worth it. I could go back

to my old job, earn a decent salary, company car, expense account, just turn up and do the work. When we'd decided to go out on our own, it had seemed like a way to an even better life though. We'd had great plans, huge ambitions and absolutely no idea that the financial crisis would deliver another kick in the proverbials. Would I do it again? Not sure. If it was just down to me, then absolutely. But watching the missus working her arse off to keep everything going while Dan and I built the company was definitely adding to the pressure. I definitely got lucky when I got Shauna. It almost made it worse that she didn't complain much, just got on with it. Unlike Lulu.

'What's happening with you two?' I asked Dan, bracing myself for the reply. Sometimes that question got a depressed shrug, sometimes a 'no fucking idea', other times it brought on a prolonged rant that felt like it was never going to end.

To be honest, I was hoping for one of the first two.

'Who fucking knows, mate.' That would do. It wasn't that I didn't care, but we'd been over it so many times and there was nothing new to add. If it were up to me, I'd move on and call it a day. Let's face it, Lu was never going to change. Not my problem or decision to make though.

Behind me, I heard the door opening and Shauna came in carrying eight bags of shopping between two hands. I jumped over to take them from her. I lifted one lot up on to the worktop, but as I lifted the other, I lost my grip and dropped them. Bugger. Had to be the one with the fruit didn't it? Fecking satsumas everywhere.

'Love it when you help out,' Shauna said, but at least she was laughing. Sometimes it seemed like we didn't do much of that any more. Definitely way less than we used to. Bracal Tech had to come in to give us some breathing space.

'Okay, I'm off again,' Shauna announced, pushing some dark blonde curls that had escaped from her ponytail back off her face. In her jeans and white shirt, she didn't look that much older that she'd been when we first met. Still gorgeous. Still perfect. The only difference was a few lines around her eyes, and a tired slump of her shoulders. I felt responsible for both causing and changing that.

'Where are you off to?'

'Back to get Beth from after-school session.'

'I'll come with you,' I offered. 'We're done for the day.'

She looked from me to Dan, then back to me. 'Shit, sorry, I forgot,' she said, weariness oozing out of her. 'Bracal Tech today. How did it go?'

I nodded. 'We're thinking it went well. If they know what's best for them, they'll already have decided to bring on the two incredibly handsome blokes with the great line in chat.'

'Aw, do you know any guys like that? Perhaps they'll cut you into the deal,' she replied, buying into the joke.

Dan got up from his chair. 'You two head off for Beth and I'll go check emails in case they've already made up their minds and let us know.'

'But they said they wouldn't make a decision for a fort-night,' I pointed out.

He sighed and raised his hands in a 'what can you do' motion. 'It's that or sit and mope over Lu. What would you prefer?'

'Go check your emails,' Shauna said, kissing him on the cheek as she passed him.

I followed them both out the back door and watched as Dan headed to the garage. What was supposed to be a short-term solution was turning into a long-term squat. Not that we minded. He was welcome to stay for as long as he wanted.

Shauna was about to get into the driver's seat when I stopped her. 'I'll drive, m'darlin.'

'Haven't you had a few beers?' she asked.

'Just a couple of sips,' I answered truthfully. 'We'd just started on them when you came in and saved us. Another couple of hours and I'd have been singing songs, telling everyone I loved them and searching for a late-night kebab shop.'

'Just a normal Friday night from 2001 then,' she retorted, with a tired smile.

We'd just pulled out of the street when she got back to the event of the day. 'So what do you really think? Will you get the contract?'

'Ah, who fecking knows. I've got a good feeling about it though.'

'You have a good feeling about everything.' There was no bitterness, just observation. I did prefer not to worry about anything until I hit the worst-case scenario. Anything other than that was a waste of energy.

'Let's go out tonight,' I told her. 'Celebrate. We'll take Beth down to that little Italian place she loves.'

'Babe, I have to be up really early in the morning. I've got a kid's birthday party at 9 a.m. in Isleworth. I'll need to prepare some of it tonight.'

'It won't be a late night. Come on, it's time we took a bit of time for us. And when we get back, I'll help you get organized for tomorrow.'

Her laughter was instant. 'Last time you helped you put pink party bags in the kitbag. The party was for a boy called Simon. There were tears.'

'Fair point.'

Her smile turned to an expression of decision, as she said, 'But sure, let's go out tonight. Be nice to spend some time together.'

It would. It's a bit of a weird thing to say about someone you live with, but I missed her. Missed spending time together when we weren't distracted doing a dozen other things. One way or another, we had to sort that out.

'Good. And as long as you supervise me, I'll still help you with the prep... prepar... preparat.... Preparrrrrr. Shit, I can't get the word out.' That had happened a few times lately. Must be those pills from the doc.

'Preperations,' she said, her voice sounding a little odd. I didn't have a chance to ask why, as we'd pulled up outside Beth's school. I reversed into a free parking space in the street. Bugger. Totally misjudged it. I tried again. Still miles off. On the third time, Shauna asked if I was going to build a bridge to get to the pavement. Damn, must be more knackered than I thought.

I finally got it right on the fourth, and we jumped out and ran through the deserted playground. The normal school day was finished an hour ago, but Beth loved the after-school singing and drama sessions. She wanted to be on X Factor. God help us.

Halfway across the grey concrete, Shauna stopped suddenly. 'Colm, are you okay?'

'Yeah, why?'

'Because you're staggering a bit. Going from side to side.'

I had no idea what she was talking about. 'No, I'm not.'

'Babe, you are.'

More than what she was saying, it was her expression that took me by surprise. She looked genuinely worried. That wasn't like her.

'How have the headaches been this week?'

I shrugged. 'Just had a couple of them. Definitely think the pills are making a difference. I'll be right as rain in no time.'

In truth, I wasn't sure if the pills were kicking in yet, but I wasn't going to say anything that would up her stress any further.

She didn't look or sound entirely convinced. 'I think you need to go back to the doctor.'

'Don't be daft, I'm fine. I feel much better.'

'Look, just humour me. I didn't want to say anything, but after that thing with your peripheral vision I started reading up on all the things that could cause this – and I'm not saying the doctor is wrong – but I just want you to double-check that nothing else is going on here. You're staggering, Colm. And you keep stuttering over your words.'

'The pills must be causing that.'

'Probably,' she agreed, still not entirely convincingly. 'But I want you to go back, and ask him to do a head scan.'

'Don't be ridiculous. Why would he do that?'

'Just to… I don't know… rule out any other reasons.'

I stopped, put my arm around her shoulders and kissed the top of her head. 'I don't need a head scan. I promise, there's nothing for you to worry about.'

'Well, I am worrying.'

'Well, I'm not,' I countered. And I meant it. Like I said, I wasn't the type to worry until we hit a worst-case scenario.

10

2001

Shauna and Colm Meet the Parents

The weather had held up, with sun beaming down from clear blue skies, so we were off to a great start on a special day. I brushed down the skirt of my cream dress as I got out of the car, then felt Colm's hand slip into mine and his mouth nuzzle my ear.

'I can't believe your parents stole our day. Damned inconsiderate.'

'I know, they should be ashamed,' I agreed, with mock sadness. 'You ready for this? Remember, it'll be... different.'

'Of course. And stop looking at me like that. How bad can it be?'

Oh, he had no idea. I'd spent the entire journey from Twickenham to Wimbledon with a growing feeling of unease creeping through my nervous system. Or was it dread? Probably a combination of both.

I was fairly sure Colm's family bore no resemblance to mine. He'd been a late baby and his father had passed away when he was a young boy, so he'd been brought up by his mum, who was now almost seventy. There was a fifteen-year age difference between him and his older brother Liam, so he'd explained that they'd never been particularly close. That said, he loved them dearly, called once a week to keep in touch, and truly cared about them.

My family dynamic was a very different splash in the gene pool.

As we started up the path to my parents' house, I could already hear the loud chatter and the music coming from the house and garden. Their twenty-fifth wedding anniversary celebration, an event that had completely slipped my mind the week before when Colm had proposed in bed with only Ben & Jerry as witnesses. Actually proposed. And I'd said yes. How could that even happen four weeks after you'd met someone for the first time? More than that, how could I still have absolutely no doubts whatsoever that I was doing the right thing? None at all. This was it. The real deal. I was actually disappointed when it transpired we'd have to wait longer than a week so that we could sort out small technicalities like churches and family gatherings, and I was totally and hopelessly in love with this man, yet – I realized as I noticed the smart black boots he was wearing with his navy suit – I didn't even know his shoe size.

However, there was no doubt this was going to be our biggest test so far. Meeting Davie and Joe had been a walk in the park – two gorgeous little guys who hadn't batted an eyelid at the introduction of daddy's new friend. Even his ex-wife Jess, in the brief exchange when we'd collected the boys, had been friendly and didn't seem at all fazed by my addition to the equation. It had been a lovely day and so incredibly easy and relaxed. I was fairly sure those words wouldn't be used to describe today.

'Remember, they're different,' I warned again.

'Ah, come on – how bad can it be?' he chuckled.

The door swung open and my mother greeted us with a gregarious, 'Darling! And you must be Calum.'

'It's Colm,' I told her, trying to sound breezy. Colm. Just as I'd told her on the phone that morning. And last weekend. And the week before that. If I kept plugging away she might eventually pay attention, but I doubted it. 'Hi Mum,' I greeted her, with a kiss on each cheek, before stepping aside and letting Colm shake her hand. I could see he was surprised. Everyone always was.

At fifty, my mum, the delectable Debbie, was twenty-six years older than me but looked like she was in her early forties, maybe even late thirties, with her blonde glossy bob, and her wide, perfect smile. Courtesy of the fact that she rarely consumed anything more filling than a salmon fillet, she also had a size eight figure that allowed her to shop in Topshop, or whatever trendy store took her fancy. However, she never went too young, keeping it classy and more or less age-appropriate. Today she was in a bright red, Roland Mouret-style dress that clung to every curve and finished mid-calf, above nude strappy sandals. She looked magnificent.

'You look gorgeous, Mum.'

'Thank you, darling,' she replied, in a breezy tone that

implied I was telling her something she already knew. Of course she did. If there was one thing my mother didn't lack is was self-assurance. 'You look lovely too, dear, even with a bit of extra weight on you.'

There it was. Barb number one, and I wasn't even in the door yet. Colm's eyes widened, but I brushed right over it. If he was going to be part of this family, he was going to have to learn that the main requirements were thick skin and low expectations.

I braced myself and carried on down the hallway and into the kitchen, looking for the one ray of sunshine that would make the day so much more bearable. She was right there, sitting at the big old oak table that had been there my whole life.

'Gran, how're you doing?' I asked, reaching down to hug her.

'Aye, I'm great, love. Has your mother insulted you yet?'

'Before I even got in the door.'

The two of us disintegrated into helpless giggles. My dad's mum was fierce, Scottish, straight to the point, took no prisoners and had a heart that was way, way, bigger than her tiny frame. She'd met my granddad, Ernie, on a weekend trip to London and never went home – something she'd always explained by shrugging and muttering, 'It was the sixties, petal.' He must have been some man to catch her. He'd been an accountant, a profession that somehow didn't fit with Annie's wild ways and daredevil personality. Perhaps it was a case of opposites attracting. He'd died just before I was born, so I'd never met him, but Annie still kept his photo by the side of her bed.

I loved her beyond words. She was the first and only call I'd made after Colm proposed. We'd told Lulu, Rosie and Dan later that night. Rosie thought it was the most romantic thing she'd ever heard, Dan was astonished and Lulu was horrified and offered to pay for my therapy as an engagement gift.

'Gran, this is Colm. Colm, this is Annie,' I made the introductions.

'Pleased to meet you, son,' she said, and I could see Colm instinctively relax as he picked up the warmth in her voice. Like a spy in some Cold War movie, she furtively looked around to check no one was within earshot. 'Congratulations. It's a bit soon, mind, but this one's a smart cookie, so you must be all right.'

Colm's face was a glorious mixture of amusement and worry over what to say next. His panic was averted by the arrival of Lulu and Rosie. I'd completely forgotten they'd be there, but of course they'd been invited. Lulu's parents and mine had been friends – more than friends, but that was another story altogether – since we were children, and since Rosie and I had met in college, she'd been a regular visitor to events that required celebration. In my mother's world, that meant just about any occasion. No occurrence was too small to throw together a soiree for thirty, at which she'd be the glamorous centre of attention. My dad was friendly enough, charismatic even, but he had zero paternal instincts whatsoever. There was no attachment. No thought given to any aspect of my life. I simply didn't enter his orbit unless I was standing in front of him, in which case he treated me like a casual but fairly welcome friend. I'd tried to explain all this to Colm without sounding like I was complaining or in any way bitter. I genuinely wasn't. It was the way it had always been and I hadn't even known any different until I was old enough to hang out at friends' houses, with parents who were more concerned with their children than themselves. Even way back then, I'd accepted that mine weren't that way inclined and I was never going to change them, so there was no point trying. Besides, if nothing else, they threw a great party.

'Hey toots, you're here.' My dad entered with a flourish, looking bright and tanned in his coral pink polo shirt and chinos. There was clearly a golf trip to Spain in his recent past.

I kissed him on the cheek and gave him a hug. 'Hi Dad. Happy anniversary. This is Colm. Colm, this is my dad, Jeff.'

They shook hands, with Colm managing not to wince at what I knew would be a knuckle-crushing exchange. It was an Alpha-male thing.

'Come on outside and join in,' Dad commanded. No chat. No 'how are you?' No 'It's great to see you, it's been weeks, is all well in your life?' Again, I wasn't bothered in the least, but Colm looked perplexed as he took it all in. 'Lulu, Rosie, you come along too. And you, Mother.'

He was the only one who didn't register Annie's eye roll as we headed out to join the other fifty or so guests on the lush, flower-bordered lawn. He immediately went into host mode, shaking hands, wandering from group to group.

'Don't eat the food,' my gran hissed for my ears only, gesturing to the buffet table. 'Your mother got some fancy caterer to do it instead of you, so we're protesting with a hunger strike.'

The champagne I was drinking caught in my throat and I choked on a mixture of bubbles and hilarity. God, I adored my gran. She knew I'd offered to do the catering and my mother had refused, telling her friends she wanted something 'a little more upmarket'. I loved that Annie was outraged on my behalf.

The rest of the afternoon passed in a flurry of social niceties and polite conversation with my parents' friends, all of which felt unusually enjoyable because I was introducing Colm to everyone. It was a tough crowd – their main subjects of conversation were golf, house prices and rising crime in the suburbs – but he handled it brilliantly and didn't complain once. Of course, my parents didn't come over to chat to us. Nope, meeting their daughter's new boyfriend didn't even come close to registering on their scale of interest. Still, Colm's effort with their cohorts was one more thing to add to the long list of things I already loved about him, while the mind-numbing boredom was one more reason to have another drink. Lulu and Rosie obviously had the same idea.

'Has Colm cracked yet and begged to leave?' Lulu asked as we met at the beer section of the bar that had been set up near the ornamental pond.

'Nope.'

'Then dump him now, because there must be something wrong with him.'

Rosie gave her a swift elbow in the ribs. 'Enough. Shauna, don't you dare dump him.'

'Where are Dan and Paul?' I asked.

'Paul is studying for his finals,' Rosie answered. 'Poor

thing is working so hard – have barely seen him for weeks.' I registered a subtle sadness in her voice and I made a mental note to call her tomorrow and check she was okay.

'And Dan said he'd rather put forks in his eyes than spend the afternoon with my parents,' Lulu said, gesturing to her mum and dad, Gwen and Charlie, who had now joined the group I'd left Colm with. I could see them making introductions, Colm still giving the impression of someone who actually wanted to be there. That was a talent.

When Lu and I were kids, we'd been far too young to understand the psychology behind it, but looking back, I could see immediately why we bonded and stuck together. Two only children, both products of parents who believed life was for their own enjoyment, and treated their offspring as mild hindrances that belonged fairly low down the pecking order. When we were teenagers, we had more of an understanding of the situation and decided that on the scale of parental importance, we came somewhere between golf and a visit to the salon for an eyebrow wax. That conclusion hadn't changed much.

I rejoined Colm, exchanged a flurry of air kisses with Lu's parents, and then listened as they resumed a scintillating conversation about the local golf club expansion plans. I was close to losing the will to live when I spotted my parents were talking to each other at the French doors that led back through to the kitchen.

This was as good a time as any to tell them. It had to be today, because I couldn't risk my gran blurting it out. I was fairly certain my mother wouldn't be particularly bothered about the news, but her nose would be out of joint if she thought Annie had gazumped her in the gossip stakes.

'Excuse me a second, can I just steal Colm?'

The flicker of relief in his expression was well-disguised but, nevertheless, I spotted it. So he was human after all.

'You're doing great,' I whispered as I led him across the lawn. 'Annie says if it gets too much she'll distract them with a conga and we can make our escape.'

He was still laughing when we reached the anniversary couple.

'Mum, Dad, can we have a quick word?' It suddenly struck me that I should probably have warned Colm about what I was about to do.

'Now, darling?' my mother asked, clearly not appreciating my timing. 'We're just about to cut the cake.'

'It'll only take two minutes,' I promised, realizing from the slight flush of her face that she was already a few glasses of champagne to the merry.

I decided to dive right in. 'Colm and I just wanted to let you both know that we're getting married. He proposed last week and I accepted.'

In my peripheral vision I could see Colm's head doing an *Exorcist* swirl in my direction. Definitely should have warned him.

The folks didn't miss a beat. 'Oh that's lovely, dear. Well done,' Mother said, like she'd just discovered I took third prize in a pie-making competition. Actually, pies would be a bit downmarket for her. It would have to be quiche.

'Well, that's a bit of a shock,' my dad said quietly, and

I felt Colm tense. He obviously didn't know my dad well enough to spot what was on his mind. Thankfully, I did.

'Don't worry, Dad, we're eloping,' I said. 'Your retirement fund is safe.'

Like he'd just been reprieved from a heinous fate, his whole demeanour switched from concerned to relieved. He had a 360-degree attitude shift, reached out and pumped Colm's hand.

'Great news. Happy for you both.'

'Thank you. Sorry, I hadn't realized Shauna was going to break the news today,' Colm stuttered, cast a startled 'what the hell?' glance in my direction. He'd thank me later. Delivering big news about my life to my parents was like ripping off a Band-Aid – best to be quick and get it over with, because if you took your time it only caused irritation. 'I'd intended to ask your permission first. And yours, Mrs. Williams.'

That was news to me. I was even happier that we'd broke the news today. Normal tradition definitely wasn't required when it came to my parents.

'Call me Debbie,' she preened. 'And our permission isn't required. Whatever Shauna wants is fine with us.' And whatever causes the least disruption to our lives is even better. I added that last sentence in my mind.

My mother's beautiful face suddenly twisted with panic. 'You're not going to announce it here today, are you?'

Again, I knew exactly what she was thinking.

'Of course not, Mum. This is your day.'

Her relief was instant. Heaven forbid anything should detract from their moment.

'Right, well I'll come into town this week and you can tell me all about it.' We both knew she wouldn't. 'Jeff, time for the cake.' And once again, the attention was back on Debbie. Normal service resumed.

Colm stared at their retreating forms, while I waited until they were out of earshot, before summarizing the situation with a dramatic but hushed flourish that only Colm could hear. 'Ladies and gentlemen, I give you Jeff and Debbie Williams. Pillars of society, social whirlwinds and lovely people, just as long as you're not their daughter. Available for conversations about golf, wine and the timeshare in Marbella. Not so much interested in aforementioned daughter's impending nuptials.'

'Yeah, they're eh…' he struggled to pinpoint the word, eventually settling for '…definitely different.'

'They are indeed. I'll understand if you want to run and save yourself before you're in too deep.' It was in jest but there was an element of honesty to it. If he was looking to marry into a loving, warm, caring family, this wasn't it. My stomach suddenly lurched at the thought that our twisted parent/child dynamic may have given him second thoughts about joining the family.

His arm slipped around my shoulders and he pulled me close. 'I'm marrying you, not that pair of crackers,' he told me. 'But I think it's a fecking miracle you turned out normal.'

I was still kissing him when a loud cough cut through the chatter around us.

'Ladies and gentlemen,' my dad's booming voice carried right across the garden and, standing next to him, my mother beamed to her audience. They looked genuinely happy and

I was genuinely pleased for them. Not many couples lasted twenty-five years. But then, not many couples had the kind of marriage that had worked for Jeff and Debbie. It was unusual, to say the least. And I was fairly sure that most of the assembled guests didn't know the half of it.

We worked our way around the lawn, until we were level with the happy couple but off to the right-hand side of them, shaded by the foliage of a huge leylandii.

'I just wanted to thank you all for coming here today, to help me celebrate twenty-five years of being married to this beautiful woman.'

Stockbroker Central gave a semi-rousing cheer.

'Of course, our time together has been made so special by the people in our lives. My mother, Annie…' He raised a glass in a toast in the direction of my granny. She put on her best fake smile as she gave him a nod, setting me off on the giggles again.

'Our daughter, Shauna,' he continued, gesturing over to where I'd been standing five minutes ago. He was too vain to wear his specs so he'd have no idea that I was now standing just across from him. Still, I'd been honoured with a mention and he'd got my name right. That might be a pinnacle in our relationship.

'And I couldn't let this day pass without thanking the two people who've been with us from the start. Gwen and Charlie, come on over here.'

Across the other side of the garden, I caught Lulu's gaze as her parents came to the front to stand beside mine. We sent each other a silent message that required no words. Lulu's mother and mine could have been sisters, both petite, blonde, impeccably groomed, while her dad, Charlie, had long since lost his hair, but not his suave charm and expensive tastes, evident from the Armani logo on his cream polo top and the thick gold Rolex watch round his wrist.

'Charlie and Gwen were our best man and bridesmaid, and I'm delighted to say they're still our closest friends.'

Another cheer.

'So, ladies and gentlemen, here's to my beautiful Debbie, our friends Gwen and Charlie and the last twenty-five fantastic years! Let's hope that there's another twenty-five ahead of us.'

The gathering toasted the happy foursome. To an outsider it must look like the perfect scenario of love, family and happiness. If only they knew. Love and happiness maybe, but Lulu and I had learned much too young that family didn't enter the equation.

Jeff sealed the moment by kissing my mum on the lips, to another chorus of whoops. Lovely.

My dad shouted something about dancing and suddenly there was music, Rod Stewart's 'Maggie May', blaring from inside the house. He must have teed someone up to switch on his sound system. It was rigged up from the kitchen to two outdoor speakers on the top corners of the conservatory and had provided the musical backdrop to hundreds of parties over the years.

Lulu and Rosie worked their way over to us, cutting through a couple of dozen people in the middle of the garden shuffling from one foot to another with various degrees of enthusiasm.

'Did your heart melt?' Lulu asked me, teasing.

'Like butter in the midday sun,' I retorted with feigned sincerity.

'So how soon do you think we can bail out without being rude?'

I checked my watch. 'I'm going to give it another half an hour and then my duty is done.'

Colm listened to the interchange with fascination. 'This is the weirdest afternoon I've ever had.'

I could see his point. Who meets the guy who's going to marry their only daughter and barely gives him a second glance? Welcome to the world of the Williams.

'Is it always like this?' he went on, and I could see he was struggling over whether to be amused or horrified.

'Pretty much,' Lulu confirmed. 'We've spent our whole lives being the less than perfect daughters of the two most self-centred couples in the free world. It breeds a certain set of survival skills. We had to get sarcastic or die.'

'Well you're doing a grand job on it.' He obviously decided to block out the bizarreness and turned to Rosie. 'How's life treating you, Rosie?'

He and Rosie had hit it off from the start. We'd all probably got together on around a dozen occasions over the last few weeks and it felt like Colm had been part of the group forever.

'It's great,' she said, her sunny tone perfectly matching her yellow forties-style sundress that accentuated her curves, and neat pillbox hat. She was the only one there in head-wear, but she absolutely pulled it off.

'Rosie, get over here and show these old ones how it's done.'

I closed my eyes and said a silent prayer for mercy to God, as my dad appeared and swept Rosie away to jive to an Elvis number.

'And we just went one step higher up the rung of crazy,' I murmured.

Although, it had to be said, despite the age difference, they were the star attraction. All those years Rosie's mother had dragged her to dance lessons paid off. The crowd formed a circle around them applauding their every synchronized move.

'Can you do that?' Colm asked.

'Nope.'

'Och, don't be modest.'

Lulu shook her head. 'She's not being modest. She dances like a giraffe on coke.'

'There you have it,' I confirmed.

When Rosie got back to us she was giggling and fanning her face with her hand. 'Your dad's got moves,' she said, hands on hips now, slightly bent over in a bid to get her breathing back to normal. It took a glass and a half of champagne before she'd fully recovered. I was glad to see her mood lift. Maybe I'd been wrong about her sadness earlier.

'Okay, so we've been here all afternoon and Colm still hasn't fled in horror, so I think I'm going to quit while I'm ahead and call it a day. Girls, I'll call you both...' I kissed Lulu, '...during the week,' I finished, kissing Rosie this time.

'Don't leave us!' Lulu wailed, laughing as she clutched on to my arm.

I prised her fingers off. 'Sorry, you're on your own. If it gets really bad there's always vodka.'

I gave them both another hug, ignoring Lulu's exaggerated petulance, and we headed into the kitchen, where Annie was holding court at the cooker, while stirring a large pot of something.

'That's us away now, Gran,' I told her, bending down to hug her tightly. She was barely five feet tall, but never left home without her heels, which took her to five foot three. Yet she had a personality that made her seem so much bigger.

'Okay, pet. I'll phone you later to tell you what I think of the boyfriend,' she said, with a wink at Colm who was standing right beside her.

'Can you make it favourable please? I'd like her to keep me around.'

'I might, but I'm not promising anything,' she said, enjoying the banter. I could see she adored him already – and her opinion was the only one that really mattered to me.

I scanned the room but couldn't see any sign of my parents.

'Any idea where Mum and Dad are?' I asked her.

She carried on stirring the pot as she gestured to the door leading to the hallway. 'I think I saw them go past there and go upstairs.'

'Okay, thanks – we'll go track them down and say goodbye.'

Wordlessly, Colm followed me upstairs, almost crashing into me when I suddenly stopped at the top.

'What...'

I immediately covered his mouth with my hand and gestured to the other side of the landing, and the open door to my mum and dad's bedroom. My dad's back was to us, his neck bent as the couple tenderly kissed.

Putting my other hand on Colm's shoulder, I silently

pushed him back downstairs, ignoring the confused look on his face. We went straight out the front door, and only then did he manage to speak.

'What's up? I think it's pretty romantic that your mum and dad are still up for a snog.'

I exhaled deeply, totally pissed off that the day had ended this way.

'Yep, my dad is definitely still up for a snog. But that wasn't my mum – it was Lulu's.'

'Lulu's mum?' he repeated, aghast, for clarification.

'Yep,' I said, suddenly exhausted. Oh the irony. A twenty-five-year wedding anniversary party, and for most of those years both couples had enjoyed open marriages. My dad's thing with Lulu's mum had been going on for over a decade, while both their spouses had been happily engaged elsewhere with a trail of dalliances of their own. No secrets. No guilt. No thought as to how any of this would affect me and Lulu. And now Colm too.

I slipped my hand into his. 'I meant what I said earlier. Now might be a good time for you to cut your losses and run.'

11

2015

Shauna Takes Charge

'You're miles away. Have you heard anything I've said in the last ten minutes?' Rosie asked, as she poured more coffee into my half-empty cup. Not half-full. It wasn't that kind of day.

I'd catered a breakfast meeting at a primary school in Fulham, then dashed over to do a lunch at the boardroom of a trendy IT company in Acton, where I watched as all these energized young twenty-year-olds discussed world domination. Or at least, software domination. I'm not sure I was ever that focussed. I must have been once, but perhaps it's just too long ago to remember.

I'd arranged to meet Colm at Rosie's café afterwards. I was actually now multi-tasking my social life. That's what it had come to.

'Sorry, hon, just a bit distracted. And tired. You know,

I'm so sick of hearing myself moan about being knackered. You have my permission to gag me if I do it again.'

She leaned forward, elbows on the table. 'Shauna, you can't go on like this. It's killing you. When was the last time you had eight hours' sleep?'

'About 2005,' I replied honestly.

'Exactly. It's got to stop. And besides that, you need to stop dressing like you're in mourning.'

'But…' Foolishly, I was about to object. I stopped myself. My zero-effort, zero-thought, zero-colour, black jeans and black polo neck jumper didn't give me much of an argument, especially against her flaming red dress, accessorized by a thick pink cummerbund and jaunty pink neck scarf. She looked like she'd just stepped off the set of *Grease*, while I could pass as an extra in a documentary about embalming.

She was right on all counts, but I didn't have the answer. Actually, I did. Bracal Tech. Colm and Dan still hadn't heard whether they'd got the contract. I sent up another silent prayer of pleading to the Gods of Business Expansion.

My eyes drifted to the huge old-fashioned station clock on the wall behind the counter. Three o'clock. Colm's appointment with the doctor was at two o'clock and I'd warned him not to come back without an appointment for a scan. I knew I was being ridiculous, but it was an acknowledged fact that sleep deprivation and stress could turn a person into a neurotic, worrying, overcautious wreck. Evidence for the prosecution right here. If he would only get the scan, it would show all was well and I'd have one less thing to fret about.

'Anyway, cheer me up – tell me about your love life.'

'It's… fine,' she replied. 'Great actually.'

'Oooh, I like the sound of great.'

'Jack thinks we should move in together.'

I sat up straighter, suddenly more alert. Techies in Acton might get energized by highbrow software discussions but exciting news in my friend's love life had the same effect on me.

'And what did you say?' I asked, already knowing what the answer would be but determined to relish the moment.

'I said I need to think about it.'

'Rosie, that's… what?' I started gushy and finished weakly, doing a 180-degree turn in my reaction when I'd absorbed what she said. That categorically wasn't the answer I was expecting.

I could see she was chewing the inside of her left cheek and she only did that when she was worried or sad.

'What's going on?' I asked. 'I thought this was what you wanted.'

'It is,' she said, her eyes wide. Was that tears nestling just inside the lower lids? 'But now that he's asked me I'm just not sure. Maybe it's too soon. Don't you think?'

'Rosie, you're talking to a woman who married a man after she'd known him for eleven weeks. Anything longer than that seems like a prolonged engagement to me.'

That at least made her laugh.

I was about to get into it further when the door opened and Colm strolled in. Maybe it was the light in the café, or the draining effect of his grey sweater, but I definitely thought he was a few shades paler than usual.

He kissed Rosie first, then ruffled my hair with a 'Hey

gorgeous,' as he sat down beside me. My smile was instant. Fourteen years and he still had that effect on me. Rosie bustled off to get more coffee and I got straight to the point. 'How did you get on at the doctors?'

He put a paper bag on the table. 'More beta blockers.'

I couldn't contain my exasperation. 'Oh for God's sake, Colm, that's hopeless.'

'Honey, it's fine. It means there's nothing wrong with me. Doc says these will do the trick.'

'Based on what? Hope and optimism? They haven't made a difference in the two weeks you've been taking them,' I bit back.

Yes, I was directing my frustration at the wrong person, but my anxiety had been escalating and I needed definite answers, not vague theories.

When he'd first mentioned the headaches and other symptoms, I'd been relaxed about it, even nonchalant. In the scale of pressing issues, it hadn't seemed like one to cause concern at all. But as time had gone on, the headaches had increased, the other symptoms had kicked in, and I'd made the fatal mistake of going back on to Google. That lack of concern had now evaporated and it had become the first thing I thought about in the morning and the last thing at night. I found myself watching him constantly. The occasional slight stagger. The flinches of pain. The odd jumbled word. The repeated blinking of his eyes when it seemed like he was trying to clear something from his vision. All small things, all infrequent, but in my head they'd grown into a huge reason to fret. That's why I'd been so clear about the path to resolution: scan head, all clear, worry ends.

Staring into my coffee cup, I took a deep breath. Why couldn't things just be taken care of? Why was everything so damn difficult?

His hand rested on my forearm. 'Darlin', you need to stop worrying about things. It's all going to work out. I promise.'

The love in his voice made a chink in my heart and I immediately regretted giving him a hard time. No wonder the poor guy had headaches. Being married to me in my current overwound state would give me a headache. 'I know. And I'm sorry. I win today's prize for overreaction.'

'You're lucky I've a particular fondness for dramatic, overanxious women,' he said, grinning, before proceeding to pick up what was left of my coffee and knock it back.

'Come on, let's go pick up Beth from school and go to the park. I think I need an hour of running around with my girl,' I told him.

He pointed out the obvious. 'It's raining.'

'I don't care.'

'Then I'm in.'

We both stood up just as Rosie reappeared with a large coffee pot.

'Are you off? I just made this fresh.'

'Sorry. We're going to get Beth.'

'Ah, give her a huge hug from me,' Rosie said, before putting the coffee pot on a nearby table, occupied by two elderly gents. 'On the house,' she told them.

'I'll call you later and we can continue that conversation,' I promised, as I picked up my bag from the floor and phone from the table, then hugged her goodbye, with a 'love you' thrown in.

We jumped into my van and headed to Beth's school. It could take an hour or half an hour, depending on the traffic. Today, it took half an hour, so when we rode down George Street in Richmond town centre, I made a sudden decision and pulled into a rare free parking space right outside a bank of shops.

Colm's bewilderment was obvious, until I pointed in the direction of the optician's shop on the corner. 'Let's go get your eyes tested in case that's what's causing the headaches.'

'There's nothing wrong with my eyes,' he argued. He was probably right. I was completely overreacting. Yet I wasn't backing down. 'Colm, you said that you were getting weird shadows in your peripheral vision sometimes.'

'That's the migraines!' Standing in the pouring rain, arguing with his wife, I could see he was getting irate.

'So let's just check,' I pleaded, then switched to cajoling. 'Come on, humour me.'

He knew when he was beaten and followed me as I navigated the puddles and the shoppers who'd been brave enough to venture out in this weather.

The bespectacled receptionist in the optician's greeted us with a cheery smile. 'How can I help you?'

'Apparently I'd like an eye test,' Colm answered in a rueful tone that immediately created the accurate impression that he was here under duress.

The receptionist began tapping on the keyboard in front of her. 'No problem. We can do next Tuesday or Wed…'

'Oh.' That came from me. 'Sorry, I didn't realize we had to book.' Damn, why hadn't I thought of that? 'It can't be done now?'

'No, I'm sorry but we're fully booked today.'

'Oh,' I repeated.

My disappointment must have triggered something in her customer service training as her eyes went back to her screen, and then…

'Except… Our 3.30 appointment hasn't turned up, so if it's okay with the optician, I could see if she'll squeeze you in now.'

My face flooded with relief, more so when she didn't even need to ask. A woman in a white coat had appeared from a side room and joined the conversation. 'Come on in. I can see you now.' She held out her hand. 'Janice Lowery.'

'I'm Colm O'Flynn, and this is my wife, Shauna. She made me come here. Forced me,' he admitted, making Janice laugh. I liked her on sight. Perhaps late fifties, her short grey hair and make-up-free face were given a flash of colour by purple-framed, fifties-style glasses that Rosie would adore.

'Don't worry,' she said, patting him on the arm. 'It's painless, and if you're really good you get a sticker.'

Someone with a sense of humour was all it took for Colm to jump in the large black leather chair with no further complaint. I slid into a small chair in the corner and as she ran through a list of questions, filling the answers in on a customer record card attached to a green clipboard, I felt myself relax. It was all going to be fine. I'd never even have to tell him the full truth. When I'd been reading up on possible causes of the headaches, I'd read that problems in the brain could be spotted in an eye test and that was why I'd really dragged him here. If he wasn't going to get a head scan, this was the next best thing. My solution to anxiety rewrote itself in my mind. Eye test, all clear, worry ends. Happy days.

Colm's personal information attained, Janice lowered the clipboard. 'So what brought you here today?'

I was about to jump in with an answer when Colm beat me to it.

'Over the last few weeks I've been getting the odd head-ache, so my dearly beloved here is making me get it checked out. I'm completely under the thumb.'

Under her exceptionally stylish eyewear, Janice didn't bat an eyelid. 'Are the headaches caused by anything in particular? Reading? Television?'

'Wife?' I added, making Colm grin. It was a small apology for springing this on him.

'Wife,' Colm confirmed.

Smiling, Janice raised the clipboard and made a few more notes.

'Any vision problems?'

'Sometimes the peripheral vision on my right-hand side seems to...' Colm thought about it before putting it into words, 'narrow slightly. Like there's a blind spot there. Or a shadow. Nothing drastic, though.'

Janice nodded, then fired off some more questions. Did he have any other medical conditions? No. High blood pressure? No. Dizziness? No. Fainting? No. Was he taking any medication? Just the beta blockers. After a dozen or so enquiries, she placed the clipboard back on the desk and slid towards Colm, the wheels on her red chair squeaking.

'Right, let's see if we can get to the bottom of this.'

Janice placed a modified spectacle frame on his face, then

began a series of tests using the chart on the opposite wall. As I listened to him rhyming off the letters in the partial darkness, my newfound relaxation went one step further and I was powerless to resist as my eyelids closed.

Somewhere between awake and asleep, I heard her say, 'Excellent! Your vision is almost 20/20. Quite unusual in a man of your age, Mr O'Flynn.'

'Can you repeat that to my wife, please?' he jested.

See. It was all going to be fine. Perfect. Nothing to worry about. Huge relief. I opened my eyes. Time to go and get Beth. I was about to stand, dust myself off and head to the car, when I saw that she was pulling a large machine in front of Colm, a steel frame with some kind of huge white microscope in the centre.

Apparently we weren't yet done.

'Just rest your chin there, please Mr O'Flynn,' she asked, pointing to a black plastic support strap under the microscope.

He did as he was asked, and she wheeled in front of him in her chair, so that their faces were only inches apart.

'Right, I'm just going to check the inside of your eyes and then that'll be you done. Now, left eye first. Look over my right ear.' Reaching over, she gently lifted Colm's lid. 'Now look up. Look left. Look...' She faltered for a second, then repeated, 'Look left.

I was instantly wide awake again. There was something in her tone, an uncertainty, maybe a concern? Or was I just being completely overanxious again?

Wheeling back, she readjusted the scope for the right eye. 'And look right.'

No hesitation this time. I chided myself. That prize for

overreaction was definitely mine today. Once again, I'd allowed my imagination to run riot.

She sat back, and I expected that to conclude the test, but instead, she readjusted the equipment again. 'I'm just going to have another look in the left eye,' she informed him. My stomach cramped. I wasn't imagining it. There was something...

When she was done, she snapped the light on, pushing her chair back and removing the steel frame that sat between her and Colm.

'Right then,' she said, in a gentle manner that was like a flashing red light warning of oncoming trouble. 'Let me come straight to the point. I think there's an issue here that needs attention, Mr O'Flynn.'

'I need glasses?' he asked brightly, totally uncomprehending of what she was saying. Blind faith and optimism strikes again.

'No, your eyesight is fine.'

I could see this confused him.

She carried on. 'The last test I did allows me to look at the nerves and blood vessels of the eyes, and gives a very clear picture of the eye health.'

I suddenly realized I was holding my breath.

She pointed to a poster on the wall beside her that had a cross-section of an eye, with a myriad of little worm-like lines feeding through it. 'Here is a picture of a healthy eye. However, in your eyes, I'm seeing a slightly different picture – a pressure is causing a swelling of the optic nerve. Can I ask again if you've ever had problems with high blood pressure?'

Still couldn't breathe. And now a creeping sensation of fear was working its way up my spine.

Colm shook his head, his expression showing that even he was slightly concerned now. 'No. At least, not as far as I know. The doctor checked it a few weeks ago and it was fine. Although as I said, he did give me beta blockers to help with the migraines.'

'Migraines. So more than just "the odd headache then".' There was a gentle, teasing rebuke. 'And you say you've been having them for a few weeks?'

'A month. Maybe two.' If I didn't know him so well, I'd say his carefree tone was conveying all the gravity of someone reading the weather forecast. Today will be breezy and fine. Over in my corner of the room, it was considerably more stormy.

'He has been under a lot of strain lately,' I interjected, sounding almost desperate. 'So that could cause his blood pressure to rise, couldn't it?'

Yes, that must be it. High blood pressure we could handle. We could fix that.

'It could,' she conceded. 'But if your blood pressure is normal, then there could be another reason behind what I'm seeing here. I think it's definitely something we need to have investigated straight away.' She picked up Colm's form and scanned the page, before lifting the phone next to her and dialling a number.

Oh bugger. She actually did mean straight away. This couldn't be good.

'Yes, this is Janice Lowery at The Eye Centre. Can I speak to Dr. Morton? Yes, I'll hold.'

Stomach churning, I checked the clock. Afternoon surgery would be over by now, and the doctor probably wouldn't even be in the building.

We shouldn't have come. We should just have waited at the school for Beth, coffee in hand, having a giggle until she appeared and we could go kick leaves in the park. This was a mistake.

'Dr Morton, hello again.' So they knew each other. That explained why he took the call. Getting to speak to a doctor at that surgery was on a par with securing an audience with the Pope.

'I've a Mr O'Flynn here. Colm O'Flynn. I've just had a look at his eyes and there's evidence of possible papilledema.'

A papilledema? I racked my mind to remember if I'd come across that word during my Google searches, but my brain was frozen, refusing to co-operate. Please make that a small thing. Nothing serious. Easily fixed. Yet Janice's end of the conversation suggested otherwise.

'I'd recommend an urgent referral. Can you take care of that please? Yes, I'll let them know. Hold on, let me check.' She picked up the form again and rhymed off Colm's mobile number. 'Lovely. Thank you doctor, I'll tell them to expect your call, and in the meantime I'll photograph what I'm seeing and email over the image.'

She hung up. 'They'll get back to you first thing in the morning. If they don't, please call them and check on it. Now, I'm just going to take a quick image…'

The machine in front of Colm was swiftly replaced with a different one, and there was a couple of clicks of a shutter.

Dear God, what was going on? What had started as

an impromptu plan to get a bit of reassurance was now backfiring spectacularly.

'Doctor…' I started.

'Janice,' she corrected me, kindly.

'Janice. What could cause this?'

'Well, it could be high blood pressure.' Her gaze moved to Colm. 'It could even be that this is your normal status and it's been like this your whole life. I have seen this before.'

'But it could also be something more serious?'

The fear that had been working its way up my spine was now choking my words.

'It could,' she conceded, again in a very calm, convivial way. 'What's concerning you, Mrs O'Flynn?'

'Could it be a brain tumour?' I could barely get the words out. Yes, it had been on my mind and the main driver in making Colm come here, but I'd been sure I was being ridiculous. Please let me be ridiculous. Please let me be wrong.

'Shauna, it's not a brain tumour,' Colm said, like it was the most ludicrous suggestion he'd ever heard. I chose not to remind him about the internet search results on the medical website a few weeks before.

Janice paused for a moment, before carrying on. 'Yes. But that would be highly unusual. In twenty years as an optician I've only seen that once before.'

'Once in twenty years. I like those odds,' Colm told her.

I didn't. If it happened once, it could happen again.

'But regardless of whether it's something minor or something that requires further attention, you do need to get it checked out.' It was no consolation that she was reinforcing the point I'd been making for weeks.

Colm was out of the chair now, shaking her hand, then taking mine, leading me outside. Only when we were back in the street, the rain pounding on our heads, did he wrap his arms around me.

'Honey, don't worry. This will be fine. I promise you. It'll all be fine.'

I wasn't sure if he was trying to convince me or himself.

There was complete silence in the van as I drove almost robotically to collect Beth, arriving at the school and taking our place next to dozens of other parents. Thankfully the rain had stopped and there was no one close by that I recognized. I was glad on both counts. School-gate chatter was definitely not what I needed right now.

A couple of minutes after the bell rang, Beth tore out of the door and ran towards us.

'Mum! Dad! I had a fa-a-a-a-n-tastic day,' she blurted, high as a kite.

Colm picked her up and spun her around and I forced myself to smile.

'So we were thinking...' I told her, with gushing enthusiasm. 'That we'd go to the park and then maybe for ice cream.'

Her eyes widened with pure excitement. 'Yaaaayyyyyy. Can we? Can I have strawberry ripple?'

Our daughter definitely did enjoyment and enthusiasm in equal measure.

Meanwhile, my internal dialogue was screaming with equal proportions of incomprehension and dread. I felt totally overwhelmed. This was surreal. Couldn't be happening. And yet it was.

'You can have anything you want, sweetheart,' Colm told

her, placing her back on solid ground. She reached up and took my hand and his, skipping between us.

'This is the best day ever!'

The best day ever.

Or the worst.

I had no idea, but I was praying for my daughter's verdict.

After all, didn't we have blind faith and optimism on our side?

12

2001

When Colm Breaks the News
to His Ex-wife

Iknew the boys would love her. There was never any
question, but she sealed the deal by doing the best
impression of Buzz Lightyear they'd ever heard. 'To Infinity
and Beyond' became their very own phrase of endearment the
first time we took them out, and now their eyes immediately
searched for Shauna when they saw me coming. Great judges
of character, my boys, even when they were knackered, as
they were now. We'd had two rounds of laser tag and a spin
on the go-carts today, after a late-night showing of a Shrek
video at my place last night. My housemate, Doug, was on
night shift, and had offered Shauna his room, while the boys
slept in with me, top and tail. Perfect.

'Right, troops, time to go home,' I told them, and was
greeted with wails of objections.

'Nooooo! That's not fair. Why do we need to go home? Is Shauna coming home with us too?'

The thing with having twins was that everything came in stereo and by the time you'd listened to every question they threw at you, you'd forgotten the ones at the start.

Shauna kneeled down and gave Joe a hug. 'Not today SuperJoe – I need to go to work. Right, let's fly!' She picked him up, swung him around, and he was so busy squealing with joy he soon forgot to be unhappy that she wasn't coming home with them.

As we left the indoor play centre, Shauna helped them on with their jackets, then slipped her hand into mine. 'They look exhausted.'

'They've had a great time,' I told her. 'Thanks to you.'

It was true. It was hard to believe she'd only known them for a few weeks. To any outsider we probably looked like mum, dad and the kids out for a Sunday day trip. I liked that idea. She was a natural at this kids stuff. It helped that the boys were easy-going little dudes, but she just always knew what to say to them. She claimed it was all the parties she catered, but I reckoned it was just her personality. Who wouldn't love her?

Out on the street I flagged down a cab, then turned to see Shauna crouched down, arms outstretched. 'Right, boys, I'll see you soon,' she told them, then almost toppled as both of them pounced on her. Their goodbyes and lists of things we'd do next week were taking so long I could see the driver getting restless.

I scooped the boys up. 'Let's go, tigers.'

'Not tigers!' Davie insisted.

'I'm Buzz! To Infinity and Beyond,' Joe yelled.

The driver was probably wishing he'd driven on past and picked up the next person standing on a street corner.

I kissed her. 'I'll come over later, let you know how it goes.'

'Okay. I'm going to go meet my gran for a coffee, but I'll be home by about six. Good luck,' she said. 'And if it doesn't feel right, you don't have to tell Jess – we can wait.'

That wasn't an option. 'I do and we can't,' I told her.

The boys were still hyper when we reached their house and charged in the door ahead of me, leaving a trail of jackets, hats and shoes in their wake.

'Hello?' I shouted, out of courtesy. This had been my house once, but not any more. Jess had completely redecorated, so it didn't even feel like the same house. Now I lived a few streets away and this was all Jess's, so I was conscious not to overstep the boundaries.

'I'm in the kitchen,' Jess shouted. 'Come on through.'

I'd be lying if I said it didn't still feel a bit weird, coming in here as a visitor, instead of kicking off my shoes and announcing that I was home. Not that I wanted to go back there. Definitely not now.

Jess was sitting at the white wood kitchen table, cup of coffee in hand, a magazine open in front of her. She always did like to keep up with fashions. Her auburn hair was cut like a model's. What was it called again? A bob. Yeah, that was it. Cut straight across in a fringe at the front, and then a sharp cut at the chin.

She always looked great, I'll give her that. She was wearing a red plaid shirt that I recognized. We'd bought it on a day in town a couple of years ago, on one of our last days out together. Some bloke had accidentally spilled a drink on her in a bar, so we'd nipped into a shop along the street and she'd picked this shirt out. She'd put it on right there and then, tied it at the waist, and we'd gone back to the pub. I had no idea the next time I saw it we'd be divorced and I'd be asking permission to come into my own house.

'They sound like they had a great day,' she said. 'Want tea?'

I climbed on to the bench at the other side of the table. 'Sure. Thanks.'

We made small talk while she brewed the tea, mostly about the boys, their week at school, what they wanted for Christmas, and what we'd done this weekend. I'd got as far as the Shrek video when she sat back down, passed me the tea and cut me off with, 'Was Shauna there?'

I knew she was trying to keep it friendly, but there was definitely a shade of annoyance in there.

'She was.'

I let that one sit for a moment, unsure where to go with it next.

'The boys seem to like her,' she conceded, calm again.

'She's great with them.'

Another pause. Problem is, I've never been good with awkward situations, so I decided to cut right through it.

'Is this weird? Are you okay talking about her?' I asked.

She put her cup down and sighed. 'Sorry, Colm. It shouldn't be strange and I didn't think it would be, but somehow it is.'

'I get it. It's another woman with your boys...' I let that one hang, not wanting to emphasize it.

For a few moments she didn't say anything, then… 'And my husband.'

That one took me by surprise. I thought about correcting her – ex-husband – but decided against it, choosing to take the opening that gave me.

'Actually, I kind of wanted to have a chat about that.'

She was looking at me intently now, eyebrows raised in curiosity. Or perhaps it was wariness. I'd never been much good at reading Jess – one of the fundamental reasons we were now divorced.

'Shauna and I, we're… getting married.'

Crap, bad timing. Should have waited until she didn't have coffee in her mouth. She immediately started to choke and splutter, taking a few pats on the back and a good twenty seconds to stop – twenty seconds that felt like half an hour.

'Holy fuck,' she finally managed. 'Married?'

'Yeah, sorry to spring it on you like that, but didn't really know how else to tell you.'

She was visibly bristling now. 'Married?' she repeated. 'Weren't you the guy who said you were never getting married again?'

'Now that you mention it…'

Her voice was raised and I found myself wondering if I could use my mug in a shield-like function. Then I decided I shouldn't be having infantile thoughts like that at a moment like this. Sometimes it was very easy to see why I was divorced.

'So what changed?'

'Shauna,' I said simply.

'But you've only been seeing her for five minutes!'

'Ten weeks,' I corrected her. This wasn't going well. It was unlike Jess to be so antagonistic. But then clearly I wasn't great at reading her or else we might still be together.

'And you've already decided to get married?' Irritation had morphed into incredulity. 'When did that happen?'

Sod it, may as well get it all out there. 'I asked her four weeks after we met.'

Thankfully, this time the shock got to her right before she took another sip of her coffee, and her cup froze in mid-air. For a moment I wondered if she was thinking about throwing it at me.

'Look, I'm only telling you all this because I didn't want the boys coming home with half stories. I'd rather tell you myself.'

That seemed to mellow her a little. 'I just… I can't believe all this, Colm,' she said, but there was no anger there, just disbelief. Okay, we were making progress.

'So when's the big day? I hope you're giving yourself some time and not rushing into anything.'

'Next Saturday.'

'Oh. Wow.' The last word was a whisper, then she got up and headed back over to the kettle, flicked it on and stood staring at it as it boiled. She still had half a cup in front of her so I had a feeling this was just a stalling tactic, a distraction from the conversation. I decided to say nothing, give her time to process everything. At least, that's what I was telling myself. The reality was that I had absolutely no idea what else to say. Since the day we'd separated, we'd kept the discussions friendly, purely superficial and only about the kids. I had no idea if she was happy, sad, seeing someone, nothing. I had absolutely zero to lead with here so the silence bounced off the walls.

It was several long minutes before she refilled her cup and sat back down again.

'Are you going to throw that at me? Only I want to be ready to duck.'

'Christ, Colm, not like you to use humour to deflect a tense situation.' Shit. Bristling again.

'Sorry, I…'

She cut me off. 'No, *I'm* sorry. That was just bitchy.'

I wasn't going to argue, so we just indulged in a few moments of respective mug-staring.

Eventually she took her gaze away from her cup. 'I've got absolutely no idea how to feel about all of this. I mean, I probably knew on some level that it would happen one day, but I never expected it to be so soon. We're barely divorced four months.'

'I know. Honest to God, Jess, I didn't plan this, I just fell in…' Using the premise that I'd rather say nothing than the wrong thing, I decided to leave that one there. Jess did too, moving swiftly on to the next question.

'Where's the wedding?'

'A tiny church in a village near Wimbledon. Her folks live out that way. It's not a big fancy do…'

'Like ours, you mean?'

I didn't, but she had a point. Jess and I had met in the first year of college, got engaged in the second, married in the third, in a cathedral in York, with 300 people there, including my whole family – aunts, uncles, cousins, the lot – over from Dublin.

This time around, my ma and my brother Liam would come over, but that was it. Small. Special. In truth, I'd be happy for just the two of us to go to a registry office, but it was the first and last time Shauna would be married so I got that she wanted to have the people she loved around her.

'No, not like ours.' I didn't elaborate. Keep it simple. Less chance of a riotous fuck-up.

Another pause.

'Does she know why we split up?'

I shook my head, but said nothing. I wasn't going to get into this again. If there was one subject that I'd happily never talk about again until the end of time, it was the demise of our marriage. No good could come of going back there and picking through the pieces. Never again.

'Okay. Right.' She seemed to be summoning up some acceptance from somewhere. I didn't push it. Hopefully, we were done chatting and I could make an exit before it all went horribly wrong. We'd survived this, let's leave it at that.

'So why her? What's so special about her?'

Fecking bollocks. Hello rock, hello hard place.

'Does it matter?' I asked, genuinely trying to avert any kind of comparison situations. I may not have the highest degree of emotional intelligence, but I realized that telling your first wife how incredible your second wife was could be a life-shortening episode in stupidity.

'I guess not,' she shrugged, then fell to silence again, until, 'Have you told the boys?'

'No. I wanted to speak to you first, see how you wanted to handle it.'

'I think you should be honest with them. Do you want to tell them with Shauna?'

I should have an answer for this. A really good answer. But I didn't. 'I don't know. What do you think would be best?'

'Why don't we tell them now? Make it like it's no big deal.'

'Sure. Whatever you think.'

She stretched over to the door. 'Boys!' she shouted.

There was a thunder of approaching feet, before Davie and Joe appeared and climbed on to the table. I'd normally point out that they weren't allowed there, but decided this wasn't the moment and, like I said, this wasn't my house any more.

'Dad has something to tell you guys.'

Shit, that was sudden. I didn't know whether she was encouraging me or ambushing me in the hope that I'd bottle out.

Two gorgeous little faces looked up at me. 'Are we getting a Scalextric?' was Joe's opener.

It was the perfect ice-breaker. Even Jess laughed. These boys were class.

'No. Well, maybe if you're good before Santa comes. But that's not it.' I really wished I'd looked up how to do this. There must be a manual somewhere. Or a book. Some self-help guide to moving on after divorce and remarrying. I didn't even care if I didn't do it perfectly, just as long as I didn't scar them for life. 'Guys, we just wondered how you would feel if daddy married Shauna?'

Davie just carried on playing with his Rubik's cube, but Joe's eyes widened. 'Will she be our new mum?'

I saw Jess wince and immediately shut that one down.

'Of course not, buddy. Your mum will always be your

mum. It just means that when you're with me, Shauna will be there too. Is that cool?'

'Yeah! She's like the real Buzz!' Joe cheered. 'Cool. Cool. Cool. Cool. Cool...'

He went off on a mantra, before suddenly stopping, yelling 'To Infinity and Beyond!' and jumping off the table. Quick reflexes caught him, and I scooped him up and tickled him.

Over his shrieks, I checked with Davie. 'Bud, is it okay with you?'

'Sure,' he said, always the more understated of the two.

Jess spoke up. 'Okay, boys, well say goodbye to your dad and go wash up. Dinner will be ready soon.'

They scrambled over me, delivering hugs and kisses before running off upstairs to the bathroom.

'That went okay?' It was more of a question than a statement. I could see she looked a bit deflated

'Yeah, but I'm glad they're happy. I am. Sorry, I was a bit of a cow earlier. Just surprised.'

I stood up, put my mug in the sink and turned back to face her. 'No worries. I appreciate you helping me tell them. I should go.'

'Okay.'

'Thanks Jess.' I wasn't sure what I was thanking her for, but I just knew this could have been a lot worse. I was halfway to the door when she stopped me, putting her hand out as I passed her.

'Colm, are you sure?' She looked up at me with the huge brown eyes I'd once stared into every day. 'It's just that...'

'What?'

'I don't know. I guess I just always thought we would...'

Don't say it. Don't say it. Not now. My internal alarm was ordering me to evacuate the premises.

She shook her head, changing tack on what she was about to say, '…Doesn't matter.'

'Okay.' Relief.

'Anyway, were you planning on having the boys at the wedding?'

'Yes. Is that okay with you?' Should probably have thrown that in before now.

'Sure. They've got those little suits we bought them for my sister's engagement party last month. They can wear those.'

'Great.'

'Let's try not to be those parents who let their own feelings get in the way and fuck up their kids.'

I had a feeling she was saying that as much to herself as to me.

I was paying attention. I just hoped she was too.

13

2015

Shauna Waits...

'Mummy, you're squeezing me!' Beth squealed, giggling, before her attention was immediately distracted by the sight of her best friend, Marcy.

'Marcy! Marcy!' she yelled. 'Wait for me!' Marcy immediately ran towards us, and I reluctantly let my girl go. How could I tell her that I just wanted to stay there, hugging her – just freeze time and feel safe, warm, giving nothing else the opportunity to hurt us.

Last night as I lay in bed next to a sleeping Colm, all I could think about was how would I tell her if something was wrong? How would this change her life? Hurt her? She was five years old and I couldn't bear the thought of anything causing her even a single second of pain or unhappiness. At 4 a.m., I'd given up trying to sleep, gone into her room and lay next to her, listening to every breath she took. This had to be okay. It had to be. Not for us, but for her and her brothers too. They were nineteen, almost men, but still guys who would roll around play-wrestling with their dad. They needed him. We all did.

Now, I spotted Marcy's mum, Lina, waving at me, but I pointed at my watch and made a rushing gesture. She nodded and put her hand to her ear to mimic making a phone call. I could go speak to her now but I didn't trust myself to talk to anyone without dissolving into an emotional mess. Instead, I jumped back behind the wheel, and drove off, Colm silent beside me.

There had been a lot of silence this week.

Every day had been surreal, like some crazy TV show had taken over our lives and transformed them into something I didn't recognize. The morning after we'd been to the optician, the doctor's receptionist had called first thing with the news that there was a cancellation at the hospital that afternoon and they'd agreed to see Colm instead. The immediacy put me right in the middle of a seesaw of comfort and terror. I'd had to stay away from Google. I wasn't going to look up papilledema. Or brain tumours. Or anything else that would freak me out even more.

'Today? I can't make it today, love. Sure, I've got the accountant coming in and then a meeting at the bank.' On the other end of the 'freak out' scale, Colm wasn't worried in the least. And his nonchalance wasn't in any way for my benefit – he just refused to even contemplate that there could be anything serious wrong with him.

'Cancel them, Colm.'

'I'm not...'

'Cancel them. Or get Dan to take them. If you don't do it, I will.'

'Okay, I'll go, but we're not telling Dan or anyone else, Shauna. Let's not make a fuss. It'll be nothing. Come on, what's for breakfast? If you make me bacon rolls I'll love you forever,' he'd joked. Joked. This may be the single most terrifying moment of my life so far and he was joking.

But then perhaps he was right and this was the way to handle it. Denial was clearly working for him and who was I to burst his bubble? So I didn't. I slapped a smile on my face, made two bacon rolls, and then called on a couple of my regular girls that I could trust to cover my bookings for that day. We could do without losing the money, but I'd make it up somehow.

The consultant neurologist, Mr Clyde, welcomed us with a curt smile and an invitation to sit, before introducing a liaison nurse and a junior doctor who were both observing the meeting. Introductions over, he asked Colm to go back to the start and explain everything that had happened, taking notes as he listened.

I tried to read his face, but he was as impassive as Colm was relaxed. A casual onlooker would have guessed they were talking about the weather. Or football. Anything but a potentially life-changing health issue. Colm downplayed everything, essentially telling the truth, but delivering it in a way that suggested there was nothing to worry about. The headaches? Sure, but they were just migraines. His mother suffered from them too. Distortions in his vision? Again, those were definitely caused by the migraines. Weird audio sensations? Not much of an explanation for that one, so he glossed right over it.

'Sometimes he staggers,' I blurted, unable to keep quiet any longer. I'd been determined not to say anything, to let him deal with this in his own way, but the doctor needed the full facts. He raised one eyebrow in question, but Colm jumped right back in with, 'Only when I've been on the beer.'

Another joke.

'No, not when he's been on the beer,' I countered softly, uncertainly, caught once again between terror and the determination to treat this the same way Colm did. If we acted like everything was going to be fine, then it would be. That's what worked for him.

When the conversation was over, he asked Colm to sit on the edge of the leather bed positioned against the wall and took a hand-held implement from the counter beside it, using it to look into Colm's eyes, one after the other. Another ten minutes of tests followed, reflex checks, reaction timings, balance studies, and with every one of them I willed Colm to do it perfectly. The doctor showed no sign of whether he had.

Eventually, he sat back down on his swivel chair and Colm rejoined us in the seat next to mine.

'Mr O'Flynn, I can't say for certain what's causing your symptoms but there are certainly abnormalities in your reactions.'

'What could it be?' I blurted again, unable to control myself.

I appreciated that he didn't seem irritated by my interruption.

'Many things. It could indeed be severe migraines. It could be a virus. But we can't rule out the possibility that it could be something more serious.'

I was suddenly overwhelmed with dread. Colm just listened, still saying nothing.

'So I suggest we organize an MRI scan as soon as possible. Jenny, can you see to that now for me?'

The liaison nurse rose and headed out of the door, leaving a stunned silence behind her. Colm eventually spoke. 'So it could be just the migraines though, couldn't it?' I could have wept for the quiet desperation in his voice, the absolute need to have a best-case option that he could hang on to.

'It could be,' the doctor agreed. 'But it needs further investigation.'

I looked from Colm to the junior doctor and read nothing in their expressions. Was it just me who was sensing the doctor's underlying tone of gravity? Was I imagining it? I wondered if they taught that reluctance to commit in medical school, although I absolutely understood why he was being vague. It was the Colm school of optimism. Don't think about the worst until it was an incontrovertible reality.

The liaison nurse, a forty-something lady with a soft voice and an air of efficiency, returned clutching a sheet of A4 paper. 'They've added an extra slot, so they can fit you in first thing on Friday morning. Does that suit?'

I could see Colm was about to object so I cut him off.

'It suits. Thank you. We'll be there.'

He realized from my definite tone that there was no point arguing.

An extra slot? And only a couple of days from now? What happened to NHS waiting lists, to all those stories in the press about appointments that took months to arrive and double-bookings that caused chaos with patient care? This felt like it was the NHS equivalent of a flume – in at the top and rushing towards the end result. Too soon. Too fast. Too high a risk of drowning.

I suddenly felt like I couldn't breathe, but then I looked at Colm. Perfectly calm. Grinning at the doctor as he shook his hand. Thanking him, like he hadn't just advised him of the possibility that he could have a chronic, perhaps even deadly, ailment.

Optimism? Bravery? Or denial? I wasn't sure which.

We made it into the car park before I stopped him, faced him. 'You okay?' I asked.

He smiled, kissed me. 'Shauna, it's going to be fine. Look, if there was something really wrong with me, I'd know. I'd feel it. This is going to turn out to be nothing.'

So that's how it was going to be. I could have argued, discussed the alternatives, forced him to open up, but I realized that wasn't what he needed. There was a pleading in his eyes that told me he needed me to go along with him on this and I decided there and then that's what I had to do.

If he wasn't going to worry, I'd act like I wasn't worried either.

If he was going to minimize it, I'd make it all seem insignificant too.

If he was going to joke, I'd joke right back.

This was Colm's head, Colm's health and the terrifying possibilities were his too – I had no right to claim them or fall apart or think about how I was feeling. This was his game and I had to take whatever role he needed me to play.

So I had.

Since that moment until now, I'd adopted a façade of normality. We'd laughed, we'd worked, we'd moaned about bills. Just another normal week, people. Move along. Nothing to see here. In front of Colm, I acted like I didn't have a care in the world. Only when he was asleep or out did I find myself in the kitchen, clutching on to the side of the kitchen worktop, my heart beating wildly, gasping for breath as some unseen force squeezed my throat.

There had only been one flashpoint, that first night, after I'd cleared away the dinner plates, and read Beth two stories in bed. On a normal night, I'd hope she'd fall asleep quickly so I could get back to work, or cleaning, or doing one of the other dozen things I'd yet to tick off my to-do list for that day. That night, I'd have read to her all night if she'd let me. When her eyes closed, I lay still for a moment, trying to calm the fears that were making the muscles in my stomach clench. Only when I was sure I could pull off something approaching normal did I kiss my sleeping Beth and head back downstairs. Colm was still sitting at the table, his laptop open in front of him, brow furrowed.

'Colm, I think you have to tell Dan.'

He was adamant as ever. 'No. Christ, Shauna, he has enough on his plate with Lulu and the business. The last thing he needs is something else to worry about. This will be fine, I'm telling you. No point in creating a huge drama for nothing.'

I felt tears prick my eyes. Frustration, panic, fear, worry... I wasn't even sure what was causing them any more. I blinked them back. The last thing this situation needed was wailing and drama.

'And I don't want anyone else to know either. What's the point? In a week, it'll all be clear and we'll have forgotten about it.'

How could I tell him that I had a horrible feeling it wouldn't be? I couldn't explain it. It was a sense. A dread. But he didn't need the negativity, so I chose not to argue.

So that was it. Case closed.

Only now, with every junction and set of traffic lights, we got closer to the hospital for the results.

His hand rested over mine in the centre console of the car, neither of us up for speaking until the barrier rose at the entrance to the car park.

'I'm taking you out tonight,' he told me. 'We'll ask Lulu or Rosie to babysit Beth, and we're going out. There will be drinking and dancing and wild sex afterwards,' he promised, with a smile that wasn't quite convincing.

So we were doing the light-hearted humour thing again. Okay, I could play along. 'For the worry you've put me through this week, there had better be diamonds too.'

'Always suspected you'd turn out to be high maintenance,' he said, his words punctuated by kisses.

I wrapped my arms around his neck and kissed him properly, softly, like it could take us back to the days when just being together, like this, entwined in each other, was all that mattered.

Too soon, we stopped, looking wordlessly at each other

for a few seconds, before he smiled, kissed the end of my nose. 'You ready?'

'Yes,' I told him.

'Let's go,' he said. 'And please stop looking so worried. It's all going to be fine, I promise, okay?'

Every particle of my being silently screamed no.

14

2001

Shauna and Colm's Wedding Day

Before I'd even opened my eyes that morning I knew it was going to be sunny, and when I threw open the curtains, I immediately felt the rays of heat on my face.

Perfect.

The phone rang and I picked it up to hear Annie's cackling laugh. 'Just a quickie. I've got nothing to wear today. Okay to come in my dressing gown?'

'As long as it matches your shoes,' I answered, giggling.

'Great! As you were then.' She hung up, still chuckling, leaving me thinking that there were no words to explain how much I loved that woman.

'Hey, gorgeous, happy wedding day.' Colm's voice was still thick with sleep, so I padded back over to the bed and climbed back in, wanting to feel his body curled back into mine. If we didn't have a ceremony to go to, wild horses wouldn't have been able to drag me away from the heaven of my bed and Colm.

'Happy wedding day. You know there's still time to change your mind?' I murmured, reaching for him under the duvet.

He laughed. 'Not while you're doing that.'

Suddenly awake, he flipped over, moving above me, guiding himself inside me.

'I thought it was unlucky to see your bride on her wedding day,' he teased, sending delicious waves of pure bliss coursing through me as his hips began slow-dancing with mine.

'I believe there's a law that states love and incredible sex trumps superstition every time.'

An hour later, we were still in bed, eating croissants from a tray. How had I got this lucky? Even if I'd planned every detail of the last three months, instead of just going with the flow and hoping for the best, we couldn't have had a better outcome. My lovely flatmate, Zoe, had announced a couple of weeks before that she was going off to Australia to live and work, solving Colm and I's dilemma over where to live. He'd moved in here and we'd turned Zoe's room into a bedroom for the kids.

It was perfect. Our own place. Just for us. At least, it was until the door burst open and Lulu and Rosie stormed in the door, both in full-length pale cream dresses. They were both so gorgeous I decided not to remind them that I'd given them a key for emergency purposes, not for bursting in like a SWAT team. Lulu had a band of flowers around her wild mane of red curls, while Rosie's dark hair was sculpted in a gorgeous retro style that suggested she'd just joined the Wrens in 1942.

'Er, hello?' Lulu's horror was obvious. 'Have I got the date wrong? Only I was pretty sure you were getting married in…' she checked her watch. 'Less than three hours.'

'Oh bugger, is that today?' I shot back, and watched her face turn an exasperated shade of red and, beside me, Colm struggled to contain his laughter.

'Get out of your bed!' she screeched, the fact that no one was taking her seriously sending her even higher up the pole of infuriation.

'I'll put the kettle on. Colm, if I were you I'd get out of the line of fire there.' Rosie, always one to avoid confrontation, bustled out of the room, a scratching sound coming from the bridesmaid's dress that rustled when she moved. I'd been delighted when we'd found the outfits in a little boutique that Lulu knew about in Kensington. They were both the same shade of cream, but that's where the similarity ended. Lulu's was off the shoulder, clung to her every curve, before flaring softly at the waist and falling to the floor. Rosie's was very much in her style, with a sweetheart neckline, cinched bodice and then a skirt that was about three feet deep courtesy of the three layers of tulle underneath. They both looked spectacular.

Realizing that Lulu was close to dragging me out of bed by my ankles, I lifted a shirt from the floor beside me and pulled it over my vest top, then got up.

Colm pushed off the blanket, about to do the same, causing Lulu to throw her hand across her face, screeching, 'My eyes, my eyes!'

'It's okay, he has boxer shorts on,' I told her through cackles of laughter. She was unreliable. Reckless. Crazy.

But she made me laugh like no one else except Colm, and I wouldn't have her any other way. Except possibly slightly quieter.

'Move!' she wailed, her hands off her face now and directing me to the bathroom.

I was in and out of the shower in ten minutes, leaving it on for Colm to jump in after me.

Back in my bedroom, I blasted my hair with the dryer and then pulled it back and fastened it with a long diamanté clasp, so that it was swept off my face, but the waves trailed down past my shoulder blades.

'I don't know why I keep you as a friend,' Lulu said, from her position, lying prone, next to Rosie, both in full bridal party wear, on top of the bed. It was one of those picture-perfect scenes I'd always remember. Why did I never have a camera when I needed one? She let out a dramatic sigh. 'No one should be able to look that good so quickly. I had to get up at dawn to do my hair.'

We both knew she was kidding.

As I applied my make-up, just a light, natural look, Colm came back into the room, shaved, dressed in smart black trousers and a white shirt.

'Come here and I'll help,' said Lulu, who saw that he was struggling as he tried to secure his cufflinks. Colm did as she said, and she had them fixed in seconds. 'Colm, are you okay?' she asked.

'Yep, fine. Champion. Why?'

'Because you don't seem to be able to look me in the eye.' She was amused rather than annoyed.

I understood the problem straight away.

'He's still mortified because he saw your mum with my dad at their anniversary party.'

'Ah,' Lulu retorted, getting it too.

Colm found his voice, but it squirmed with discomfort. 'I just think that must be really hard for you guys. I mean, the whole swapping thing is just... different.'

I'd tried to explain, but – like many things in my family – I realized it didn't make much sense to anyone else. It didn't even make sense to Lulu and I, and we'd lived with it for most of our lives. My dad and her mum had been having an affair for as long as I could remember. Her father, Charlie, responded by shagging anything that took his fancy, my mother pretended not to know, valuing her friendship with Gwen over her need for fidelity, and the four of them just got on with it, went on holiday together, spent weekends together, lived their lives together, all of them getting exactly what they needed from the relationships. I didn't pretend to understand why it worked, but I just knew that it did. It was a four-way, convoluted, complicated dynamic that was wrong on every level, but one that appeared to suit them all.

'You're so sweet,' Lulu told him sincerely, 'but I promise, we're fine. We got over it a long time ago.' And we had. Somewhere around the middle of our teenage years, we'd decided to stop being horrified and accept it. However, what was odd was the difference in how it had affected our personalities. As a result of our backgrounds, Lulu treated sex as a currency, needed a constant stream of affection and put no value on monogamy. I differed on all counts.

'Anyway, if it helps, I think there's been a shift in relationships back at the ranch,' I added. 'My mother has gone off on an

140

artist's retreat. I'm fairly sure that means she's now shagging someone who's a dab hand with a paintbrush.'

At my side of the room, Rosie, the hopeless romantic sighed. 'I just think that maybe none of them has met the right person. I mean, perhaps they all settled, found a way to trundle along, and it'll only be when one of them finds real love that they'll all make a change. I think that could happen, I really do.'

Lu immediately countered, 'But let's face it, who'd want them? "Hi, we're Jeff, Debbie, Charlie and Gwen, available for new relationships just as long as you don't mind the fact that we've been having an inter-couple sexual relationship for decades." Not exactly a tempting personal ad, is it?'

Rosie stood up, her argument defeated, ready to get back to the love and romance of the day, even if we weren't sticking to pre-wedding traditions.

'You know, this is all highly unorthodox,' Rosie pointed out as she helped me into my dress.

'I know, honey. Colm, can you throw over my shoes?'

Unorthodox it may be, but it was exactly how I wanted it. No stress. No fuss. As little formality as possible. I honestly couldn't give a damn about photographs, and favours, and big fancy cars. All I cared about was marrying Colm, in front of people I loved. Nothing else mattered.

I froze as I noticed that everyone else was staring at me. 'What? What is it?'

Nobody spoke. Crap, my dress must be ripped. Or stained. Sod it, I could wear something else. I could…

'You look beautiful,' Colm said, perhaps the first time I'd ever seen him being completely serious.

I grinned and moved over to check myself out in the wardrobe mirror. He was right about the dress being beautiful, but it was also absolutely simple. Just a white crêpe sheath, off the shoulder, straight down to my ankles, with a split at the back so that I could take steps of more than eight inches. I loved it.

'You don't look too shabby either, Mr O'Flynn,' I replied, my jaws hurting because I couldn't stop smiling. 'Ready?'

We all piled in to my flash wedding car, otherwise known as Rosie's rickety old camper van, and we set off, detouring via Teddington to collect the boys, as arranged, from Jess's parents' house. They both looked utterly adorable in their matching suits and I was grateful to Jess for making the effort with them.

A hundred verses of 'The Wheels On The Bus' later, we made it to Wimbledon and I could see my parents standing waiting outside the church. At least they'd turned up then. We poured out of the van, to the surprise of my dad and the wide-eyed horror of my mother. She didn't do informal. She didn't do relaxed. And she definitely didn't do bloody old camper vans.

Kissing me again, Colm headed on into the church with the boys, stopping to greet an elderly lady and a young guy who looked vaguely like him at the door. I guessed that must be his mum and brother. They'd flown in that morning from Dublin and Dan had collected them and brought them straight here.

Yes, it was bizarre that I was meeting my husband's family for the first time at our wedding, but between work, the boys, and the fact that we'd only been together for what seemed like five minutes, there just hadn't been the opportunity to get over to Ireland.

My mother waited until everyone else was inside and then went off to make her entrance, guaranteeing the whole congregation would get a great view of how fabulous she was looking. She was welcome to her moment. Right now, every nerve in my body, every piece of my heart, was bursting with happiness and excitement.

'Sorry, sorry, sorry!' a panicked voice from behind me, beside me, in front of me, ended with a quick kiss and a 'God, you scrub up well, gorgeous' before my old catering college chum, Vincent, flew on in, a very pretty redhead teetering behind him.

And then there was perfect peace.

'You're getting married,' Rosie cooed, her eyes filling up as she and Lu came in for a group hug.

My dad waited until we were done, and then held out his arm.

'Good to go, Shauna?'

No, 'you look beautiful'. No teary sobs of emotion. No obvious unbridled pride. Just time to go.

Yes, it was.

I took his arm and we walked up the steps to the door, Lulu and Rosie behind us. Dan was waiting there to greet us, holding the door open to let us through, his handsome smile directed first at me, and then at Lulu. Despite their wild, volatile relationship, I had a feeling it wouldn't be long until they were following us up the aisle.

Annie had chosen the songs for the service, persuading the vicar that 'He's Got The Whole World In His Hands' was the perfect start to married life. She was the first person I saw when we got inside, standing next to Vincent, the redhead girlfriend having been dispatched to the row behind. I'd no idea how Annie had managed that but it didn't surprise me – she's always had a soft spot for tall, dark and handsome. She winked at me, setting off an irrepressible fit of the giggles that lasted the whole way up the aisle.

There, with Davie on one side and Joe on the other, was Colm. Waiting. Every pore of him matching my happiness. I'd never been surer of anything in my life. I loved this man. We belonged together. We were going to have the most incredible lives. Nothing, absolutely nothing, could touch us or take this away.

The vicar made the introductions and moved straight on with the ceremony.

He lifted my hand and placed it on top of Colm's.

'Colm, repeat after me…'

The vicar's words faded into the background, as Colm and I's eyes locked, saying so much more than just the words that we were repeating.

'I, Colm O'Flynn, take you, Shauna Williams, to be my wife, to have and to hold from this day forward, for better, for worse, for richer, for poorer, in sickness and in health, to love and to cherish, till death do us part.'

The vicar spoke up again. "And now, Shauna, could you repeat the same words."

'I, Shauna Williams, take you, Colm O'Flynn, to be my husband, to have and to hold from this day forward, for better, for worse, for richer, for poorer, in sickness and in health, to love and to cherish, till death do us part.'

Davie and Joe burst into an excited round of applause, sending a ripple of hilarity through the gathering. It was perfect.

Colm scooped up Joe and I lifted Davie, just as the vicar announced, 'I now pronounce you man and wife. You may kiss your bride.'

'Yuk!' Joe exclaimed. The boy definitely had a gift for comic timing.

Colm leaned over and kissed me. 'I love you, Mrs O'Flynn.'

'I love you back,' I whispered.

So, so much.

And I had no doubt I always would.

Until death do us part.

15

Colm and Shauna Wait to Hear...

The waiting room, a large open space with rows of chairs, was packed, so Shauna and I stood against one of the cream-painted walls. To be honest, I was glad that it made conversation impossible, because I had nothing to say.

A slow, tight knot was forming in my stomach as I looked around the room. A sign said this was the waiting area for the neurology and maxillofacial departments, but the sign wasn't necessary. In every row was a person with a wound, a scar, a dressing, so many of them with partially shaved heads, their skin pale and drawn. *These* were sick people. I wasn't sick. I was fine. That's what I kept telling myself and Shauna, and here I could see it was true.

Bugger this. Waste of time, it was. I actually felt guilty taking up the time of the medical experts when clearly these poor souls needed it more.

Shauna was staring at her feet, her hand gripping mine. This last week had been hard on her, but I didn't know what to say to make it better. If I said it would be okay, she asked me how I knew that. I didn't have an answer. I just had to keep believing it, stick to my mantra that I'd worry when there was something concrete to worry about.

'Mr O'Flynn.'

Shauna's head shot up and we both turned to see the liaison nurse we'd met on the first visit. What was her name? Shit. Felt like I couldn't remember anything these days. Too much on my mind. Julie. Julia. Jessica. Jenny. Jenny, that was it.

We crossed the room to join her and she led us along a corridor and into a side room, where Mr Clyde and the same junior doctor as the last time were sitting. Another bloke was with them now, though. Serious-looking guy with grey hair, his shirt and tie crumpled.

'Mr O'Flynn, this is my colleague, Mr Miller.'

I shook his hand then sat down next to Shauna, putting my fingers over hers.

Mr Clyde cleared his throat.

'So Mr O'Flynn, since we last spoke, have you had any other symptoms?'

'Just a couple of headaches.'

He nodded and made a note on the pad in front of him, then hit me with a load of other questions, many of them the same as last time. Visual issues? Audio distortions? Seizures? Loss of consciousness?

I answered no to everything. It had only been a few days since I'd seen him last, and I could honestly say that this week had been much better. I was on the mend. Definitely recovering. I'd even taken on the twins at tennis and beat them both, one after the other. Two hulking big teenagers, and their forty-one-year-old da' had conquered. Could an ill man have done that? Nope.

And Beth. Jesus, she was five. She couldn't have a sick da' who wasn't able to take care of her. That just couldn't happen. I was fine. Top of the world. Just grand.

When he'd exhausted his questions, the doc leaned over and flicked on a switch on a white panel on the wall next to him, illuminating a black and white image, clearly some kind of X-ray of a brain.

'Mr O'Flynn, this is the result of your MRI scan.'

Beside me, I could hear Shauna's breathing coming thick and fast, as we both stared at the screen, trying to make sense of it. I couldn't. There were areas of light and shade, lines and curves, but I had no idea whether this was how it was meant to look.

The doc took his pen and held it an inch or so in front of the screen.

'Let me get straight to it, Mr O'Flynn.'

Fuck. Straight to what? Did that mean there was something wrong? There couldn't be. I wasn't sick. I was fine. Totally fine.

Shauna's nails were digging hard into my palm now but I barely registered the pain.

'This area here...' he continued, swirling his pen over the top of the image, 'is called the occipital lobe. It's in this section of your head.' He was demonstrating by pointing to the back of his head now, about halfway down, just left of centre.

He took his pointer back to the screen. 'And this shadow you see here...' More swirling of the pen. '...I'm afraid, is a tumour.'

What? Seriously, what?

'Oh God,' Shauna whispered.

'I have a brain tumour?' I said, in total disbelief. There had to be a mistake. I was forty-one. I'd played five-a-side football last weekend. How the fuck could I have a brain tumour?

'You do.'

He paused for a moment, perhaps to let us absorb what he was saying, before charging right on.

'The reason it's affecting your vision is because it's infringing on the point in your brain where your optic nerves meet.'

'So... so...' I couldn't form the words.

'What does that mean?' Shauna finished for me, her voice barely louder than a whisper.

He put his pen down and turned full on to face us.

'The tumour is fairly large, around the size of a small fist.'

No. This had to be a mistake. How could something like that be in my head without me knowing?

'It's what's been causing the headaches and the audio dysfunction, and as I said, the pressure on the optical nerves has caused the visual disturbances.'

Another pause. Shauna and I said nothing. Stunned.

He carried on. 'We have two options. It's in a position that should be accessible, so the first option is surgery. We could go in, debulk the tumour, try to remove as much as possible, perhaps even all of it. But obviously that comes with considerable risk.'

I wasn't liking the sound of that course of action at all. I could feel sweat beads pop out on my forehead.

'What's the other option?'

'We could wait and see, monitor it, make the decision further down the line.'

That sounded like a far more acceptable plan – until he went on, 'But doing that comes with major concerns and fairly high-level risks too.'

'What risks?' Shauna asked before me. Her voice was so faint I didn't even recognize it.

He addressed her question, but was looking back at me. Stop fucking looking at me. I'm not sick. This is a mistake.

'Your sight could be damaged, perhaps severely and irreparably.'

What was he saying now? 'Could I go blind?'

'Yes. And the other risk comes with not knowing what kind of tumour it is. Until we get a biopsy under the microscope, we can't ascertain that for certain. It could be benign, and that would be the best outcome. However, if it's malignant and a particularly aggressive one, we may lose our opportunity to operate in a fairly short window of time.'

'And then I'd…' I froze. No more words.

'That would be fatal,' he said, correctly interpreting what I was trying to ask.

A gasp from Shauna, and ironically, the one fecking time in recent months that my peripheral vision was completely clear, it was allowing me full view of the two silent tears that were running down her face.

'But… but… it could be… benign? And he'd be… fine?' Shauna stuttered, the desperate hope in her voice was heart-breaking.

'That's a possibility,' Mr Clyde replied, but I didn't detect confidence. 'In a man of your age, that's certainly the more probable outcome.'

My hope rose.

'But, again, being completely frank, I would usually expect a benign tumour to have certain markers that I'm not seeing here. That's not to say it isn't – I just can't make any conclusions until we've analyzed it.'

I took a deep breath, trying to calm the sickening feeling that I knew what he was going to reply to my next questions. 'So what should we do? What would you advise?'

'I think we need to operate. And quickly. That's why I invited my colleague, Mr Miller.'

He gestured to the grey-haired guy in in the corner seat. I'd forgotten he was even there.

'Mr O'Flynn, I'm the consultant neurosurgeon and I concur with Mr Clyde's analysis. I think we need to know what we're dealing with here and sooner rather than later. I have checked my schedule and I'd like to arrange your surgery for next Monday.'

'Next Monday,' I repeated, trying to digest what he was saying. Next Monday. Christ, they weren't hanging around here. 'And you're what? Going to open my head up?'

'Would you like me to explain the procedure?' he asked.

Fuck, no. Absolutely not.

'Yes,' Shauna answered.

He looked to me for confirmation and I nodded, fighting that gut-twisting terror you get when you're at the top of a huge roller coaster and about to plummet to earth.

'We'll make an incision across the back of your head in almost a horseshoe shape. That will allow us to remove the back section of your skull, then enter the brain and debulk – that just means remove – as much of the tumour as possible. Hopefully all of it. We will then reattach the skull using metal screws and close the scalp. Mr O'Flynn...'

'Call me Colm.' I've no idea why I blurted that out, other than something told me that if he was going to actually be inside my brain at some point, it was probably fine to be on first-name terms.

'Colm... I have to advise you that the surgery also comes with not insignificant risks. We're dealing with the brain, which is never an exact science.'

'Give me the worst-case scenario,' I told him. Shauna's hand was gripping mine like a vice, her nails digging into my palm so deeply there should have been pain, yet I couldn't feel anything. All I could see and hear were the doctor and his words.

'Given the area we will be working in, blindness is a small, but notable possibility. Seizures. Paralysis. And worst-case scenario,' he said, repeating my words, 'is that all surgeries, including this one, can be fatal.'

'So I could die if I do it and die if I don't?' I asked, trying desperately to understand. This couldn't be happening. It was a joke. *Jackass* cameras were here somewhere.

He nodded solemnly. 'Yes. But in our opinion, the chances of a fatal outcome are considerably higher if you don't.'

'Can I think about it?'

'Of course.'

'We don't need to think about it,' Shauna said, voice cracking, as she spoke. 'Colm, if you don't have surgery, there's a considerable probability you will die. If you have surgery, there's a very good possibility that you won't. Am I understanding that correctly?' She was looking searchingly at the doctors now.

They were both nodding, but it was Mr Clyde who said, 'You are.'

'Then you have to do it, Colm.'

I knew she was right. It wasn't really a choice, because there was only one viable option. But still... his description of the surgery was replaying in my head. Cut scalp. Remove skull. Take out part of my brain. Screw skull back together. I was now crashing to earth on that roller coaster and fairly sure I was going to vomit. I swallowed hard. I couldn't do this. I couldn't. Sod it. I just wanted to get up and walk out of there, rewind the last hour and go back to normal life, forget this ever happened. What was the worst that could happen?

I would die.

And soon.

So there wasn't really a choice here.

Shauna was right. If I wanted to stay alive I had to do this. I was all out of options.

'I don't really need to think about it, do I? Go ahead and book me in.'

He nodded and Shauna clutched my hand even tighter. Out of the blue, I had a flashback to our wedding day, to the ceremony, when she'd stood next to me, so incredibly beautiful and I'd felt like the luckiest guy alive when she'd said, 'Till death do us part.'

Suddenly, that didn't make me feel quite so lucky any more.

16

2002

Four Go to Bali

Lying on my front on the sunlounger, I could feel the sun beating down on my back, turning the little gold charms on the shoestring of my bikini red hot. Probably not the best choice of swimwear, but Lulu had persuaded me that it looked great, and since it was that or the Speedo costume I wore to take the kids swimming on the weekends, I brought the bikini.

I felt Colm's hand move across my back, carrying a scent of coconut, until it crept under my bikini bottoms and stopped.

I flipped my head up and turned to face him. 'Did you just put suntan lotion on my back as an excuse to grope my arse?'

'Indeed I did,' he murmured, leaving his hand where it was.

His deadpan reply sent me into fits of giggles. Today

was day three in the closest place to paradise I'd ever experienced. Bali had been Lulu's idea, or was it Dan's, and we'd gone for the Sheraton resort on the recommendation of the travel agent, who'd come here on her honeymoon. It was the perfect choice. The rooms were decorated in cool creams with traditional Balinese dark wood furnishings, the bars served up an endless stream of delicious cocktails and the hotel was right on the beach, so when it got too hot we could head into the sea for some kite-surfing or waterskiing to cool off.

That's where Lulu and Dan were now, about 100 yards out on a pedalo. Probably the best place for them. They'd been bickering since we'd arrived – at least when they were out there they'd be forced to talk to each other and neither of them could stomp off in a huff. I understood that some people – including Dan and Lulu – thrived on a tempestuous relationship, but to me it just seemed like too much hard work.

But then it wasn't any worse than the life poor Rosie was having. I could see her sitting in the outdoor bar with a Jackie Collins novel and a large glass of something red, with a pineapple sticking out of the top. Ten more blissful minutes lying here next to Colm, then I'd go keep her company for a while.

Two little kids walked by and I had a sudden pang. 'Missing the boys?' I asked.

'Absolutely,' Colm fired back. 'However, if they were here, I would be playing footie, building sandcastles, and I wouldn't be able to lie with my hand on your arse, so that's keeping me going.'

I pushed up on to one side, dislodging his hand and earning a mutter of objection. I consoled him by leaning over to his sunlounger and kissing him. He tasted of a holiday blend of salt and cold beer, which was strangely sexy. As was the fact that he was lying there in black swim shorts, he'd been working out, and in the harsh glare of the sun you couldn't quite see that he was covered in factor seventy because he'd burnt his chest, nose, and forehead the day before. That pale, Irish skin was not made for the midday sun.

Maybe it was the cute kids playing in the sea, or the realization that I was missing the boys too, but without much thought, I announced, 'I think we should have a baby.'

At the sound of Colm choking on his beer, the lifeguard spun around, obviously fearing that someone was in trouble in the pool. He looked relieved when he saw that no one was drowning, nor did anyone require the administration of the Heimlich manoeuvre.

'Could you give me a bit of warning before you spring life-changing announcements on me please?' he spluttered, as if I'd just announced something shocking and not entirely welcome.

I was genuinely surprised and a bit puzzled by his reaction, although I wasn't sure why. It wasn't that we'd discussed the subject in depth. There had been a vague 'I'd like kids one day' and a 'yeah, that would be great' conversation before we got married, but in the three months since we walked up the aisle it had never come up.

Despite the temperature, I felt goosebumps pop up on my arms. Surely he wanted children? And how could I not be entirely confident of the answer to that question? I was the worst married woman ever. How could I not know such vital, major information about my husband's hopes, plans and opinions? I should really check which political party he voted for too.

But the kids subject came first. Surely I'd misunderstood his reaction?

'Colm, do you want more children?'

I was expecting a 'yes, absolutely'. Perhaps even a 'can't wait!' Instead, I got a shrug, and a weak, 'Eh, hadn't really given it much thought.'

I spun my legs around so I was sitting on the edge of my lounger, facing him, in full combat position. This was unbelievable. We weren't so much on different pages as in different books.

'But we talked about it before and you said you did.'

'When?'

'Before we were married. We were talking in bed one morning and...'

'Ah, were you naked?' he said, grinning. 'I'm not responsible for anything I agree to when you're naked.'

He thought this was funny. For once, I didn't.

'Colm, please don't joke about this. I really do want kids. I had no idea you didn't.'

My tone must have penetrated his jocular attitude, because he seemed to finally spot that I was serious.

'Look, it's not that I don't want kids. But it's just... well, we've got the boys.'

'But they're *your* children.' He blanched at that, but I wasn't for backing down. 'Come on, Colm. I love them to bits, but having them doesn't mean I never want to have children of my own. If anything, seeing how brilliant they are just makes me want to add to the family.'

Colm thought about that for a moment, then shrugged. 'Okay. I understand what you're saying and if it's important to you, then we'll do it.'

'Now I feel like you're just agreeing to appease me.'

I was getting irritated, and his expression told me he was matching the sentiment.

'It's not that I'm appeasing you, I guess that it's just not that important to me. If you want to have children, then we will, but if you don't I'd be cool with that too.'

Why did that annoy me? He was ultimately saying that he would be on board with my wishes, yet his non-committal attitude was putting my hackles up. Did he take nothing seriously? Since we met it had felt like one big long party of discovery and love, but now, for the first time, I wasn't liking what I was discovering.

The sunshine had faded for me, despite the fact that it was probably the hottest point of the day.

'I'm going to go chat to Rosie for a while.'

I didn't even give him a chance to argue, just stood up, grabbed my drink and walked off, ignoring the fact that the hot sands were scalding the bottom of my feet. I should really go back for my flip-flops, but I was too busy being petulant. I never claimed to be calm and reasonable 100 per cent of the time.

Rosie looked up from her book and smiled when she saw me stomping towards her. She started speaking before I even sat down. 'You don't look happy. I thought it was supposed to be me who's miserable on this trip.'

'Sorry, honey, I'm climbing into that pit of misery with you. Did you know that Colm didn't want kids?'

The laughter came first. 'Erm, no – but then I think that since he's *your* husband, attaining that kind of information might be your responsibility, not mine.'

'Fair point,' I acknowledged. 'Just wish I'd thought of it before now. Anyway, sorry, enough about me. How are you doing?'

'I just hope they've got a good library here, because I've just about finished this and it's only day three.'

'At least your book matches your kaftan,' I said, gesturing to the fact that the novel's leopard-print cover was almost identical to the chiffon of her top. 'That's a mean skill for accessorizing right there.'

That at least made her smile. I tried to do better.

'You know you can come lie with us. Or we can go do stuff.'

'I know, but to be honest I'm probably crap company just now. I'm feeling the need to mope a little. I realize that makes me pathetic.'

'Not pathetic – just hurt. Have you heard from him?'

She shook her head. 'I've kept my mobile phone switched off and in the safe. Don't trust myself not to call him.'

My annoyance at Colm immediately transferred on to Paul, Rosie's boyfriend, who'd just finished his zoology degree and announced he was moving north, to work in Chester Zoo, and leaving her behind. Urgh, I was furious. Not only was he walking out on her with no warning, after she'd more or less supported him since they met, but he'd told her the day before they were supposed to travel here with us. 'I mean, how bad must it be when he can't even wait until after a five-star holiday to dump me,' she'd wailed at the airport. 'Was he just using me all along for somewhere to live while he was at uni?'

'Tell you what, why don't we go to the spa and get a couple of treatments and discuss how men are thoughtless bastards?' I suggested. I didn't mean it – actually, after my discussion with Colm, perhaps right now I did – but I thought a bit of sisterhood solidarity might cheer her up.

She finished her cocktail in one sweeping motion. 'Oh, I think I can manage that. I have plenty of material.'

The beautiful girl in the spa showed us through to a massage room where two equally stunning women gave us massages that sent us both to sleep. When they were finished, I had to crawl off the bed, before heading to the nail section of the spa for a mani-pedi.

'Thought I'd find you in here!' Lulu's voice was very slightly slurred. Obviously a few lunchtime cocktails had been consumed.

'Hi!' I greeted her. 'Sorry, we'd have told you we were coming but you were out on the pedalo. I knew you'd track us down. Is everything okay?'

She flopped down on a free seat at the other side of Rosie, her sexy black strappy swimsuit barely covered by a sheer kaftan that clung to her every curve. Her long red curls were pulled up in a high ponytail and she had oversized Gucci glasses on her head. It didn't matter where she went or what she did, Lulu always looked sensational.

'Dan's driving me crazy,' she said. 'We just seem to fight constantly.'

'Nooo, really? I hadn't noticed,' I said, my face a picture of innocence.

That made her laugh. 'Oh, okay, Mrs Perfect. Just because you and Colm agree on *everything*,' she teased.

'We just had out first fight,' I countered, watching as her eyes widened. 'Did you know he didn't want kids?'

'No.'

'Me neither. I'll have the sugar baby pink, please,' I said to the manicurist who was holding up a pale pink and a deep plum for me to choose from. What must these ladies think about these conversations? They must hear everything coming from these chairs.

'Wow. How do you feel about that?'

'I'm not thrilled. He says he'll have them if I want them, but somehow that makes me feel worse.'

'I get that. And what about you, Rosie? Are you sure you don't want me to round up a posse and go have a word with Paul?' This time it was Rosie who was smiling and it even looked genuine.

'Thanks, you're a pal, but no. I'm moving on. I'm giving myself the rest of this holiday to feel sorry for myself then I'm going to go home and forget about him. I'm only twenty-four. There's plenty of other guys out there, and there must be one who won't be a dick to me.'

'Absolutely,' I reassured her. It was so ironic that we'd all been friends forever, and it had always been Rosie who'd dreamt of marrying young and having a huge family, and yet somehow Lulu and I, the two more independent free spirits, were the ones who had settled first. Or at least, I had. I still had doubts about Lulu.

'Is Dan still alive or did you drown him at sea?'

'Alive. But I was tempted. He just can't get over his suspicions that I've been seeing someone behind his back.'

Both Rosie and I had the same head-swivelling reaction to that one.

The thing was, she *had* been seeing someone. And not for the first time. It was a regular occurrence. Whether it was a quick snog with an Australian barman or an occasional quickie with the guy who serviced her car. The problem wasn't that she'd had a fling, it was that Dan had caught her.

This time around Tim was – oh, the cliché – her tennis coach. They'd been having extra sessions for the last couple of months, doing the kind of workout normally seen on TV channels that require a pin number.

'Don't look at me like that. You know the thing with Tim means nothing. It's just a… distraction.'

'It's the kind of distraction that is going to break Dan's heart though,' I told her, trying to get through, but fearing I was wasting my breath.

'I know. I know. God, what's wrong with me? Why do I always do this? I'm a fucking train wreck.'

The questions were purely rhetorical. Lulu was a smart cookie and a million conversations over the years had left her in no doubt why she did this. She just needed the constant validation and the relentless thrill of those first stages of a relationship. Or, more correctly, first stages of an affair. Some would say she was living life to the full. Others would say there was something inside her that was broken, snapped by a messed up family that viewed shagging as a communal hobby. I thought the truth was somewhere in the middle, but no matter how much she infuriated me, I loved her – in all her flawed, funny, traitorous glory.

'It's got to stop, Lu,' I said, gently. 'For your own sake and for Dan's, it has to stop. You need an honest relationship and you can't keep doing this to him. He's a good guy and the only reason he's stuck around is because he loves you.'

'And he's never found any conclusive proof,' Rosie added.

'Eh, okay, Miss Marple, thanks for your input,' Lulu barbed. Her eyes closed and her whole body deflated as she exhaled. 'But I know you're both right. Dan deserves better than this. I either need to call it a day with him or stop seeing other people. The lies will stop. I promise.'

I highly doubted it. It was like hearing an alcoholic swearing off vodka. Or a crack addict going cold turkey. I had a horrible feeling that in ten years time she'd still be trying to break the habit.

It was late afternoon by the time I got back to the room, to find Colm already there, lying flat on the bed watching some thriller movie on TV. I wasn't sure of the title, but Bruce Willis was involved.

'Hey,' he said.

'Hey,' I replied, demonstrating a distinct lack of originality.

I decided to just go lie in the bath, stay out of his way, make the point that I was still pissed off and wasn't ready to discuss it any further – but then I decided that I was rubbish at sulking, so it was better just to clear the air.

'Colm, I'm sorry about earlier, but you just took me by surprise. I didn't realize that was how you felt.'

He muted Bruce Willis.

'Me neither. S'pose I hadn't really thought about it. Come

here.' He opened his arms and I climbed on the bed beside him, my sticky, post-massage skin hot against his cool, air-conditioned body. 'I'm sorry too, m'love. I didn't mean to piss you off, and I meant what I said – if it's important to you, then we'll have ten kids.'

I laughed. 'I was thinking more along the lines of two.'

'Two it is then. In fact...' His hand pulled the string of my bikini top and it disintegrated immediately. 'We could start now if you're not too busy.'

'Actually, I was thinking we'd wait a couple of years and then start trying.'

'Good plan. I'll just check I've got the basics of what we're supposed to do.'

His mouth closed on mine and I melted into him, every shred of tension and irritation being smoothed away by his touch. Fight over. Normal service resumed. Love wins.

We were almost late for dinner, an alfresco feast at a restaurant a little further along the sands. When we arrived, Lulu, Dan and Rosie were already there.

'Hi! We thought you'd had a better offer,' Lulu slurred, refilling her wine glass as she spoke. Oh dear. I had a horrible feeling there'd only be one relationship left in the group by the end of the night. Looking at Dan, I wondered if he thought the same. His jaw was set in irritation, his eyes jumpy. This wasn't the best start to a relaxing and enjoyable evening.

The waiters took our orders, supplied more drinks and retreated off, leaving us almost alone on the edge of the sands, just the sound of breaking waves for company. It should be beautiful. Romantic. Blissful. But the atmosphere between Lulu and Dan was twisting the ambience, and as

I met Rosie's eyes, I saw we were both thinking the same thing – awkward. How many nights had we spent like this, with a fight or tension between Lulu and Dan casting a cloak of anxiety over everyone? I adored them both, but this couldn't go on. Some people just weren't meant to be together and they really needed to put an end to this, no matter how sad that would be.

Dan interrupted my thoughts by clearing his throat. 'Okay, I have something to say.'

Oh God, he was going to finish it now. Noooo. Not now. Later. In private. His next words made me wonder if he was reading my mind.

'I was going to do this later, when Lu and I were alone, but I suppose we all spend so much time together this makes more sense.'

No it doesn't. It really doesn't. My thoughts went unspoken. It was like watching a car crash about to unfold and being unable to scream a warning.

'The thing is… Lu and I have been together for three years now and it's never been easy.'

My eyes flicked to Lulu, who was watching him intently, her face giving nothing away. I knew her so well. She'd never, ever show that something was hurting or scaring her.

I shot a warning glare at Dan. Don't do this. Don't break up with her. Don't humiliate her like this.

He suddenly stood up, sending his chair toppling backwards. He couldn't do it, couldn't say it, so he was leaving. It was probably for the best. They could talk later, when they were both ready, sort it out in private and find a way to move on as friends.

But he didn't walk away. He came round to Lu's side of the table, dropped on one knee, pulled a tiny box from the pocket of his trousers and popped it open to reveal a huge, round solitaire diamond.

'Lu, I love you. You drive me insane, but I absolutely could not live without you. Marry me.'

Oh. Fuck. Oh. Fuck. Oh. Fuck.

I could feel panic rising. Why was there never a fire alarm when you needed it? Or a shark? Or anything that would head off the moment when my best friend told the man she was cheating on that she couldn't possibly marry him because she was a screwed-up mess?

Lulu opened her mouth, tried to form words, taking what seemed like a lifetime to co-ordinate her brain with her vocal cords.

'Yes,' she whispered.

Oh dear God, yes? Yes? Just when I thought this couldn't get any bloody worse, she said yes to the poor guy she'd been unfaithful to for years?

Shark! Shark!

17

2015

Two Go to the Hospital

The forced joviality was almost more heartbreaking than our honest emotions, but we all went along with it because it was the only way to deal with this.

'Right, Beth, have you got your bag and your scooter and your private jet?' Lulu asked.

Beth guffawed with laughter. 'Auntie Lulu, I don't take a private jet to school!'

'You don't? Oh. Well we'll just have to take my car then, I suppose. Right, say goodbye to mum and let's go.'

I was beyond grateful to Lulu for keeping everything upbeat for Beth, who was now waiting for me, arms wide open. I kneeled down to give her a huge hug, and if she noticed that I hung on longer than usual, she didn't say. She was almost out the door, when she turned back with an afterthought of, 'Will Daddy be back with his new head when I get home?'

'Not today, honey,' I managed, fighting to hold it together. 'Another few days.'

'Can you ask him to hurry up? I miss him.'

'I will.' He only went in last night, to prepare for the op today, and she was missing him already. I knew how she felt.

Lulu looked back at me with such a tortured expression that I almost broke.

'Here's your lunch, sweetie,' Rosie said, handing over Beth's *Frozen* lunch box.

'Right, come on, Beth O'Flynn,' Lulu chirped, 'our private jet is waiting.'

'It's not a private jet!' Beth giggled before skipping out the door.

I exhaled, holding on to the kitchen table for support. Don't crumble. Keep it together.

Telling Beth had been horrific on the inside, flippant on the outside. We'd told her in as casual a way as possible that daddy had a lump in his head and the doctor had to take it off. That was it. Nothing more.

'Like when I fell over on my roller skates?'

'Yes, just like that,' I told her. 'Only this lump is on the inside, so the doctors have to do an operation that will leave daddy with a big bandage around his head afterwards. He'll look like a mummy from *Scooby Doo*.'

At this point, Colm had pretended to transform into a zombie and chased her round the room, to her screaming delight.

Telling Rosie, Dan, and Lulu had been tough too. No cartoon dog could soften the blow. The night before last, Beth had gone for a sleepover at her friend Marcy's house.

I'd asked Rosie and Jack round on the pretence of a mid-week catch-up, but Jack was working, so Rosie had come on her own.

We'd also lied to both Lulu and Dan to get them in the same room, inviting them round separately. They had been completely avoiding each other since the last fight over Dan calling in the lawyers. Married for years, then nothing. No contact. No dialogue. She was still living in their home and he was still in our garage. They'd just cut each other out of their lives altogether. I couldn't get my head around their actions at all.

No surprise then that when Lulu walked in and saw us, Rosie and Dan already there, I could see she thought it was some kind of marriage guidance intervention. I only wished it was.

'I'm not staying here if...'

I cut her off. 'Don't, Lu. Just sit down.' Something in my voice must have shocked her enough to comply.

'Is it the Bracal Tech contract? Did we not get it?'

'We haven't heard yet,' Colm said, before taking a deep breath.

Colm and I had agreed that he would say the words, and I was grateful because I wasn't sure I could do it. Typically, he'd gone right for it, making it sound totally flippant.

'Right. You know these headaches? Well, turns out I have a brain tumour. They're operating on Monday to take it out. It'll probably be benign and I'll be fine, so I'm not worried.'

I let the 'probably be benign' go. This was his story to tell it in whatever way he wanted. He'd be fine. He would. And if that's what he wanted to say, then I wasn't going to contradict with anything that would shake his confidence. I just wish I felt it too.

There were questions. Lots of them. And tears. Rosie's ran down her face, Lulu wiped hers away, mine were blinked back. Dan just sat, stunned, pale, speechless, before kicking in to practical mode. 'Right, what can we do? What do you need?'

Colm shook his head. 'Nothing, mate.'

'Maybe just some help with Beth,' I'd added. Lulu and Rosie immediately worked out a schedule of drop-offs, pick-ups and play dates that would keep her so occupied she wouldn't even notice, much less be affected by, the fact that daddy wasn't there.

Logistics sorted. I just wished there was such a painless solution that would mend Colm's damaged head and my broken heart.

'What about the twins?' Rosie had asked. 'Have you told them?'

Colm spoke up again. 'No. They're away on that exchange visit in France. Eight weeks. So I'm not telling them until they get back and it's all over. They don't need to be worrying about this.'

We'd debated that one long into the night, and I wasn't 100 per cent sure we were doing the right thing, but I just hoped they'd understand our actions came from a good place. Davie and Joe had been looking forward to this trip for so long. Two months in Paris, between their first and second year at university, helping out teaching English at a camp. They'd only been there for a couple of weeks but we'd been getting daily texts and calls telling us how much they were loving it. Neither of us wanted to take that away from them, to end an incredible experience. Hopefully, they wouldn't be upset that we hadn't told them. They'd grown into great kids – mature and funny, with Colm's sense of adventure. I couldn't stand the thought of causing them heartache.

'And just so you know, I'm not telling my mam or my brother either. Since my mam's stroke last year, she's not been well and, Jesus, this could kill her.'

Whenever he spoke about his family, his Irish accent got stronger.

'So there it is. Brain tumour. Out Monday. Over and done and back on my feet within a week,' he summarized. 'Right, who wants a beer? If I'm going to have a headache, I may as well make it a hangover.'

Wide-eyed and stunned, the others had gone along with it, somehow managing to change the subject and carry on with a night that descended into stories and laughter and ended with drunk singing at 3 a.m. Even Lulu and Dan managed to keep it civilised.

Optimism and denial, mixed with friends and craic. The Colm O'Flynn technique for surviving a brain tumour.

When we woke up in the morning, heads predictably sore, I'd tried to talk to him. The practical side in me – the one that ran this house, this family, my business, the one that made all the decisions, sorted the problems and made sure that everyone was where they needed to be, the one that took care of everyone – *that* one needed to talk, to process, to make plans. None of those functions came under Colm's remit in our day-to-day lives, but surely these were exceptional circumstances? In the last couple of days

I'd read loads of stuff online about people's reactions to life-risking surgery. According to most of the accounts, they got their affairs in order. Talked to everyone they loved. Wrote letters of forgiveness or acceptance. Tried to come to terms with what was happening.

So far, Colm had nipped to Tesco for a case of beer and thrown a party. There had to be more and he needed to know I was here for whatever he was truly feeling on the inside.

'Babe, you know you don't have to act like this is nothing. We can talk about it,' I said.

He winced as he tried to sit up, but I wasn't sure if that was due to the subject or the consequences of last night's overindulgence.

He lifted his hand and ran it down the side of my face. 'Darlin', there's nothing to talk about. It's going to be okay. I truly believe that, and you need to as well.'

There were a million things I wanted to say to that, but I didn't. Instead, I curled into his chest and closed my eyes. He needed me to be strong. He needed me to handle this in the same way he did. He needed me to get a grip and ignore how I was feeling and make this bearable for him. He needed glib denial and surface humour. I decided that as long as we were in the same room, that's what he'd get. And if I crumbled to my knees elsewhere, he would never know about it.

I opened my eyes and reached for the remote control. 'Okay, in that case, let's stay in bed all day and watch a movie. Chick flick?'

'Nooooo.'

'Sorry, you don't get a choice. Only people without brain

tumours get to vote.' For him, I could play funny, no matter how much it hurt.

He was still laughing when I found a rerun of *Dirty Dancing* and clicked 'play'.

'Dear God, take me now,' he chuckled.

That stung, but I didn't flinch. As far as he was concerned, I was all signed up for laughs, humour, denial and optimism.

I kept it going all day, even when we picked up Beth and took her out for ice cream, then an hour of riding scooters in the park. I even managed to keep it going after we'd put her to bed and Rosie arrived to sit with her so we could go in, the night before the op, as instructed. We drove all the way to the hospital, passing people heading out to bars, going for dinner, walking dogs, and the whole way, we sang along to some naff eighties rock anthem CD. Bon Jovi had never been murdered quite like that.

I smiled when the nurses welcomed Colm and talked him through the admission form. I laughed when he put on the pyjamas and slippers I'd bought the day before from Marks & Spencer's. I warned him that he'd better not stay up all night chatting up the nurses, and then doled out a wail of comic outrage when the matronly nurse within earshot told us that would be fine by her.

The staff let me stay for a few hours, and when I said goodbye, I kissed him like I didn't have a care in the world.

Laughs. Humour. Denial. Optimism… until I got back to my car, in a dark hospital car park, under a perfect full moon, and I buckled over and cried until I was hoarse.

I didn't remember the drive home, but both Lulu and Rosie were waiting for me in the kitchen, Beth upstairs fast asleep.

I poured a mug of coffee – didn't want to drink wine because I'd be driving again in just a few hours – and sat at the table.

For the first time I could say what I really thought, vocalize the fear that was making my chest hurt and my hands tremble. The words caught in my throat, strangling my voice, pushing a torrent of tears down my face.

'Tell me we won't lose him,' I begged.

'We fucking won't,' Lulu vowed, her whole body shaking with emotion and defiance, while Rosie put her head on my shoulder and we sobbed, all three of us, making a blur of promises, and pleas and assurances that weren't ours to make until the darkness outside became light.

I went upstairs, and crawled in with Beth for the last hour before the alarm sounded, spooning her, holding her tight. She couldn't lose her dad. I wouldn't let that happen. I'd do anything. Say anything. Make any bargain that would keep him with us.

'Mummy, you're here,' she said with a sleepy smile, turning so that her arm went round my neck and our cheeks touched. 'Where's Daddy?'

'He's at the hospital, remember?'

'Ah, I remember.' She reached over and picked up Sully, the *Monsters Inc* furry creature she slept with every night. 'He should have taken Sully so he wasn't lonely.'

A wrecking ball hit my chest and I put my teeth into my bottom lip to stop the tears. I wouldn't cry in front of her. I wouldn't. She wasn't going to feel even a single tremor of this pain.

All morning I'd managed to keep it together. After Lulu

and Beth headed off, I wobbled, buckled, then bit back the anguish. I had to, this time for Colm's sake. I couldn't go in there with a puffy face and red-rimmed eyes.

'Are you sure you don't want me to come with you today?' Rosie asked for the tenth time.

I shook my head. 'Thanks, honey, but honestly, no. They said it'll be around four hours, so I'm just going to take a book and hang out in the waiting room.'

I appreciated that she wanted to be with me – Lulu and Dan had offered too – but I knew I'd be stronger on my own. These were our friends and they were worrying too – selfishly, I only wanted to think about Colm today, and not have to consider how anyone else was doing. Did that make me a terrible person? Maybe. But it was how I handled things best, by myself, toughing it out, a façade of confidence and calm forcing me to hold it together. At the first sign of sympathy or someone else's pain, I knew I'd crumble.

Like the journey last night, the drive to the hospital passed in a blur, the walk to his ward the same. I felt pure relief when I walked into his room and saw him there and… I froze.

It was Colm. He was sitting on his hospital bed, in a surgical gown, his legs encased in what looked like thick white tights, but at his side was a nurse, a different one from last night, and she was just popping a razor back into a bowl of water, leaving my gorgeous, handsome husband with only a narrow strip of hair on the top of his head.

His expression was searching, trying to gauge my reaction, so I fought past the shock to make a quick recovery.

'I think you're too late to audition for *Last of the Mohicans*.'

Weak. But it was the best I could do in the circumstances. Colm immediately grinned and I saw his shoulders relax.

'My wife,' he explained to the nurse, who smiled warmly.

'I'm Cass. I'll be looking after him today. Does he have any disgusting habits?' she asked with a wink.

'Too many to mention. I'll have to write them all down.'

'Ugh, I always get those ones,' she said, hooting with laughter as she left the room.

I kissed him for a long time, then sat on the side of the bed, my hand in his.

'When are they coming up for you?'

'Should be any time now. The anaesthetist has already been round for a chat and I've signed a pile of forms. They said they're taking me earlier than planned. The person that was supposed to be before me isn't having his op now.'

We both chose not to speculate as to why that might be.

'Ah, here you are.' Mr Miller, the neurosurgeon came in, his manner quiet and efficient. Given the option, it was probably preferable to a surgeon who was blasé or bombastic. 'Morning Mrs O'Flynn.' Smiling, he gave me a brief nod. 'Sorry to rush this man away, but his surgery has been moved up in the schedule.'

No. Don't take him yet. Please don't take him away. I beg you. I'll do anything. Please give us more time.

But I said nothing. I couldn't. If I started to plead with him, I'd never stop.

Instead, I just slipped my hand into Colm's and stood by as the doctor spoke to him. 'Right, Mr O'Flynn...'

'Call me Colm,' he said, just as he had on the day of the diagnosis.

'Ah yes. Quite. Right, Colm, we're just about to take you down now. Do you have any further questions?'

'Nothing. I just hope you've got a steady hand today, Mr Miller.'

'Steady as a rock,' the surgeon replied, and I ached with gratitude that he was going along with Colm's attitude. 'Right then. The porters will be up in a few minutes for you and I'll see you downstairs.'

Colm waited until we were alone. 'You okay?'

'Yeah,' I replied. 'What about you?'

'I'm not worried,' he said confidently.

We both knew I was lying, I suspected he was too.

'I was talking to the doc last night and he said this kind of surgery can cause some personality changes. I just wanted to tell you that. You know, in case I come out of this a miserable bastard.'

I kissed his lips. 'Can I put in requests? Can I ask him to tweak the part that controls romantic gestures and buying excessive gifts for your wife?'

'I'll ask him to make a note of that when I get down there.'

That chipped a piece of my heart, but I was determined not to cry, determined that as long as he was smiling I would be too.

'Look, Shauna…' he hesitated. 'I'm not going to die.'

'I know.' Don't cry. Don't cry.

'There's no fecking way God will kill me while I'm wearing these tights.'

It was too much. A whole avalanche of unstoppable laughter and tears descended, taking my breath away, an internal monologue screaming so loudly it was deafening.

Don't take him. Please don't take him. Please don't take him.

I burrowed my head in his shoulder, let him wrap his arms around me.

'I love you,' I whispered. 'You're everything.'

'I love you too. And you're more.'

I heard the unspoken worry, the fear, the emotion in his voice, felt his arms pull me tighter.

'Mr O'Flynn.'

The voice came from the doorway, and stole the moment.

On the inside I was pleading again, wishing time would stop, begging the world to leave us be. Don't take him from me. I'll do anything, give anything, just please don't take him.

'I am indeed,' Colm replied, suddenly restored to forced cheeriness.

The porter came to the top of the bed, flipped a lever at the back and pulled up the side bars. 'Off we go then.'

Colm's hand held on to mine for a few more seconds. 'I'll see ya later,' he told me with absolute certainty.

'You will,' I replied, then watched as a hospital porter took away the husband that I'd loved since the moment we met.

18

2006

Lulu and Dan's Wedding

I groaned as I rolled over, picked up a book from the bedside table and threw it at the alarm clock. I missed. Bollocks.

Beside me, Shauna opened one eye. 'I think the idea of putting the alarm clock at the other side of the room was so that we'd actually get up and turn it off and not just hit the snooze button and go back to sleep. Or launch my book at it.'

'It was a good plan at the time,' I told her, wincing. Shit, my head hurt. That's what tequila shots at 5 a.m. did to a man. A best man, at that.

I'd been made up when Dan asked me, even happier when they announced the wedding was going to be in Spain. To be honest, a few times over the last few years we thought it might not happen at all. Shit, those two could fight. And fall out. And make up. I couldn't be arsed with the drama, myself, but hey, it was Dan's call and no amount of tequila would make me get in the middle of that one.

'Right, Colm O'Flynn, time to get your gorgeous buttocks out of bed,' Shauna told me. 'Or you could stay right here and have holiday sex with your wife. Your choice.'

'I'd definitely go for the second option if I wasn't an alcohol-poisoned shell of a man,' I told her, groaning. 'Still will, if you do all the work.'

She smacked me on the face with a pillow. 'Nothing new there then,' she quipped, then moved above me, kissing me, not even caring that I must smell like a pub carpet. That was devotion. Five years married and she still kissed me when I was hungover, and laughed at my shite jokes. That was pretty good going.

Her hand had just slipped under the sheet when her phone rang.

'Leave it,' I whispered, but I was too late, she was already reaching for it.

'I can't. It might be my gran. She said she'd call this morning to express her outrage yet again about not being invited.'

Even through the hangover, that made me laugh. Shauna's gran was a class act. A gem. And it was just as well, because her parents were the most uncaring, self-centred bastards I'd ever known. I'd asked her about it right at the start, wanted to know how she managed to put up with the way they treated her and she'd just shrugged. 'I decided a long time ago that you can't make people love you if they don't. My mum and dad should never have had kids – they didn't mean to, I was an accident – but they had me and they deal with me in the only way they know how – blind indifference and barely concealed disdain. And yes, sometimes I feel like telling them how I feel, but what would be the point? They're not going to change. You can't force someone to love you. Besides, I've got Annie. She loves me enough for all of them.'

If Shauna could live with it, keep it civil and pretend not to give a toss that they didn't care, then I could too, but it didn't stop me being entirely fecking outraged at their indifference. And don't even get me started on their messed-up relationship with Lu's mum and dad. Jesus, that was all kinds of twisted, but again, none of my business. I would just do the same as everyone else, keep a lid on my opinion, keep everything friendly on a surface level, and avoid mentioning the herd of elephants in the room.

'Oh, not my gran, it's Vincent. Hang on.'

She climbed out of bed and grabbed a bottle of water from the table by the window. 'Hi Vincent, what's up.'

Vincent. Bane of my bloody life. Nice enough bloke, but his timing was relentlessly crap. For the last month, since they'd launched the new company, every time I sat down with my wife, every time we fell asleep, every time I wanted to make hungover love to her in a villa in Spain, he bloody called. It had been Shauna's idea, going into business together, the two of them joining their catering companies together to capitalize on clients and cut down costs. It had been a good move, but Christ, he must be eating into their profits with the amount he spent on mobile phone calls to my missus.

'No, it's banoffee pie. Yeah, it's in the storage centre all ready to go.'

I got out of bed and headed for the shower, switching it on and then searching the marble unit for the shower gel.

I was sure Shauna would've packed it. Yep, there it was, right next to my razors, shaving cream and… I squinted to read the packet… pregnancy test.

So it was that time. Again. I sighed as I leaned my forehead against the tile wall, hoping the cold surface would eradicate the thumping head, made even sorer by the new possibility of another kind of headache. It was two years now since she came off the pill and sometimes it felt like getting pregnant was all she thought about. Every month she was disappointed, every month she picked herself up, shook it off, and crossed her fingers for the next time. And every time I tried to act like I shared her sadness. I just couldn't tell her that I didn't.

The door opened and she came into the bathroom behind me, laughing at my pathetic head/tile stance. 'That bad?'

'Worse. What did Delia Smith want?'

She flicked my buttock. 'You really need to stop calling him that. You're going to forget and say it to his face one day. Anyway, he was just checking today's function.'

'All okay?' I tried to seem interested, but we were talking about mini-quiche and vol-au-vents here.

'Fine. He's great. Teaming up with him was such a good move. And stop pretending to care,' she said, flicking me again.

I saw her gaze go to the white box on the worktop. 'Shall I do it now? I'm a week late tomorrow.'

I thought about it and then made the right decision. 'Leave it until tomorrow, love. If I'm going to find out that I'm going to be a dad again I don't want it to be naked in a bathroom, with a hangover, a banging sore head and an erection.'

She looked down then back up. 'I can do something about

at least one of those things,' she told me, pulling me towards the shower.

As it happened, the fact that she'd also packed painkillers, extra water and my best suit took care of all of the issues, so when I headed to Dan's suite at one clock, dead on time, I could almost pass for human.

Rosie's new boyfriend, Mark, was there already. That didn't surprise me. He'd told us the night before that he had to get an early night because he was getting up to do yoga at dawn. Rosie was a lovely girl, but I had serious reservations about her taste in blokes. This one had been around for a while, though, so she was obviously into him.

Lulu's dad and Shauna's dad came in at my back, the whole male contingent now complete. Charlie and Jeff looked knackered, probably because they'd still been up doing shots with Lulu and Rosie when I'd crawled to my bed. Last thing I remember was Jeff and Rosie singing Doris Day songs until Shauna's mother got out of her bed and read the riot act.

'All right, mate?' I asked Dan, who was sitting on the couch looking extremely catalogue model in his pants. I didn't pretend to understand his relationship with Lulu. The bloke could have anyone and he was no pushover, yet he put up with all Lulu's drama. It was like some weird force-field attraction shit.

'Yeah, I'm good.'

I'm not the most perceptive, but there was something about the way he said it that was off. Before I could ask him what was up, someone opened another magnum of champagne and got things started again.

I was tempted to join in, but I saw Dan slip into the bedroom and followed him.

'You okay?' I asked as soon as I was out of earshot of the others.

'No,' he answered.

Shit. Not what I was expecting.

'What's up?'

He shook his head as he shrugged. 'Am I making a huge fucking mistake here?'

'*What?*'

Now he thinks he's making a mistake? On the morning of the fecking wedding?

'I mean, let's face it, we both know she's a nightmare. I woke up this morning and just thought, fuck, what if this is how it's always going to be? What if she's always a nightmare? I always thought she'd calm down, because you know, I think a lot of what she does is out of some twisted insecurity, and no wonder given she grew up with The Cockswappers. I don't even mind that she doesn't want kids…'

'What, never?'

'Nope. Says her folks put her off the whole reproduction concept. Her words. I'm cool with it. I just hate all the other crap. I kinda figured that if we got married then she'd settle down. Cop on. But what if she doesn't? What if I'm still checking her phone and wondering if she's shagging the guy behind the bar when we're eighty?'

For the first time in my life, I genuinely, absolutely, was speechless. Dan and I had been mates for the best part of ten years, but shit, we talked about football. Maybe a bit of golf. We liked a drink and we knew how to party.

At no point did we ever have heart-to-heart, bare-your-soul, in-depth conversations about the psychology of his relationship with Lulu.

Christ, I needed another drink, but his expectant expression told me this was an occasion on which I needed to form coherent sentences, so I gave it my best shot.

'I don't know,' I told him, honestly. 'I really don't. Look, I've never pretended to understand your thing with Lu. I know you love her.' I floundered. I was rubbish at this. Zero out of ten for constructive advice so far. 'But I suppose the bottom line is that you need to decide if you can live without her or if you love her enough to stay – even if that means you have to put up with all her crap. Either way, you have to decide now, and either way, I'll back you up.'

Okay, I was hitting a flow now.

'If you don't want to do this, you can just walk out and I'll tell everyone for you, you don't need to look back.' I had no idea why I said that and I really, *really* hoped he didn't do that because I was in no way equipped for that kind of responsibility. 'Or I'll go get her and you can talk to her.' Choose that one. Definitely that. 'Or if you decide to go through with it, we'll never tell anyone we ever had this conversation.' That one! That's definitely the top option!

He went quiet as he thought about what I'd said. Choose door number three. Dear God, please.

'Did you ever have any doubts about Shauna?'

'No.' Honesty again. 'Not a single one. But that doesn't mean we're perfect. We fight. We argue. We disagree on loads of stuff. But like I said, when it comes down to it, I wouldn't want to live without her.'

Thirty-two years old, and this was the first time I'd ever had a conversation like this with another guy. Maybe Shauna was right when she said I had the emotional intelligence of a shagpile rug. She was so much better at this stuff than me. I wanted to put the current situation on pause, phone for her advice on what to do, then come back and execute a perfect save. As it was, I went for the more natural stance of crossing my fingers and hoping for the best. It clearly wasn't working. Dan was staring out of the window now, his hands on his head, face a mask of serious.

'All good in here, boys?' Lulu's dad picked that moment to stick his head in the door, already dressed in his white shirt and trousers. The all-white thing had been Lulu's idea. Personally, I thought we looked like a Boyzone reunion on a summer special of the *X Factor*.

'Yeah, all great, mate,' I told him. 'Just working on the speeches.' It was the first thing that came to mind, followed by 'shit, speeches!'. We really did need to work on the speeches. I'd been planning to wing it by talking about their unquestioning devotion to each other, but I think I might just have lost the bulk of my material.

'Champion!' he said, giving us a thumbs up before retreating back to the lounge, to sit with his best mate, Shauna's dad, the man that was screwing his wife. But hey, one fucked up relationship shitstorm at a time.

'What do you reckon, bud?' I asked Dan, not wanting to be pushy, but aware that the guests would soon be heading to the sands, and the groom wasn't meant to be the last to arrive.

He sighed, turned around. 'I can't call it off,' he said.

I wanted to punch the air with relief. 'If I'm walking into a disaster, then I'll just have to deal with it when it happens. I love her.'

That was it. So simple. Job done.

'Thanks for listening, Colm.'

'Any time,' I assured him, while thinking, 'or preferably never'.

'Okay, let's go get married,' he said, pumped up now.

'I don't want to throw any more issues in, but I think it might go better if you were wearing more than your boxers.'

Half an hour later, we were on the beach, and Lulu was walking towards us, holding her dad's hand, her mother walking behind her with Shauna and Rosie. All of them were dressed in white, Lulu's dress long, the others shorter. I know all eyes should be on the bride, but I couldn't take mine off Shauna. Her blonde waves were flowing over her shoulders and she had pink flowers in her hair that matched the bunch of roses she was holding. If this was our day and she was walking towards me looking like that, I'd marry her all over again.

I winked and she returned it, then we both played our part in the ceremony to perfection. Shauna took Lulu's flowers, fixed her dress, squeezed her hand. I managed not to drop the rings.

Dan never wavered once. His voice was strong and certain, and he got through all his vows without doing a runner into the ocean and taking off in a speedboat. Pretty much all we could ask for.

As they both said I do, I glanced over at Shauna and tears were streaming down her face. It wasn't like her.

I could count on the fingers of one hand how many times I'd seen her cry, and even then it was only at movies and the occasional advert featuring neglected dogs. She was tough, Shauna. I'd loved her on sight, but I'd loved her even more when I learned how independent she was, how she just got on with stuff, made it happen, relied on no one to help her or fix things, while at the same time, making sure she took care of everyone else. She was the one who made sure Rosie was okay, the one who told Lulu when she was out of order. And the one who was always thinking ahead, making sure our lives were as good as they could be, planning stuff, making things happen.

Except for the whole kids thing. The fact that hadn't happened was definitely stressing her out.

'I now pronounce you man and wife. Dan, you may kiss your bride.'

Cue cheers and applause as Dan scooped Lulu up and kissed her. Deciding that for now, my job was done, I wandered over to Shauna, who still had tears dripping from her face.

'Hey baby,' I said, putting my arms around her and kissing the top of her head. 'What's with the waterworks? You getting all windswept and romantic in your old age?'

She shook her head, using the palm of her hand to wipe away her tears. Then she laughed, and said, 'Have I got mascara all down my face?'

I kissed her nose, then one cheek, then the other. 'No, you're fine. Especially if you want to form a tribute act for Kiss.'

She nudged me with her elbow. 'Colm O'Flynn, you are so lucky that I love you. It's a miracle, really.'

'I know, you're right. I'm blessed,' I said, teasing her. That's when I noticed that the tears were still coming. 'Right, you're milking this with the whole weeping thing you've got going on there.'

She laughed again, yet the tears hadn't stopped. Behind us, a man with a camera was taking photographs of Dan and Lulu and her parents and I had a feeling they'd soon be giving us a shout. Probably not the best timing since my girl was still breaking her heart.

'Are you going all soft on me? Are you going to be reading slushy books and forcing me to watch romantic films?'

'No,' she whispered, wiping the tears away for a second time. 'I'm sorry. I know I'm being pathetic. It's just that... It's just that... I'm not pregnant.'

19

2015

The Operation

It sounds so clichéd, but it really had felt like time stood still. Four hours, that turned out to be seven, that felt like forever. I tried to read, tried to sleep, tried to eat. In the end I just sat, until eventually the nurse popped her head in and said he was now in recovery and they'd bring him up when he'd come out of the anaesthetic.

What did that mean? Had it worked? Was he okay? Was he damaged? I asked, but there were no answers, just kind smiles and promises that the doctor would speak to me soon. I thought about calling someone but there were no words to describe the terror that was crawling through every vein in my body.

So I just sat a while longer.

When the door eventually opened, the man who came back looked nothing like the one that had come into the hospital last night. That man had been healthy. Strong. This man was pale, looked sick. His shaved head had dressings round it, with two drains protruding from the bandages, both filled with blood. It was horrific. This wasn't my Colm. It was someone else.

Then he forced open his eyes, pulled that crooked smile and whispered, 'Hey m'darlin.' And he was my Colm again.

I stroked his face, his eyes, put my fingertips to his mouth, as if I needed touch to reinforce that he was there. 'How are you feeling?'

'Like a guy took a saw to my head.'

'Nothing gets past you,' I said, genuinely smiling for the first time since the day we'd walked into the optician's shop in Richmond nearly two weeks before. His sense of humour was still there. That was a win.

He was fine. It was all going to be fine.

'How long can I stay?' I asked the nurse, who'd introduced herself as Karen when she'd come on shift an hour before.

She looked at her watch. 'Visiting is in an hour and lasts until 9 p.m., so you can stay until then. I'll pull the curtains closed to give you some privacy. I'll be bringing some food shortly – can I get you something?'

'No thank you.' It somehow felt wrong to impose, when I could just nip down to the coffee shop on the ground floor later. Besides, I didn't have much of an appetite.

Colm slept for another twenty minutes, waking – in a stroke of perfect timing – just as Dr Miller walked in the door.

'Mrs O'Flynn,' he greeted me pleasantly, before turning to the person who mattered. 'How are you doing there, Colm?'

'Good. Yeah, good. I think.' His voice sounded husky and I wondered if that was from the surgery. Had there been a tube down his throat? Or did that just happen in *ER* and *Grey's Anatomy*?

'How did it go?' I said, not even sure what I was asking. Were the results quantifiable? Would he already know the outcome?

'Well, there are many positives.' Many positives? Did that also mean there were negatives?

'I'm not dead,' Colm croaked.

'Yes,' Dr Miller almost laughed, 'that would be the main one. Other than that, we got out everything we could see. Now, that doesn't mean that we got it all. The very nature of this kind of mass means that there were almost certainly cells left behind. And as I said before, we won't know the nature of these cells until they've been examined.'

He took a pen out of his pocket and held it up in front of Colm's nose.

'Colm, I want you to follow this pen and tell me when you can no longer see it.'

He ran it to the left, to the right, up and then down, stopping each time when Colm gestured that it had gone out of sight. My heart was in my mouth, as I watched his reactions, praying that he'd pass whatever test the doctor was setting.

'Okay, the good news is that you still have your central vision, but part of the tumour was attached to the optic nerve. That's what was giving you the incidences of loss in your peripheral vision. I'm afraid the damage on your left side is considerable, perhaps permanent, but the positive there is that – with no new tumour growth – it won't get any worse than it is now.'

No worse. That was good. Great.

I watched as Colm moved his eyes from side to side of his own accord, then up, down, circle. 'I can handle that,' Colm said. His positivity made me want to weep.

'Other than that, there seems to be no paralysis, no weakening of body function or loss of cognitive skills. All in all, I think we've had the best result we could hope for so far.'

Happiness soared from the centre of my chest and I wanted to punch the air. Best result. I'd take it. But I still had questions.

'Mr Miller, Colm said this morning that personality changes are a possibility?'

'That's true. This has been major surgery to the brain, and as I've said before, it's not an exact science. Post-surgery personality variances are impossible to predict but something that we see in many cases.'

I didn't care. I honestly didn't. He was here, he was almost in one piece. That was all that mattered.

My next question was the one that had been on my mind since he walked in the door. 'Can you tell what type of tumour it was?'

He shook his head. 'I'm afraid not. It's been sent to the lab, but results will take up to a week.'

I'd researched the subject so intensively over the week of sleepless nights that I now felt like I could give discussions on the many varieties of brain tumours. The range was vast, from benign to malignant, from low grades to high. The symptoms and effects depended on where they were situated. The occipital lobe, like Colm. The frontal lobe. The parietal lobe. The temporal lobe. The brain stem.

Then there was the biggest variant – the specific type of

tumour. There were over 120 different kinds, but for some reason, a few of them stuck in my mind. Meningioma. Ependymoma. Oligodendroglioma. And the one that came with flashing red lights, the glioblastoma. That was the one with the lowest life expectancy and the lowest long-term survival rate. Some patients got six months. Some got eighteen. Some longer. Very few of them got anywhere near years in the double figures. But thankfully, those were rare, especially among men of Colm's age. The facts backed up Mr Miller's earlier summation, that the likeliest outcome was a benign and treatable mass, one that would have little or no effect on his life expectancy. I'd take that one, please.

'So what will happen in the meantime?' I asked.

'All going well with his recovery, Colm will be fine to leave here in three or four days. I've made an appointment for you at my clinic two weeks from tomorrow to discuss the results.'

'So we won't know anything until then?'

'No.' He turned back to Colm again. 'For now, just concentrate on healing and building your strength up. We've had a good result so far – I don't see any reason for that to change.'

It took a whole sentence to deliver just one word. Hope. That's what he was saying. Hope Colm had no post-op complications. Hope he healed well. Hope the tumour was benign. Hope we could get our lives back. Hope he didn't die.

'Well, I'll leave you now. If there are any problems, the team will call me, but I don't expect that to be the case. I'll see you on my ward round in the morning. Well done. It was a good day.'

'Thanks, doctor,' Colm said, his voice a little stronger now.

'Thank you so much. I can't tell you how much we appreciate what you did for him today.' My eyes filled up again, and I furiously blinked the tears away as always. I'd cried more in the last two weeks than I'd done in my entire life, but after everything Colm had been through in that time and today, I resolved that there would be no tears here tonight. Colm was still here. We still had him.

Laughs. Humour. Denial. Optimism. Say it again.

The nurses came round with food as promised, then ran some quick tests on Colm's blood pressure, temperature and pulse, marking the results on a chart. Next they pulled back the bedsheet.

'See you kept your tights on,' I teased.

'They kept me alive today,' he fired back, grinning. I didn't care if he wore those tights for the rest of his life, as long as he was with me.

The nurse checked his reflexes, then ran a pen-like rod along the soles of his feet. I've no idea what she was hoping for, but she seemed happy with the result. Outside the door, we saw visitors arriving for the patients in the other rooms and wards, some clutching flowers, presents, kids. Real life. All of it here.

I was back at the side of the bed again, one hand in his, the other playing with a loose thread on the blanket.

'So I've been thinking…'

'Oh God. Will it cost me money?'

'Quite probably. You know that conversation we keep having?'

'The one where you say I'm the biggest shag you've ever seen?'

He was bringing out all his favourite lines and I'd never been so happy to hear them, but I still needed to have a different conversation.

'No, the other one. The one where we talk about our work/life balance.'

'Ah, that one. My second favourite after the shag one.'

'There has to be a lesson in all this, Colm. All these years, we've been working night and day, putting everything else off just to pay bills and survive. It has to change, babe. I want to enjoy life again. I want to do things, go places, spend time with each other and Beth, and Davie and Joe, just doing nothing. We need to look at this as a chance to change things. A lesson learned. I don't want to waste another day of our lives.'

I felt my voice cracking, so I stopped. Composed myself. Waited for one of his usual wisecracks. It didn't come.

'I know, you're right,' he said. 'This morning, when I was waiting downstairs, I just kept thinking about the last few years and all the shit that's happened. I know it needs to change. You, me, Beth, the boys... I think we lost sight of what matters, going after a life that we don't really need. I let you take way too much pressure, left everything on you.'

'It's okay,' I told him.

'It's not. It's really not. I'm so sorry.'

'You don't have to be sorry for anything.'

'We both know I do. When this is all over, we're going to make sure we have great lives. The five of us. Nothing else matters.'

Maybe it was the after-effects of the anaesthetic, but this new Colm was saying all the right things and sounding like he meant it. He'd spent his whole life keeping everything jocular on the outside, but perhaps it took something like this for him to take stock, to realize that we'd gone down the wrong road and needed to back up.

The daylight had dimmed outside when the bell rang for the end of visiting and I kissed him for a long time, reluctant to leave, desperate to just crawl into bed beside him and hold him all night.

Only when the lovely nurse had popped her head in the door for a second time did I say goodbye. 'I'll be back in the morning. They've said if you're still in this room and not moved to a normal ward, then I can stay all day.'

I could see he was getting sleepy again, his eyes dropping. When they closed, I silently left the room and headed outside. I'd come in first thing this morning terrified and devastated, now I was leaving exhausted but relieved. He was okay. He was going to be fine.

I waited on the lift with hordes of other people, then drifted out to the far corner of the car park where I'd left the car. I got in, closed the door, put my seat belt on and rested my head against the headrest, replaying the last few hours, seeing his face, hearing his voice.

'When this is all over, we're going to make sure we have great lives,' he'd said.

The positivity I'd felt when he'd said that returned... but only for a second, before it was ambushed by another thought, the one that had been gripping my heart in a vice all day, while I ignored everything it was saying, determined not to let it take hold.

Now it was loud and clear.

What if we didn't get that chance? What if the results of the tests showed that this was the kind of brain tumour that didn't give second chances?

20

2008

When Shauna Returns
to Where It All Started

'What time is Vincent picking you up? And is he still single? Open to a bit of an illicit affair?' Annie asked me, with a twinkle in her eye.

'Gran!' I feigned outrage. 'He's picking me up at nine and I'm a married woman!'

Her turn to feign outrage. 'I know, dear. I was just hoping he might be interested in a wild fling with an older woman.'

I laughed so hard I almost dropped my tea. Visiting her tonight had cheered me right up. I tried to get over at least once a week, but with the twelve- and fourteen-hour days we'd been putting in, sometimes seven days a week, I didn't always make it over. It had only worked this week because we were catering a fortieth birthday party in a very grand home in Wimbledon, not far from Annie's little cottage. I'd left to come here as soon as the food was served, and Vincent had stayed behind to oversee the clear-up.

I had absolutely no idea what I'd have done without him. Vincent was the kind of guy who showed up. No bullshit excuses. No erratic crap. He pitched in. Made it work. Teaming up with him was the best business decision I'd ever made and it was beginning to pay off financially.

'Seriously, I do like that boy. He's got honest eyes.'

'Gran, he's thirty-one. But you're right, he does have honest eyes. He's a really decent guy too.'

'Does Colm not get jealous?'

'Of what?'

'Oh come on, ma love, there isn't many that would kick that lad out of bed for making crumbs with his custard creams.'

I giggled. 'You are so shallow, but so right. And no, Colm never gets jealous. He was born without the capacity for jealousy, worry and cleaning dishes. Besides, he knows I have zero attraction to Vincent.'

'Are you dead? Shauna, he's gorgeous.'

'Yeah, but I just don't see him that way.' It was true. Vincent made me laugh and I enjoyed his company, but he had zero effect on my libido. I appreciated the whole 'Younger Ben Affleck On A Good Day' thing he had going on, but I'd honestly never wanted to jump his bones.

'He's my friend, Gran. He's never been attracted to me and I've never been attracted to him. It's called "platonic". And "loving my husband".'

'Aye, well there was never anyone else for me but my Ernie, God rest his soul, but I might have made an exception for this one. Anyway, how's my boy Colm doing?' Gran loved my husband. They had that same irreverent, quick, dark humour. 'If I was forty years younger and he needed specs...' she said every time we discussed him.

'He's doing great. He's thinking about setting up a company, going into partnership with Dan. A management consultancy.'

She paused, Bakewell tart midway to mouth. 'And what do you think of that?'

'I think it's a great idea. They work together now anyway, so I don't have any worries about their partnership. I know there have been warnings about the economy, but business in that sector is still booming. Only thing is that it'll force our hand with the house. We've been renting up until now, but if we're going to buy we'll have to do it before he becomes self-employed or we'll struggle to get a mortgage.'

Annie took this all in. 'You'll work it out and do the right thing, love. You always do. You're the smartest of all of us, especially that feckless father of yours.'

'Gran, that's your son!' I don't know why I was protesting. She'd made her disapproval of my father perfectly clear to me my whole life. Like me, she kept everything amicable on the surface, but that congeniality floated on a pool of disapproval. Years ago, after a few too many sherries, she'd explained why. 'Can't stand the way he treats you, Shauna. Selfish. All he cares about is himself and that mother of yours. I don't understand it. That's not the way he was raised. His father was a decent family man, God rest his soul, and after he died I taught our Jeff better than that. Don't know where I went wrong with him, but by God, I did.'

It was the one and only time she'd ever gone deeper than calling him a 'useless lump that's far too fond of himself', and I never probed further. All that I cared about was that she loved me and I loved her back. She'd brought me up, been more of a mother to me than Debbie ever had. We had an understanding. A likeness. 'Two peas in a pod, me and you,' she always said. 'But thank Christ you didn't get my legs.' Then she'd roar with laughter, lift her skirt above her knees and do a jig across the kitchen.

'And what about, you know, the other thing?'

'Gran, why can't you say it?'

'Because I don't want to upset you.' The situation upset me. Annie talking about it didn't.

'Thanks Gran, but avoiding the word "pregnant" doesn't make a difference when we're actually talking about me not being pregnant,' I told her, keeping my tone light as I helped myself to another square of her beloved Turkish delight.

'S'pose,' she said, pensive, before starting again. 'So. Not pregnant yet then?'

'No,' I replied. 'I promise you'll be the first to know. After Colm. And the rest of my street, who'll be alerted by the brass band and the Red Arrow display.'

She wasn't buying my joviality. I could see the concern in her eyes. 'Och, pet, it'll happen. It took a long time for me too, and I only had the one. Makes it all the more upsetting that he turned out to be a useless lump that's far too fond of himself.'

And there it was. When I'd stopped laughing, I got back to the subject of the discussion. 'I'm thinking of trying IVF. It's been almost four years since I came off the pill and nothing. Don't get me wrong, I love the twins, but I want one of my own, Gran. Does that make me selfish?'

'No, of course it doesn't, love.'

We'd had this conversation a hundred times before so I knew her answer, I just needed to hear it again. That was the toughest thing about this whole process – I struggled to find anyone else to talk to about it. My mother wasn't in the least interested. I didn't think it was fair to wallow over the subject with Rosie, when she too desperately wanted kids but couldn't get past the relationship that lasted longer than the two-year stage. Lulu and Dan were absolutely resolute about not wanting children because Lulu claimed, in her words, that she was having 'no part of anything that required the wearing of clothes that didn't need dry-cleaning'. Yes, she was glib, but her sentiment was honest. Kids just weren't something she was interested in. She trotted out dismissive lines for people who asked her at dinner parties, but the truth was, she'd announced when we were about twelve that she didn't want children, in case she 'fucked them up the way our lot had fucked us up'. I wasn't sure that that angry young girl had ever left Lulu's soul.

I realized my gran had asked me something that I'd missed.

'Pardon?'

'You said "I'm".'

'What?' I asked, not understanding.

'You said, "*I'm* thinking of trying IVF", not *we*.'

Wow. She was like the granny division of the CIA – chief interrogator, using the powers of observation, tea and Turkish delight.

Her laser-strength perception, as always, cut right through the facts and went straight to the heart of the problem. Colm. Colm, who I loved with all my heart. But who, I'd also learned, had absolutely no capacity to dwell on things that weren't going well. He didn't get it. He just didn't understand my longing, or my monthly disappointment. However, what hurt the most was that, as much as he tried, he couldn't make it matter to him. It wasn't on his list of life wishes, therefore if it didn't happen that was okay.

In my world, it wasn't.

I tried to condense and minimize all that for my gran.

'Did I? Oh. It's just that… well, he doesn't mind so much. It's different for him. He's got the boys, he's happy. There's no biological clock deafening his ovaries. Sometimes I think he'd be happier if I stopped thinking about it and things just stayed the way they are now.'

It was true. It was also consistent. He'd had the same point of view since that day in Bali when we'd first discussed it.

Annie thought about that for a moment. 'Shauna, if this is important to you then don't let it go. And if Colm doesn't see how much it means to you, you've got to help him understand it. And no, you're not being selfish. It's about time someone else cared about your happiness. God knows those useless lumps of parents never did.'

She was off again, but thankfully, before she could get into full rant mode, a horn beeped outside.

'That'll be Vincent,' I said, grabbing my bag off the floor, then kissing her as I headed to the door. 'I'll be back over next week, Gran.'

'Great, love. And don't forget to ask him if he likes older women!'

I was still shaking my head with amusement when I climbed into the van. It was a new investment, a shiny white

204

Fiesta van with Constant Cravings written in jaunty green letters on the side. It had taken us ages to come up with the company name and we still lived in dread of a letter from K.D. Lang's copyright lawyers.

'What's funny?' Vincent asked, checking his side mirror as he pulled away from the pavement.

'Annie wants to know if you'd consider a fling with an older woman.'

'Only if she takes me to the bingo,' he retorted.

We both knew that it was hilarious because it was about as far from the truth as you could get. If Colm was a down-to-earth, grounded bloke, Vincent was his metrosexual opposite. Back in catering college we'd been best mates, a relationship that worked because he was easy-going, uncomplicated, and – mostly – because it was only ever going to be platonic. He wasn't my type and I definitely wasn't his. I liked quirky guys and upfront humour, while he paid his way through college by modelling, and only went for the tall, gorgeous girls he worked with, all of whom inevitably fell in love with his chiselled dark looks and gym-buffed body.

His suggestion to join the two companies together had come over a beer at our annual catch-up, and I saw immediately that it made sense. Our collective company revenue had increased tenfold, mainly because his involvement gave me time to focus on marketing and expansion, while his ideas were brilliant, his food was sublime and he was so damn good-looking we were getting tons of repeat business. Sod political correctness – if the objectification of my partner led to more profit for us, it was all right by me.

The debrief on the job he'd just left took us halfway

to Twickenham, and discussing the bookings for the next couple of days took us the rest of the way. We were getting close to home by the time we got on to personal stuff.

'Crap, I'm sorry, I haven't even asked you how things went with Carole today.'

Carole. Vincent's girlfriend. Lingerie model. They'd had a lunchtime meeting that day to discuss their future and he hadn't had a chance to give me the update.

'Ah, it could have gone better.'

I smiled.

'Why? What happened?'

'She says she wants a commitment.'

'Ouch.'

'Exactly.'

'And what do you want?'

'Am I being too shallow if I say the love of a good woman and incredible sex?'

'Not if you do it in that order.'

'Then that'll do me,' he laughed, but I could see the tension around his eyes.

'So what's the problem?' I probed, gently.

Without pretension or thought, he ran his fingers through his dark hair, then over his two-day stubble.

'I'm not there yet. Not ready to go to the next level,' he said, then rolled his eyes, ruefully as we stopped at a set of traffic lights on the outskirts of Richmond.

'She says I have commitment issues. It's not exactly a newsflash, is it?'

I instinctively railed against the picture he was painting of himself. This wasn't some flighty guy who messed people around. He was solid. Reliable. Decent. And if he wasn't ready, then it wasn't because he had issues, it was because he was being honest. 'Don't be hard on yourself. Sometimes it takes one person a little longer to get to the right place.'

'I don't seem to remember that happening with you and Colm.'

I laughed. 'Touché. But we were young. Crazy.'

'I remember,' he said, smiling.

'So what's missing?' I asked him. 'Love?'

He shook his head. 'No, I definitely love her, I just don't know if it's enough. You know that thing you had with Colm, where you couldn't live a day without him? I'm not feeling that. God, I sound like a girl. Can you check if my testicles are still attached?'

I punched his arm. 'Eh, avoid the sexism please.'

'Sorry,' he grinned. 'I'm much better with cars, sport or the pricing structure of a finger buffet.'

'You'll die a sad and lonely old man,' I teased. 'Watching rugby on the TV with a fridge full of sausage rolls.'

'Don't mock. There are worse ways to go than death by sausage roll.'

As we reached the centre of town, the Richmond streets were still busy. I decided it was too early to call it a night. Colm was away and I wasn't ready to go home to an empty house. Besides, Vincent didn't often open up about stuff, and I wanted to know more while I had him on a roll.

I had a quick look at the clock on the dashboard. 'Do you want to go for a quick drink?'

'Absolutely,' he replied, needing no persuasion whatsoever.

'Do you want to phone Colm and see if he wants to come meet us?'

'No, he's in Manchester with Dan tonight – group training session tomorrow – so I'm home alone. That sounds like a good title for a Joe Pesci movie.'

Vincent shook his head. 'Your jokes are beyond lame.'

'They are,' I agreed. 'That's what makes me adorable.'

'Indeed. So where to?'

'Why don't we just head to the bridge and choose when we get there.'

Instead of turning into my street, he kept going straight, over Richmond Bridge and then slipping into a free parking space just as we turned on to Hill Street.

Jumping out, I gestured to the Pitcher and Piano.

'Let's go there. Haven't been in for years. That's where I met Colm, you know.'

'If you're going to get all dewy-eyed about Mr Wonderful, I'm not coming in.'

'Okay, I'll get dewy-eyed about your relationship issues instead. How does that sound?'

'A tad sad, but acceptable.'

He put his hand on the small of my back as we crossed the road, always so gentlemanly. Colm's level of chivalry was to shout, 'Run!' and hope we made it to the other side.

The pub was still busy, despite the fact that it was ten o'clock on a Sunday night.

One of my favourite songs, Stevie Wonder's 'Superstition', was playing on the sound system as we made our way through the crowd to the bar. I'd forgotten how much I loved this place. It represented so much that was special to me:

my twenty-something youth, a thousand nights out with Lulu and Rosie, meeting Colm.

'What would you like?' Vincent raised his voice over the sound of the music.

'Gin and tonic, please. And crisps!' I hadn't eaten all day except for Annie's home-made scones and Turkish delight.

While he ordered, my attention flickered to the open doors that led out on to the balcony, to the exact spot that I'd been standing in when I met Colm seven years before. Seven years – yet it felt like we'd been together our whole lives. What would have happened if I hadn't gone out that night? Or if I'd left five minutes earlier as I'd been planning to? It horrified me to think we could have gone through this life without meeting. Or perhaps that wasn't how it worked. Maybe in any life we'd have found each other and…

I lost my train of thought, distracted by what I was seeing now through those same doors. The image wasn't computing. How could that be?

'Shauna,' Vincent said pointedly, interrupting my thoughts and taking my attention. 'Here!' He thrust a drink into my hand, then asked, puzzled, 'Are you okay?'

'No. Look.'

I gestured to the open doors, but he was at a different angle from me and struggled to get an adequate view. 'Can't see their faces, but do you mean the couple kissing?'

I nodded, wearily.

'So what's the problem?'

'The problem is that's my friend. And the guy she's with isn't her husband.'

21

2015

The Prognosis

'Do you need some help there?' Shauna asked, as she watched me search through the wardrobe for my jacket. It was there last week. Or was it yesterday? It was definitely bloody there.

'No, it's fine.' I know I snapped at her. Didn't mean it. But it was just so... aaargh, where the fuck was my jacket?

I saw her back off and turned to say something, when I spotted the jacket, hanging on the hook on the back of the bedroom door. Shit. I was sure I'd already looked there.

I pulled it on and headed downstairs.

'Ready, honey?' she asked brightly, like I hadn't bit her head off two minutes before. How did she do that? She just let everything bounce off her like she was made of Teflon.

'Shauna, I'm sorry, I...'

'It's fine. Come on, let's go. Traffic might be heavy on the way there.'

Out in the driveway, I was halfway round the car when I remembered, and doubled back, climbing into the passenger side instead. I didn't drive any more. Just one more kick in the nuts to add to the others. According to the DVLA, I'd be banned from going behind the wheel for at least a year, possibly longer, depending on the results of the meeting today.

I didn't even want to think about what that would mean for my work or my day-to-day existence. Couldn't drive to meetings. Couldn't jump in the car and pop to the shops. Couldn't nip to the school to pick up Beth. On the scale of things, it wasn't life or death, but it was bloody inconvenient.

Life or death.

That's what today was all about, but I already knew the answer. It was all going to be fine. Benign. I was already feeling much better than before the op. A few pills, a bit of recovery time, a couple of inches of hair growth and I'd be on the road back to normal life – even if it was on the bus.

'You okay?' Shauna asked me for the 3423rd time.

'Yeah, I'm fine.' It was like a role reversal. All these years, she'd answered 'I'm fine' to questions when she clearly wasn't, yet now I was doing the same. And, just like I used to do, she was pretending to accept it.

I knew I was being rough on her but I just needed to get today over with. Turn the corner. Put all this behind us.

It was two weeks since the op and the wrap-around bandages were off my head now, but that left me with the physical version of a split personality. From the front I looked like a normal guy with a bad haircut, but when I turned round I looked like a man who'd lost out in a fight with an axe.

I'd kept the dressing on the wound and pulled a hat on so I didn't scare kids. Thankfully, Beth hadn't been fazed at all. Made of the same strong stuff as her mother.

We drove most of the way in silence. There had been a lot of that this week. Shauna had wanted to talk stuff through, discuss how I was feeling, the treatment, the changes to our lives, but I wasn't having it. What was the point? Let's deal with things as they happen. Get the facts, sort them, move on. What was the point of thinking about the potential downsides when they weren't going to happen? And anyway, how many times did I have to tell everyone it was going to be fine? I'd never understand the whole obsession with thinking through potential scenarios or preparing for the worst. Sod that. Stay positive, don't worry about a thing, it'll all turn out for the best.

When we parked up, she put her hand on top of mine. 'It's going to be fine,' she said, her grin wide and gorgeous. See, she was coming round to my way of thinking.

'It is, don't worry,' I agreed. 'Although I'm definitely suing them for this haircut.'

Her hand was on the door handle when she stopped, turned back to me. 'Colm, I love you.'

I'd heard that a million times before but for some reason the way she said it just caught me at the back of my throat.

'I love you too, m'darlin.'

'I know.'

The waiting room in the neurology department was just as busy as when we'd gone there the first visit, but this time it was different. This time, I realized, I was one of them, one of the sick people. A fortnight ago, I hadn't given a second thought to the fact that this world existed and yet now I was living in it, using words like radiotherapy and chemo and prognosis. As we crossed the room, I saw eyes glance towards me, registering the hair, the dressing. Too late, I wished I'd kept the hat on instead of stuffing it in my pocket when we entered the building.

An hour later, fifty minutes past the time of our appointment, we were still sitting there, eyes trained on the corridor that led to the consulting rooms.

'Do you think I should go ask at reception, double-check they know we're here?' Shauna asked, biting her bottom lip, her hand holding on to mine so tightly her knuckles were turning white.

'They know,' I told her. 'They'll come for us soon.'

Just as I said it, I saw a couple come from the corridor, a tall guy, his eyes red-rimmed, his wife sobbing, only the elaborate headscarf she wore giving away which one of them was undergoing treatment. They both looked weary, worn, his arm around her waist, supporting her as if her legs could give way at any moment.

Beside me, Shauna took a sharp breath. She'd seen them too, their devastation playing out for the whole waiting room to see.

'Poor buggers,' I whispered, so only Shauna could hear me.

'Mr O'Flynn?' I saw Jenny, the liaison nurse, scanning the room, then nodding as she spotted us.

She waited until we reached her before starting down the corridor. 'How are you? You're looking great,' she told me, while I searched her face for clues. She must know. She must have full information on what we were going in here to be told, yet she was giving away nothing. That must mean everything was going to be fine. I knew it.

Inside the stark pale greens walls of the room, Mr Miller was waiting, sitting next to a guy I hadn't met before. He introduced himself as Mr Johns. Oncologist. So what did that mean? Why was he here? Out of nowhere, tiny tingles of anxiety started in my chest. Oncologist. The specialist who dealt with radiotherapy and chemo for cancer. Didn't necessarily mean he was here to speak to me though. Perhaps he just sat in on the clinic all day. I was one of dozens of people Mr Miller would be seeing today, all of them in different stages of treatment, with different tumours, so maybe he was there to consult only for those who needed him – like those poor souls who'd been in before us.

No, he wasn't here for me. I was fine. Fine.

Introductions over, Mr Miller lifted his pen. 'So Colm, tell me how you've been since the operation? Further vision issues? Headaches?'

No, no, no, no. That wasn't how today should work. I was here for answers not questions. Just tell me. Tell me I'm okay and then I'll answer questions for a fortnight. Forever.

But none of that came out of my mouth. Instead I said, 'Just a few headaches, but I think they're more to do with the wound. Mr Miller, please don't think I'm being rude, but can we please get to the point and tell us about the tumour? I'm fine, right?'

He put his pen down on the desk and turned so that he was facing us straight on. I'm not sure if it was me or Shauna who was holding on tighter, but I could no longer feel my hand.

'Colm, we've had the results back from the lab and I'm afraid they're not what we hoped. The analysis shows that your tumour is what we call a grade 4 glioblastoma.'

Glioblastoma.

Oh fuck.

I remembered that word. I'd seen it weeks ago, when Shauna had been researching brain tumours. It was cancer. Not benign. Cancer.

I couldn't breathe. Couldn't make my lungs work. Couldn't understand what he was saying. Everything was shutting down and all I could hear was white noise. Chaos. The thudding of my heart pumping out blood.

'I'm sorry. I know this isn't what you wanted to hear. Do you need a moment or shall I carry on?'

'Carry on.' It was Shauna's voice, not mine, and it was a choked whisper.

'Okay. I'm suggesting we implement a treatment plan immediately. We removed as much of the tumour as we could see, but as I said post-op, that doesn't guarantee there were no cancer cells left behind. We need to start a six-week programme of radiotherapy, followed by a chemotherapy regime. That's why Mr Johns is here. He'll talk you through the plan.'

Mr Johns started speaking. Saying words. At least, his mouth was opening and closing, but I was hearing nothing. Just more white noise. Glioblastoma. Grade 4. I knew this wasn't good. Oh fuck. We were definitely not fine.

I realized he'd stopped talking and either time had stood still or they were waiting for me.

'Colm, do you have any questions?' From the way he

said it I could tell he was repeating it. I hadn't heard it the first time.

'Is it curable?' I think it was my voice...

Something rearranged the doctor's features for the briefest second before he spoke. Sadness? Pity?

'I'm sorry, it is not.'

'So... So...' My voice again, working independently of my brain. My fucked-up, broken, bastard of a brain. 'So what? It will kill me?'

'It is incurable. Yes.'

'When?'

'I'm afraid there is no quantifiable answer to that. What matters is that...'

'I need to know when,' I repeated, cutting him off.

'Colm, we prefer not to discuss timescales. They vary so widely and there are no definitives.'

Shauna spoke up, reading me, knowing what I needed, smart enough to ask the question in the right way, even though tears were flowing down her face and she had to pause between words, her voice failing her.

'Mr Miller, I think I read on the internet that a glioblastoma has an average prognosis of twelve to eighteen months. Is that true?'

Twelve months. A year. That couldn't be correct. She was mistaken.

'In some cases, yes. But Mrs O'Flynn, I must emphasize that's not a fixed term. Many people outlive that prognosis.'

'How many? Exactly how many outlive that prognosis?' I pushed.

He paused again before answering.

'Research shows a five-year survival rate of around six per cent.'

Six per cent.

So that meant ninety-four per cent of people with this tumour died within five years.

My beautiful, crazy, brilliant Beth was five years old and he'd just told me I wouldn't see her grow up.

This was worst-case scenario. Worst. Fucking. Case. Scenario.

22

2008

The New House

The front doorbell rang and I instinctively looked at the kitchen clock I'd just hung five minutes before. Five o'clock. Jess was bang on time as always. She was great like that. Unfailingly dependable and reliable.

'Colm, Jess is at the door!'

No answer.

'Davie, Joe! Your mum is here.'

Still nothing. Bugger. I bent at the knees, the way they advise in Health and Safety videos, and put the huge cardboard box I was carrying down on a clear space on the floor. I'd much rather the Health and Safety video said, 'Don't even consider carrying huge cardboard boxes, especially when there are big strong men who could do the job for you.' However, it seemed like the 'big strong men' were nowhere to be seen.

Annie and Rosie were unpacking stuff in the kitchen and

I knew Vincent was in charge of organizing the garage. Lulu and Dan were missing in action. And Colm was...

I heard a scream from the back garden and looked out of the window.

Colm was chasing Joe and Davie with a water gun. Great. It was the day of the move into our new house, we had a whole host of grown-up jobs and he was out playing with the twelve-year-olds while two large trucks, still half-full of our entire worldly goods, sat in the driveway.

Not that I was keeping score, but I'd found this house, organized the mortgage, dealt with the lawyers, the estate agents and the banks, arranged the removal vans, packed up the old flat, cleaned it for the next tenants, arrived here at dawn this morning, cleaned it from top to bottom, went back to the old flat, co-ordinated the loading of the vans, arranged drinks and food for everyone who was helping us, pitched in with the unloading of the vans at this end and I was now humping bloody great big boxes while Colm, who'd contributed zero to the process so far, was outside chasing the kids with a bloody water pistol.

And worse, his ex-wife was ringing a doorbell I didn't even know we bloody had.

'Do you want me to get that?' Rosie shouted from one of the other rooms.

'No, it's fine, but could you go shout the boys and tell them their mum is here? They're in the back garden.'

It would be rude to keep her waiting any longer.

Smile on face, hair hastily smoothed back into less of a riot, I opened the door.

'Hi Jess. You found us!' I kissed her on each cheek, ignoring the contrast between us. There was I, old ripped jeans, a baggy white T-shirt, hair looking like I'd been electrocuted, while Jess was in immaculate white trousers, with a fitted grey shirt and her deep chestnut hair gleaming as it tumbled in a Jennifer Aniston style bob to her shoulders. I chided myself for the trite comparison. Jess was a good person and a great mum – she deserved to have gleaming chestnut hair.

'Would you like to come in? The boys won't be long.'

'No it's fine. Steve is waiting in the car,' she gestured to a silver Mercedes further along the road and I gave Steve a wave. They'd been a couple for a few years now and – although we only interacted at pick-ups and drop-offs – he seemed like a really nice guy. More importantly, the boys loved him.

'Thanks for coming to get them. They were dying to see the new house and they were actually really helpful this morning. They've got longer attention spans than Colm.'

She smiled ruefully, 'Yep, ain't that the truth.'

As always, we'd gone straight for our common ground – Colm and the kids. Sometimes I wondered if we should try to establish a more personal relationship, but Colm didn't see the point. We were never going to be the kind of co-parents who went on holiday together or sat round the table having Christmas dinner. However, on the infrequent occasions when we met, it was amicable, friendly. We chatted when there was anything to discuss, called each other if plans had to be changed, but other than that, Colm generally did the exchanges and they were a quick but friendly five-minute affair at the door.

'Hey Jess, how're ya doing?' Colm materialized behind

me with the kids, who immediately did that thing that kids do.

'Please can we stay longer, Mum. *Please?*'

Jess shook her head, smiling patiently. 'Sorry, guys, Steve is in the car and there's a pizza at Pallino's that just won't wait.'

'Pizza! Yaaaaaaaay! Let's go!' Joe yelled and took off down the path, his brother right behind him as they headed for the car.

'Oh, you're good,' I joked with Jess.

'Yep, how easily they're coaxed,' she laughed.

'I'd happily go racing to the car for a pizza right now too,' I admitted, only half kidding.

We waved until they were out of sight, and were just about to retreat back inside when another car slipped into the spot that Steve and Jess had just vacated.

Lulu and Dan got out and were heading towards us. I immediately scanned their body language: stomping footsteps, hard-set expressions, no physical contact. So that explained why they were six hours late.

'Don't say it,' Lulu greeted me. 'I'm sorry, I'm a crap friend...'

'Indeed you are.'

'And I know we're horrendously late and we've been no help whatsoever.'

'Nope, none.'

She held up a carrier bag. 'But we've brought food and wine. Forgive me.'

It was impossible not to. The strain on her face was visible, her eyes puffy. I had no idea what was going on, but it clearly wasn't good. Behind her, Dan hadn't shaved and his eyes were bloodshot. Another day, another drama. What was it this time? Couldn't be the whole 'kissing in the pub' thing – as far as I knew, that had blown over months ago. It hadn't taken long for it to get back to Dan. Someone other than me had seen her in the Pitcher and Piano that night, they'd told someone, who'd told someone else, who knew Dan's sister, who'd told him. When he confronted Lulu, she'd admitted that it had been a meaningless fling and begged him for another chance. Eventually he'd agreed. Clearly it wasn't going smoothly. And no wonder. I wouldn't blame Dan for walking away. He'd put up with more than anyone deserved and, despite all her promises, Lulu obviously wasn't going to change. Loving someone who was hell-bent on self-destruction was one thing, but surely there had to be a limit before self-preservation kicked in? I loved Lou – but I loved Dan too and wanted him to have a chance at real, long-term happiness.

We joined Annie, Vincent and Rosie in the kitchen, where we ate the fish and chips straight from the paper, with cardboard boxes as tables, and drank wine from plastic cups. Barring the fact that the new arrivals had added a touch of frost to the atmosphere, the happiness was palpable. Our first real home. Sure it was a huge risk. We'd stretched ourselves to afford the mortgage, but my business was going so well and Vincent and I felt sure it would continue, and we had to buy before Dan and Colm carried out their plan to set up their own company later in the year. It was all going to work out, I could feel it. Colm's life motto of blind faith and optimism was contagious.

'Oh, this is so good,' Rosie cooed, holding a chip up in front of her face and admiring the view. 'Don't tell Mark I'm eating this or he'll have me on a week-long juice cleanse to recover.'

'So how's it going with Yogaman then?' Colm teased, earning a flying chip in his direction.

'Still going,' she said brightly, but my spider senses tingled. If there was a scale of conviction, her tone was only sitting around eighty per cent. And we were getting to the two-year mark of doom.

She was still speaking. 'He's really smart. And funny. And bendy.'

'Bendy is good,' Lulu offered and we all ignored the fact that Dan scowled.

'And I've finally got the hang of the whole yoga/vegan thing.'

'You've gone vegan? Rosie, you're eating fish!'

'I'm a selective vegan. Only when Mark's around.'

We all laughed, but I did feel another twinge of worry. Every boyfriend that came along brought about some major change in Rosie. At college, there had been Sy, the fun-loving party animal that Rosie loved so much she stayed out every night and blew her final exams. Paul the zoologist loved indie music and staying home, so Rosie slipped right into his reclusive lifestyle. Now Mark, aka Yogaman, had her on mung beans and the downward dog. It seemed like she always had to morph into the guy's idea of a perfect woman, instead of just being herself – the lovely, kind, funny, smart woman that she was – and being loved on her terms.

Vincent was the first to stand up and scrunch up his chip

papers. 'Right, well, much as it's been a slice of heaven, I'm going to bail out and leave you to it.'

'Hot date?' I asked.

'And is it with me?' Annie added hopefully, with a cheeky wink.

'Sorry, Annie, someone else got in there first.'

'Story of my life, son. Tom Jones said the same thing. He'll be back when he realizes his mistake.'

'I'm going your way if you want a lift though,' he added thoughtfully. God, if he didn't work it out with Carole, then whichever other stunning babe with forty-four-inch legs that finally landed Vincent was going to be a lucky lady. He'd covered our jobs this morning, come straight here afterwards to help out. He had a brilliant creative eye, and now he was chauffeuring my granny home to Wimbledon. I made a mental note to ask how it was going with his commitment issues. Actually, that was a crap and wholly incorrect label. He didn't have commitment issues, he was just being cautious. Making sure. Careful with her heart. And in a way, that said more about him than if he'd just waded on in there with reckless promises that he might break further down the line.

In the meantime, at least he was putting a smile on Annie's face.

'Go on, Gran. You've been a great help, and we're not going to do much more tonight anyway.' I was honest on the first count, lying on the second. Annie had barely stopped since this morning, cleaning, sorting, organizing, making endless cups of tea for everyone else. She was twice the help my feckless parents could ever have been if they'd deemed to show up. Which, of course, they hadn't.

I was grateful I'd inherited her grafting gene, although I knew that was why I'd still be unpacking at 3 a.m. if necessary. If I let her, she'd stay until then and do the same, but I could see the tiredness in her eyes. I didn't want to exhaust her. It was so easy to forget she was in her seventies.

'Are you sure, love?'

'I'm sure, Gran. I'll call you in the morning.'

When the door closed behind them, I picked up Colm and Dan's chip papers and tossed them in the black plastic bag that was hanging from the kitchen doorknob. 'Right, gents, your mission if you choose to accept it… Actually, scrub that, you're not getting a choice. There's a set of wardrobes in each bedroom just dying to be built up.'

Colm groaned, but Dan, looking slightly more alive than when he'd arrived, got to his feet. 'Come on, O'Flynn, let's go.'

I had a feeling he'd rather be anywhere else but here in this room. As soon as he'd left, Lulu exhaled, like a weight had been lifted off her shoulders. Here we go. It's not that I didn't care, because I did, but bloody hell, this was the busiest day of my life and it was going to get hijacked by yet another Lulu and Dan drama. Right, no matter what this was, I was nipping it in the bud and getting back to unpacking crockery.

'He's seeing someone,' she blurted.

The crockery would have to wait.

'No!' Rosie exclaimed. 'He wouldn't.'

Lulu shrugged woefully. 'He is. The girl in the flat next door. Cabin crew. Fucking typical – she always looks great.'

It wasn't time for comparisons, but sitting there in a black cap-sleeve T-shirt and capri trousers, her wild mane of hair flowing loose, Lulu looked pretty great herself.

'Has he admitted it?'

Lulu nodded. 'Yep. Says it's just started, but I'm not sure. I think it might have been after... after...'

Holy crap, this was a first. Dan? Loving, understanding, faithful, upstanding, putting up with more nonsense than any husband ever should have to, Dan? After Lulu's serial indiscretions, it shouldn't be a surprise, yet somehow it was.

'When? After he found out about that guy you were snogging in the pub that night?'

'That's the one,' she admitted. 'I thought we'd got over that, but I guess not. Or at least, Dan hadn't.'

Wow, their obsession with each other was matched only by their inability to let the other one go. Now it seemed that perhaps Dan was finally slicing through the ties with a chainsaw.

'Don't say I deserve it...'

'I wasn't going to,' I countered, although there was an acorn of truth in that. How many times would anyone take that kind of betrayal before returning the hurt? 'So what are you going to do?'

Lulu shrugged. 'He says it's over. That he only did it because he was so pissed off. He still wants to make things work with us.'

'And do you?' Rosie asked.

'I think so.'

'Lu, you two can't keep doing this to each other,' I said, pointing out the obvious, repeating the same thing I'd said to her a dozen times before.

'I know. Maybe I just don't know how to do a proper relationship, Shauna. Maybe I just don't have it in me. I mean, look at who taught us what was normal.'

I understood the point she was making but I didn't want to hear it.

'Enough, Lu,' I scolded her, but gently. 'We're not our parents. We don't need to make the same choices, and at some point we need to stop blaming them for our lives and just get on with it.'

'She's right, Lu,' Rosie spoke up for the first time. 'Your parents made mistakes but that's all in the past.' I was astonished. Rosie generally kept quiet when it came to any discussion about our parents, but she'd decided to speak up. Maybe Yogaman was doing wonders for her confidence after all. Although, she had exhaled deeply when she saw from Lulu's expression that she didn't appreciate the input.

'Lulu, you know we're right. You have to get over yourself.'

I was well aware I was coming across hard on her, but it was the truth and it needed to be said. Yes, we'd grown up with parents who had a skewed relationship with monogamy and an even more dysfunctional relationship with parental care. And yes, to an extent that had shaped who we were. But surely there must be a statute of limitations on using that as an excuse for shit decisions?

'Sometimes I wish I hadn't gone through with it.' And again with the maudlin self-pity. On the day of the wedding, she'd decided to call it off and I'd talked her out of it. It was only later that I found out that Dan had his doubts too and Colm had talked them through with him. Perhaps we shouldn't have interfered. 'But I feel like we can still make it work. Besides, I fucking hate the idea of him with someone else. He's a good man. I just don't know why that never seems to be enough.'

I didn't have the answer to that, but I could guess what would probably happen next. They'd go on an incredible holiday, spoil each other with gifts, treat each other like they were the most special person on earth, and then it would slowly fade and we'd be back here again in a year, or two years, or five.

She stood up. 'C'mon, I can't talk about it any more. It only makes me want to smash things and I wouldn't do that to your new house.'

I gave her a hug, then pointed her in the direction of a room that needed attention.

We worked on for a couple of hours, with Rosie The Almost Vegan finishing the unpacking of the kitchen while Lulu and I sorted out the bedroom so Colm and I would have somewhere to sleep that night. At 2 a.m. they left, Dan and Lulu avoiding eye contact with each other, their hostility still simmering, and I headed back to the bedroom with two cold bottles of beer. Colm was lying starfished on top of the duvet. 'Okay, so I'm going to keep going because I want to get more done before I head out on that job tomorrow.'

'You're going to work all night? You must be joking,' Colm asked, horrified. 'Darlin', I love you, but count me out. I'm knackered.'

'Don't worry, I'm happy just to work away on my own. Couldn't sleep anyway,' I told him, climbing on the bed. 'I'm totally buzzing. I can't believe this is ours.' I clinked my bottle against his. 'Cheers.'

'Cheers. Here's to our new house. May the roof hold up and the mortgage rate never increase,' Colm added, grinning.

His hands were grimy, his hair was ruffled, he hadn't shaved and he was wearing old jeans that wouldn't look out of place in an eighties tribute act, yet I still thought he was the sexiest thing I'd ever seen. My libido suddenly kicked my intention to carry on working into touch, and I reached over and slipped my hand under his T-shirt.

'So I was thinking that before I go back downstairs, this house really needs to be christened.'

He smiled, stretched up and gave me one of those dismissive kisses. The peck. The one that said, 'Great idea babe, but can we do it some other time.'

'Great idea babe, but...'

I interrupted him, desperate to head off the rejection I knew was coming. 'Come on, honey, it's ovulation week and...'

Wrong move. Over the last few months he'd been getting more and more indifferent to any conversation that included the words ovulation, pregnancy or fertility, while I'd been getting more and more stressed that I wasn't getting pregnant.

He reached up and kissed me again, more than a peck this time, but still dismissive. Like a resolute and very definite full stop on the end of a sentence.

'I promise we'll christen it in the morning, love.'

Ouch. A complete knock-back. There was a confidence boost. Looked like I'd be going back to work after all.

I could have argued, but I wasn't going to. What was the point? I was fairly sure that nagging a man to have sex didn't count high on the turn-on scale of foreplay.

As I left him, eyes closed, to head back downstairs to work, I reflected on the irony of the situation. Lulu and Dan, on the brink of divorce, swept up in a torrent of destruction and despair, were probably having wild, crazy sex right now.

Meanwhile, over in what was supposed to be the land of the happy marriage, I was working on my own, moving house on my own, trying to have a baby on my own, running every aspect of our lives on my own, dealing with the problems on my own, while Colm sailed through, letting none of life's little niggles so much as touch him.

I loved Colm with every beat of my heart, but...

For the first time, I realized, there was a 'but'.

23

2015

A Rubber Ring in
a Stormy Sea

Nobody was saying anything.

We'd been friends for a million years, and we'd never had a speechless moment, yet now no one could find words to say.

My parents had come to pick up Beth for her first ever weekend at Granny and Grandad's house. My mother had been horrified when I'd asked her. I'd used the excuse that Colm was still weary after the surgery, but even that didn't dent her irritation at the inconvenience of having to cancel her planned spa break. Thankfully, they'd had a change of mind. I've no idea why or how. All I know is that my mother went off the phone, told my dad about our conversation, and then for the first time ever – and I mean *ever* – he had called me and said that they'd be happy to help out. In fact, he even offered to come collect Beth. After a lifetime of coming to terms with their general parental crappery, perhaps there was hope for them yet.

I was about to go to shout Beth through from the living room when Colm spoke. 'Look, for God's sake, someone say something. Nobody's died. At least not yet,' he joked, pulling a couple of bottles of Bud out of the fridge and handing them to Dan and my dad.

'So that's it? There's nothing they can do? I mean, come on, for fuck's sake…' Dan realized he'd just sworn in front of my mother. 'Sorry Mrs Williams.' He turned back to Colm. 'But… man, there must be something?'

'There is,' Colm replied, still sounding like he was talking about the football, or the shopping, or anything else other than the fact he'd just been told he was dying. 'Radiotherapy. Chemotherapy.'

'But that won't cure it?' Rosie asked, her face stricken with horror and disbelief.

'No, but it could give me years. Och, I'll outlive all you lot yet.'

Our gaze met across the table and I smiled, knowing he could read what my eyes were telling him. I love you. I'll always love you. My heart is breaking. And I can't even think about a time when you won't be sitting there, pulling out beers and bad jokes. That one caught in my throat and I stifled a gasp, determined not to let him down. I would not buckle. I couldn't. He needed a wife who was strong and positive. If I caved to my deep, desperate wish to buckle over and sob until dawn, then I was making it about me. It didn't matter whether I wanted to scream or cry or howl at the moon, I was going to be whatever he needed me to be.

Two big fat tears rolled down Rosie's face and I wished that Jack was there to support her. He was life coaching for a company up north. Or was it down south? I couldn't remember, but she said he'd be gone for a while. Crap timing. Rosie was an emotional soul and his love would have been a comfort.

As if he sensed this, my dad leaned over and hugged her. It was a spontaneous, kind gesture that took me by surprise. Displays of empathy weren't usually his thing, so it was touching that he was making an effort. My mother, not so much.

'Well, we'll hear how you get on, dear,' she told Colm, standing up and reaching for her bag. She was obviously desperate to leave. Maybe she had highly important plans. Like lunch. Or a manicure.

We'll hear how you get on? Seriously? I felt a lifetime of fury bubble up from my gut. Not 'what can we do to help?' Not 'what do you need us to do?' Not 'we're here for you no matter what'.

Christ, Colm wasn't applying for a job. Or going on a sponsored fucking walk. Her son-in-law of ten years had just been handed a death sentence and her reaction was, We'll hear how you get on!

I wanted to scream, but Beth chose that moment to burst in the door, all crazy blonde curls and gorgeous in her bright blue fairy dress, fizzing with excitement at the prospect of a weekend away. 'Are you ready, Gran? Are you? Are you?' She was big on repetition when she was excited.

I scooped her up, gave her a huge sloppy kiss, tickled under her chin, making her chuckle, and made her pinky-promise to have a great time. It was only two nights, but I'd miss her so much. She'd become my solace. Every night, I'd read her a story, then cling to her as she slept, desperate to protect her from the pain of what was ahead. We still hadn't told her how sick her dad was. And until we had absolutely no choice, until the time came to prepare her for the worst, I never would. I wasn't putting that kind of sadness and worry on my daughter until I absolutely had to.

In the meantime, I truly hoped my parents would make this fun for her. Despite everything, I wanted her to develop a relationship with her grandparents, especially now. They weren't much, but they were all she had as family in the UK. We went over to visit Colm's mum a couple of times a year, now that she was too frail to travel here, and he wasn't particularly close to his brother, the age gap too wide for them to have built a relationship in their youth. Colm still hadn't told them and they deserved to know. I'd raise it with him again soon, but not now.

As the door closed behind my parents, Lulu shook her head. 'They are un-bloody-believable. Colm, just as well you're not relying on them to be bastions of support and encouragement because you'd be well and truly fucked. Not that you're not already fucked.' From anyone else it would be harsh or unfeeling, from Lulu, said with eye-rolling irreverence and brilliant comic timing, it was perfect. Colm dissolved into laughter and took the rest of us with him, Rosie's giggles punctuated with so many tears, it wasn't entirely clear whether she was laughing or crying.

'Don't you sugarcoat it there, Lu,' he chortled, sending everyone off again. It was bizarre. Surreal. Almost hysterical, in every sense of the word. A horrific moment in our lives, yet we were clinging on to laughter like a rubber ring in a stormy sea.

Lulu had exactly the kind of no-nonsense, straight-down-the-line candour that Colm needed right now. This was what he wanted to hear – not sobs and platitudes and clichés, accompanied by pitying looks and hand-wringing.

I felt a wave of gratitude to Lu for saying and doing the right thing. Who knew that being devoid of a sentimentality gene would make her great in a health crisis?

'Right,' Lu went on. 'So what can we do then? When are your radiotherapy sessions?'

'Daily, starting week after next,' Colm replied. 'I've to go get some kind of mask fitted on Monday. It'll keep my head steady while they're zapping me. Then the sessions start the following week, every afternoon, Monday–Friday, two o'clock.'

Lulu nodded. 'Okay, so Shauna, I take it you'll struggle to drive him there and back every day with work and the school run?'

It was something I'd already thought about but hadn't discussed with Colm yet. Of course I wanted to be with him every day, but that came with consequences. I had standing lunch bookings every day of the week and if I didn't do them, I'd need to hire someone else in. At some point I'd have to work out how I was going to make it work when Colm… I gulped… wasn't here. But not yet. One day at a time.

'No, it's fine. I'll get someone else in to help. Maybe I'll take someone on full-time.'

There were a couple of uncomfortable looks around the

table and I knew what they were thinking, their minds going back to a past time and a person who was no longer part of our lives. My stare told them not to go there. Vincent was a closed chapter now, no matter how much I wished he wasn't, how much I regretted what happened to us, how much I wished I could go back and change…

That was for another time.

'That doesn't make sense, though,' Lulu argued. 'You'll just be losing income that way. I'm not doing anything anyway, so I'll come and take you there and back every day, Colm. I can bring my laptop with me and work while you're getting your treatment. It honestly doesn't matter to me whether I'm working in the office or in the waiting room at the hospital. Besides, the hospital probably has better coffee. That stuff in our place is atrocious.'

I could see Colm thinking about it and he was about to agree when Dan stepped in for him. 'Good idea, Lu. That's… kind of you.'

She barely registered that he'd spoken. They were keeping things civil and had called a ceasefire for Colm's sake, but things didn't seem to be improving there. I hadn't even had a chance to ask her what was going on with them now, but as Dan was still resident in our garage, I assumed there hadn't been a windswept reunion. I wanted to wring both their necks and tell them to stop being so bloody stupid. Hadn't life just doled out a killer demonstration of why it was too short to waste on destructive crap?

Colm was speaking now. 'Magic, Lu – that would be great. I mean, you'll drive me insane, but at least you'll be cheaper than a taxi.'

'Sometimes I feel so special,' Lulu bit back. I loved their relationship. Sparky, sarcastic, but there was fifteen years of history there, and much as Colm was definitely in Dan's corner, he loved Lu too.

He turned to me, 'That okay with you, love? Seems like the easiest thing all round.'

'Yeah, it's great. Thanks Lu.' I blew her a kiss. An unreliable, disaster of a friend she may be, but I loved her and she was pitching in when it counted.

I was devastated that I wasn't going to be by his side through every appointment and session, but a tiny knot of tension – one of the many – unravelled in my stomach as that was resolved. The last thing I wanted to be right now was pragmatic, but the truth was we had a mortgage to pay and we were barely making it every month. If my earnings dipped, we'd soon be in trouble – and right now we didn't need more stress.

We hadn't even talked about the consequences for Colm's work. Did he even have a job any more? He and Dan had no back-up plan for this scenario, never thinking for a moment that this could happen. It was as if Dan read my mind.

'And you know, Colm, we'll keep everything going at our end. I'll take on your jobs and make it all work somehow. Don't worry about a thing, mate, I've got it covered.' I could see he meant it and I knew he would do everything he could to keep that promise. But there was a reality here, and that was that if Colm wasn't out drumming up business and taking his share of the workload, revenue would fall, and there were no reserves to take an income from. We had no savings. The house was in negative equity. We could potentially have to live on my earnings alone and that wasn't enough to support us. That little knot of tension that had slackened, snapped back like an elastic band, taking several layers of my stomach lining with it. I ordered my cardiovascular system to breathe. Just breathe. One problem at a time. The Bracal Tech contract would come in and all would be fine. It would give us a guaranteed income and that breathing space Colm was always talking about. Right now, that was all I wanted him to be thinking about – one breath after another, just keep breathing.

This time, it was Colm who was on my wavelength. 'Thanks, Dan,' he said, his words showing a wobble of emotion for the first time tonight. 'And when the Bracal Tech contract comes in we'll bring a couple of guys on board on an ad-hoc basis to get us up and running.'

Until what? I wanted to say. Or rather, I wanted to avoid saying. Would he ever go back to work? Would he want to? Was his professional life over? Should we make up a huge and completely unreasonable bucket list and go off bloody surfing in Hawaii and bungee jumping off buildings? What were we going to do? How were we going to live? And... I struggled to breathe again as the rest of the sentence formed in my mind... How long was he going to live for? His prognosis was terminal, but the doctors had explained that he could feel well for some time, that many people felt going back to work, carrying on with normal life, helped them to cope by keeping them focussed on living instead of dying.

'You okay, Shauna?' Rosie asked, taking my hand under the table.

'Yeah, fine,' I whispered, zoning back into the conversation and immediately realizing that there was a weird vibe going on between Colm and Dan.

'Yeah, that's what we'll do,' Dan was saying, but there was an underlying uncertainty in his words.

Colm had spotted it too. 'Dan?' he questioned, not really sure what he was asking.

I mentally backtracked in the conversation. They'd been talking about the Bracal Tech contract. Taking on extra help. Making it work.

'Dan...' Lulu repeated, her tone completely different from Colm's. It carried a warning, a rebuke, emphasized by her raised eyebrow and her steady stare. She looked like a mother shooting a knowing warning across the bows of a teenager who wasn't telling the truth.

'What's going on?' I asked, a chilling sense of foreboding taking grip.

'Nothing, it's... nothing,' Dan started.

'Dan!' Lulu's eyebrow was up again, ordering him to spill whatever secret he was determined to keep to himself.

Dan looked at Colm, then me, helplessness and dread written in every line of his devastated expression. 'The Bracal Tech contact – we heard from them yesterday. We didn't get it.'

Colm closed his eyes, steadying himself before reacting. My gorgeous man, his head covered with dressings, his face pale, dark circles of exhaustion under his eyes, the man who had dealt with more this month than anyone should ever have to deal with, and now there was this.

Since the very first day he'd felt unwell, we'd been living from one cliché to another. It'll all turn out fine in the end.

Let's not worry until there's something to worry about. What doesn't kill you makes you stronger. Try to look on the bright side. Every cloud has a silver lining. Don't let the bugger get you down. You'll get through it, just hang on in there. Nothing's ever as bad as it seems.

And now the one that seemed to have become the story of our lives – just when you think things can't get any worse, they do.

24

2009

Rewind to the Early Days
for Colm and Dan

'Jesus, man, remind me why we thought this was a good idea in the first place?' I asked Dan, putting my feet up on the desk and stretching in the hope that my spine would forgive me for sitting in the same position for the whole day.

He answered by taking a bottle out of the mini-fridge in the corner of the office and tossing it over to me. 'Because you can drink beer and you won't get a bollocking off the boss.'

'Good point. It was all worth it,' I admitted as I cracked the top off on the corner of the desk. If I did say so myself, the first official office of our newly formed company wasn't too shabby. We'd managed to get a deal on two rooms on the ground floor of a converted townhouse just off Richmond Green, about a hundred yards from Dan and Lulu's house. After we quit our jobs, we'd worked from his kitchen for the first couple of months, but it wasn't viable long-term.

We needed somewhere we could bring clients for meetings and host training sessions, so an office space was essential. These rooms were ideal. White walls, grey carpets, and we'd managed to get a great deal on a couple of desks, a boardroom table and some filing cabinets at an auction. Knowing there was a rent payment coming off at the end of every month was an extra motivation for hitting the phones and drumming up business. Lulu was usually there to help us do that, but she'd headed off early to go see our accountant and get some advice on extending the start-up loan.

In all honesty, business had been slower than we'd expected. A few of our old clients had come with us, but we were just getting to the closing stage with new ones we were pitching for. Without a track record, and with long, drawn-out tender processes involved with any companies connected to the government, we hadn't hit our projections yet, but I was confident we'd turn it around, despite the fecking bastard that was the global financial crash. It wasn't killing us, but it definitely made it tougher out there.

It would all come good, turn out fine in the end. That was my mantra and it had worked for me so far.

The phone on my desk rang and I considered ignoring it. No one would be calling at 6 p.m. at night unless it was a cold call or someone looking for money.

'Answer the phone, you lazy git,' Dan moaned.

'Hello, COMP Consultants.' COMP. Channing O'Flynn Management Practices. Dan and I had used a professional, scientific method to decide whose name should go first – he won on the third round of rock, paper, scissors. To be fair, OCMP Consultants didn't roll off the tongue quite as well.

'Mr O'Flynn?' Formal. Must be looking for money. 'This is Cathy Rett at Masters Young.' My feet slid off the desk and I immediately gave this one my full attention. Cathy was the managing partner in a national distribution company I'd pitched our services to the week before. I'd thought then that it was fifty-fifty whether we'd get the business, and asked her to let us know either way. Now it looked like she was following through.

Across the room I could see Dan looking at me quizzically so I flipped the button to put the call on to loudspeaker.

'Cathy! How are you?'

'Excellent, thank you. You?'

'Grand. How can I help you?'

I couldn't read her voice so it was impossible to tell if this was a 'we're giving you the contract' or a 'sorry, we're going elsewhere but please re-tender next year' call.

'Sorry, to call so late in the day…'

'No problem at all…'

Dan was out of his seat now, crossing to my desk, eyes wide and hopeful.

'I said I'd let you know the result of your tender as soon as possible…'

'Yes?'

'Our management team has just reviewed all of the applications…'

Christ, she was stringing this out.

'And we've decided to award the contract to your company.'

I immediately shot out of my seat and joined Dan in a move that involved a wide-open mouth, a dance and repetitive punching of the air. All of which was done in complete silence, while I maintained a professional, formal tone as I said, 'That's wonderful news, Cathy. Many thanks for letting me know. I'll have the contracts drawn up and couriered over to you tomorrow.'

'Lovely. I'll call you if I have any questions.'

'Please do, Cathy. And thanks for calling – I appreciate it.'

'You're very welcome. Goodnight.'

As soon as the dial tone clicked in, our yells matched our movements. Yesssss! This was a major score for us. It wasn't going to pay off the starter loan or cover the expenses, but it was a step in the right direction.

'Come on, let's head over to the Slug and celebrate properly. I'll call Lulu, you call Shauna.'

'Ah, she's working. Bollocks. She's catering a charity thing in Fulham. Call Lulu and have her meet us, and then we'll let Shauna know to drop in on the way home.'

'Sounds like a plan,' said Dan, reaching for his phone.

The adrenalin was kicking the end-of-day fatigue out of the way and replacing it with pure excitement. This was brilliant news.

Shauna would be knackered – this was the seventh night in a row that she'd worked. She'd been slogging her guts out since we formed the company, pulling up the slack in our finances. We'd known that was going to be the case for the first few months, but I guess neither of us had realized how tough it would be. She and Vincent were doing breakfast meetings, lunches, parties, dinners, weekend events, anything she could get in the diary. But no matter how tired she was today, I knew she'd be totally up for celebrating this

She answered on the first ring.

'Darlin', it's me. Listen, we got the contract with Masters Young.'

'That's fantastic! Well done, honey, you deserve it. You really do.' She sounded tired, like she was trying really hard to sound enthusiastic, but not quite getting there.

'So look, we're heading out to celebrate at the Slug,' I said. 'Come join us when you're done.'

There was a pause on the other end before she finally spoke, sounding even wearier now. 'Honey, I can't. I've been up since 6 a.m. this morning and I won't get done here until after ten. Then I need to get home, unpack the van, repack it for tomorrow and be back out in the morning at six.'

'Come on, love, just a couple of drinks. It's a celebration! Can't you leave Vincent there to do it himself?'

'Colm, are you kidding? Vincent is working the same hours as me. The two of us are like the walking dead over here. I'm not bailing out and leaving him to do the function and then clear up by himself. Don't be ridiculous.'

I was getting pissed off now. Okay, so she was doing this to pay our bills, but couldn't she just make a bit of an effort here for me? Didn't she want to share in this?

'Fine. Don't worry about it.' I wasn't going to beg. She didn't want to come, fine by me. I was perfectly capable of celebrating on my own.

'You've forgotten, haven't you?' she was saying now.

'Forgotten what?'

'Tonight.'

Shit. Bollocks.

'It's important, Colm.'

'Shauna, I'm not saying it isn't, but it doesn't mean we have to put our lives on hold until…'

The click of the phone told me I was no longer speaking to anyone on the other end. I tossed it on the desk and lifted my beer, chugging back what was left of the bottle.

'So that sounds like it went well then,' Dan jibed, before following up with, 'Sorry, just want to savour this moment. Usually it's Lu and me who are killing each other. Good to see Mr and Mrs Perfect ain't so perfect.'

'Shut it,' I replied, closing him down, before casually adding, 'Anyway, I'm still perfect. It's just the missus that's got issues.'

I was joking, but there was no point going into it all – not when we'd just had the best news since starting the company. I'd sort it out later with Shauna, but in the meantime, we had some celebrating to do.

Dan cracked open two more beers and handed one to me. 'Lulu is going to meet us there in half an hour, so time for one more here. She's with Rosie, so she's coming too. Apparently it's all off with Yogaman, so she's up for a cocktail or six.'

'Ah bugger, what happened this time?' I said, taking the beer.

'No idea. Lu didn't say. Anyway, on the same subject, what's the deal with Shauna just now then? Feel free to tell me to shut my face, but things seem a bit tense lately.'

If there was ever a way to burst the bubble of happiness over landing the new deal, this was it. I contemplated changing the subject. Dan and me had spent most of the last ten years together and I was pretty sure the number of deep, emotional discussions we'd had about relationships added up to… yep, that one, solitary profound exchange on the morning of his wedding. But hey, we had half an hour to kill, and if there was anyone who could give an expert take on dealing with tough spots, it was him.

'Och, just a rough patch.' It was weird even saying that. The first eight years of our lives together had been so great it still felt strange that we'd got to this point. I remembered it from when I was with Jess. The stage where you said something and it was taken the wrong way. Or didn't say something and that was taken the wrong way too. Either way, couldn't win. In saying that, with Jess and me, it went too far for us to fix. This wasn't the same. Just a bit of a dip. A rough patch, not a relationship-ending situation.

Dan laughed. 'Is that it? Is that your idea of baring your soul?'

'Absolutely. I'm happy in my emotionally stunted self,' I replied.

'Is it that Vincent guy?' he went on, in full-scale detective mode. 'There's no way I'd let him anywhere near Lu. I'd never see her again.'

'Nah, Vincent and her have been mates forever. If anything was going to happen it would have been long before we met. They're just mates. And even if he fancied her, Shauna wouldn't go there. No way she'd mess around. She's too decent – not her style.'

Too late, I realized that could be taken as a criticism of Lu. And him. Things seemed to be okay with them since they worked out the last issue a few months ago. Not that that meant much. The two of them careering to the brink of divorce was pretty much an annual event. But to his credit, Dan let it go.

'So what's the problem then? If you want, I can track down a couch and you can lie on it while you tell me your problems.' Now he was really taking the piss, so I decided to go for it.

'Okay, then, but you'll regret asking,' I warned him.

'Bring it on. Whatever it is, Dr Dan can take it.'

I decided to test his confidence on that.

'She's knackered, so she's touchy. I don't remember the last time she had a day off. She totally grafts day in and day out. But it's the whole kids thing that's stressing her out. It's the wrong time to have a baby now, what with us starting up here, but we've been trying for so long that she didn't want to give up. They've got her on some fertility drug and I don't think that's helping with the stress, but before you and I set this up, we'd agreed to give it a try and she still wanted to go ahead with it. Anyway, feel free to cover your ears if this bit is too much information, but tonight is the first night of ovulation so we were supposed to... you know.'

'Perform on demand?' Dan offered smartly, enjoying this whole thing way too much.

'That's it. Tough job, but someone's got to do it,' I joked. There was a twinge of reality in there too though. All that 'shagging to a timetable' had changed things. It used to be that we couldn't keep our hands off each other anyway, but in the last year things had changed – probably around the time she started putting her legs up the wall straight after sex and filling herself full of hormones. It's not that I didn't want more kids, but if it didn't happen, it wouldn't be the end of the world for me. We'd be fine, just the two of us. Great holidays, no sleepless nights, no hassles with childcare.

So now I was stuck with a decision to make. Two choices – go out, have a long overdue night on the town, or go home, wait for Shauna and probably end up in a fight anyway.

No contest.

I tossed the empty beer bottle in the bin and grabbed my jacket off the back of my chair.

'You ready to go?'

25
2015

Making Memories

Rosie filled the kettle and flicked it on, while I got two cups out of the cupboard and then opened the fridge and pulled out the plate of eclairs that had been left over from my afternoon booking today. It had been an eightieth birthday party for a lovely man in a nursing home in Acton.

'Did the party go okay?' Rosie asked.

I stopped, put the eclairs on the kitchen worktop and rested my head against the wall cupboard, desperately hoping that the coolness of the wood would salve the pain of the memory.

'It wasn't my finest moment,' I replied.

'Oh God, what happened?'

What happened? I really wasn't sure. Since Colm's illness, I'd learned that no one explains how this living grief thing works, or gives any warning of the flashpoints to look out for. No one tells you that you'll be perfectly fine, going about some daily task, and then before you've got time to catch yourself, you've slid down a wall and you're helpless to do anything but hold your stomach and roar until the pain subsides. Or that you'll be driving along and suddenly notice that tears are streaming down your face in a torrent that forces you to pull over and weep, pitifully breaking your heart, until your throat is raw and you can barely breathe.

No one tells you any of that, but I've been finding it out by myself, every day, every night, in the six weeks since Colm's operation.

Today I was ambushed. 'Turns out the birthday gent was an Elvis fan. I've no idea why that matters. But he blew out his candles and the next minutes we were all singing "Blue Suede Shoes". And then "Jailhouse Rock". "Viva Las Vegas" was a spectacle involving his lady friend and some nifty dance moves.'

'This is all sounding great so far,' Rosie said hopefully.

'And then I looked at him, dancing away, singing his heart out, making sure the party was in full swing, and I thought... that's exactly what Colm will be like when he's that age. Then I realized...' I stopped to shove the palms of my hands in my eyes to stem the torrent that was stinging once again. '...I realized that he won't be. He'll never do that. He'll be gone.'

We'd never grow old together. I wouldn't bake him a cake when he turned eighty. Or seventy. Or even fifty. We wouldn't get those years, all those Christmas Days, the summer holidays. He wouldn't be at Beth's wedding, and our grandchildren would never know him. He'd be gone. A memory. And every day took us closer to the moment we'd say goodbye.

The pain was so acute it felt physical, the stab of a hot blade of loss inserted between my ribs and twisting, slowly, making sure every sinew screamed for it to stop.

Rosie wrapped her arms around me and held me until I had to step back. That's the other thing no one tells you – sympathy makes it worse. I can be holding it together, strong and coping, and then someone is kind, or understanding, or puts a hand on your arm and says they're sorry, and your heart is right back down on the floor, broken in two, bleeding on the pavement.

I exhaled, blowing the pain out, roughly wiping my face, desperate to get some composure back before Colm came home. Today was his last radiotherapy treatment, a cause for celebration, he said.

'How's Colm been?' Rosie asked, back on the task of pouring tea. She brought the two steaming red mugs over to the battered but loved oak table and sat across from me.

'He's been Colm,' I answered truthfully. 'He doesn't want to talk about it. Says he's feeling better every day.' On the outside, the physical changes would back that theory up. He now looked so much better than he had a month ago. The radiotherapy had taken out a letter-box of hair across the back of his scalp, a loss that the doctors said would be permanent. But that aside, the rest of his hair had grown back and the wound had healed, he'd regained the weight he lost after the op and he was looking more rested and stronger than he had for months.

'Do you think he's in denial?' Rosie asked.

I shook my head, sure that it wasn't the case. Every spare minute over the last month and a half I had spent researching this tumour and the effects on the patient, both physical and psychological. Denial was a typical reaction. As were anger, fear, depression, sorrow, resentment and rage. Colm had definitely shown flashes of anger. There was no doubt there had been a personality shift towards irritation and intolerance, and I wasn't sure if that was caused by the operation, the tumour or the medication he was taking. Whatever it was, I could handle it. I was pretty fucking angry too. However, other aspects of his behaviour were less easy to wrap my head around.

'I don't. I think it's more complicated than that. You know, over the years it's not always been easy to handle the way Colm shrugs stuff off. Doesn't let it touch him. Just sails through life on an even keel, blocking out anything that is in the least bit uncomfortable. It's always driven me crazy.' I wasn't sure I was explaining it well, but Rosie had known Colm for as long as I had, so she'd been a spectator to his determination to meander through life avoiding pain and staying far away from anyone else's heartache. Once upon a time, that's how I handled life too. Before responsibilities and necessities made me grow up.

I kept going, needing to talk, 'When sad things happen, it's like he shrugs it off, doesn't let it stick to him. Oh the fucking irony that the saddest thing of all has happened to him. And that's how he's dealing with it now. It's in a box in his mind, and he's not for opening it. Compartmentalized. Move along people, nothing to see here. Everything's under control. I'd almost wish he raged or made a plan or cried or did something that let me communicate with him, work through it, but he doesn't want that. He just wants normality.'

I lifted an eclair, realized I didn't have the stomach for it and put it back on the plate.

'So I just get up every morning, slap a smile on my face, and get through the day. Pretending there's nothing wrong, when it couldn't be more so. Inside, everything is screaming at me. What's going to happen to him? How could we possibly live without him? Will he hurt? Will he need special care? How will Beth cope with losing him? What impact will this have on the rest of her life? How will we tell the boys? How can we help them deal with the grief? And this one's way down the list, but how will I support us on my own in my negative-fucking-equity house with our outstanding business loan and credit card debt that could take down a small nation? How will we pay the mortgage and the bills? I just want to make everything okay. But most of all, I just want him to live, to be here. I want to fix this, Rosie, but I can't.'

That summed it up. I couldn't fix this. Early in our relationship, I'd slipped into the fixer role, become the person who organized, planned, solved problems, sorted out everything in this family, and yet here was the biggest problem we'd ever faced and I was powerless to resolve it.

Rosie's face was etched with concern. 'What are you going to do?'

'Just... love him. Every day. And hope. Maybe drink a lot of wine, too,' I said, desperately trying to add a light-hearted moment. God, I was getting as bad as Colm, joking when completely inappropriate. Fourteen years and he was finally rubbing off on me.

'Anyway,' I said, shoulders back, gasping for a breath of

normal air. 'Enough about the sadness. I need to go collect Beth soon, but first I want to know, when are you going to tell me about you?' I asked, with mock reproach.

'Tell you what?' She actually looked worried.

'What's happening with Jack? Are you going to move in together?'

She lowered her eyes as she shrugged. 'Urgh, I don't know. I really don't. It just doesn't feel... right. I think maybe I'm not the settling-down type.'

If I wasn't sitting in the middle of a bench, I may well have fallen off my seat.

All Rosie had ever wanted was to meet the right guy, get married, raise a family in a white house with a picket fence and have adequate pension provisions. She'd craved that her whole life, but now she wasn't ready? It didn't make sense. This was like a mid-life crisis in reverse.

I held my mug to my chest, warmed by the heat.

'Right, what's going on?' I demanded, intrigued.

'Nothing,' she protested, laughing. 'Can't a girl be independent and reject a guy's proposal?'

'Of course! But it's just that you've always wanted to do the whole marriage and babies thing.'

'Maybe once...' she said. I didn't have time to probe deeper, as at that moment, Lulu and Colm arrived, bursting through the back door with a sledgehammer of energy and hilarity.

For the millionth time, I thought how lucky Colm and I were to have Lulu. In truth, she may not be much of a wife, but she was a great friend and she was throwing herself into her new role as Colm's chauffeur with real gusto. She was cheering him up, making him laugh, and was there every time he – or I – needed her.

'Ta-da!' Beth exclaimed, bursting out with jazz hands from behind Colm's legs.

'Baby!' I greeted her, holding my arms wide open and bracing myself for the incoming charge as she rushed towards me. My favourite moment of every day, no question. 'I was just coming to get you!' I told her, puzzled. Had I arranged something else? God, I was so tired this was like being back in those days after she was born and I was so sleep-deprived I would find my hairbrush in the freezer.

Colm tossed his jacket on a chair. 'Yeah, we were literally passing the school, so we thought we'd pop in and collect her a little early. Teacher said it was fine. I told her we had an emergency situation.'

'What emergency situation?' He looked fine. They were laughing. Please don't let that be an act. Please don't let there be something else wrong. Come on, nothing else.

Colm shrugged and scooped Beth off the floor. 'I needed to see my girl! That was the emergency!'

'It was only a white lie, Mummy. Our secret. Just can't tell Mrs Rodgers.'

I decided these were exceptional times. Taking your child out of school early and lying to teachers? Not acceptable in normal circumstances. Colm, happy, upbeat, after his last day of radiotherapy, picking his daughter up early to celebrate? Go right ahead, savour every moment, because there was no knowing how many more days they'd have like this.

Lulu flicked the kettle on, then slid into a chair next to

Rosie. Meanwhile, Beth jumped on my knee and I hugged her tightly.

'How was your day, honey?

Fantaaaaaaaaastic!' she raved. 'The very best ever!'

'Oooh and why's that then?' I asked her, tickling her stomach and making her squeal with delight.

'Can't tell you,' she said, before creasing into an adorable fit of the giggles.

'Pardon? Of course you can. You can tell your mamma anything.'

'Can't,' she said.

'Can.'

'Can't.'

'We could be here all night, baby.'

That moved her off message, and she turned to Colm, eyes wild and pleading.

'Can I tell her, Daddy? Can I?' she begged. 'Auntie Lu, let me tell her please!'

'What are you all so buzzed up about? What's going on?'

'We're going to Disney World! We're going to see Mickey Mouse! And Minnie. And I'm going to be a princess!'

'We are?' I kept the smile on my face, while raising a questioning eye to Colm.

He said, 'You know, I decided we needed a fantastic holiday. A holiday of a lifetime. Give us some great memories to look back on.'

The smile stayed put while the shot of pain ransacked my guts. I got it. Oh God, I got it. Memories. For Beth. He wanted our daughter to have a lifetime of knowing her daddy took her to Disney.

The pain in my guts reshaped into a ball of steel wool and lodged in my throat.

'Thought we could book it online tonight,' Colm was saying now.

'Of course we can,' I managed to force out, before reality dawned. In cartoons, some people had an angel on one should and a devil on the other. I had a small disapproving accountant sitting on both of mine, and right now they were just about having heart attacks.

I silently argued with the accountants' silent disapproval. Disney. Paris. A couple of days. I'd find the money. I'd cut back on costs, work a couple of extra shifts, maybe try to sell some of the stuff that was cluttering up the back shed. I'd find a way.

'Good idea,' I enthused, 'let's do it! After Auntie Lulu and Auntie Rosie have had a cup of tea, I'll get right on it.'

'Yaaaayyyyy!' Beth cheered. 'I can't wait to tell Marcy. She's always wanted to go there.'

'But, honey, Marcy went to Disney last summer.'

Beth stuck out her bottom lip, suddenly serious, as if she had great knowledge to impart. 'No, Mummy. Marcy went to France. Daddy says we're going to Florida. For two weeks!'

Keep breathing. Keep smiling. Keep breathing. Keep smiling.

My gaze went back to Colm. 'Really?' Still breathing. Still smiling. It was like every thought I was having was getting stuck on a repetitive loop, playing again and again until my brain managed to absorb it.

'Yeah, well I thought we may as well do it properly. What do ya reckon?'

I reckoned he'd already told Beth. I reckoned he needed this. I reckoned he hadn't thought any of this through. I reckoned that even if it killed me, I'd find a way to make this happen because he wanted it and that was all that mattered.

'Well…' I could see he was bracing himself for objections, while Beth was watching my face expectantly. 'I reckon it's the best idea you've ever had.'

26

2009

Broken Hearts and Promises

There had been a time when he would shout my name when we made love, and then he would stay, his skin on mine, our limbs wrapped around each other. Our eyes would be locked, our lips inches apart.

'You're everything,' he would tell me.

'You're more,' I'd reply.

We would talk, laugh, fight over who was going to go get drinks, or shower first, or make breakfast the next morning. Mostly we'd just talk. Just be.

Tonight, as soon as it was over, he slid off me, gave me a brief, meaningless kiss, muttered something about it being great (it wasn't) and then lifted the remote control for the TV from the bedside table. He flicked through the channels until he found something he wanted to watch and then slipped his arm around my head, nudging me into his chest.

The message wouldn't be any clearer if it flashed up on

the television. Cuddle in, keep quiet, chill out, don't bother me with waves that will disrupt my still pool of peace and harmony. Classic Colm. Sure, he'd make token enquiries, with the occasional, 'Good day?' or 'How's things?' but I'd learned over the years that unless there was an impending apocalypse, an imminent death or the TV was broken, he really just wanted to hear 'fine'. Every now and then, I'd test him by going off on a rant about something and he'd invariably zone out within a minute and a half. Colm wanted upbeat fun, an easy life, and a good laugh – and didn't see why he couldn't have all of those things on an ongoing basis. It was a big part of the reason I'd fallen in love with him. And he was right. Except when he wasn't.

I pushed away from him and – keeping my knees tight together – spun around so that I could put my legs up the wall. I nudged a pillow under my buttocks to help tilt my pelvis in the right direction. The fertility guide recommended that this position was maintained for half an hour, but I usually stretched it and tried for at least an hour. I know it irritated him, and in turn, he irritated me because I didn't understand why he was irritated! It wasn't *him* who was filling himself full of fertility drugs and *he* wasn't the one who was spending half their life checking ovulation charts and pregnancy tests. *He* hadn't discovered that he had a condition called polycystic ovaries, which meant he rarely or never produced eggs. This didn't make *him* feel like a total failure. And no, *he* didn't have to lie with his legs up a bloody wall. Yet *he* was irritated?

'The treatment finishes this month,' I mused aloud, hoping he'd be up for talking about it. It was all I'd been able to think about for days. The treatment plan had consisted of taking a fertility drug that was our big hope, but had so far only brought us huge disappointment.

Now we'd hit the recommended limit of three courses, the doctor was reluctant to prescribe more due to the possibility that overuse of the drug could raise the chance of ovarian cancer later in life.

If this didn't work, it was back to the drawing board. More tests. Different drugs. Investigating other options. We'd discovered I wasn't a candidate for IVF because I didn't have any eggs to fertilize, but we could look at the possibility of using donor eggs or a surrogate, or perhaps even abandoning the pregnancy process altogether and considering adoption.

So much to think and talk about, yet Colm was watching *Match of the Day*.

'What, love?' he replied, not taking his eyes off the screen.

'The fertility treatment. This is the last month we can take it and then we have to look at other options.'

'Okay.'

Still hadn't looked in my direction.

'Okay?'

'Yeah.'

I could feel a wave of anger whipping up a storm in my stomach. I fought to stay calm.

'So I take it from your reaction that you don't want to talk about this then?'

He sighed and finally turned to meet my gaze. 'Now? You want to talk now?'

'When else do we have, Colm? Between my job and yours,

we're lucky if we get to spend a waking hour together every second day.'

I wasn't exaggerating. Since he'd set up the business he was travelling a lot, pitching for clients, while I was working round the clock to keep us afloat. I wasn't complaining – I knew it was part of the deal and I'd agreed to it. I wanted him to have his dream. I just didn't expect it to come at the expense of mine.

He pressed the off button on the remote control and threw it on the bed, clearly irritated.

'Okay, shoot.'

'What do you mean "shoot"?'

The wave of frustration and anger at his attitude was rising and I wasn't sure how I was going to stop it. It was in my throat now, ready to let loose. I could honestly say Colm and I had had maybe three or four major fights in the entire time we'd been together. Unless I could get this under control, we were on course for adding to that tally.

He sighed. 'Shauna, you're the one who has all the opinions on this subject, so you tell me – what are we doing?'

'You mean you can't even be arsed having an opinion? Is that where we're at now? I hear you talking about a bloody football game with Dan for hours upon endless bloody hours, and yet you can't even be arsed talking about this for five minutes? This is not just me we're talking about here, Colm. It's us. Our family.'

'We've already got a family,' he shot back and something inside me snapped. Actually broke.

'I don't!' I was definitely shouting now. 'I don't have a family. I know we have the boys, and I truly love them, but

263

they're not mine. My parents couldn't give a fuck. And there was you... there was always you... but what's happened, Colm? What's happened to us? When did you become so detached that you couldn't even be bothered talking to me about something that's important?'

'When it became all you talked about!' he yelled back, making me flinch. Colm had never shouted at me. Not ever. It could have snapped me out of my fury, but it didn't. It made it worse.

'Because I'm trying to get you to care! You act like it doesn't matter, but it does. It's our future.'

He twisted to face me now, eyes blazing, body language screaming conflict. 'So why does it have to include more kids? Look, I'm not adverse to a baby. If it happens, fine. But I'm not going to lose sleep over it and I wish you'd just fecking drop it and let us get on with our lives. It's become like a bloody obsession.'

'Because I feel like I'm doing it on my own!' I screamed. 'Just me, Colm. On my fricking own. Trying to make something happen that's important to me. And no matter how hard I try I can't get you to share it.'

'Why do I have to?' His face was pure fury now, a look I didn't recognize, had never seen before. Oh God, this was a fight on a whole different level from anything that had gone before.

'Because... It matters. I want this. I've asked you for nothing since the day we met, and now I'm asking you to do this for me.' I couldn't make my mouth stop moving and I knew with absolute certainty that I was about to cross a line, but I couldn't pull back. 'I take care of your boys every weekend, have done for all these years. I look after them, I love them, my money contributes to their maintenance and I never complain. I NEVER FUCKING COMPLAIN. I do that for you. And for them, but mostly for you. Yet you can't do the same for me.'

I paused, took a breath, then fired on.

'You wanted to set up your own company and that means I have to double my income to pick up the slack, so I'm on fourteen-hour fucking days, not because I want to but because it's important to you. It's your dream, just like having children is mine. I'll do anything to help you make it, Colm, anything at all, because that's what you do for people you love. Their battles become yours. You fight for them. Do everything you can to make their lives as amazing as they can be.' I took a gasp of breath, my chest hurting with the sheer exertion of trying to force all this out past a huge boulder that had lodged somewhere around my heart. 'But you seem to think that doesn't apply to you, that you get it all on your terms. Well you can fuck off. Seriously, Colm. Enough. I've spent my whole life with parents who couldn't give a crap how I feel, who wouldn't go out of their way to do something for me if their life depended on it and I'm not going to spend the rest of my life doing it with you. I've got to be worth something, and if I'm not, then I don't want to be here.'

I jumped out of bed, needing oxygen that wasn't available in a room that suddenly felt toxic. He said nothing, not a word, as I flew downstairs.

In the kitchen, I poured a coffee from a pot that was off, but still warm, then opened the doors to the garden. It was almost a relief to feel the cold air, my vest and pyjama trousers no match for the night-time chill. I sat on the step, staring out at the hut Colm never painted, the greenhouse he never repaired and the empty space where he'd never build a swing set or a paddling pool. Empty. Void. An exact mirror of how I was feeling now that the anger had gone. No tears. No wails. No pacing up and down. Just cold empty stillness seeping into numb pores. I had a fleeting longing to call Annie, dismissed because a midnight call would startle her and I didn't want to break her sleep.

Maybe half an hour, perhaps an hour passed, time lost in the vacuum, before I heard him approach behind me.

'You'd really leave?' he asked, gently now, and as he sat down beside me everything about him suddenly felt familiar again.

'I don't know,' I replied honestly, still staring forward, unwilling and unwanting to see his face.

'I could hide all your shoes so you couldn't go.' A tentative joke, his message hopeful, almost pleading. I could have ranted that this was no time for jokes, that he wasn't listening, that I was buckling under the pain of this, but none of it would have meant a thing because this was the man I married, the one who made my heart melt on that first night, and who I'd loved because no matter what life threw at us he was that positive, funny guy. Even through the chaos of conflict, I knew that I couldn't have it both ways. I couldn't love that attitude, but hate it when it applied to me. It was who he was.

'I'm sorry,' he said. No jokes. No witty banter. Just a serious man that I wasn't sure I'd ever met before. 'I know I'm crap at this and I know I haven't been fair. You're right to want me to support you but, Shauna, honestly, I don't know how to change how I feel. It's not that I don't want to. If I could somehow switch on a desperate longing for another child then I would, but it's just not in me.'

I wanted to argue, but I also wanted to let him keep talking, fearing that if I cut him off during the first real conversation we'd had about this then he'd never start again, and the chance to resolve this would be gone. I just stared straight ahead, his silhouette mirroring mine, and listened as he carried on.

'You know, I think in life that there are givers and takers, and you're a giver. You can put other people before yourself, and you're brilliant with the boys and you're always the first person to pitch in when anyone needs help. You're constantly wondering how other people are feeling and you genuinely care if there's something wrong with them. I think you're the best person I've ever known. And the kindest. But I can't be like that. I just can't.'

'Not even for me?' I asked, my voice struggling to raise above a whisper.

'Shauna, I love you with all my heart,' he said, deflecting the question. 'But how I feel is how I feel. I can go along with what you want, but I won't pretend I have a burning need for it to happen and I won't be devastated if it doesn't. The thing is, it seems that the more you want this, the more I lose my wife, and I know that's made me avoid the situation and maybe even challenge it. I know I've been unsupportive and have been an arrogant prick.' There was an embarrassed smile of honesty as he said that. 'But I just want my wife back, the one that was happy with us, the one who woke up smiling and who lived for today, just happy because we were together. Shauna, I think that if we carry on this way it could cost us everything.'

His voice cracked as he said that last line, a raw honesty dripping from every word. I heard him.

'I don't know how to fix this, Colm. I love you. You know I do. But this is my life and...' I needed to just say it. 'I need more than you in it. I want to be part of something...'

'You are part of something.'

'I'm not. Not in the way that I want to be. I love my friends, but when it comes down to family, let's be honest, I have Annie and you. That's it. And of course, I've got the twins, and I'm so grateful to share them, but they belong to you and Jess. I want more than that. I want to be part of a unit and to create the kind of family I wanted so badly when I was a kid, to have someone that calls me mum and who will be the missing part of this life we're living now. I can't give up on that. Not even for you.'

That brought us back to silence for a few more moments. Eventually, he sighed. 'Okay.'

Okay what? Okay, you don't have to give up your longing for a family, but I'll just pack and go now? Okay let's have another go at making a baby this instant? I waited for more.

'Okay,' he repeated, more resolute now. 'I understand how you feel and I'll do anything to keep you, Shauna. I promise I'll stop being a dick.'

Even through the apprehension and sorrow, that made me smile.

'I'll get on board with this but can we just...' He struggled to find the words. 'Just pause for a minute?'

'What do you mean?'

The hands that were under his chin, supporting it, now pushed through his hair as he exhaled. 'Just give ourselves some time? I feel like we've lost each other and we need to get back to being us again. And let's be honest, with the business and the finances the way they are, this isn't the right time. We'd be financially screwed if you couldn't work. You know that's true.'

I did, but I didn't care. That was the difference between us.

'So what do you want to do?'

'Just take some time off the baby thing. This round of treatment is finished, so let's just wait a while before doing anything else. Let's get the business up and running properly, then you can cut back to working normal hours and we can get some cash in the bank, a bit of security so that if you do have a baby you can take maternity leave and we won't be stressing. Let's just take the heat off the urgency, and in the meantime, let's just be us again. I know we're knackered and up against it with work, but let's drop all the bullshit stresses and try to make time for each other again, remember how to love each other without all the resentment and the strains. And when the time is right for us, I promise I will do everything I can to make this happen.'

There were a whole lot of promises flying around here, none of them coming with guarantees. I could see that every word he said made sense, but I wasn't sure it was that easy. How did I switch off this deep, inherent need? How did I look at him again without feeling let down? But then, how could I live without him? I loved him.

He was still in full flow. 'I'll make my body available

for sex twice a day and I'll wear loose boxers to help the swimmers. I'll put my legs up the wall too.'

I couldn't help laughing. 'I don't actually think that you doing that makes a difference in the process.'

'Doesn't matter, I'll do it anyway just to keep you company.'

Oh God, he was so sweet and funny he made my heart break. My Achilles heel, this man. The only person I'd ever known who could change how I was feeling with just a look or a word.

'You know, when I see that family I want it's always with you,' I said, vocalizing my thoughts without editing them first. 'I can't imagine ever having that with someone else. I love you. If that's what we need to do then I can do it.'

Even if it had to be on his terms, I knew there was no other option than to try.

As I turned to face him properly for the first time since he sat down, I saw his face flood with relief.

'I'm not saying it's going to be easy though, Colm. I don't think I can just snap out of this and go back to being the way we used to be. It'll take some time, a bit of adjustment, but I'll try.'

My mind flicked back to what he said earlier, about me being a giver. He had to know that I wasn't giving everything over to him here. He had to understand that this was conditional.

'But, Colm, when I think the right time has come, it won't be up for debate. I'll take a break for you, but when it comes, you've got to be ready to be there for me.'

His arm slipped around my shoulders and for the second

time tonight – this time with so much more feeling – he gently pulled my head into his chest. I could feel the thudding of his heart and the change in my breathing as it synchronized with his.

'I will be, I swear.'

I believed him, even if I wasn't sure he believed himself.

It was going to be okay. I could do this. We could make it work. That positivity wasn't entirely mutual.

'Think I'll still hide your shoes, though, just in case.'

27

2015

The One Before

Jess put a mug of coffee on the table in front of me, passed another to Steve, and then sat down opposite me at the kitchen table.

'Thanks,' I said as I lifted it. I took a sip, and blurted, 'Oh feck, your coffee is still terrible.'

'It is,' Steve agreed, laughing. 'Stuff will kill you.'

I saw Jess's immediate reaction of horror, before Steve clicked on to what he'd said and started to stammer. 'Sorry, Colm, I mean... I didn't mean... em...'

I put my hand up in a conciliatory gesture and smiled. 'It's fine, honestly. Don't worry about it. I'm far more likely to get run over by a bus.'

The two of them laughed too much, grateful the awkward moment was over. It was one of thousands in the last few months and I'd developed pretty good brush-offs for all of them. People made innocent comments or jokes, realized they could have significance to a dying man and all of a sudden you were sliding down a chute of discomfort to a whole big pit of mortification.

Steve stood up. 'I'm off, anyway,' he said. 'Need to pop into the office for a couple of hours.'

He shook my hand. 'Take care of yourself, Colm,' then headed out the door. Even a blinkered, socially unaware, emotionally stunted man like me found several things odd about this situation.

He had barely looked at Jess.

He hadn't said goodbye.

No kiss.

No details about when he'd be back.

And he was going into the office on a Sunday afternoon.

He was some kind of property developer – not an occupation that normally required weekend shift work.

'Is everything okay with you two?' I asked tentatively, aware that none of this was any of my business and Jess and I had kept our conversations purely about the kids for the last decade. It was only in the last few weeks, since we'd broken the news to the boys, that I'd started popping in when I dropped them off or picked them up. Sometimes just for ten minutes, other times I'd have a beer and pass an hour or so.

'Yeah, he's just under a bit of pressure right now. Things have been tough with the whole financial crisis. Rubs off at home a bit when he's got a lot on his plate. Not that it's anything compared to what you're going through. I mean… erm…'

There it was again. Two said-the-wrong-thing-squirms in the space of five minutes.

I halted her right there. 'Jess, you need to get over the whole "worrying about offending me" thing. I promise they didn't replace the bit that was cut out with a sensitivity chip. I'm still pretty much unoffendable.'

'Thank God, because Steve and I seem to be doing pretty well at testing that theory.' I noticed the smile didn't reach her eyes.

'You sure you're okay?' I asked again.

'Positive. How were the boys this weekend?' she asked, changing the subject.

The boys. That made them sound like kids. The reality was they were both over six feet tall, and thanks to a fondness for the gym, almost as wide.

'Great,' I told her, honestly. 'We stayed in a lodge out by Henley. Just played football all weekend and chilled out at night. They'll tell you all about it, but they were on good form.'

'Any more questions?'

'Nope, and I know it's not because they're afraid to ask. I think they're just okay with the details for now.' I shrugged my shoulders, grinning, 'Jess, they're my sons. They don't have the DNA for emotional depth and introspection.'

'That is so true,' she replied. 'They've been the same here. Obviously the way we told them helped. They seem to be handling it really well, but I'm keeping an eye on it. Have spoken to the university as well, just flagged it up in case there are any issues there.'

It struck me that I should probably have thought of that and been the one to broach it with the others involved in my sons' lives, but as always, it hadn't occurred to me.

What did occur to me was how lucky I was to have married two smart women. In many ways they were so alike and that had shown over the last few months. Shauna and I had been careful about what we told Beth, settling on a sanitized version of the truth, omitting the ultimate detail that the tumour was incurable and I could… well, you know. I didn't like to even give that thought headspace. Quite literally. It went along the lines of 'Daddy had a sore head, the doctors have fixed it, so we hope it won't get sore again.' At which point Beth kissed the top of my head 'all better' and skipped off to watch *Frozen* for the 3321ˢᵗ time.

Jess and I decided to take the same approach with the boys, only the language being more teenage-appropriate. Brain tumour. Operation. Radiotherapy. Chemotherapy. Feeling great. Hoping it'll stay that way for a long time.

We answered their few questions, at no point telling them the type of tumour, so that they couldn't look it up on the web.

'But it won't kill you, Dad, will it?' Joe asked.

'I've no idea, son – I could get knocked over by a bus tomorrow. But I'm not worried. People live for twenty years with brain tumours.' Absolutely true. No lies. People might think it was the wrong approach, but it's what was right for us. I didn't want the kids' first thought every morning to be that I might die soon, didn't want them worrying, fretting, getting stressed, treating me differently. So far it had worked. It helped that by the time the boys came back from the exchange trip to France, I was through radiotherapy, done with the first round of chemo, and looking so much better than I had in the midst of it all.

'You know, you look great,' Jess interrupted my thoughts with a point that was taken straight from my wavelength. There was an irony in there. Over a decade divorced and we still thought along the same lines. I knew she wasn't bullshitting me because I agreed. I looked exactly the same as before, only with a bit of a tan from a few days on the golf course. As long as no one studied the back of my head, they'd never know there was anything wrong with me. That's the way I wanted it to stay.

The liaison nurse had suggested a support group, but I'd declined. I honestly didn't need one. I was fine. Doing great. What was the point of talking about what was going to happen if I couldn't change it when it did? And besides, maybe it wouldn't. I understood the prognosis, I'd read the statistics, but if you looked hard enough, the internet was full of stories about patients with my tumour that outlived the odds by miles. I'd take that option, thank you, and in the meantime, I wasn't going to worry about the alternative.

'How's Shauna doing?' Jess asked.

'She's grand. She's one of those people that no matter what life throws at her she just keeps on going. I got lucky with her. With both of you,' I said, vocalizing my earlier thought.

'I'm not...' she stopped, as if the words had caught in her throat, and I could see that her eyes had filled with tears. She hastily wiped them away with the back of her hand and sniffed. 'Sorry Colm, it's just that... fuck, I hate this. It's so fucking unfair. After everything that happened to us and now this. How much heartache are we supposed to endure? I can't stand that this is happening to you and not just because of how it will affect our boys but because you don't deserve it.' She paused, forced a smile. 'Are you checking for the nearest exit yet?'

It was an old joke, one I couldn't believe she remembered. Jess had always been quick to show her emotions, wore her heart on her sleeve, and she used to say that the minute I spotted tears, I'd scan the room for an emergency exit. There was admittedly a grain of truth in there, but not tonight.

I got up and went round to her side of the table, slid into the seat next to her and put my arm around her. 'I'm sorry.'

'What are you apologizing for, you crazy person?' she smiled, while still crying, a bittersweet combination that took me right back to fifteen years ago, when it seemed like we couldn't have a conversation without heartbreak. Looking back, I probably let her down, not equipped or willing to deal with a relationship that was unravelling quicker that I could stop it.

Not that I'd suddenly become some kind of new man, enlightened and in touch with his inner soul, like that bloke Rosie used to date. Couldn't remember his name. Not sure that I ever called him anything other than Yogaman. However, I'd progressed enough to know that she didn't need me to fix this, just needed me to be here. No need for a swift exit this time.

Joe picked that moment to wander in the door, then froze when he saw us.

'Has someone died?' he asked suspiciously. Even I got the irony there.

Jess wiped her tears away again, with both hands this time. 'No, darling, everything's fine.

'Yep, looks it,' he said, with all the nonchalance and deadpan delivery of... well, me. Even if the brown wavy hair and the identical green eyes didn't prove the case, there was no doubt that boy was my son. Momentary concerns swept aside, he went to the fridge, pulled out some ready-made sandwiches on a plate and headed back for the door, making a final show of both care and flippancy as he left.

'Sure you're okay, Mum?'

'I am, Joe. Just having a moment. I'm fine.'

'Ok. S'pose at least it makes a change.'

'What's that?' she asked him, bewildered.

'It's usually Steve that's making you cry. At least this time it's Dad.'

Maybe it was time for a swift exit after all.

28

2009

The Revelation

'So are you going to talk about it at any point?' Vincent asked me, in between laying out a tray of lobster tails and plopping a trough of summer salad next to it.

This was a sixteenth birthday party in Chelsea. Very few carbs, but plenty of excess. The manicurist, the massage therapist and the make-up artist were setting up through in the lounge. A stylist was there with a long rack of clothes and boxes of accessories for the girls to choose from. I'm sure I spotted the Louboutin logo on one of them. The limo would arrive in an hour to take fifteen impeccably made up teenage girls to a One Direction concert at the O2, backstage passes and hospitality thrown in. Naturally. Add on the gifts and the overnight stay at the Mayfair Hotel, and the whole party was probably going to cost what I earned in six months. Not that I was jealous. Actually, perhaps I was a bit. Or a lot. What would it feel like to have someone treat you to that kind of celebration? For my last birthday, Colm bought me a card and a bottle of perfume, and even then he only remembered to give them to me the next day.

'Talk about what?' I asked, genuinely unaware of what he was referring to.

'About the fact that you've had your very own small dark cloud above your head for weeks.'

Sighing, I put the last bright pink silk napkin in its crystal holder. 'Have I?'

'Yup.'

'Bugger. Sorry.'

'It's okay. I'm thick-skinned. I can take it. So what's going on?'

'Nothing, I'm fine.'

'Fine?' he replied, only his version had added scepticism.

I swatted him with a bright pink silk napkin. 'Absolutely fine! Dear Lord, it's finally happened…'

He paused, dangling a tray of salmon blinis in mid-air. 'What?'

'You've turned into Annie. You have to know every detail and you're not giving up until you get them. You'll soon be swigging sherry and complaining about the shocking price of tights.'

I thought he'd leave it be after my attempt at deflection, but he wasn't so easily deterred.

'Look, if you're going to make me spill my guts about my issues with Carole, it's got to be a two-way street.'

'No, it really doesn't. I'm helping you develop emotional intelligence and depth. I'm already fully developed, thanks. Spilling my guts won't help.'

Later, as we removed all the savoury foods and replaced them with a wonderfully elaborate cupcake pyramid, he took another pass at the interrogation.

'Why?'

'Why what?' I asked.

'Why won't you tell me what's wrong? How long have we been friends?'

'Since catering college. About twenty years.'

'Exactly. So spill.'

I stopped, mid stacking of small pink cakes with strawberry toppings.

'Oh for God's sake. Vincent, it involves my ovaries. Do you really want to go there?'

I hadn't realized that two sixteen-year-olds at the makeshift grooming bar were within earshot and one was so entranced by our conversation that there was a sudden 'Ow!' as she burnt her scalp with her hair straighteners. The other one, a tall girl with waist-length blonde hair, cheekbones that could cut glass, and a swagger that belonged on a catwalk, had been subtly flirting with Vincent since we got here. I didn't blame her. If I was a teenager and confronted with this walking, talking, funny, *GQ* cover guy, especially in tonight's outfit of tight black jeans and a slim-fitting tailored white shirt, I'd fancy him too. Now she blatantly watched, waiting for his response.

'Not literally,' he quipped, 'unless I decide to switch specialties from pink sparkly cupcakes to gynaecology.'

I lowered my voice so the two nosy young ladies in the corner couldn't hear.

'Don't. If you made a mistake and confused the two

you might have to explain to a patient why she woke up vajazzled.'

He struggled to keep a serious face. 'Stop deflecting.'

'I'm not.'

'You are, Shauna. You're a nightmare. Are you like this with Colm?'

'Like what?'

'All closed off so that he never knows what's going on with you? Bet he spends his whole life trying to guess how you're feeling.' He was teasing, but it stung a little. A cynical voice inside me doubted that the amount of time Colm spent caring or guessing about how I was feeling stretched to much more often than when he was horny, bored or he noticed there was no food in the fridge. I told the cynical voice to hush up.

'Okay!' I exclaimed in muted tones, moving along the buffet table and out of earshot of any of the guests. 'Fine. If you insist. Are you ready?'

He nodded solemnly. 'Go for it. I can take it.'

I took a deep breath. 'We've stopped trying to have a baby. I'm trying to be okay with it, but I'm struggling to get there. I know this is completely the wrong time because the guys have just started up the business, but after almost eight years I was still hoping it would happen. Colm doesn't have any kind of burning desire to have more kids anyway, but I do. I can't believe my traitorous bloody lady bits won't bloody work. How're you doing so far?'

'Hanging on by a thread,' he replied. 'The "lady bits" might have been a step too far.'

'Okay then, to conclude, Colm and I agreed to take some time off the pursuit of pregnancy and just focus on being a couple again. Colm is relieved and just wants to get on with having a great life, however I'm in a different place. One that requires a lot of questions from interfering people that you work with.'

I was about to say more when my mobile phone vibrated in my back pocket. I slipped out of the door to answer it.

'It's me, m'darlin.' I immediately felt bad for talking about him to Vincent. Not that I'd said anything terrible, but it was private, between Colm and I. And Lulu. And Dan. And Rosie. And the nice doctor at the fertility clinic.

'Hey, love, how's things?'

I could be so pissed off with him, or devastated over something that had gone wrong, and I'd hear his voice and all at once things didn't seem so bad. Most of the time. Giving up on having children for now was going to take a bit of time to get over, but what were my choices? After a few weeks of hidden sadness, I'd realized I could either continue to be miserable, or pull myself together and get back to enjoying life without ovulation charts and monthly devastation. I was trying to go for the latter. Really trying. And a big part of that was trying to reconnect with Colm, go back to being that upbeat, positive person that had made our relationship so great at the start. The simple truth was that I still loved him. Sure, we'd been dented by the strain of the last few years, but not enough to walk away from him.

What was that saying? Fake it until you make it? Right now Fun Shauna was faking her way back to happiness.

'Good. The party went great, I'm jealous of the wealth of a sixteen-year-old and I seriously need to have a word with myself about my attitude, but other than that I'm smashing.'

He roared with laughter. 'I like your attitude.'

'You hang on to that thought when I'm arrested for stealing a limo and a pair of Louboutins from a birthday party. Anyway, where are you? Are you on your way to meet us?'

'Darlin', we're not going to make it. The meeting ran late and we're just leaving Birmingham now.'

I felt a crushing weight of disappointment. I'd been looking forward to tonight. Rosie was now seeing a bearded, Metallica T-shirt-wearing roadie called Zak and his band were playing in a club in Soho. I bit back the urge to moan. No point in falling out about it – wouldn't change a thing. And besides, since the fertility deal, I was getting highly adept at supressing my true feelings to Colm.

'Poor thing, you must be knackered. Don't worry about it. I was just looking forward to seeing you. Feels like it's been so long since we were out.'

'Way too long. I'll make it up to you. How about tomorrow night?'

'Sorry, hon, got a wedding job on. And a christening on Sunday. We'll talk about it later. I'll go to the club for a while and then head home early.'

'Sounds like a plan. Love ya.'

And he was away. I headed back in and got back to work, turning up the speed so we were cleared and in the van within half an hour. Vincent pointed us in the direction of Soho.

'Is Carole meeting us there?' I asked. Rosie had invited Vincent along too, so naturally his girlfriend was coming along. I'd only met her a few times and I could see why they were together. She was gorgeous, funny and incredibly direct, unafraid to say what she thought. I liked her style and I didn't blame her for wanting more from Vince. He was a catch.

'Yeah, she should be there shortly. I told her to go find Lulu and Rosie if we're not there.'

'Have you sorted it out with her yet?'

He shrugged. 'It's a work in progress. I just don't get the rush, you know? Why can't we just take it easy, see where it goes, instead of forcing it?'

'You're right. Just don't wait too long in case she gets a better offer. She's pretty hot,' I laughed. 'And you're not too shabby, but I've seen better.'

'You haven't though,' he winked, feigning smarm and making me laugh. 'Come on, admit it. You must have fancied me once.'

'Never!' I screeched.

'Never? Great, there's my ego decimated. Can we go back to talking about your ovaries?'

Still laughing, I turned the stereo on and the retro, dulcet tones of James Blunt singing 'Beautiful' filled the van. 'I know it's meant to be romantic,' I said, sighing, 'but this song makes me want to bang my head on something until I slip into unconsciousness.'

I flicked the dial and got Bruno Mars with 'Uptown Funk'. 'Now you're talking,' I said, dancing in my seat. I knew every word. That's what happened when you spent day after day, driving from job to job with the radio on as loud as possible to keep you awake because you're living on a few hours' sleep a night.

Vincent joined in, doing a disgracefully bad duet until the song was over.

By the end, my ears were straining to cope with just how atrocious we were. 'I think it's just as well we're great cooks, because we're never making it as singers.'

'Speak for yourself. I think I have potential,' he said, feigning indignation. The music started to fade and I realized he'd used the buttons on the steering wheel to turn it down. 'I'm sorry about what happened,' he said, flipping back to seriousness for a moment. 'I know how much you wanted the treatment to work.'

'Thanks. Just wasn't meant to be. At least not yet. Probably for the best.'

'Do you believe that?'

I thought for a moment. In many ways it was true. Since Colm and Dan started their business I'd been working double shifts, seven days a week, to pay the mortgage. It would be impossible to sustain that workload with a baby, so then we wouldn't be able to pay the bills and we'd be screwed. It made absolutely no sense to do it now. Yet... 'No.'

'Didn't think so.'

I'd have found a way to make it work. It was that simple. I felt my throat begin to tighten. I really didn't want to do this right now. 'Vincent, can we go back to bad dancing and worse singing?'

'Sure,' he said, and I could see he understood that it was too sore on my heart to talk about it any more.

He gave my hand a squeeze. 'But I'm always here for you, you know that?'

I did and I was grateful that he cared. Grateful that he was there. And oh-so thankful that right now we were on our way to a bar, because all I wanted to do was drink a couple of beers, listen to loud music and be normal. No worrying about the bills. No stressing about work. No moping about negative pregnancy tests that had chipped a piece off my heart.

The club was packed when we arrived, so we jostled our way inside. Luckily, the combination of Lulu's flaming red hair and skyscraper heels meant she was always easy to spot in a crowd. Another couple of minutes of manoeuvring through bodies and we made it over to them.

'Wahey! The cavalry's arrived,' Lulu cheered, hugging us in turn. 'Thought you were never going to get here.'

'Sorry! It wrapped up a bit later than we expected.'

I kissed her, before hugging Rosie and then Carole, who headed off to the bar with Vincent to get drinks. 'So where's your man then, Rosie?' I yelled in her ear. Either this was really, really loud or I was getting old and out of practice. That said, it felt good to be out for the night, especially at an event where I wasn't hovering in the background with a tray of coronation chicken vol-au-vents.

Rosie was sporting a whole new look tonight – she had a leather jacket over a black ribbed stretchy dress that went down to her ankles. I've no idea how she could walk or breathe, but she looked great. Like a gothic goddess. I just hoped the change in her style was nothing to do with trying to please the new man. If she didn't find a great guy soon, I was going to pick one for her. If Vincent wasn't already going out with Carole, he'd be my top choice. Vincent and Rosie. Their names even sounded sweet together – like a flower shop. Or a cruise-ship duo.

'There he is over there!' Rosie shouted, pointing just to the left of the stage. Roadie? Tick. Beard? Tick. Metallica T-shirt? Tick. That would be Zak then. From the couple of times I'd met him, I thought there might be hope of this one lasting. Let's hope that underneath that imposing exterior there was a sweet, lovely man dying to get out and make my pal happy.

Vincent and Carole returned from the bar with the drinks. From the way she was gently swaying, in a black leather mini dress and black suede boots that put her well over six feet, she'd obviously had a couple of cocktails already. Hint of alcohol consumption aside, she looked like she'd just stepped off a Bond movie, and Bond, James Bond, would be putty in her hands. He wouldn't give me a second look, especially now that I'd changed in the toilets, swapping my black trousers, charcoal shirt and smart shoes for jeans, biker boots and an old but beloved Guns N' Roses T-shirt.

'I see we've been ditched by our menfolk yet again,' Lulu complained, making it clear she was seriously pissed off. I had a feeling of foreboding. Her and Dan had been doing great since the last blip. That seemed like such an innocuous way to describe their affairs. The IT guy. The tennis coach. The personal trainer. The barman. The interior designer. The… I stopped. The list was too long. And of course, for Dan there'd been the air hostess. Lu still refused to fly Virgin. For the moment, though, they seemed okay, although I was definitely worried. I could live with being in a relationship in which I saw my husband for five minutes every second full moon, but Lulu would never accept that. She needed regular contact, regular validation, and if she wasn't getting that from Dan, there was always the risk that she would look elsewhere. I made a mental note to suggest to Dan that he limit time away as much as possible. Not even a new business was worth sacrificing his family life. Yes, I saw the irony in that thought.

The song the band was playing ended and they left to a rapturous applause, crossing with the main act who were storming the stage. This was the band that Zak roadied for and it was an incongruous match. These were very definitely an indie, almost folky group, while Zak, with his extremely ripped physique and Metallica T-shirt, was more on the heavy-metal side of the music divide. But he immediately proved me wrong, by starting to move his head in time to the music, clearly getting in to it.

Book. Cover. Never judge.

Rosie took advantage of the break to go search out Zak, while out of the corner of my right eye I saw that Vincent and Carole were now in deep discussion and it didn't appear to be topping the romance scale. I zoned it out, deciding I'd had enough relationship trauma of my own this week. Even though Colm wasn't here, tonight was going to be about music, drinks, laughs, dancing and fun with my friends. No drama. No hassle. No stress. Bring it on.

'What's up with those two?' Lulu asked, spotting the heated debate.

'No idea,' I responded, deciding it wasn't my place to discuss Vincent's love life. I liberated another bottle of beer from the drinks shelf next to where we were standing. This wasn't the type of place for fancy glasses and mirrored tables.

'You know, I so would,' she said, gesturing to Vincent.

At that moment the song ended and the volume levels in the room crashed, making my yelp of 'Lulu!' much louder than I intended.

She responded with a cheeky shrug. 'What?' she retorted, like I was the one who had just said something outrageous. 'Don't bloody give me that disapproving look. He is gorgeous. I could suck grapes off that torso until the end of time.'

'Lulu!' I repeated, not caring that heads were now swivelling in our direction. 'That's... that's...' Bugger, I couldn't keep the disdain up any longer and succumbed to a helpless cackle of laughter. She was so wrong on every level, but I bloody loved her unashamed outrageousness. I just wished it wasn't aimed at my business partner. 'You keep your hands off, Lulu. I thought you were a happily married woman this month? Or was that last month? It's hard to keep up,' I teased.

'I am a happily married woman,' she pouted. 'But I'd be so much happier if I was doing naked yoga with Vincent. Tell me you never considered it? Not even once?'

'Nope,' I answered truthfully.

'You're not human,' Lulu sneered.

She may have been right, but I preferred a more anthropological explanation. When Vincent and I met at college I'd assumed he was gay, because I felt no tingle of attraction there despite the fact that he was the Brad Pitt. The Ryan Gosling. The Johnny Depp. He was the bloke that was so devastatingly, exquisitely handsome that every girl flirted with him. Except me. I always preferred the cute and funny guy who made me laugh. In truth, I was glad there had never been an attraction between us because it meant that we could just go straight to being friends, with none of that tentative awkwardness on the way. He went through half a dozen relationships over the time we were in college and ultimately broke up with every one of them, while his break-up tally with his very best female pal remained at zero

'Oh dear, she's leaving. Check it out. Trouble ahead. Incoming. Incoming.' Lulu gave a military-flavoured running commentary on the scene unfolding with Vincent and it was so irresistible I had to look. Yep, Carole had strutted away from him, leaving his brow furrowed and his arms wide with exasperation.

Given that we were standing between them and the door, she was stomping towards us and would pass us in about two seconds. I braced myself for what to say, rearranging my face into an open, friendly smile. She mumbled something as she got within a few feet of us but I couldn't hear what it was.

'Sorry, Carole? What was that?' I asked, guessing that it was something to do with her premature exit.

'I'm done. I'm not competing any more.'

Lulu and I were immediately engrossed. 'Competing with who?' Lulu asked, and if I wasn't mistaken there was an underlying glimmer of hope in her expression.

'You!' Carole blurted, as if it wasn't even in doubt. It took me a stunned moment to compute. That outburst could only be aimed at Lulu but for some strange reason Carole was looking at me.

'What are you talking about?' Lulu got in there first.

'Don't bloody stand there acting all innocent,' Carole ranted, eyes still on me, and I wasn't entirely sure if it was her or the alcohol that was now trying to make a very heated, direct point.

'Carole, I've no idea what's upset you, but...'

'What's upset me?' she raged. 'How about the fact that my boyfriend, Mr... Mr...'

Her brain obviously wasn't passing the information on to her mouth.

'Mr Bullshit over there...' Ah, got it now. 'Has been with me for the last year, A YEAR...' she yelled that bit for emphasis, '... of wasted bloody time because he was just stringing me along, passing time, because Mr Bullshit...' it was rolling off the tongue now, 'is in love with YOU!'

Oh crap. It was definitely the drink. I tried to appease her.

'Carole, I promise you, he's not. I'm really sorry I've been monopolizing him lately, but it's just that, well to be honest, Colm and I are struggling financially so I've been taking on loads of extra work and obviously that encroaches on Vincent's time too. I'm so sorry. I didn't think that one through. Look, I'll bring in other help for some of the jobs and find a way to make sure Vincent cuts back and gets more time with you.'

The top half of her body swayed backwards as her hands went on to her hips, her face an exquisitely beautiful picture of annoyance.

'Are you lying or being incredibly thick?'

Lulu's gaze flipped quickly to me as she made an O-shape with her mouth and raised her eyebrows in expectation. Meanwhile I had a whole internal dialogue going. Okay, self, just take a moment to consider this situation. On the one hand, you would normally never, ever, in a hell-will-freeze-over-first, million years let anyone get away with talking to you like that. On the other hand, she's drunk, she's your partner's girlfriend, she'll probably be mortified in the morning and you'll have to see her again at other events, so it's probably best for you to suck this one up and be the bigger person.

I took my own advice, albeit I delivered my reply in a deadly calm, very direct tone.

'Carole, I'm married and I'm in no way attracted to Vincent. We're friends. He's not in love with me. He's not attracted to me and he never will be. Let's just forget about this and I'm sure we'll laugh about it tomorrow.'

An Elvis sneer appeared on her perfectly plump lips.

'Ha! You just answered my question. If you really don't think he's in love with you then you are really, really, really...'

The words all slurred into each other.

'...thick.'

With that she stomped off and left Lulu and I open-mouthed and gobsmacked. When the shock wore off enough for my motor skills to return, I turned to look at Vincent, who was already staring straight at me, with a weird, defeated expression I didn't recognize.

In love with me? I'd never heard anything so ridiculous.

Or had I just won top prize for being thick?

29

2016

Balancing the Books

I banged each button on the calculator so hard my fingers actually hurt. We were financially screwed. No matter what way I added up, subtracted, juggled or manipulated the figures, there was no way to make them balance.

The one consolation in all of this was that now Colm was at home, I didn't have any childcare issues or costs. Thank God. That would be the overdrawn straw that broke the bank manager's back.

However, even the minimum payments to the credit cards were huge, thanks to Colm's newfound thirst for travel. 'Creating memories,' he called it, and he was right. Unfortunately, the consequences of those memories were now creating nightmares.

There had been the fortnight in Disney World. The city break to Amsterdam. The week with the boys in Paris. And then, the lodge at Henley last weekend. Every time he said he wanted to do it, I'd smile, nod and then go spend two hours trying to find the most economical way of making it happen, while he went and sought out the swim shorts and the scuba set.

I wasn't going to say no or point out that the holidays were making a serious dent in the overdraft and credit cards. I'd done that briefly the first time, the night he and Lulu had ambushed me with the Disney idea. When we'd booked it that evening, he'd chosen five star all the way. 'Babe,' I'd said hesitantly, reticent to burst his bubble of enthusiasm. 'Maybe we should look for somewhere a bit more reasonable? I'm not sure how we're going to pay for it all.'

'Bung it on a credit card,' he'd said glibly. 'When I get back to work we'll pay it off.'

Dan, the good friend that he was, had agreed to allow Colm to keep taking a basic salary despite the fact that he was off sick, but with only one income coming in to the company accounts, it came nowhere near what he'd been earning before, and even that hadn't been great. But that wasn't the issue now.

I hadn't said what I was thinking, but he'd read it in my expression. 'And if I don't get back to work,' he'd countered flippantly, with more than a hint of impatience, 'that means there will be a life insurance payout and you can pay it out from that.' It wasn't true. We both knew the only life insurance policy he had was a tiny one from his last job and it would only pay out a few grand. He and Dan had never got around to setting up new policies. That wasn't the point, though. His comment injected toxic reality straight into my gut. He was going to die. My love was going to die.

And whether his bravado came from denial, or bravery, or a mixture of both, the thought of him so flippantly admitting it almost broke me.

That was the last time I mentioned money. Since then I'd made it my mission to keep on top of the finances, and with all the extra jobs I'd taken on, sometimes four or five in a day, we would have been just about keeping afloat if it wasn't for the damn holidays. The irony was, wherever we went, I was too bloody stressed about money to enjoy it, spending half my time on the phone and online trying to drum up more work. I'd have been happy to savour every one of these days at home, in the park, just hanging with our friends, but – for the zillionth time, I chided myself – this wasn't about me.

It didn't matter if I was freaking out in the inside that I was going to be left with mountains of debt I had no way of paying back. Or that we could lose our negative equity home because I couldn't pay the mortgage.

No matter how scared I was, how sick to my stomach those thoughts made me feel, I wasn't the one that was dying. I didn't get a vote. Colm got to choose to spend his days wherever he wanted because he was the one that was running out of time.

Colm wanted memories, he'd get memories, and sod the cost that would come after he was gone.

After he was gone.

The thought was on a loop in my head.

After he was gone.

When I wouldn't have a husband.

After he was gone.

When Beth would grow up without her dad.

After he was gone.

When Davie and Joe wouldn't have him to buy them a drink at their weddings, to teach them to drive, to see their children born.

When he would always be in the past.

I was suffocating, choking on my grief.

The knot of tension in my stomach was twisting tighter and the depressingly familiar, excruciating wave of panic and pain rose until it felt like my chest, my neck, the back of my scalp were on fire.

'Hey m'darlin, you coming down? Lulu's here already.'

I hadn't even heard him approaching the door. My smile was on instantly. 'Absolutely. Two minutes. Just let me get finished up here.'

He eyed the pile of paperwork in front of me. 'Everything okay?'

'Absolutely. Two mins,' I repeated breezily.

That seemed to satisfy him and he padded off down the hall. My gorgeous man. The half of my heart. Everything.

He'd be gone.

Like a diver deprived of oxygen for several minutes, I took an overwhelming gasp and buckled over, a silent scream ringing in my ears. This is how it was. Coping. Coping. Coping. Crash. Always in private. My internal rage and sorrow building until I blew, like a pressure cooker valve being lifted to let out the steam just in time to avoid an explosion.

When it finally ended, it took a few moments for my hands to stop shaking and the pain in my throat to subside. Breathe. Just breathe. My mantra.

Of course, I'd known it was going to be tough, but I could never have anticipated the conflicting emotions. The pain and sorrow. The anger. The resentment, immediately followed by self-hatred for thinking that. Admiration for his bravery. Fury over his state of denial. The overwhelming love. The gratitude that he was still here. The panic that he wouldn't be. And – although I'd never admit it to a soul – the desperation for him to notice that I was suffering too.

He was a man dying from cancer. But I was a woman whose husband was dying from cancer. Yes, his devastation trumped mine by a million miles, but in this new reality I wasn't allowed to hurt. Or bring down the mood. Or moan about practicalities. I was the supporter. Get on with it. Smile on face, let's go.

I waited until some strength had returned to my legs, then headed downstairs, smile and light-hearted demeanour back in place.

Lulu and Colm were already at the kitchen table, both of them laughing hysterically over some private joke. I didn't ask. I was just glad that she was there for him, keeping his spirits up and his mind distracted by raucous nonsense and a steady stream of frivolous entertainment. I thought again how she'd really stepped up to this. I owed her.

'You going like that?' were Lulu's opening words and they weren't said with a softly-softly air of consideration and compassion.

Amused and indignant, I decided that perhaps I wouldn't bother owing her anything.

'Why, what's wrong with me?'

I scanned my jeans, flip-flops and pale blue T-shirt and

contrasted it against her slinky black dress and killer heels. We were very obviously reading off different dress codes.

'Nothing, but it's Rosie's big night. A bit of an effort wouldn't go amiss.' She was only half teasing but I let it pass. The truth was that all I wanted to do was go crawl into bed and get more than five hours' sleep for the first time in months. Effort? It was taking all I had to remain upright and stable.

Dan appeared through the back door, cutting off any retort my frazzled mind could have come up with. I saw Lulu's eyes flicker but nothing more. I had absolutely no idea what was going on with those two now but at least they weren't completely ignoring each other. The occasional polite but cold word passed between them.

'Okay, we ready?' Dan asked, his car keys still in hand.

'Yes.' Lulu picked up her bag and grabbed a black leather jacket off the back of her chair, then threw it round her shoulders. Effortless class.

'So what do you think of the news then?' Dan asked me. The atmosphere in the room immediately plummeted below zero.

'Erm, we hadn't actually said anything to Shauna yet,' Lulu countered, her eyes blazing. I had a feeling I was witnessing another nail in the coffin of their marriage. But what did that have to do with me? And why was Colm suddenly looking shame-faced?

I leaned against the wall, glad of the support. 'Said anything about what?'

It was Colm who eventually spoke up. 'I'm going to go back to work.'

There was a distinct sound of thunder in my ears and

I didn't trust myself to utter anything more than a weak, 'What? Why?'

'Because what else am I going to do, Shauna?'

A list suddenly popped up in my head. Rest. Take it easy. Enjoy spending more time with your daughter and sons. Be here when I come home after a working day that feels like it will never end. Make love. Talk. Hold me.

'I feel fine,' he went on, an exaggeration of the truth, but I let it slide. 'The treatment is working and, let's face it, I know we need the money.'

'We're managing,' I countered, stopping myself from pointing out that he was already taking a basic wage, so while going back to work might increase that in the long-term, it wouldn't have a massive impact on our finances until he went out, found more work, brought it in, got paid. That could take months. In the meantime, I'd need to find and pay for childcare for Beth. She was at Marcy's again tonight, but that was an occasional sleepover situation.

He looked at me sceptically. 'It'll take some of the pressure off you though.' So he'd noticed. Not enough to ask me about it, to ask how I was coping or to sit down and talk about how this was affecting me. None of those things. He just waved me off with a smile every day and greeted me with one when I got home. All is well. We're all fine. Shauna? Shauna just gets on with it. That was his attitude. She's fine. Och, she's grand.

An internal voice screamed in my head to shut up.

Resentment fought with bitterness for top billing and then, almost instantly, shame killed them both. That maelstrom of conflict was back. What kind of bitch was I, to have feelings like that when he was the one facing the end of his life? He was the one who was dealing with the worst scenario of all and I was the one feeling sorry for myself? Get a grip. Get a fucking grip.

'I just want to go back to normal,' he added, then turning to Dan. 'It's not fair that I'm taking a wage and not earning it.'

'Mate, you know that's not a problem,' Dan interjected.

'But it is for me,' Colm argued. 'I don't want to feel like I'm stressing you out, bud.'

That one brought a wave of resentment and bitterness right back. He didn't want to stress Dan, I got that. But was I being vile by wishing he gave me the same consideration?

His attention was back on me now. 'I need to do this, Shauna. I need some normality.' There was a challenge there, or perhaps it was the desperation of a man who was determined to ignore what was happening to him. Either way, I knew I wasn't going to argue, because the truth was simple. I would never stand in the way of anything he wanted to do for however long he had left.

All eyes were still on me, waiting, expectant. Lulu took a breath, ready to say something, to make a case, but I cut her off, my eyes on Colm, an expression of what I hoped was encouragement on my face.

'Okay,' I said, hoping my tone was encouraging. 'When are you going to start back?'

I needed time to get things in place, arrange childcare, rearrange my schedule. Maybe a month. At least three weeks.

His grin was wide and triumphant. 'Next Monday.'

'Yayyyyy!' Lulu cheered, spontaneously hugging him. Yay, indeed.

Over Lulu's shoulder, he met my eyes and I winked, never dropping the smile for a second. I could do this. I'd find a way to make it work. Somehow.

'Right, let's get off then or Rosie will be on the rampage,' Dan jested.

As it turned out, she wouldn't have noticed. The party to launch the newly renovated Doris's Day was in full swing, at least sixty people packed into a café that had just been extended to seat forty. Other than four cosy booths that lined the new entrance, all the chairs had been temporarily removed and the new white tables pushed against the freshly painted caramel-coloured side walls, all of them now groaning under the weight of drinks and a feast of savoury and sweet snacks. The budget didn't stretch to champagne, but there was Prosecco, water, beer, jugs of juice, and next to them, huge cream platters of mini burgers, chicken satay sticks, salmon parcels, vegetable samosas. On the dessert table, tiny Victoria sponges, intricate chocolate eclairs, cute carrot cakes, mountains of chocolate-dipped strawberries and tiny pots of mousse in five different flavours. It looked spectacular. Rosie came towards us, her happiness obvious, making my battered, damaged heart swell, thankful that something she'd worked so hard on had paid off.

'You're glowing!' I told her, hugging her.

'Ah, that might just be the heat in here,' she said, deflecting the compliment as always.

'Nope, it's definitely just you. Congratulations, honey, we're so happy for you,' I told her, squeezing her tightly.

I stood back to let the others do the same, scanning the crowd for familiar faces. Over in the furthest corner, there were a few unexpected ones. 'My parents are here. Yours too, Lu,' I told her.

'Really?' Lu said, obviously surprised. 'They didn't say. But then, that's not exactly a surprise, is it?' She had a point. I tried to remember the last time I'd spoken to my folks. Two weeks ago? Maybe three? Four? I had no idea. Maybe it was the time they'd come to collect Beth for that one and only sleepover at their house. Calling to check in or to enquire after our well-being had never been their strong point and the trifling issue of Colm's brain tumour hadn't changed that.

As Rosie disentangled herself from Dan's embrace she picked up on the tail end of our conversation. 'Your dads have been helping me get the place finished. So kind of them. Honestly, they absolutely saved the day.'

I'm not sure if Lulu or I was more dumbfounded but I decided to take the award. 'My dad's been here?'

Rosie nodded. 'For a couple of weeks. Both of them. They've been great.'

Two thoughts. First of all, my dad had been conspicuously absent in everything we'd ever done. He didn't show up for house moves. Or when Colm and Dan moved into the new offices and they needed decorating. Or when Beth was born and we had a room to prepare. Or when my husband was diagnosed with terminal cancer. Second thought? My dad had been just fifteen minutes away for the last couple of weeks and hadn't popped in to see us even once. How were we? How was Colm doing? How was Beth? How were we coping with the worst thing that had ever happened in our lives? Dad of the Year trophy to the man in the salmon pink shirt.

'You thinking what I'm thinking?' Lulu hissed. 'All these

years and neither of them have lifted a finger to help us and yet this? They must be getting bored with golf breaks to Marbella.'

'Absolutely,' I retorted. 'Remind me to book their services next time I'm painting the kitchen.'

The music changed and Patsy Cline's 'Crazy' oozed from the speakers. Apt.

'Guys, come get drinks,' Rosie said, taking Colm's hand and leading him and Dan towards the buffet table.

'We'll wait here – return with wine,' I pleaded, backing into an empty booth, aware that if we moved someone else would take our spot. I wanted to have a look around, and I should really go say hello to the parenting squad, but right now exhaustion was eating at my bones and I just wanted to sit down. Lulu slid into the red leather bench seat across from me.

I noticed her eyes following the guys as they headed away from us.

'So what's going on with you two then?' I asked, suddenly aware that it had been a while since we spoke properly on our own, meanwhile Dan was still in my garage.

'What? Nothing!' she shot back. Her words bristled with defensiveness.

'And the architect?'

A flicker of comprehension. 'Oh. He's gone. Done.'

I felt optimism rising. 'So you and Dan…' I left it hanging, hoping that she'd latch on and take it to a place of happy endings.

Instead she shrugged. 'I don't know. We're… cordial. Civil. I think what's happened to Colm has had an effect on that. Seems petty to be causing drama around him when you guys are dealing with so much more. And obviously, Dan's even more motivated to make the business work, so he's seriously putting in the hours. Between you and Dan, it's like being in the land of the workaholic,' she joked, but it was a reminder that Colm and I weren't the only ones affected by what had happened to him. Our friends, Beth, we were all in this together and it was touching everyone's lives. Except my parents, obviously. Dan was slogging to help financially, Lulu was making it her mission to keep Colm entertained, I'd come home every night and there would be fresh cakes, baked and delivered by Rosie, who picked up Beth from school every day then passed a couple of hours with Colm before I came home. The people over in the corner may be responsible for my DNA but this group was my real family. I noticed Lulu's eyes returning to where the guys were standing with Rosie and she carried on, 'I think we need more time before we decide what to do. Need to know for sure what I want. Or who.'

Before I could ask her any more, another familiar face walked in the door.

'Jack!' I exclaimed, rising to greet him with a kiss on both cheeks. Lulu did the same. I had a real soft spot for Rosie's latest man and couldn't help hoping that her happiness with the new café would be swiftly joined by the relationship security she'd always craved. On top of that, he was cute. There weren't many forty-five-year-old men that could carry off a ponytail and white linen trousers.

'Come, sit with us,' I offered.

He didn't make a move to do so. 'Thanks, but I'm just

popping in for a minute to congratulate Rosie and then I'm off.' This wasn't the demeanour or words of a man who was here to share in his girlfriend's success. Or the confident, assertive manner of a life coach who always took steps based on solid aims and positive outcomes. This guy was nervous. Sad. Definitely uneasy.

Although Lulu hadn't seemed to pick up on that.

'Congratulations!' she bellowed. 'I'm so thrilled about you asking her to move in with you. Glad you recognized a good thing when you saw it. Although, of course, if you hurt her we now know where you live, making it easy to hunt you down and break your legs.'

My neck was starting to hurt from looking upwards, but not enough to distract me from the confused mottling of his brow.

'You don't know.' It was a statement, not a question. Or rather, it was a sad, angst-filled admission.

'Know what?' I asked, hoping I was misjudging this.

'She said no. Didn't want to move in with me. Ended things a couple of weeks ago. I just came in tonight because I wanted to see how she's doing. Clearly she's fine,' he observed, gesturing to Rosie, who at that exact moment threw her head back, laughing at something Colm had said.

Lulu and I looked at each other, dumbfounded. She'd said no? I racked my brain for our last conversation about it. Sure, there had been a hesitation, but I'd assumed that was the 'moving in together' equivalent of pre-wedding jitters. She said no? Why didn't I know this? God, I was a crap pal. I'd been so wrapped up in my own problems I was unaware of major things happening to my friends.

'Can you tell her I was here? And I wish her well?' He made a move to go, but I stopped him.

'Jack, I'm so sorry. We had no idea,' I said, wanting to ask more, but realizing it would be rude to probe.

Lulu had no such qualms. 'But what happened? You two were perfect together.'

He sighed helplessly. 'I thought so too. But... look, I'm just going to be honest because, let's face it, I'll probably never see you again...'

That one caused a twinge of dismay. Hopefully he was wrong about that.

'The truth is, I'm pretty sure she is seeing someone else. Actually, looking back, I think she might have been seeing someone else all along,' he studied us as he said it, no doubt trying to gauge from our reactions if there was any truth in that.

'Noooooo!' I argued, the whole notion preposterous. 'That's ridiculous. Trust me, Rosie isn't having an affair. We've been like sisters for a million years and we'd know. Wouldn't we, Lu?'

No answer. I realized Lulu's gaze had drifted over to where Rosie and our husbands were still in deep conversation. Lulu watched for a few seconds, before finally sharing her thoughts.

'I really don't know if we would.'

30

2009

No Time for Goodbye

'Line dancing.'

'What?'

'I'll be at line dancing, my lovely, but you're welcome to come with me.'

I tried to keep the hilarity out of my voice. Class. Sheer class.

'Gran, when did you take up line dancing?'

'When I got bored rigid at Pilates. There's no point to it at all. I fell asleep last time I was there, and some strange and very flexible gentleman with his hair in a bun wasn't best pleased.'

Hilarity won, as I exploded into giggles.

'There are no words to express how much I frigging love you, Gran.'

'Try, dear. I need the ego boost,' she cackled.

'So, line dancing it is. What time do I need to be there?'

'Eight o'clock.'

'Okay, I should be done around seven, so I'll pick you up on the way.'

'Lovely. Oh, and you need to bring cowboy boots. And a Stetson. And Vincent.'

I hung up, still laughing, and shouted to Vincent, who was over the other side of the kitchen preparing trays of chicken wings, nachos and mini burritos for the Tex-Mex bowling party we were catering at a huge house on Richmond Hill at 6 p.m. It was food delivery only, no serving or clearing, so we'd be done by half past. Tomorrow morning, we had a breakfast event in Wimbledon, so it made sense for me to stay at Annie's house tonight, especially as Colm was away for a few days in… in… I actually had no idea where he was. I'd lost track of where he and Dan were working these days.

'Annie says I've to bring you to her line dancing class tonight.'

He grinned. 'Is it just me who suddenly got the best mental image in living history?'

'Does it involve Annie and a large cowboy hat?'

'It does.'

'Then no, it's not just you. Please tell me I'll be like her when I grow up.'

'That's never been in any doubt,' he confirmed, putting the final piece of chicken on the tray and then slipping off his gloves. 'Okay, we're set. Ready to go?'

'Yup.' I grabbed my jacket and slid on my backpack. Handbags were out of the question in this job, as I always needed two hands to carry trays. 'Would you mind dropping me at Annie's when we're done and picking me up there in the morning? Colm's away and I don't fancy going home to an empty house.'

'Of course not. Here...' he handed me the burrito tray. 'I never want to see another one of those for as long as I live.'

'Aw, I'm feeling your pain,' I teased. The burritos were a sore point. He'd dropped the first lot, burnt the second lot and these were the third attempt. So far it was looking good, but I concentrated on getting them to the car before I brought up the question I'd been dying to ask for ages.

'Heard from Carole yet? Or is she still treating you like a cold-caller trying to sell her pet insurance for a dog she doesn't have?'

'Fido is alive and well,' he retorted dryly, before answering the question. 'And no, not heard a word since she moved out and called me an emotional fuckvoid. I've no idea what that means. Anyway, I tried to call a few times, but I've given up.'

'Are you sure you want to do that? If you just explained that she got the wrong end of the stick...'

'Do not give her a stick,' he warned ruefully. 'Give her nothing that can be used as a weapon.'

He was joking, but I knew it had to sting. After the nightclub fiasco last month he'd been mortified, but there was a little indignation thrown in there too.

The next morning, I'd pouted dramatically, sweeping my hand to my forehead like a forties movie star. 'So you're not in love with me?'

'You're great with a piping bag, but no,' he'd assured me, laughing. The official verdict was therefore in – I wasn't thick. Not that there had ever been any doubt.

'What about Colm? Things any better?' he asked now.

I shrugged. Were they? I had no idea. We were fighting less, so that was good. But we were like two people floating in the same zero-gravity situation, occasionally bumping into each other and passing the time of day. I was still faking it, I suspect he was too. I wasn't sure that either of us had the energy to change that. Right now, we just needed the energy to work to pay the bills that were starting to suffocate us. I glossed over the subject and then flipped to talking about next week's bookings. The diary was full, which was great for the balance sheet, but I was increasingly aware that Vincent and I were so tired we were almost running on empty.

The delivery took half an hour and then we headed to Annie's house. We were almost there when I said, 'Vincent, thanks for doing this. I don't say that to you enough.'

'For doing what?' he asked, puzzled, indicating to turn at the approaching set of traffic lights.

'For working every single day and night with me. I know you're giving up a lot. I could bring someone else in to help though,' I told him for the millionth time. 'Just because I have no life doesn't mean you should suffer too.'

He rolled his eyes. 'Shauna, stop saying it like it's such a hardship. Sure, the hours are crap, but I'm taking home half of everything we earn so I'm profiting too.'

There was no time to discuss it any further, as we pulled up outside Annie's house and she stormed out like an ageing SAS when she saw the van. And oh dear God, she hadn't been kidding about the Stetson.

'Vincent, you have to come. I swear it'll be the biggest thrill those ladies have had since before the menopause.'

'I don't have a hat,' he argued weakly. She took hers off and plumped it on his head. 'You do now, son.'

He was powerless to resist the passive-aggressive demands of my seventy-something Glaswegian powerhouse granny. It wasn't a surprise. I'd never yet met anyone who could.

A few hours and a whole lot of heel-tapping later, 'Achy Breaky Heart', 'Boot Scootin' Boogie', and my personal favourite, 'Honky Tonk Badonkadonk', were just a few of the tunes that stuck in my mind. Annie knew every step, every turn, every holler, while Vincent and I tried desperately to follow, like the two new kids on the yeehah block who didn't have a clue what was going on. We were hopeless. Embarrassing. Yet it was the most fun I'd had in as long as I could remember.

'Gran, you totally put us to shame,' I told her on the way back to her house.

'Aye, there's life in me yet, love,' she preened. 'The day I can't spin around a dance floor you can shoot me.'

'Gran! Don't say that. Anyway, you can't pop your cowboy boots until you've taught us how to do those bloody dances. Vincent, we were officially rubbish.'

Annie sighed. 'Aye, thank God you're good-looking, son, because you're never going to get a woman with those dancing skills.'

Vincent hooted with laughter. Sometimes there was really no answer to my gran.

At the house, she persuaded him to come in for a nightcap. The woman was incorrigible. It was near midnight and she still wanted to keep the party going.

Inside, she headed to take her coat and boots off while Vincent and I went to the kitchen to make tea.

'So, not exactly how I anticipated tonight unfolding,'

he said, deadpan. 'Kidnapped by Annie, forced to dance for my life, scarred by my inability to co-ordinate my arms and legs.'

I plopped two sugars in my gran's tea and poured her two fingers of her beloved Maccallan nightcap. 'Are you traumatized?'

'Absolutely. But I don't think I've ever laughed more. You're some team, you two.'

I took that as a compliment.

Picking up the tray, I headed to the lounge, Vincent at my back. I'd only taken a few steps in, when I stopped, forcing him to crash into the back of me.

'She's sleeping,' I whispered, nodding to Annie, in her favourite chair, eyes closed, a hint of a smile on her lips.

I put the tray down on the table and lifted a throw from the couch to keep the chill off my gran when…

I stopped. Something wasn't right. A look. A sense. I flew over to her side.

'Gran. Gran! Vincent call an ambulance! Call an ambulance now!' I screamed.

He dived to the phone while I slipped my arms under her and lifted her over to the couch, her frame tiny, but even so, requiring strength I never knew I had. 'No, Gran. Oh God, please no.'

With shaking, furiously fast fingers, I checked her pulse by pressing on her neck. Nothing. I listened to her chest. It didn't rise or fall.

'No, no, no, no! Come on Gran. You can't do this. You can't. Come on!' This couldn't be happening. She had been bloody dancing only an hour ago.

I placed my hands on her chest, one on top of the other, and I pressed. One. Two. Three. Four. A steady rhythm.

'Don't leave me, Gran. Annie, wake up. Please wake up. Oh God, please...'

Vincent was at my side. 'Ambulance is on the way. Let me take over.'

'No, I can't.' Twenty-five. Twenty-six. Twenty-seven. Twenty-eight. Twenty-nine. Thirty presses, then I moved to her head, gave two breaths into her mouth. Still nothing. Back to her heart. Steady beats, 100 a minute, just like I'd been taught on every first aid course I'd ever been on. Thirty presses. Back to her mouth. Two breaths. Nothing. Back to her heart. One. Two. Three.

'Come on Gran. Please. Please. Please. You can't. Not you. Please not you.'

'Shauna, let me...'

'No! Go outside and wait for the ambulance in case they can't find the cottage. Flag it down,' I gasped. Twenty-one. Twenty-two. Nothing. No response. No movement. No sound. No beat of her heart.

Again. Again. Head. Heart. Press. Head. Heart. Press. Nothing. Again. Again.

Hours passed, days, weeks. Head. Heart. Press. Again.

No response. Had to keep going. She'd come back. She'd never leave me. Not Annie. Never. Keep going. Had to keep going.

Vincent ran in, two guys in hi-vis jackets following him.

'Shauna, they're here. Let them take over.'

Head. Heart. Press. One. Two Three.

'Shauna, you need to let them...'

Ten. Eleven. Twelve. Had to keep going.

'We've got this, love.' A voice I didn't recognize.

Twenty-one. Twenty-two.

'Shauna…' Arms around me, pulling me back, gently, forcefully, holding me to him as we sat on the floor. Two men moving to Annie's side. Oxygen mask. Head. Heart.

I fought to get back to her, but Vincent was too strong. 'Gran. Gran!' I screamed.

They pressed. They counted. They worked on her until one looked at the other and I knew. I was still on the floor, Vincent was holding me and I pushed him off, crawled to her. The men moved to let me in.

I wrapped my arms around her and I lay my head on her motionless chest.

'Please don't go,' I whispered. 'Please….'

She didn't answer. Didn't laugh. Didn't touch me. Didn't run her fingers through my hair. Didn't hold me. Didn't tell me everything would be okay.

It would never be.

I stayed there, held on to the woman I loved more than any other and I wept until there was nothing left.

31

2016

Counting Days

'Goodnight, gorgeous girl,' I crooned, as I lifted the duvet off Beth and slipped in beside her, making her squeal as I covered her face in kisses. I'd probably just added half an hour to the time it would take her to fall asleep but I didn't care. I got so little time with her these days that I needed to make every moment count. That fucking brain tumour wasn't getting this. It wasn't taking one ounce of joy away from my girl. Fake it until you make it. A few years ago, when Colm and I were having problems, that was the slogan I lived by. That was before this incredible little girl made an appearance, but I could still go with the concept. As far as Beth would ever know, I was happy, fun, giggly, silly mum when I was with her. Exhausted, worried, stressed, miserable me only came out to play when Beth wasn't around.

'I love you right up to the moon, past Mars, round Saturn, through Venus, and then back,' she told me solemnly, the list getting longer the more she learned from the book we were reading about a little boy who visited all the planets.

'I love you to all those places and back too. Twice.'

She giggled again, and was rewarded with another round of kisses before I finally said goodnight and headed through to our bedroom.

Colm had his suitcase open on the bed, packing in a couple of shirts, extra shoes, toiletries.

'That's Beth just nodding off if you want to go say goodnight,' I told him.

'Yeah, I will,' he answered, distracted as he foraged in a drawer.

'What have you lost?'

He stopped, irritated. 'My black belt. I'm sure it's in here.'

'It's already out, babe,' I said gently, pointing to the pillow, on which a strip of black leather was resting. This happened a lot. His memory was definitely erratic, his attention span even more so. His sense of humour, temperament, communications, all in the same boat, tossing on the waves, sometimes high, sometimes low. I wasn't sure if it was the personality changes the doctor had warned us about, or if it was the strain of dealing with the prognosis, or if it all came from tiredness, from the long-term exhaustion that was often the result of a trauma to the brain. Or was there something else? Something I was missing?

He didn't say anything, just lifted the belt and tossed it in the case.

'Colm, are you sure you want to do this?' I asked for the tenth time this week, before going on, 'Dan said he could go and...'

'I don't want Dan to go. I'm doing it.'

The trip to Manchester was a pitch for a new client, one that Colm had been working on before he got sick. Dan had taken over but the deal still hadn't been sealed. Now, Colm was jumping back on it, determined to bring it in, even though it meant a couple of exhausting days of trains and taxis. A cab was picking him up at 8 p.m. to take him to Euston for the 9 p.m. train, then he was heading straight to the hotel at the other end, so he could get a night's sleep before meeting the client tomorrow morning. I'd at least made him accept that doing it all in one day would be way too tiring. Even a half-day in the office was exhausting him and I was worried that this would push it too far.

'But Colm…'

'Shauna, stop treating me like I'm fucking dying,' he blurted and I felt myself physically recoil, like my face had been slapped. This wasn't the old Colm. The old Colm didn't yell. He didn't rage at me. There was a time when I knew his every gesture, every feeling and reaction, but no longer. Sometimes I felt like this tumour was already starting to take him away, bit by bit.

I opened my mouth, but there were no words.

In front of me, Colm exhaled, his two hands going to his hips, head down. It was a few seconds before he lifted it again. 'I'm sorry,' he said, his whole body sagging with whatever combination of emotions were in play.

'It's okay, you're just…' I was planning to go with 'tired' but I didn't get a chance to finish.

'It's not okay. Christ, I'm a prick sometimes.'

Two choices – honesty or conciliatory humour. As

always, I went with the latter. 'Yes, you are indeed,' I told him. 'Thankfully, I have high tolerance levels in the world of prickdom.'

That made him smile.

'C'mere,' I said, climbing on to the bed and reaching for him. He took me up on it, moving his suitcase to one side to clear a space. He didn't speak until our heads were on the pillow, faces inches apart, arms and legs entwined.

'I'm sorry,' I said. 'I'm not deliberately mollycoddling you.' I phrased it differently from him, unwilling to use the 'd' word.

'I know,' he said, that tidal wave of anger now settled to a moment of mild disconcertedness on a rippling sea. 'It's me. It's just so… Fuck, I hate this, Shauna.'

'I know. Can we talk about it?'

'What is there to talk about? It is what it is. Talking about it changes nothing.'

Just when I hoped he was opening up, the cell door slammed shut. I'd read all this stuff about how this kind of event in life pulls people together, bonds them. I didn't feel very bonded right now. I loved him, more than words, but this tumour had infected the connection between us and it was eating it away, so that no matter how hard I tried I couldn't reach him. We still laughed, still hugged, still kissed, still said 'I love you' ten times a day, but it all felt so surface, like it wasn't permeating the soul.

I wanted to tell him I was struggling, wanted to wail and rant about the unfairness of it all, but all that would achieve was bringing him down, reminding him what was ahead of him. I couldn't do it.

But weeks, months, of acting this way and I felt… Oh God, the boulder in my chest was back, cutting off my airways, making it impossible to block out the emotions that were winding around my heart like wild triffids attacking a tree, choking the life out of it with every second that passed. I had to say something. It had to be now. I tried to keep my voice even, controlled.

'I know, but Colm, I feel like we're losing each other. I feel like I'm fighting my battle and you're fighting yours, but we're not doing it together, taking strength from each other.' I hoped I was making sense and knew I only had a few more moments before all my breath was gone. 'I miss you. I miss what we had. We were always a team, and now, when it's harder than it's ever been, you won't talk, so I feel like I'm doing it on my own and so are you. We need to change this.'

As I said those last words, I watched his expression darken. 'Change it how? Isn't that the point? I can't fucking change this. None of it.' The waves of anger were back. He climbed off the bed, continued throwing things into the case, making it clear that as far as he was concerned the conversation was over.

I already regretted saying anything. I should just have kept quiet, carried on doing what I was doing, just being in the background, allowing him to play everything out his way.

'Colm, I'm sorry, I…'

He wasn't listening.

'You don't always get to be the hero, okay?' he raged. 'You don't always get to be the one that fixes things, that steps in and sorts everything out and solves all the problems.'

I couldn't understand what he was saying. None of it was making sense.

'What are you talking about?' I gasped, struggling for air.

'It's always you. When we were setting up the company, you were the one whose income facilitated that. We couldn't get pregnant, you kept on trying everything until it happened. When Annie died, you took care of everything. And now. Do you think I don't know the problems this has caused? I know how bad the money situation must be, but you just keep on swooping in, fixing things, taking control and solving the problems I'm causing. Me, Shauna!' He was properly yelling now. '*I'm* causing the problems and I know that. I can't drive, so I can't even pick up Beth. I can't plan stuff for the future. I can't take you out because you're always working. And there's not a fucking thing I can do about it except watch you keep it all going, stepping in to sort out my failings. Do you know how hard it is to watch you do that? And you act like it's all a fucking breeze.'

Something inside me snapped. 'A breeze? Hard to watch me? Are you kidding me?' Blind, white-hot fury, months of suppressed frustration and pure, raw, visceral grief took over. 'I'm screaming on the inside every sodding minute of every day! There isn't a moment since we found out about the tumour that I haven't had a knife in my gut, slowly twisting, ripping out my insides, but I knew that didn't matter. All that mattered was keeping everything going, making sure you had everything you wanted, playing it out your way! I wanted to keep a happy home for Beth and to do what I could to help you, so I just put a smile on my face and did it. But don't you fucking dare say it's a breeze, because

321

every single day I have to stop myself from screaming at the unfairness of it and begging you to help me deal with what's happening. I'm not playing the hero. Do you want to know the truth, Colm?'

He didn't reply, his face red with fury.

'The truth is that you don't get to do this. You don't get to refuse to open up to me, to demand it's played out your way and then resent me when I go along with it. You don't get to feel so bloody sorry for yourself that you can't see that you are breaking me in the process. You don't get to do this to us.'

'Yes I do! Because it's happening to me, Shauna! Not us! Me! I'm the one who's sitting here counting the days until I die!'

Tears blinding me, I staggered out of the room, scared of what I'd say if I stayed. No more. I couldn't do it any more.

But… did I really have a choice?

I was almost past Beth's room when I heard a murmur, so I backtracked and went inside, fearful that our shouts had woken her. Damn, how had I let it get so out of control?

Opening the door, I saw she was still sleeping, but restless, her beautiful face shadowed by a frown. In an instant all the rage dissipated, the pressure cooker had opened, and all that was left inside was pure, sodden grief. My legs buckled, so I held on to the wall, let it guide me to the bed, to my girl. I slipped in beside her once again, my face immersed in her blonde curls and I stayed there, until her hair was soaked with tears, until my love for her soothed me.

I heard a car horn outside, then the banging of the door, and only later when it was dark, and everything was completely still, did my thoughts clear enough for me to realize that he hadn't come to say goodnight to Beth.

On any other night that wouldn't be a problem.

But tonight that seemed like the biggest hurt of all, because something inside me understood what was really happening here. He was detaching himself from us. Letting go.

Or perhaps he was already gone.

32

2009

The Funeral

The room was packed with people, yet the volume was a low murmur, with the occasional sob, the occasional laugh, coming from different groups. Shauna was speaking to a gathering of elderly ladies, attempting to smile, but even from here I could see that her eyes were dead.

Dan wandered over and stood next to me. 'How is she doing?'

'I don't know,' I answered honestly. 'It's like she's going through the motions, saying the right things, doing what's expected, but it's almost...' I searched for the word, '...robotic. It's like she's still in shock.'

Dan shook his head mournfully. 'She probably is. To have to do what she did and then for it to be...'

He didn't finish. Didn't have to. Shauna had fought to keep Annie alive and the post-mortem had shown that it was all pointless. A massive stroke. Death was instant. Nothing

Shauna could have done would have saved her. Knowing that didn't stop her from blaming herself though.

'I don't know how to help her. To be honest, I'm not much good at this kind of stuff. Nothing I want to say sounds right.'

Dan shook his head. 'Then I hope you're a quick learner, because I think she's going to struggle. She told Lulu she can't contemplate a world without Annie. She's heartbroken.'

I sighed. 'She was all the family Shauna had. You can't count those two.' I nodded over to the other side of the room, where Shauna's mother was talking to Lulu, while her dad was in deep conversation with Rosie. It was good of the girls to step in and support her. They always did. Took the heat off me.

I'd tried, but the truth was that some people knew what to do in situations like this and some didn't. Seemed like whatever I did it was wrong. If I tried to cheer her up, she snapped at me. If I gave her space, she simply stopped speaking to me.

I just didn't know what to do. And if one more person told me it would get better in time, I may well resort to violence.

I saw her excuse herself from the group and quietly move away, heading through a heavy oak door to the foyer of the golf club. The venue had been Shauna's dad's choice, and he'd chosen to come here, despite Shauna's objections that Annie hated this place. 'Full of jumped-up tossers with an overinflated opinion of themselves. A bit like you, son,' she'd say to Jeff. She'd add a wink on to the end to soften the blow, but everyone knew she meant it. In all the time

I'd known Annie, she'd never backed down, never shirked the truth or turned her back on anyone who needed help. Shauna was a lot like her.

'Back in a minute,' I told Dan, then headed out after Shauna. Through the door, I looked left to the reception area and right to the corridor that led to another bar. Shauna was nowhere to be seen. I opted for left. I crossed the foyer, and headed to the entrance, two heavy, mahogany antique doors befitting a grand old building like this. I pushed one open, stepped out, the green grass of the practice area directly in front of me. I'd been here before, setting off on my annual round of golf with my wife's father. The irony was that for a shit parent, he was great company. Full of the chat and hilarious anecdotes. Full of the charm if there were ladies present. I couldn't work the guy out at all. Funny guy, crap father, Shauna always said, and she was absolutely right.

There was no sign of her and I was about to go back inside when I spotted the long bench off to the left, where the golfers stopped to make their final preparations before going on to the first tee. There were two people on it, their backs to me, facing off into the distance. I didn't need to see their faces to know who it was.

Shauna. Vincent.

Fair play to the guy, he'd been great. He'd told me what happened that night and I was so grateful that he was with Shauna, that she hadn't gone through that on her own. Since then, he'd called, dropped by, been there for her, and yes, I was well aware that some of those tasks should have been mine, but Vince seemed to do it so much better.

Like now. I could see Shauna's shoulders move, shudder,

and I guessed she was sobbing. Vincent put his arm around her and her head fell on his shoulder. That was it. No talking, no drama, just a quiet moment of solace.

I considered going over, but what would that achieve? Vincent was doing a great job of comforting her. Like I said, he did it so much better than me.

If nothing else, I knew my limitations, knew when I didn't have what someone needed. Coping with the death of a loved one rated pretty high on that scale. I didn't do death. I couldn't. A searing memory made an attempt to surface, and I pushed it back down. I wouldn't go there, wouldn't be one of those people who constantly relived the past, killing themselves with a million small cuts. No. Not today. Not ever.

So I backed up, slipped through the door and headed back inside, thankful to Vincent for taking my place.

33

2016

Going Back in Time

The cab driver was prattling on but I had absolutely no idea what he was saying. I'd zoned out before my arse hit the leather of the seats, grateful that he'd come early and got me out of there.

Fuck. Where had that all come from? One minute I was packing and the next we were screaming at each other and I was saying...

I can't even remember what I was saying, but I knew it hurt her. I could see it on her face, in the way she backed away. Disgust. That's what I saw. Maybe pity. Whatever it was, I couldn't deal with it, so I was out of there. Glad to be away, and just for one night I didn't have to watch her clear up, worn out, trying to pretend she was fine while looking like she'd rather be anywhere else but there. Well, me too.

My phone buzzed to signal an incoming text and I was tempted to ignore it. If it was Shauna, I didn't want to get into it again. I just wanted to be normal Colm. Not the husband with the brain tumour. Or the guy who was relying on his wife to pay the bills. Just me.

Eventually I looked. Not Shauna. Jess.

Hey Colm, can the boys come hang at your house this weekend? Sorry to spring this on you but bit of a situation here and would appreciate your help.

I had to read it twice. Bizarre. In all the years we'd been co-parenting, the only time I could ever remember Jess asking for help was when she was ill – once with flu, another time with a broken leg after falling off Joe's bike, and the third occasion, in hospital having her appendix removed. And they were nineteen now, so it wasn't as if they needed looking after.

I checked my watch. I'd already booked the taxi for way too early in case traffic was bad, and he'd turned up fifteen minutes before time. We hadn't hit a single jam so we were ahead of schedule. Sit at Euston for at least half an hour before the 9 p.m. train, or do a quick detour to check on Jess, see my boys and be bang on time for the later train at 9.40 p.m.? No contest. I'd do anything to wipe away the bad taste of what had just happened with Shauna.

'Change of plan, mate,' I told the driver, before giving him Jess's address. After she'd married Steve, they'd moved from Notting Hill to a swanky house overlooking Regent's Park, which was practically on the way to Euston

I let the taxi go at the gate, hoping Jess or Steve would give me a lift the rest of the way later.

Jess answered the door and I saw immediately I was right. Definitely ill. Her eyes were swollen and red, bloodshot too. Her skin was pale and her hair, usually shiny and straight, was pulled up into a riot of curls on top of her head. For a moment she looked nineteen again, the age she'd been when we met – no make-up, messy hair, always giggling. But that was before we got married, had the boys, before we lost… before we lost it all.

'Colm, what are you doing here?' her voice was thick and hoarse.

'Okay, so this isn't a line but I was, literally, passing when I got your text, so I thought I'd stop by, check everything was okay, see the boys.'

'They're not here,' she said, so quietly I strained to hear. Even I couldn't fail to miss the fact that my arrival was unwelcome though.

This wasn't turning out quite as I'd expected. Typical. The one time I decide to be spontaneous and check on someone else's well-being, this happens. Life was much simpler when I adhered to the more familiar territory of being a self-centred prick.

Awkward. 'Okay, well I'll just go and…' I wasn't sure what came next. I was standing on the doorstep like a pillock with my overnight bag and in possession of no plan whatsoever. I could just flag a cab. There was sure to be one passing any minute.

'Do you want to come in?'

Or I could just go in and have a cup of tea and scrounge a lift to the station off Steve, as per my original plan.

'Okay,' I replied.

I followed her to the kitchen, where she flicked the kettle on and took two cups from the cupboard. No sign of Steve. Bugger. I'd have a quick cuppa and phone a cab.

'So when did this come on you then?'

'When did what come on me?' she asked, spooning sugar into my cup. Too late I remembered her track record on hot beverages and wished I'd asked for a soft drink.

'The flu. How long have you been sick for?'

The spoon paused in mid-air and, bizarrely, she began to laugh, the kind of laugh that builds until its close to hysterics and there are tears running down your face – just like the ones she was wiping away now.

'Jesus, Colm, you really are frigging hopeless.'

'Why? What have I done?' Och, bollocks, what now? I couldn't do anything right today.

She composed herself enough to hand over my cup and I placed it on the table in front of me. I'd psyche myself up to drink it in a minute.

'I'm not sick, it's just been a bit of a tough week and today it got the better of me and I've spent most of it alternating between organizing stuff and indulging in some serious weeping. Don't judge me. You know I've always been a crier.'

That was true. It was the biggest difference between Jess and Shauna. Jess would blub at the slightest thing, while Shauna only spilled a tear under extreme circumstances. The only time I remember her truly breaking her heart was when Annie died. I wasn't sure she'd ever get over that, but of course, the days and weeks moved on and she did – although, only after Beth was born did the red-rimmed eyes finally become a thing of the past.

'Are the boys okay?' I asked, suddenly concerned that her state of upset was something to do with them.

'They're fine,' she reassured me, as she sat down on the leather stool next to me at the breakfast bar. 'I've sent them to my mother's for the night.'

'You could have sent them to me. They could just have stayed at our house all week. And by the way, of course they can come over this weekend. Just send them over when they get back from your mum's.'

'Thanks. I hope Shauna doesn't mind. I know she must have enough on her plate right now...'

That made me bristle slightly. Why would Shauna mind if they were there?

'Of course she wouldn't. She loves having them around.'

'They love her too. I don't know if I've ever told her, but I'm thankful for how great she's been to them.'

'I'll tell her you said that – she'll appreciate it.'

There was an uncomfortable pause, which I ended by jumping right in. 'So are you going to tell me what's happened here?'

'Steve and I have split up,' she said and puddles of tears filled her lower eyelids again. When a couple dropped down her cheeks, she wiped them away with the sleeve of her grey sweatshirt. 'Sorry. I don't even know why I'm crying. It's not like it's new or as if it's not what I want.'

Little cogs were clicking into place in my mind. The last time I was here... his behaviour... the trip to the office on a Sunday.

'He's seeing someone else?' I said calmly.

She nodded. 'He is. He swears he didn't start until after we split but I'm not so sure. Don't suppose it matters.'

'Of course it matters!' I didn't know the guy particularly well, but I thought he was better than that.

She shook her head dolefully, 'I really don't think that it does, and to be honest, I wouldn't blame him. It was me who ended it.'

That surprised me. I took a sip of tea and immediately spluttered. Sod this. 'Do you have any booze? A beer?'

'I've a bottle of tequila in the fridge.'

'That'll do nicely.' The train journey to Manchester would be a blur, but that probably wasn't a bad thing. I waited until she'd filled two shot glasses and we knocked them back. It burned the mouth off me, but it was still less painful than her tea.

I didn't understand any of this. They'd always seemed happy. Content. This didn't make sense.

'So why?' I asked, when my vocal cords recovered from the shock of the liquid.

'Why what?'

'Why did you end it?'

Jess shrugged. 'I didn't love him any more. I'm not sure that I ever really did. No, that's not true. Maybe in the beginning...'

'But you've been with him for years. Why stay if you didn't love him?' I tried to work out how long they'd been together. Ten years? Twelve? More? I couldn't remember, but it was definitely long-term.

'Because there was no reason not to. He loved me, we had a nice life, he was great with the boys. We were happy.'

None of this was making sense – or changing my firm conviction that there were some emotional situations that would forever be unfathomable to me. I knocked back another tequila. The heat as it passed my throat went straight to my nerve endings, forcing them out of the foetal position they'd been in since the fight with Shauna. I stretched my neck from side to side, enjoying the warm feeling as the muscles relaxed.

'So what changed?'

'You,' she told me, staring straight at me.

That one required another shot, before proceeding.

'Me? How?' Oh crap, what had I done? Had I said something? Caused a fight? If I had it wasn't deliberate and, shit, how was I going to explain this one to the kids?

'You got sick,' she said simply. 'And I saw how quickly and unexpectedly it could all be taken away and I decided…'

Another shot.

'I decided that I'd regret living a life where I never felt the kind of love you and I had ever again.'

That one came right out of left field. I had no idea. None. And I had no clue as to how to respond.

A single tear ran down her left cheek and this time it was me who leaned over and wiped it away. The timing sucked, but I really needed to go. I was going to miss my train if I didn't get out there and get a cab right now. Yet I felt like the biggest arse for leaving her like this.

'That was a different time, Jess. We were young. Had no worries. No cares. It was before life came and gave us a kicking.'

'I know,' she shrugged, almost embarrassed. 'But I have to hope it's out there and I'll find it again. Otherwise, what's the point?'

Again, I had no answer. She wanted to recreate something that was long gone, yet I understood that. How many times since the day I sat in the surgeon's office and heard him say 'brain tumour' had I wished I could go back, do stuff again, have another chance to relive the best bits? So many. It must have been the tequila but suddenly my eyes were stinging, my throat was tight, something deep inside me was hurting, a physical pain.

'Oh God, Colm, I'm sorry.'

'For what?'

She didn't answer. She just leaned towards me and stroked my cheek, and that's when I felt the wet tears, tasted the salt as they touched my lips, realized that they belonged to me.

Now Jess was wiping them away, and holding me as my shoulders shook, rubbing the back of my neck and...

My lips were on hers and I was kissing her, my tears mingling with hers, my desperation matching her need for me.

The train to Manchester left the station without me.

34

2009

After Annie...

Colm leaned over and kissed me. 'Right m'darlin, see you later – assuming you don't get a better offer and leave me for someone far more attractive.'

'That would never happen,' I objected. 'However, if it was someone with more money...'

He laughed as he opened the door and jumped out, grabbed his bag from the back seat, then stuck his head through the open window.

'You sure you're okay?' he said, serious this time. Concerned. What was I to say? No, I'm not. I'm dying inside. Sometimes the pain of Annie being gone hurts so badly I feel like my heart will stop and that would be a mercy. He didn't want to hear that. This was Colm. He wanted flippancy and cheer.

'I'm fine. Honestly. Now go.'

He blew me a kiss and headed off, throwing his bag

over his shoulder as he headed into Richmond station, the first leg of a journey that would end with two days of motivational training for an IT company in Brighton. Yes, the irony was glaring. Colm, the guy who liked an easy life, who preferred to take the stress-free, effort-free path and hope that everything would work out in the end, training other people in motivational techniques

I drove off, dread and depression blending with the relief of not having to keep a smile on my face for a second longer. I'd miss him, but the truth was I welcomed space to breathe. The car journeys on my own had become treasured moments of respite, the only time I could allow myself to feel. Sometimes it would overwhelm me and I'd pull over and just sob, buckled over in my seat, head thudding off the wheel until the physical pain overtook the one in my heart.

Today, I just kept going, driving towards the inevitable. Vincent had suggested that he do this job alone, but I'd refused. It was an eightieth birthday lunch for a darling lady I'd worked for before. When I'd taken the booking a couple of months ago, I'd commented on the coincidence.

'May 19th!' I'd exclaimed. 'That's my grandmother's birthday too. She'll be…' I quickly counted it up. 'Seventy-five this year.'

'Ah, a young thing,' Penelope had said, laughing.

There was no laughter now. Penelope had made it to eighty. Annie hadn't made it to seventy-five.

I felt my heart begin to race and a scalding heat work its way through me. I couldn't do this. I just couldn't. I should be picking my gran up today, taking her to lunch, maybe on to a show. Or throwing a party for her where she'd sing and dance and tell inappropriate jokes. Then at the end of the night, we'd drink tea and gossip until our sides hurt with laughing.

Suddenly, I couldn't face the void of having absolutely nothing to do but think about her. I was about to call Vincent, tell him I wasn't coming, but I stopped, Annie's voice echoing in my head. 'You just need to get on with it, love. No one else is going to do it for you. Just pick yourself up and keep going. You're a strong lass, Shauna, there's nothing you can't do.'

All my life I'd heard her say those things to me, or variations of them, and every time I'd roll my eyes and... well, get on with it. She'd instilled it in my DNA. The Annie gene. The one that was making me put my phone back down and drive to Penelope's house.

If Vincent was surprised to see me, he didn't show it. I was grateful there was no time to talk – we unpacked the food, set it up, served it, cleared it away, wished her a happy birthday, hugged her and left with her grateful thanks ringing in my ear. The whole time, I ignored Vincent's quizzical glances, answered his concerns over my well-being with a breezy, 'I'm fine.' I smiled at the relatives, admired their love for their matriarch, and closed my eyes when they threatened to burn with tears, before opening them, shaking it off, and carrying on, Annie still with me, talking, cajoling, reassuring, repeating her encouragement over and over. 'You just need to get on with it, love. No one else is going to do it for you. Just pick yourself up and keep going. You're a strong lass, Shauna, there's nothing you can't do.'

So I did it. I carried on. And I managed to do it until I

got out of the house, where Vincent had finished packing up the van.

'You did great today,' he said and we both knew why it mattered, but I was hanging on by a heartstring and I knew if he said one more sympathetic thing it would snap.

'Thanks. You too.' Bright. Breezy.

'Are you sure you don't want to come back to my house and hang there this afternoon? I've got no plans other than movie, food, very attractive snoring on the sofa while wearing nothing but my pants. Although obviously if you come I'll remain clothed.'

'Thanks. Tempting, but I'm fine. I'm just going to go home and chill.'

It was a lie. The truth was I didn't want to infect him with my sadness.

'You sure?' Concern and care were in every crease of his gorgeous face.

'Absolutely. I'll see you tomorrow.'

I jumped in my car and I drove off, waiting until I got to where I was going before I stopped, choked, let the grief consume me, rip me to shreds, dismantle me like Lego, piece by piece, until I was just skin and bones, and muscle, my heart and soul eviscerated.

Annie's grave had a simple headstone. Black. Gold writing. In the vase in front of it, the lilies I'd left there last week. They were wilted now. Next to them, the plant I'd left the day we buried her. A sunflower. It was her favourite. Nothing from anyone else. I doubted my parents even remembered where she was.

I sat on the grass. Just sat there. Closed my eyes. Formed a picture of her in my head. She was there. Laughing. 'How're you doing, my darling?' she was saying.

'I don't know how to do this without you, Gran.'

In my mind, she rolled her eyes, shook her head, a sad smile.

'Of course you do,' she said. Not harshly. Quietly. But in a way that conveyed she absolutely knew she was right. And then her image left me. I tried to get it back but it was gone. I ached with the loss, the feeling of unwanted solitude, a pain that was compounded by the distance that had grown between Colm and I.

Our crippling workloads and the fertility struggles hurt, but they were pushed aside by the pain of losing Annie and he wasn't the guy who could give emotional support. He just didn't have it in him. He tried to make me laugh when I wanted to cry. Tried to ignore my pain when I wanted to talk. Behaved like nothing was wrong, when nothing was right.

And all the while, the ache was still there.

So now I sat. Unable to move. Broken. Minutes passed. Hours. Still I sat. Staring. Numb.

At some point, I'm not sure when, I went back to the car, started the engine, pulled away. I've no idea how it knew where to go, or who was driving. I felt nothing. Made no decisions. It just happened. It moved until I was sitting at the end of the path, then I was out of the car, walking, banging on the door. It opened.

His face.

I didn't say a word.

Vincent opened his arms and I walked into them.

35

2016

Forsaking All Others

It was dark when I woke up, and for a moment I couldn't understand why I had warm breath on my neck and soft hair on my cheek. Beth. The smile was automatic, but followed by a pounding in the front of my scalp, the one that comes when you've fallen asleep crying.

Then I remembered. Colm. The fight. The things he said. The things I said.

My stomach churned with instant regret. How had that happened? How had we gone from packing a suitcase to screaming at each other with such malice, saying such cruel things?

I knew he didn't mean them. I didn't either. The words had come from his damaged brain and my fragmented heart. Damn. I just wanted to rewind yesterday and have him here with me.

I pushed myself up and rearranged Beth's cover so that

she was snuggled up in the warmth of the duvet, then padded out of the room.

Downstairs, the house was in darkness, so I flicked on the kitchen light as I searched for my mobile phone. Found it. I checked the screen. There were a couple of messages – one from Lu, one from Rosie, one from Joe. I quickly read them, then checked the time – after midnight. Too late to call or text back.

Nothing from Colm. For a moment the hurt resurfaced but I pushed it away. How could I judge or criticize anything he did? How was a dying man supposed to act? There was no handbook or guidelines. Sure, he'd lashed out at me, but that's what happened in any lifetime – people in pain took it out on those closest to them. And this was so much more than that. It was a guy facing the certainty of losing a future. And how had I responded? By fighting back, unloading a whole load of petty, self-centred stuff that, while true, I should have been smart and strong enough to handle. Bugger, what an idiot. All I wanted to do right now was hear his voice, hold him, make this right.

I dialled his number, not even thinking through what I was going to say, other than the fact that it would start with 'sorry'. No answer. It rang out then went to voicemail. Maybe it was on silent. Yes, that would be it. He'd have put it on silent on the train, in case he got an incoming call that disturbed the other passengers. Or maybe he left it on the train. His memory was getting worse by the day.

I did a calculation in my head and realized Colm would have checked into the hotel, a five-minute walk from the station, half an hour ago. He'd still be awake.

I searched my phone for the copy of the confirmation email, then dialled the number. It was answered immediately and I asked to be put through to Colm's room.

There was a pause on the other end, and I heard the click of nails on a keyboard. 'I'm sorry, but Mr O'Flynn hasn't checked in yet.'

'Are you sure? It would have been about an hour ago.'

'Absolutely positive. I've been here since ten o'clock and he definitely hasn't arrived.'

'Okay, thank you.' I disconnected, a creeping sense of unease rising. I chided myself. Don't panic. The train must have been late. Of course, that was it.

Back on my phone, I connected to the internet and checked the real-time arrivals for Manchester station. 9 p.m. train, arrived on time.

The unease escalated, a chill of anxiety added on for good measure. I'd known this was a bad idea. Why had I let him do it? He could have collapsed, maybe had a seizure – the surgeon had said seizures were a possibility. Or maybe he was so exhausted that he'd fallen into a deep sleep and was now lying on an empty train in a deserted Manchester station.

I tried his phone again – still no answer.

Full-scale panic now. What to do? I couldn't phone the police. They'd laugh when I said he'd been missing for an hour. I tried the hotel again and recognized the same voice as before. 'I'm really sorry, but it's me again. Has my husband checked in yet?'

'I'm sorry, but he hasn't.' Her voice oozed sympathy.

My heart was racing now, my legs shaking. What should I do? I had nothing. No clue. Who could I call at this time?

I settled for texting the only person I knew who'd be up.

Are you awake?

Send.
Lulu replied immediately.

Yep. You okay?

No. Can't find Colm. Prob overreacting but he hasn't checked into hotel. Am freaking out.

Send.

I'm coming over now.

No, don't! Like I said am probably overreacting. Will call hotel again. You don't need to come. Don't want to create a drama.

Send.
My heart was already racing, hands shaking.

'I'm here.' That wasn't a text. It was Lulu's voice, behind me, marching in the back door, in men's boxer shorts and a gent's shirt, wearing a pair of Converse trainers several sizes too big. 'Sorry, it was this or the sequined mini-dress I was wearing when I entered your garage two hours ago.'

'You're spending the night with Dan?' I asked, astonished.

'I know. Go figure. I bumped into him at a bar tonight, and yes, I realize there's humour in having a one-night stand with your own husband.'

'But why didn't you go to your own house?'

'Dunno,' she shrugged. 'Here was closer and we were horny and…'

'Stop! I beg you. I don't need details.'

'Sorry. So what's happened?'

The panic that had been temporarily assuaged by the surprise of her arrival came flooding back. 'Colm's train arrived in Manchester just after 11 p.m. It's less than a five-minute walk to the hotel, but he's not there yet.'

'The train could have been late?' she suggested.

'Nope, I checked. It arrived on time. He's not answering his phone. He hasn't checked in. What if something's happened to him, Lu?' The pitch of my voice was strangled by the thought. 'We had a huge fight tonight. Huge. The worst ever. He stormed out and… where is he, Lu? I need to find him. I need to say sorry, to tell him that I…' Pause. Another realization. 'This was the first time I can ever remember not telling him I love him as he went out the door.'

'Shhhhhh,' Lu murmured, with uncharacteristic softness as she wrapped her arms around me. 'We'll find him. There will be a simple explanation and we'll laugh. I promise. It's going to be fine.'

The logical side of my brain knew that assurance was based on absolutely no fact or knowledge, yet the synapse that controlled desperation grabbed on to it. It was going to be fine.

'Okay, fire up your laptop for me,' she said, and call the hotel one more time.

I did both. He still wasn't there.

When the screen came alive, Lulu clicked on to the

MacBook Air's internet browser and I watched as she double-checked the train times. 'It definitely arrived on time,' she said, telling me what I already knew. She clicked on to a couple of news sites, then the Manchester police Twitter feed. Nothing to report.

She sat back for a moment, thinking. 'Do you know the password for Colm's iTunes account?' she asked.

'Lulu, I don't want to listen to music. I just want to find...'

'It's not for the music,' she cut me off, her fingers manipulating the silver pad on the keyboard, the curser heading to the search bar, where she typed in iCloud.com.

The sign-in box came up and she entered Colm's email address, then paused at the next box. 'What's his password?'

This felt wrong. It was an invasion of privacy. A step over a line. But I was worried sick that he was lying somewhere, ill or hurt, or – I tried to block the thought but it came anyway – worse. There was no line I wouldn't vault over to find him.

'Beth2001,' I told her. Our daughter and the year we met.

'Okay, we're in.'

I wasn't religious, but thank God.

She flicked across the screen of icons and clicked on a green square, labelled 'Find My iPhone.' Click.

'How do you know this stuff?' I asked.

'I'm an unfaithful woman with a suspicious mind. You've no idea the stuff that I've learned over the years. Dan can't fart without me knowing about it.'

Back on screen, a map appeared, then the focus zoomed in to a circle in the middle, going around, contemplating the answer. Eventually the map moved again and the circle stayed still. I tried to understand.

'Zoom out,' I asked, and Lu adjusted the screen. London. He was still in London? How could that be? Oh God, did he not even make it to the train? Did the stress of our fight cause some kind of blood pressure overload and he'd passed out somewhere? Was he in hospital right now only minutes away from here?

Lulu zoomed in again, and this time I registered the street that the circle had rested on. A4201. Outer Circle. The road that ran around the perimeter of Regent's Park.

'Hang on, that can't be...'

Yet it was. Lulu switched to street view, and yes, there was the gorgeous crescent of houses, one of which was inhabited by Colm's ex-wife and children.

'He's with Jess?' I said, my comprehension struggling with the information.

Lulu was equally perplexed, but slightly more pragmatic. 'He must have gone to see the kids. Perhaps there was a problem. Or one of them was unwell.'

'They're fine,' I said, using words that sounded so detached it was like they were coming from someone else.

'How do you know?'

I pressed a few buttons on my phone, opened the text I'd received earlier from Joe.

Hi Jess. Can you tell dad we're staying at gran's house tonight? If he wants to play pool he can come over.

I let her read it before clarifying. 'It came in while I was sleeping. The boys are at Jess's mum's house. Nowhere near Regent's Park.'

Lulu could see where I was going with this and tried to head me off. 'Shauna, don't. Colm would never do that. And besides, Steve will be there. Colm probably popped in, ended up having a beer and crashed on the couch.'

I shook my head, still trying desperately to make some kind of sense of this. 'They've split up.'

Lulu's eyes widened. 'What? You're kidding.'

'Nope. I overheard the boys talking at the weekend. Davie was telling Joe that Steve was moving out this week, but that their mum didn't want anyone to know yet. I'd assumed I'd heard wrong, but now it makes sense. Colm is with Jess.'

And there was no outcome to this that could be good for us.

The thought that he'd run to her after we'd had a fight hurt.

The other possible conclusion was... I couldn't even finish the thought. He wouldn't. Surely, he could never do that.

Both our eyes returned to the tiny circle, on a map. The one that had just exploded a bomb in my life.

36

2009

Shauna and Vincent

Wordlessly, Vincent took me through to the lounge, where he sat me down, wrapped a soft throw around my shoulders, then knelt in front of me, his arms enveloping me. He held me, the silence only broken by our breathing, no words needed or wanted.

I was numb. Void. Until slowly, with exquisite pain, an honesty unfurled inside me and I knew why I was there.

'I need you,' I whispered.

I felt his body flinch, before he eased back, to see my face, to check what he'd heard. He saw that he was right.

'Shauna, you don't. Oh God, I wish you did. I so wish you did.'

'Vincent…' I reached over, put my hand on his heart, felt it beating under my touch, fast, hard.

'Don't do this, Shauna. Not like this.'

I could hear what he was saying, but I wasn't listening. 'Please…'

'No.' It was soft, thick with sorrow. He ran his fingers through his hair, groaned, then touched my face. 'I love you,' he said simply, but he didn't have to because right then I realized that I knew. Even before Carole told me. I'd always known. 'I've been in love with you for so long I can't remember a time when I wasn't. But I don't want it to be like this,' he said. 'Not when you're vulnerable and hurt. It would feel… wrong. Like I was taking advantage of your pain. And I know… Don't worry, I know. You love Colm. You always have. And I hate that he doesn't see you, doesn't know what he has.'

'Vincent, please…' I stopped, the words refusing to form.

He stood up. 'I'm going to go to bed now, before either of us says or does something that can't be undone. And tomorrow, we'll pretend this never happened, smile and carry on like everything is fine. The way you do every day.'

Ouch, that last one stung, the puncture mark deeper because we both knew it was true.

I watched him go, then lay back, closed my eyes. He loved me. Right now, right here, I felt like he was the only one who did. My parents gave nothing. Annie was gone. Colm and I were in a warped existence where I no longer knew what was real and what was fake.

Vincent loved me. And just for tonight, no matter how selfish that made me, I needed to know what that felt like.

Without making a sound, I stood up, crossed the room, climbed the stairs, leaving behind a trail of clothing as I went. His bedroom door was open, and I saw him in the half-light, lying on top of the bed, his head turning to me as he registered that I was there.

I walked to him, naked, raw, every nerve, every sense needing to touch him, lie with him, feel him next to me, inside me.

'Shauna…' he whispered, before I silenced him with the gentlest of kisses.

This time he didn't say no.

37

2016

Colm and Jess

It was the light streaming in the window that woke me, but the pounding headache that immediately followed was what delayed the realization of where I was. When it came, I felt an overwhelming groan permeate from every pore. Fuck. What had I done?

The space beside me in the bed was empty, so I got up, and then had to put a hand against the wall to steady myself. My head was actually spinning. Thank you, tequila.

I couldn't see my clothes, so I grabbed a towel from the en suite and wrapped it around my waist, then headed out of the door, not even sure how to get downstairs. Bollocks. I was supposed to be in Manchester and instead I was in London, in my sons' house, waking up after spending the night with their mother. This was so many levels of wrong, it made my head pound even harder.

'Morning,' Jess said, as I entered the kitchen. In bare feet and denim cut shorts, a white baggy T-shirt and her hair tied up in a ponytail, she was fresh-faced and functioning so much better than me. She clocked my outfit. 'Sorry, I was going to bring your clothes up. They're on the chair.'

She gestured to the seats at the breakfast bar, where we'd been sitting last night. Oh fuck. We'd had sex there, on the counter. Then I'd carried her upstairs, with her laughing as she gave me directions on which way to go, and we'd made love again in bed. Her bed. Twice.

Again. Fuck. What had I done?

She slid a coffee in front of me, but I didn't lift it. The irony wasn't lost. A hot drink was how this had all started last night. Actually, that wasn't true. The fight with Shauna was how it started. Oh God, Shauna. A flashback delivered snippets of what I'd said to her last night and I groaned.

'Flashback?' Jess said, sitting across from me this time. Her tone was tentative, almost sad.

'Yeah,' I replied.

'Thanks. Men always groan with horror when they realize they've slept with me.'

'No, no, it wasn't that!' I rushed to clarify, even though I knew she was taking the piss. 'It's Shauna. Last night. We had a fight before I came here.'

'I know.'

I tried to remember if we'd discussed it. 'Did I tell you about it?'

'No, but maybe you should.'

I shook my head. 'Somehow that would feel... disloyal.' Even as I said it, I realized how stupid it sounded. Yeah, repeating a conversation was disloyal. Screwing your ex-wife? A trifling misdemeanour.

'Okay, let me have a shot at it,' she said, softly, like she was teasing a thorn from my flesh and talking to me gently to take my mind off the pain. 'Since you found out you have the tumour, you've gone to that place between denial and numbness, where you ignore the problem, pretend everything is going to be okay. You've convinced yourself that it doesn't exist, even though something inside knows that it does. And it's that bit of you that makes you angry, makes you want to push everyone away because you're hurting. But you cover that up, act like it's all easy, life's a joke and you're not going to accept the alternative.' She stopped, looked at me. 'How am I doing so far?'

I didn't need to answer. She could see the truth on my face.

She carried on, 'Every time you look at Shauna it reminds you of what's happened and what's going to happen. So not only do you back off from her, but you get irritated, block out her feelings. You're pushing her away with your indifference and you know she's hurting but you can't bring yourself to help her or be there for her because that means acknowledging the reality of what's happening. If she shows even a glimpse of vulnerability, you close it down, brush it off.'

She stopped, waited for a response.

'How do you do that?' I asked, aware that we both knew the answer.

She told me anyway. 'Because history repeats itself.'

We both sat with that one for a moment, the honesty of it searing, yet in a strange way comforting. There was something in the fact that Jess knew all this about me, knew my worst flaws, and yet we were here, two decades later, sitting round the table, pretending to drink her coffee.

Although, there was nothing comforting at all about what had happened here a few hours ago. Christ, what had I been thinking?

'Jess... last night.' It was as far as I got, before I ran out of words.

'Last night was incredible,' she said softly. A boulder of guilt came crashing down on top of me, only lifting when she went on. 'I'm not even sure how or why it happened. The alcohol didn't help, but I think I just wanted to...' she paused, thinking it through, '... feel like I used to. Only I didn't. We both know it was a one-time thing. We're not those people any more. We're not the teenagers who fell in giddy love. I'll always love you, Colm, but I don't want to go back there with you. I don't think you want that either.'

Once again I was struck by the wisdom of this woman that I'd married and somehow let go. 'No, I don't.' But it wasn't that simple. I struggled to find the right words to convey how I felt about her. In the end, I went for the truth. 'You're amazing,' I told her honestly. 'Except when you make coffee.'

That made her laugh, but only briefly, before her body language became a rueful shrug.

'Not feeling amazing right now. I don't know that I'll ever come to terms with sleeping with another woman's husband. Not my finest moment,' she admitted, tears pooling in her eyes again. 'What are you going to do about Shauna?'

'I don't know. How do I tell her this? She doesn't deserve

it. Jesus, I'm a prick. I can't even begin to explain how much she's put up with, everything she's done... But that's the problem. She said last night I resented her for coping, for taking care of everything. I think she's right. Now I think maybe she wasn't coping as well as I thought.'

'She was being strong for you,' Jess added, as always going straight to the truth of it.

'I see that now, but at the time I think that made me feel... The truth? I think it dented my ego, because she was the one taking everything on and not me.'

Jess nodded. 'But she couldn't win, because if she'd fallen apart and looked to you for support, you wouldn't have been there for her because you're doing what you always do. Bad stuff isn't happening. What was it you always used to say? "Blind faith and optimism".'

'Christ almighty. What a prick I am,' I said again. I could keep saying it all day, yet it still didn't begin to cover my stupidity. 'How did I ever get you two to fall in love with me?'

'You have an unusually large penis.'

'Do I? How did I not know this?'

'No,' she retorted, giggling. 'You really don't.'

Suddenly I was laughing, then in an emotional repeat of last night, there were tears. Nothing for twenty years then twice in twelve hours. What was happening to me? There was more I wanted to say, stuff I suddenly needed to share, but I knew that I would be sharing it with the wrong woman. I needed to see Shauna.

I needed to tell her what I'd done, tell her how I hated myself for it, beg her to forgive me. I loved her so much and I'd completely fucking blown it, right from the minute I'd walked out the door last night, being a stubborn dickhead. I hadn't even told her I loved her before I left. I couldn't stand the thought that she wouldn't believe me after this.

'What am I going to do, Jess? She'll never forgive me.'

'Don't tell her.'

'I have to.'

'Why? To make yourself feel better? To salve your conscience? Telling her will only cause her even more pain and you've no right to do that. Go to Manchester this morning, have your meeting, come home, and love your wife. Make it right. Don't add to her heartache. She doesn't deserve it.'

She was right. I knew she was. I just didn't know whether I could live with the guilt… or die with it.

38

2009

Then There Was Everything

I kneeled on the grass and closed my eyes, waiting for the image to come, so that I could tell her my news. My incredible news.

When I woke up this morning, this wasn't in the plans. Colm had rolled over and hugged me, kissed me good morning and then we'd made love.

That happened sometimes. It was all part of the healing that had started five months ago, on that night with Vince when we... I didn't finish the thought. Vincent had been right in everything he'd said that night, every reason he'd given that we shouldn't go there was true. I should have listened to him, but I'd been too damn selfish. Or maybe I just hoped it would be the answer. Perhaps all those years, when Vincent was always there and I thought of him as nothing more than a friend, maybe somewhere deep inside I was wondering what it would be like, how it would feel.

Now I knew.

The morning after I spent the night at his house, I'd woken up, and my answer was there.

He wasn't Colm.

Vincent was beautiful, and caring, and he'd stayed right by my side when I needed him. He'd shared the most painful thing that had ever happened to me, held me up, refused to let me drown. And perhaps for a moment I'd thought there should be more than we already had. Maybe even hoped…

But even through the tidal wave of guilt, I knew that I didn't love him the way I loved Colm. Colm was my heart, he was everything. No one else had ever, or could ever come close.

Silently, I'd slipped out of bed, left before Vincent opened his eyes, regret and overwhelming guilt leading the way. Later, he'd come to the house, let himself in and stood, lines of tiredness on his beautiful face, leaning against the door frame, a few feet away from where I sat at the kitchen table.

'Hey…' he said.

'Hey.'

'You left.'

'I'm sorry. I had to.'

The flicker of pain across his eyes told me he understood. It took a moment before he spoke with resigned sadness, only a hint of a question in there. 'It was only once?'

I sat there surrounded by my life, by Colm's things, by the world we'd built together. Sleeping with Vince had been a mistake, a desperate mistake, but a foolish one nonetheless. Slowly, I nodded. 'It has to be.'

'Okay,' he said, his jaw set, as if forbidding him to say more.

'Please don't hate me, Vincent. I know it was selfish, I know…'

'Shauna, stop.' He sighed, not moving, still standing feet away, unwilling to be near me. 'I don't hate you. But last night, I meant what I said and I don't know how to take it back. I just wish… you know.'

I did. And in a different way, I loved him too. My life was so much better when he was in it, but inside, in that place I'd been trying to numb when I was with him, I knew I'd used him. Like a desperate person cuts their flesh to ease the pressure of a deeper pain, I was self-harming my life with Colm, eviscerating it in the hope that the new scab would cover the old wound until it healed. It hadn't. It was Colm I should have gone to, not Vince.

'I know,' I said. 'But I won't leave him, Vincent. I love him. I shouldn't have come to you, and I'm so sorry…'

'Me too.' I could see he wasn't going to plead, or try to change my mind and I was so grateful.

The vacuum between us swallowed our words until many more seconds ticked by. Vincent was the first to find his voice. 'I can't even regret it. I guess at least now I know.'

'Would you ever have told me?'

'I doubt it. Not while you and Colm were still together. I wouldn't have forced you to choose in a competition that I knew I'd lose. I guess that's what's happened now.' The corners of his mouth turned up in a sad smile. 'But I don't know where to go from here.'

I exhaled, heart aching. I'd thought about this since the moment I'd left his bed. Twenty years of friendship had made him part of me, a part that I didn't want to live without.

'I don't deserve your forgiveness, or your friendship, so it's up to you. I'd like to keep going, just be who we were, do what we were doing.'

'Pretend it never happened?' Another sad smile, but no bitterness in his voice.

'Yes.' I knew I was being brutal, asking too much. I had no right to ask anything more of him.

Another vacuum, then a despondent sigh. 'Okay. I don't know how that's going to work, but I think it's the only thing we can do...' he shrugged, saying nothing, saying everything.

'Me too. Vincent... thank you.' I meant it. With every ounce of me, I meant it.

We'd loved each other – maybe, we knew now, in different ways – for two decades. Somehow, we'd find a way back from this.

And in a way, we had.

Since May, we'd carried on, never spoken of it again, and sure, there were moments of awkwardness at the start, but we'd got over them. Within a couple of weeks it was back to normal on the surface, both of us refusing to dive underneath the calm seas.

A brief chapter in my life had closed.

This morning, on a bright October day, a brand new one had opened.

After Colm and I made love this morning, I'd watched him leave, then closed my eyes, hoping to snatch another couple of hours of sleep before he returned with the boys.

I'd almost dozed off, when my eyes flew open, an awareness rippling through me. I knew. I spent the next hour checking, but it only confirmed what was already a certainty.

I left a note on the kitchen table for Colm and grabbed the keys to the van, driving slowly, carefully, my need to share the news balanced by the need to adjust to the new reality.

When I reached my destination, I jumped out, slammed the door behind me and I ran until I got there, sunk to my knees, the wet grass causing stains that spread across the denim of my jeans.

'Gran,' I said, reaching out to touch the hard granite, my fingers skipping past the details, only tracing the words on the three lines that meant the most to me.

Bethany 'Annie' Williams.

1930 – 2005.

Forever loved.

'It's me,' I said, just like I always did, every week when I came, sat here, talked to her.

'Something's happened,' I told her. 'Although, you probably know already.'

I could picture her now, cowboy boots and a cigarette, tea in hand, waiting for me to continue.

'Gran, I'm pregnant.'

My hand went over my mouth and was immediately soaked with tears.

Pregnant. After all this time, after the drugs, and tests and the legs up the bloody wall, I'd finally fallen pregnant when I'd given up hope.

'I think you had something to do with it. I can't believe that you didn't. So thank you, Annie. With all my heart. Thank you so much. I promise you, I'll make this baby's life amazing.'

In my mind, Annie threw her head back and let rip with that raucous cackle of pure joy.

This was everything. The whole world. But I knew it had to come with a trade.

One love for another.

39

2016

Secrets and Lies

I was there. I was knocking on the door and praying there would be no answer. Yet I wasn't walking away. If I left right now, this would go no further, but if I didn't, it couldn't be undone. Still, I stayed. Banging on the door now. Desperately hoping no one would come.

The door opened and I spoke with a calm that contradicted everything I was feeling inside.

'You slept with my husband.'

Jess said nothing for a moment and I was sure she was trying to come up with a plausible lie, or a deflection that would give her time to lodge a defence.

'I did,' she said, like she was admitting to spilling milk or skipping a queue, while those two words had just shredded my life. She stood back to let me enter and as I passed I felt a fleeting urge to punch her, but I resisted. What would be the point? She closed the door and I waited until she led the way to the kitchen. She looked younger somehow. Perhaps it was the jeans and the simple blue T-shirt. Or the fact that her hair, usually so sleek, was piled up on top of her head in a messy bun. Or maybe it was just that she fucked my husband last night.

I'd looked after this woman's children for fifteen years. I'd never once caused waves. Even when Colm and I barely had the cash to eat, I'd made sure she got her maintenance payments. Yet she'd had no compunction in taking away the one thing that was mine. I was losing him already, but this was different. At least the other way, I could have pretended to myself he wanted to stay. Not now.

I'd spent the whole night just staring at that green dot on the map. I'd been tempted to go round there to confront them, but I hadn't. I couldn't bring myself to face the truth. Maybe that made me a coward. Instead, I watched the dot, my heart breaking when it finally moved at 7 a.m. Euston station. Then north. Stopping at Manchester. That's where he was right now.

I had no idea where he was coming back to. Our home? Here?

He must have seen my missed calls by now, yet he still hadn't contacted me.

Was it over?

'Would you like tea?' How pathetically civil.

'No.'

I couldn't even sit. I just leaned against the polished black granite of the breakfast bar. A thought stabbed my heart. Had Colm fucked her on there? Or in the chair in the corner? Or in the hallway? Or did they wait until they got upstairs and christen every room? Hell, maybe they'd done it before. Maybe they'd never stopped. Perhaps he'd been shagging her since the day they got divorced and it was a miracle I hadn't found out before now.

'How long?' I hated that I sounded like a cliché.

'Just last night.'

My expression told her I didn't believe her.

Sighing, she pulled out a high leather chair and climbed on to it.

'Shauna, I'm not going to lie to you, but let me start by saying I'm so, so sorry. It was once, I swear. I'll answer everything you need to know.'

'How could you?'

That stumped her.

'You think that because you've split with Steve you can just swoop right in and take Colm from me?'

She didn't ask me how I knew.

'No. I'm not trying to take him. Last night wasn't the start of something.'

'So what was it?' I saw tears spring to her eyes and I wanted to scream. *She* slept with *my* husband and *she* was the one who was crying? I don't fucking think so.

'It was... desperation. Unhappiness. Sadness.'

So now she was just throwing out nouns.

I was pacing, unable to stand still, unwilling to touch a single surface in this house in case my husband's flesh had been there. Right now, the husband that I loved, disgusted me.

She carried on talking. 'Have you ever been so desperate, in so much pain, that you would reach out to anyone who was there, just to feel someone touch you?'

That stopped me, an image from the past flashing in front of my eyes. Six years ago. Vincent. Me. Naked. Hungry for each other, every movement fuelled by a craving for solace on my part, for reciprocation of love on his.

She was watching me, saw that her words had resonated.

Suddenly, I was wrangling with a new question. Why did I get to sleep with someone else, yet here I was, raging at Colm for doing the same? What utter hypocrisy. And back then, I'd blamed the pain of loss, but that had to be surpassed by what Colm was facing now.

I was a lying, cheating hypocrite, so perhaps I had no right to judge anyone.

'But why you? What could you give him that I couldn't?' I demanded, my fight weakened, but still there.

'Nothing,' she replied.

The adrenalin was wearing off and my legs were beginning to feel like they might not hold me much longer, so I relented on the seat, taking the one that was furthest along the breakfast bar from Jess. Deflated I may be, but I still didn't trust myself. 'Then why?'

Jess exhaled sadly. 'Maybe a bit of nostalgia. The chance to feel like we were nineteen again. No worries. No cares. It wasn't me he wanted, Shauna, I promise you. It was the chance to be that person again, be that young guy, just for one night, to feel that his life could still have an amazing future.'

I hated that I understood that. I hated even more that he chose to claw that feeling back with Jess and not me. Why her? Why now? If he wanted to revisit the past, why didn't he want to try to recapture the bliss of our early days together?

I stared at my hands, entangled so tightly that my knuckles were white. 'So what now? Does he want to be with you?'

'No. He really doesn't. He was in a complete state this morning – devastated over what he's done. Please don't let this come between you. He loves you. Only you. And I know I said it already, but I'm so sorry, Shauna. I've never been that woman before and I never will again. I'm not proud of myself, but for a moment, through a tequila haze, I saw a chance to have a resolution that we never got when we parted.'

'Did it work?' I so hoped that it didn't.

'No.'

'Good.' I didn't want her to have any satisfaction at all.

My jaw was starting to ache from clenching my teeth together to stop me from screaming, shouting, crying.

There was a long pause, neither of us rushing to fill it, both unsure where this was going now. I'd come here furious, apoplectic with hurt and grief, and yet now there had been a shift in the narrative and I wasn't sure how I felt any more.

Had Colm cheated on me under normal circumstances, we would have been having a different conversation. With no one to fall back on, no other family in my life, I needed the stability of unconditional and unassailable trust in a relationship. Now Colm had broken that, I should be gone.

Yet I knew that my time with Vincent made that a double standard.

Before Colm got sick, infidelity would probably have been a deal-breaker, but this life we were living now was no longer black and white.

I realized that Jess was staring at me, waiting for my next attack. In almost fifteen years, the longest conversation we'd ever had was about her screwing my husband. I'd never have seen that one coming.

Something else was replaying in my head. A comment that raised an unanswered question.

'What did you need to resolve?' I asked her, going back to what she'd said a few moments before.

She thought for a moment. 'When we split up we were so angry. Cancel that. *I* was so angry with him. I thought he'd destroyed every shred of love I had for him, but now I realize that I just didn't understand him. I didn't know him well enough. Maybe now I'm a bit wiser. I see him acting the same way now with you and I recognize it and know that it's not out of a lack of love or care, but because when the worst things happen in life, he simply doesn't know how to act any other way. I think I needed to forgive him.'

'By screwing him?'

A tired, apologetic shrug. 'I didn't say it made sense.'

Another silence while I processed that, not sure that I understood.

'Why were you angry with him? What had he done?'

For the first time, there was a question in her calm demeanour. 'He never told you why we split up?'

'He just said you grew apart.'

Her whole body visibly shuddered and I could see more tears showing up, just ready to flow. 'We lost a baby. A girl. Daisy. She was stillborn. A perfect, beautiful, little girl.' Jess had to stop, take a breath.

Sympathy overwhelmed me. Oh God, poor Jess. Poor Colm. Why had he never told me? I reached out, took her hand.

'You don't have to…'

She cut me off. 'I do.'

For many moments there was nothing but the sound of her sobs before she went on, her voice cracking with pain, her words floating on a sea of sorrow.

'It was after the twins. It seemed like life was perfect. We were so in love and we had these two incredible little boys and it was everything we had dreamt of. When I fell pregnant we were overjoyed and when we found out it was a girl… I can remember wondering how I got so lucky. How we had managed to build a perfect life. We wanted her so, so much. There was no warning. Everything was so good, so happy, and then suddenly it wasn't and we never knew why. Her heart stopped when I was in labour, they did everything they could, an emergency C-section, they took her out, tried to save her, tried to bring her perfect little body to life, but she couldn't come back, couldn't stay with us.'

Instinctively, without questioning, I was out of my seat and my arms were around her and I had no idea where her tears stopped and mine started. We both cried. For that little girl. For us. For Colm.

The world changed before either of us spoke again. I saw now. I understood so much more.

Only when she was still did I let her go.

'After Daisy died…'

I put my hand on hers. 'Jess, you don't have to tell me any more.'

'I want to,' she said. 'After Daisy died everything changed. I was inconsolable, lost. I couldn't function, couldn't exist without her. Colm handled it so differently. He wanted to move forward, block it out, act like it hadn't happened. He couldn't deal with my grief and I hated him for not sharing it. Of course he did, somewhere inside, but he wasn't capable of showing it and even less capable of supporting me. When he looked at me all he saw was a pain that he couldn't take away. He couldn't bear to watch my suffering so he shut me out. It got so that I couldn't stand to be in the same room as him.' She rubbed her palm across her sodden cheek. 'We couldn't recover. Couldn't make it work.'

My mind raced to absorb everything she said, so much of it revealing reasons, providing explanations. Colm's reluctance to have more children. His inability to deal with heartbreak. A hopelessness that manifested as a lack of care. Jess had worked through it all and come to a place of understanding and acceptance.

Somewhere deep in my soul, I knew that I could too.

'I'm so sorry, Jess. Truly.'

'Thank you. I am too.' It took a few seconds for that to sit before she lifted the tone, moved back to more recent ground. 'But none of this excuses what I did and I don't think that it does. I want you to know that.'

'I know. But it explains so much. Not just about last night, but about our life together. Kind of wish we'd had this conversation ten years ago,' I said, squeezing her hand. 'I need to know, though. Do you want to be with him?'

She didn't hesitate. 'No.'

The wave of gratitude that crashed over me was all-consuming.

'Why not?'

'Because it's you he's in love with, not me. And because...' she stopped, choosing her words. 'Because I couldn't lose him twice.'

The bolt of pain cracked my heart, followed by a surge of empathy I could never have anticipated. We were no different, Jess and I. We were both losing our husband, an imperfect, infuriating, but special man, and the only difference was timescale.

Pragmatism kicked in and I needed to know what was next, how to move on, now that I knew we had a future, however short. I just needed to get him back.

'How was it left this morning, Jess? Did you discuss what happens next?'

'Yes. There will be nothing between Colm and me, I promise. He's yours. And I told him not to tell you what happened last night, but I don't know if he can do that.'

I immediately knew that she was right. There was too much pain, too many boundaries that had been irrevocably broken. If we had to wade through the mire of our mistakes we'd never make it to the other side. We had to keep it all in a box, sealed tight, buried under the seabed, never to be reopened.

'He has to. If he gets in touch with you today, tell him again to say nothing to me. Tell him it would affect the boys, it would cause too much damage... anything. Just make him promise not to tell me.'

'Can I ask why?'

It was time to match her truth and, strangely, I had no qualms at all about trusting her. 'Because a long time ago I did something I regret. If Colm tells me about you, then I'll have to go there too and we might not have time to recover from that. I can't have whatever time he has left wrecked by deceit and mistrust and more pain. I love him too much to let that happen. He's dying, Jess. Counting days. There's nothing to be gained from the truth here. And I need you to help me, make him see it's the only way.'

For a moment I thought she was going to ask what I'd done to regret, but she didn't. Instead, she just cut straight to agreeing to help.

'Okay, I will. You know, he's lucky to have you.'

I wasn't sure that was true. I'd betrayed him by sleeping with Vincent, and I'd regretted it every moment since.

I hugged her again. 'Thank you. I can't believe I'm about to say this, but in a way, I'm glad this happened. I understand so much more now. I just hope it's not too late to make everything all right again.'

'It's not,' she said, with more confidence than I felt. I was about to reply when a ringing phone interrupted my thoughts. 'I think that's yours,' Jess said.

I scrambled in my pocket, found it, checked the screen. 'Unknown number.'

'It might be Colm. If his battery has run out he might be using a different phone.'

She was right, but I couldn't help a twinge of irritation over the reason that she knew he hadn't charged his phone last night. I was going to accept this, but I didn't say it was going to be easy.

'Hello?'

'Shauna, it's your mother.' I was struck by how unlike my mother it sounded.

'It's your dad. He's in hospital. Hammersmith. You have to come now.'

'But Mum, what's…'

'Just come now, Shauna.'

The line went dead.

40

2009

Saying Goodbye

I pressed the doorbell, and there was a loud buzz from somewhere deep inside the house. I heard a woman's voice. 'It's okay, I'll get it. I'm going now anyway... Oh.'

The last word was a sneer, delivered without hesitation or embarrassment as Carole and I came face to her perfect face. Bugger. I hadn't expected her to be there.

'Seriously?' she asked, a question that I had no idea how to answer, given that I had no knowledge of the reference point.

'Hi Carole,' I grinned, and threw in a cute wave. That seemed to annoy her more.

'Urgh,' she uttered, strutting past me and down the path.

I waited, not sure whether it was okay to enter or not. This was the first time I'd been back since that night, and I wasn't sure of the boundaries until Vincent ambled down the hallway, in nothing more than a pair of jeans, surprise registering in his expression when he saw me.

'Hi. Is everything okay?'

Yes. No. Absolutely. Where to start? I answered with a shrug and a weak, 'Yeah, I just wanted to… talk to you. Just for a moment. If you're not busy.'

More puzzlement from the incredible-looking man in the jeans and naked torso. The sudden thought that Annie would love this view made me smile.

'What's funny?' Vincent asked, his smile now mirroring mine.

I giggled. 'I just had the sudden thought of how much Annie would love this sight right here.'

The laughter, like the smiles, was contagious. He opened the black gloss cupboard above the sink and took out two mugs, slotting them both into position on his high-tech, NASA-standard coffee maker, and pressing a few buttons. In seconds, the machine began to expel two streams of steaming liquid into the cups.

He looked over in my direction and the glance became a stare, 'Why are your knees dirty?'

'Oh.' I hadn't even realised that they were. White jeans probably weren't the best choice for kneeling on grass.

'I was at the cemetery. Went to talk to my gran.'

He responded with a soft smile, a memory of a special woman shared.

When the coffee was done, Vincent lifted them both and handed one over. 'Want to sit outside or inside?' he asked.

'Outside.' Inside felt claustrophobic, what with Vincent, me and the ever-present guilt that came with us.

'Good call.'

It was still warm, the unseasonably warm October sun beating down on us as we sat on the loungers side on, so we were facing each other.

'Carole looked pleased to see me,' I said breezily, making him splutter his coffee.

It took him a few seconds to recover. 'Yeah, she's hoping you'll be very best friends,' he said, carrying on the joke.

I took a sip of the Columbian roast, felt my stomach lurch a little, and wondered if that was a hint that perhaps coffee would be an issue in the next few months.

I put the mug down on the table that sat between the top ends of the loungers. 'So is it all back on then?'

Vincent made that face he always did when he was deliberating. 'I don't know. She's moving to New York, wants me to go with her, says we'll have a better chance over there without "that bloody woman" everywhere.'

'I'm "that bloody woman"?'

'Yep. Don't take it personally,' he grinned. 'Anyway, obviously moving to the US isn't feasible, so it's a moot point.'

'Would you want to go? If it wasn't for the business?'

I expected a firm 'no', but he hesitated. 'Honestly? I don't know, Shauna. Look, I know we agreed not to talk about...' he pondered the right words, '...*what happened*... but if we're going to discuss this we need to lift the ban.'

I didn't like to say that we were about to completely blow the ban to smithereens once we got on to talking about the reason I'd come here, so I just nodded.

'Ban lifted,' I agreed.

'Okay, so…' Suddenly he was floundering, his whole demeanour going from cocky and funny to deflated. 'I don't know if I can be happy here any more. How can I move on and love anyone else when I'm seeing you every day? You'll never leave Colm, Shauna. I accept that. I really hoped you would, even after we were together, but I knew I was wasting my time. Going to New York makes sense on many levels. It would give Carole and me a chance to see if we could make it work. It would be a new start, a new city, a place where every damn thing didn't remind me of you.'

His stream of consciousness ended there, and took a moment to adjust to a different viewpoint. 'But obviously we have the business here, and we've worked so hard to make it a success. If I left now it would leave you totally in the lurch and I wouldn't do that to you, especially when you and Colm are still struggling financially.'

I realized that I hadn't thought about our overdraft or the implications of the latest development on our finances. Money no longer seemed to matter quite as much.

A bird landed on the ground at the end of the lounger and hung around, eavesdropping.

'I think you should go,' I said, my gaze meeting his as his brow furrowed.

'You do?'

'Yes. I think Carole's right. Please don't tell her that. But I think you need to see if a new environment changes things. You might discover after a week that you didn't love me at all and I was just a habit. Like smoking. Or vodka shots.'

And, I added silently, that would make what I came here to tell you so much easier.

He feigned pensive thought, then nodded. 'You could be right. It took me a while to realize vodka shots were not the route to happiness.'

'Vince,' I said, serious again, 'please go.'

'Why are you so insistent?'

It had to be now. 'Because I'm pregnant.'

The jokes, the conversation, the world, changed. His head reeled back liked he'd been slapped.

'You're… is it mine?'

I'd known he would ask. Of course he would. And it broke my heart that there was a tiny hint of hope in his question.

'No,' I whispered. 'I'm sorry, but it's not. I'm only about two months gone.' It was October now. We'd been together in May, five months ago. There was no question. 'It's Colm's baby.'

He closed his eyes for a long moment before he went on. 'I hope he realizes how lucky he is to get this life, Shauna. You, a baby… that's an amazing future right there.'

He leaned over, gently slipped his hand on to my neck and then leaned over and kissed me lightly on the lips.

'Congratulations, honey. I'm so glad you got your wish.'

I knew he meant every word. Just as I meant every word later, when I told him I loved him and walked away, knowing that I'd never see him again.

I did love him. As a friend, a partner, a person.

But I was in love with Colm and our child. Our child. Mine and his.

In a perfect world, Vincent would have different feelings and we'd have been able to carry on working together, seeing each other every day, rubbing along as we built our company – but you couldn't have everything and I'd take what I'd just been given over everything else. A proper family.

I was choosing a new life… and that meant knowing when it was the right time to say goodbye.

41

2016

The Hospital

Less than half an hour after I'd left Jess's house, I burst through the doors of Hammersmith Hospital's A&E department and saw my mother, directly ahead, sitting alone in the midst of a pile-up of cuts, bruises, wounds and wails. Despite the chaos, she sat ramrod straight, staring forward, ignoring the human suffering around her. Her stoic isolation was almost pitiful.

I dashed across the room, but when I got to her side realized I didn't know what to do. We'd never been a 'hugging' family. We didn't do sharing of emotion or demonstrations of affection. I'd never seen her stricken like this, and I had no idea of how to respond. After a hesitation, I sat down beside her and put my hand on her arm. 'Mum, what happened? Is he okay? What's going on?'

It was just a little movement at first, a slight undulation, then it became a steady pendulum of pain as she rocked backwards and forwards, no tears, no wails. I could see a man in the next row watching us with interest – this middle-aged woman, perfectly groomed with her blonde bob, pink jeans and chic leather jacket, looking woefully out of place in this setting. Beside her, an exhausted companion, all dressed in black, displaying confusion and awkward body language.

She finally answered my question.

'They're working on him now. They say it was a heart attack. Unresponsive in the ambulance. No way of knowing how he'll be.'

Still staring forward, no emotion, just backwards, forwards, backwards. I'd never seen her upset before, so close to dissolving that pristine, impenetrable façade.

'Mum, it's okay,' I told her. 'He's going to be fine.' Of course he was. My dad was what? Sixty-four years old? Sixty-five? It was a sad indictment of our relationship that I couldn't recall his age. He was still a fit, healthy strong man. This must be a pulled muscle. A faint. Something simple. Not a heart attack. No way.

'What was he doing when it happened? Was he on the golf course?'

She turned to look at me, her expression very strange, like I should already know or like it was obvious. At least she'd stopped rocking. I felt a pang of regret. Or perhaps it was resolve. After this was all over, I really had to talk to her and my father, find out what was happening in their lives. I don't think we'd had any more that a four-sentence conversation in the last ten years.

I realized she'd answered me, but it was a whisper that I didn't quite catch.

'What was that?'

'He was with his girlfriend,' she said, perfectly calmly. Oh God. This couldn't be good. Lulu had told me years ago that our parents were no longer sharing partners, but that must have changed again. Bugger, Lulu's mum must be traumatized. I really hoped that when it happened they weren't in the middle of having... urgh, I couldn't finish the thought.

'So where's Gwen now?' I asked.

My mother stared back blankly. Damn, she was totally altered by this.

'Gwen? Gwen isn't here.'

'But you said...'

'I know what I said,' she snapped. 'He was with his *girlfriend*. She's over there.'

Oh for Christ's sake. Not only did she have to deal with my dad being ill, but his bloody girlfriend was here too. I looked around for Gwen. Lulu would go crazy at her mum for this and I had a good mind to tell her to piss off.

'Gwen? Where is she?'

My mother flinched, then a sad smile. 'Not Gwen. That seems like so long ago.' Her tone suddenly hardened. 'Her replacement.'

Well this was news.

Slowly, perplexed, my head turned in the direction of her stare and there was... no.

No way. This couldn't be right. On unsteady legs, I got up, crossed the room to where she was sitting, on her own in the corner, bent forward, her arms around her stomach as if she was hugging herself. I hadn't even noticed her before. Now, she looked up at me, eyes pleading, apologetic, scared.

'Rosie?' A question, born out of incomprehension. Then realization. 'You're my dad's girlfriend?'

'Shauna, I'm so sorry, please…' Begging now. I tried to sit, but it was more of a fall into the seat beside her.

'Oh dear God. I don't believe this. You're seeing my dad.' No longer a question. An accusation. A pissed off, outraged, furious accusation. 'Since when?'

'About fifteen years ago.'

If she'd revealed she was shagging Brad Pitt I wouldn't have been any more shocked than I was now.

'It was at their anniversary party. Their twenty-fifth. You were there with Colm.'

I flicked through the memories in my mind, turning back time.

'But I saw him with Gwen that night.'

She nodded. 'We got talking later, and that grew into… something.'

No. This didn't make sense. It just didn't. Another flashback. Rosie and my dad dancing, a crowd around them, her flushed face as she rejoined us. That was the start of something that had lasted fifteen years? I tried again to understand.

'But, Rosie, all the guys you've met since then? You so wanted things to work out with them.'

She sighed, sadness enveloping her like a thick cloud.

'I did. Jeff said…'

My mind interrupted with a scream. Jeff? *Jeff?* Not bloody Jeff. My dad. MY DAD! The thought didn't make it out of my mouth.

'…that he would never leave Debbie.'

My mum. MY FRIGGING MUM! Again, my objection was only on the inside.

'So I went out with other guys. Jeff wanted it that way, didn't want me to be sitting at home waiting for him. So I didn't. And every time I met someone I wanted it to be the one who would make me want to change this, the one that I'd love more that Jeff. I tried so hard to make that happen, but it never did. I always loved him more,' she whispered.

Another memory raised its head. Jack, at Rosie's party, telling us he thought she was seeing someone else. He'd been right and we'd dismissed that theory out of hand. He'd sensed it, while we'd remained absolutely clueless. Fools. Fucking fools. How had we missed it?

'I'm sorry, Shauna, but I couldn't tell you.'

I understood that. How did you even start that conversation? 'Hey chum, we've been best mates forever, but guess what? I'm shagging your dad.'

This was surreal. It felt like I had been transported to a parallel universe or the set of a TV show, anywhere other than my own life. How should I react to this? What was the accepted response? I plunged to the depths of my emotional reservoir and came up with…. Nothing. Numb confusion.

All these years of friendship, based on a lie. We'd shared every aspect of our lives, lived like sisters, and all the while I'd no idea there were shades of incest going on.

My father. Rosie. This wasn't some cute Michael Douglas/ Catherine Zeta-Jones twenty-five-year age difference love match. This was my dad and my best bloody friend.

'Do you hate me?' she asked.

'I'm not sure I know how to feel. My relationship with my

dad has always been... complicated.' A bitter laugh escaped this time. 'Who am I kidding? It wasn't complicated, it was non-existent. There was no love there, Rosie. Not like a normal mum and dad. Sometimes I think that the only good thing to come out of my relationship with them was that their indifference made me tough, independent. I'm not sure I could have coped with everything that's happened to us if I wasn't as strong.'

She didn't respond, let me ramble on until I wasn't sure if I was talking to her or myself. I took it back to her.

'But that's what I don't get, Rosie. All these years you've listened to me talk about him, you've watched how he treated me, saw what that did, and yet you were screwing him?'

That was the betrayal, right there. He'd hurt me. Ignored me. Made me feel that I didn't matter. And she'd rewarded him for treating me that way by loving him? Sleeping with him? How could she do that?

Nausea overwhelmed me and I fought it back until I could speak again.

'I just can't believe I didn't see it. Does my mum know how long it's been going on?'

'Yes.'

Bloody hell. 'She's always known?'

Rosie shook her head. 'Not right at the start. Back then she was in a thing with Lulu's dad. Now there's someone else. Her personal trainer.' My mum and Lulu's dad. So it had been a full-scale wife swap situation. Lulu and I hadn't sussed that one.

'Welcome to my family, people,' I said, utterly depressed by the thought. 'I'll never understand why they stay together.'

Rosie's whole face crumpled. 'Jeff says they love each other. They just don't consider sex to be part of that. He loves me too, but there's a loyalty to Debbie that he won't break. They'll never separate; never break up the lives they've built. I don't understand it either, but I've learned to accept it.'

'So you're going to go through the rest of your life waiting for him? Always being second choice? Being on your own while they're pissing off to Marbella every second month?'

'It won't always...'

'Of course it will! Rosie, how could you think... what?'

I realized that she was no longer looking at me. She was staring at my mum, or rather, at the doctor in the white coat, who was now speaking to her. The doctor put out his hand to help my mum stand and she did as she was beckoned.

I stood too, went to follow, Rosie stayed put.

'I'll wait here. Can you tell me how he is?'

My anger was tempered by the almost palpable anguish that seeped from her. How could she have been so foolish? So blind? So secretive? Yet if I pushed aside the fact that he was my father, she was just one of my closest friends, utterly devastated because the person she loved was ill.

Pity made me agree to her request, before I followed the doctor and my mum through a door that required an entry code, then into a side room. There were two small sofas, sitting at right angles, a small white plastic coffee table in front of them with a jar of cut peonies. My dad's favourite flower. I don't know how I knew that.

He spoke to me first. 'I'm Dr Wilson.'

'Shauna,' I replied. 'Jeff's daughter.'

I had to spit out the words. Daughter? The man didn't know the first thing about being a father. He was a conniving, odious manipulator who had cheated me out of a proper family and cheated Rosie out of fifteen years of her life. How would I ever come to terms with that? How could I ever start to move past it?

The doctor's voice brought me back to the moment.

'Shauna. Mrs Williams,' he said, his attention back on my mum. 'We brought your husband in and it was clear there had been a cardiac event. We attempted to resuscitate him but I'm afraid we were unsuccessful. Mr Williams passed away ten minutes ago. I'm so very sorry for your loss.'

I had no idea if I'd ever have forgiven him – but now I wasn't going to have the opportunity to find out.

42

2010

Another Hospital, Another Time

I paced. Paced some more. Paced again. Fuck, how much pacing did a guy need to do? The hospital corridor stank of disinfectant and panic, the latter being all mine.

I'd tried to stay inside the delivery room but Shauna was screaming, in so much pain, and I couldn't do it. I was there, back there, all those years ago, with Jess, and the screams were attacking me, ripping me apart.

I should have told Shauna about Daisy, the perfect, beautiful baby Jess and I lost. Of course I should have. But how? When? At what point do you say my wife and I split up because we lost our child and I couldn't handle my wife's grief, couldn't be there for her, and the resentment between us grew until it suffocated our love? I could never pinpoint the right moment, so instead I just erased it from my history. The truth was I couldn't tell anyone else because I was too busy lying to myself. Blocking it out. Today, I couldn't lie.

It was confronting me, right in my eyeline, front and centre in my world.

I couldn't do it. Every time Shauna screamed, I was back there, excited, hopeful, with absolutely no idea that everything was about to implode. Jess and I had held Daisy for hours, this perfect, peaceful, beautiful little girl who'd never had the strength to take a breath. I'd told her everything about our hopes and dreams and the life we'd so wanted to have with her. And then we said goodbye.

The last time, I lost my daughter and my wife and I couldn't deal with the possibility of that happening again with Shauna. So yes, I'd tried to avoid the subject of having kids, tried to delay it in the hope that she'd change her mind or it just wouldn't happen. The irony was that doing that to her nearly broke us anyway, yet I still couldn't tell her. Couldn't reopen the box that kept that nightmare contained.

But now I was reliving it, watching Shauna lying in that bed, in so much agony, no idea what was ahead, knowing the worst that could happen and I could lose everything again.

'Colm, go for a walk,' Shauna said, between gasps. 'Babe, I love you, but I can't look at that face any more. You look like it's you who's in pain.' From her amused, sympathetic grin, I could see she thought I was just being typically me. Hopeless in emotional situations. Crap at dealing with drama. Switching off from anything resembling pain or suffering.

I did all of those things. It was who I was, but only because I knew just how bad it could be. So I left, went out into the corridor and I paced. One hour. Two hours. Every step anther stab of torment, of sheer terror that on the other side of that door, my whole world could be about to come crashing down.

'Mr O'Flynn,' the nurse said, her head popping out the door. 'It's almost time.'

She looked at me expectantly, but my legs wouldn't move, my feet rooted to the spot.

'Mr O'Flynn?'

I had to go, had to move, couldn't miss this moment. I had to be with Shauna and if the worst happened…

'Colm! Get. In. Here.' Shauna was gasping, panting, yelling through gritted teeth.

I moved, one foot in front of the other, steady does it, keep going.

'Right, Shauna,' the midwife said, 'let's meet your baby.'

No. Panic took a sledgehammer to my chest. I wasn't ready for this.

The midwife was still speaking to Shauna. 'I want you to push when I say. Okay?'

Shauna nodded, her blonde curls soaked, stuck to her pale, waxen skin. She'd never looked more beautiful. I stayed by her head, the view of what was happening at the other end blocked by her knees and gown. Her hand gripped mine, my knuckles cracking under the pressure. Even my frigging joints were spineless.

'All right, Shauna, here we go. Now… push.'

The roar was deafening, blood-curdling, excruciating.

And then… nothing. Silence. Oh fuck. Not again. Not again. Not again.

The loop of thought was suddenly pierced by another wail, and there she was, full of life, being lifted towards us, placed on Shauna's chest, skin on skin, still attached to her mama, arms and legs trembling as they felt the rush of air in her new world. A nurse quickly covered her with a blanket and she was quiet again, at peace, contented.

She breathed. One tiny breath after another. Every rise and fall of her chest making my heart thunder with the joy I couldn't even describe.

'Hey, little one,' Shauna whispered, tears coursing down her face. 'I'm your mum. And this is your daddy. He's a bit of a weakling around hospitals, but you'll love him.'

Laughter mingled with the tears as I leaned over and stroked my daughter's face. 'I have good points too, beautiful girl,' I told her. 'I'm great on a skateboard. I'll be a pushover if you want anything. Anything at all.'

Anything. Because this time my girl had made it and I'd never stop being grateful.

Shauna's smile couldn't have been wider.

'She's perfect,' I murmured. 'Thank you.' I had to clear the blockage in my throat before I continued. 'You know what this means? You're down the list. She's number one in our house now.'

'I think I can handle that.'

I knew she could. How many times had she told me that she could only be with a man who loved his child more than anything else in the world? She wanted to give our daughter the father she never had. Break the cycle.

I wouldn't let her down. For the rest of my life I'd love and protect her, make her laugh and shoot any boyfriends that came to the door. I was going to stand by her side every day and never, ever leave her.

Shauna was gently stroking our daughter's face, mesmerized by every line and curve. 'What are we going to call her then?'

I'd refused to discuss it before now. I told her it was superstition, but I knew it was fear.

'I don't know,' I said truthfully. 'Any ideas?'

She carried on stroking that perfect face. 'Tomorrow is Annie's birthday.'

'There could never be another Annie, m'darlin.'

'I know. But Annie's full name was Bethany. How about… Beth?'

'Beth,' I repeated, realizing immediately that it felt right. 'Okay, Beth,' I spoke to my daughter. 'How do you like the sound of that? I'll take silence as a yes.'

She didn't make a sound.

43

2016

Going Back

It was dark by the time the cab pulled up at the house. I could see a dim light radiating from the side of the building, so that meant Shauna was in the kitchen. If I thought there was any chance he wouldn't have called the police, I'd have ignored the taxi driver's cheery, 'There you go, mate,' and just sat there, eyes straight forward, killing an hour, maybe two, before I had to go in there.

I had to tell her.

This morning, Jess had begged me not to, listed all the reasons I shouldn't do it. It would wreck our lives. It would destroy Beth's childhood. Affect the boys. Devastate Shauna. Snatch away any shred of happiness that we would have from now until…

As always, I didn't finish that thought. Maybe acceptance of this illness would come soon, but it wasn't here yet so I wasn't going to let it eat into my life even a day sooner than it had to. Shauna couldn't understand that, but it was honestly how I felt. I'd read more on brain tumours than I ever wanted to know. Yes, I was looking at a high probability of a year, maybe two, but that wasn't a fixed sentence. It came with exceptions. 'Statistic outliers' they call them. People who survive longer than the odds, for no specific reason. They just do. Right now, I was feeling fine, so I was going to trust that I was a statistic outlier until something or someone told me otherwise. I was going to believe that I'd live to see my girl sing in ten Christmas shows, finish primary school, high school, get married…

A huge mass formed in my throat. I wouldn't give up on the future. Fuck this disease.

But I couldn't focus on staying positive and willing myself to live if I was drowning in guilt.

Jess was probably right. I should wipe it from the memory and move on.

But I couldn't.

I couldn't look Shauna in the face, kiss her, make love to her, and know that I'd been with someone else. My phone had been out of charge all day. That's what happened when you stormed out of a house without packing a charger. It was probably just as well, because I'd thought about phoning her a dozen times. Coward's way out, I know. Now I was going to have to man up and confess everything, and watch her face as I obliterated our entire lives.

It was a familiar mantra, but fuck, I was an idiot.

I wasn't even sure what I was hoping to achieve. Her forgiveness? What were the chances of that? And if she did find a way to forgive me, would it be because of the tumour?

We couldn't live like that. The only thing worse than her leaving me would be her staying with me out of pity.

What the fuck had I done?

I just had to hope that she could find a way to love me after this. I couldn't lose her. For whatever time we still had, whether it was one year or ten, I needed her to be with me – not because she felt sorry for me, but because she loved me enough to overcome it.

'Mate?' The taxi driver was getting restless.

'Sorry,' I blustered, thrusting forty quid towards him. It was probably his biggest tip of the day, but I wasn't above buying karma anywhere I could.

I walked slowly up the path. Dead man walking. In more ways than one. It was after 9 p.m, so Beth would be in bed. I desperately wanted to see her, but at least this way there would be no distractions, no little face running towards me, her life about to be decimated by the fact that daddy had been a cheating bastard. I'd open that door, Shauna would be there, I'd tell her.

Suddenly I was back in the doctor's office, waiting for the next conversation, one that I knew had the potential to change my life. That one hadn't gone well. I had no reason to think this would be any different.

The cold metal of the door handle stuck to the palm of my hand as I paused, took a breath, then pushed it open.

'Hey, m'darlin, how...'

I stopped.

I'd expected her to be bustling around the kitchen, cooking or cleaning. Or perhaps sitting at the table, doing paperwork with a huge mug of coffee by her side.

Instead, she was curled up in the armchair in the corner of the room, her chin resting on the knees that were pulled up against her chest, her skin pale, her eyes red-rimmed and swollen.

She knew.

Shit, she knew.

How had she found out? That didn't even matter.

She knew.

'Shauna?' I dropped my bag, crossed the room in two strides and then I was on my knees in front of her.

'Shauna, I'm so...'

'My dad died,' she whispered.

44

2016

No Going Back

Icould see it in his face the second he opened the door. He was going to tell me.

Goddamn his inherent honesty and screwed up integrity.

I couldn't decide if he was the bravest or the most foolish man I'd ever met. Probably both.

And yet I understood how he was feeling. I'd wrestled with telling him about Vincent for a long time after it happened. A few times, the words had almost spilled out, but I'd stopped them just in time, desperate to give us a chance to make it work. That doubt ended the moment I discovered I was pregnant.

I wasn't going to rob my child of her father because of my mistake. If that meant I lived with the guilt, then that was what I'd do, because she mattered so much more than I did. My child deserved to be with the father who I knew would adore her every day of her life.

Colm and I loved each other, and we could make an incredible home for her, create the family I'd never had. I had no right to take that away from her.

So I never told him, and honestly? I never regretted that for a single moment.

Maybe that made me a terrible person, but I would rather live with the consequences of my choice, than blow up my family by doing what other people would consider to be the right thing.

I still believed it was for the best. It hadn't tainted our marriage and it hadn't complicated Vincent's life either. The last I heard, he'd married Carole, they were living in New York and happy. It may have taken a twisting path, but he'd found his love.

And so had I.

It was Colm who was on his knees in front of me now, his arms around me, holding me while I sobbed. Not for the father I had lost, because the truth was I'd never really had one. I cried for the dad my daughter could lose. The man I could lose.

I couldn't let that happen. At least, not before his illness took that out of our hands.

I wanted every day from now until then to be as perfect as it could be. If he told me, yes, of course, I'd forgive him, but it would always be there, a wedge between us. I knew him. He thought it would ease his guilt but it wouldn't erase it completely, and he'd always wonder whether I stayed because I loved him or because he was dying.

The doubt and regret would drown our days and shadow our nights.

'Shhhhh,' he soothed me, stroking my hair. Only when my shoulders stopped shaking and my trembling hands were still did he ease back from me, take Beth's blanket from the back of the chair and wrap it around me.

He stayed on the floor, his face so earnest that I wanted to reach down, caress his cheek.

'I'm so sorry, Shauna. What happened?'

'He had a heart attack. He was with Rosie.'

I saw the confusion, then he went with the most obvious conclusion. 'He was at the café?'

I shook my head. 'No. He was…' My lungs ran out of breath and I had to pause to refuel them. 'He was having an affair with Rosie – has been for as long as we've been together.'

His initial reaction, like mine, was overwhelming disbelief. 'What? No. No way. Rosie wouldn't.'

'She did.'

'Shit.'

'They were together this afternoon when he collapsed. She phoned an ambulance, took him to hospital, called my mother…'

'Your mother knew about Rosie?'

'She did.'

'Jesus wept. I'll never understand them.'

'I won't either,' I said. The sorrow was choking me but the irony was hard to miss.

My parents had spent their lives ignoring their indiscretions, an aspect of their behaviour that I'd always despised. Now I was choosing to do the same.

Perhaps it should make me feel more compassionate towards them, but it didn't.

They chose to ignore the infidelities for themselves, I was choosing to do it for the family I loved and the child that I cherished. If that made me a hypocrite, I'd take it.

'How do you feel about Rosie?' he asked, still astonished.

I shrugged. 'I don't know. This afternoon I was furious. Raging. How could she do that? How could she be with him and also be the friend I spoke to every day, yet those two lives were separate? But if I put the fact that he was my dad to one side, she sacrificed years of her life for a man she couldn't have. That's beyond tragic. Now I just feel... sorry for her. She's lost fifteen years on someone who wasn't worth her heart.'

I pulled the blanket tighter around me to stop the shivers. He reached over, pushed back my hair, stroked my face.

'Losing him must hurt,' he said softly. 'I know you weren't close, but he was still your dad.'

Emotional preconceptions. My father had died, so I should be grief-stricken. Colm had been told he had terminal cancer, so he should be inconsolable. Yet neither of us was playing by the rulebook. Maybe nobody ever really did.

'I'm sad that someone's life has ended,' I told him honestly. 'But I don't feel like I lost a father, because I can't mourn something I never had. Does that make sense?'

Colm nodded wordlessly, just listening, letting me talk.

'I feel... angry. I know I shouldn't, that probably makes me a heartless bitch, but I do.'

'Why?'

'Because he never pretended. Was I not even worth that? Could he not even have acted like he cared, called me up once in a while, took an interest, told me I mattered? Even if he didn't feel it, even if we both knew it was a lie, I just… I would have taken that. I would have convinced myself it meant something and I would have been able to live with it. Why couldn't he just have pretended to love me?'

There were no tears left now, just my voice, distorted by heartache. Colm knew better than to make false protestations about my father's feelings for me. He'd been around for over a decade of my life, he'd lived through my parents' disinterest in me and in Beth and there was no denying it. Still, he tried to look for explanations.

'Perhaps he didn't want to lie to you.'

'He should have.' The words were more forceful than I intended. I took a breath. 'Sometimes it's not about honesty, Colm. Sometimes loving someone, truly caring for them, is about protecting them from the truth, guarding their heart. Even if the person you're protecting them from is yourself.'

His beautiful green eyes were locked on mine now, and I saw the recognition, the understanding, the very moment of realization.

He knew. The conversation was about my father. But we were actually talking about us.

45

2016

Moving On

Fifteen years ago, I walked up the same church aisle.

Back then, the first person I saw was the gloriously indomitable Annie, in dramatic purple and a hat that resembled a frisbee, disguising her tears because she was born of a stoic generation that was disdainful about crying in public. Now she was no longer here. A hole in my heart that I knew would never heal.

I saw my parents. The woman who gave birth to me was preening, loving the attention being mother-of-the-bride brought her, while breezily overlooking the fact that she'd shown no interest whatsoever in her daughter's wedding.

Today, that thoughtless insouciance was gone, replaced by a woman whose soul was a void of loss and stony solitude. I wasn't sure she would ever feel anything again. My whole life she'd refused to share her love with me. That hadn't changed now that I was all she had left.

At my back the last time were my best friends, Lulu and Rosie in matching pastel elegance. Now I saw Lulu, sitting next to Dan, their hands entwined. On the other side of Lulu was Rosie, her face swollen and distraught, a beautiful woman who had been broken. We'd survive this. I wasn't sure how, but somehow we'd find a way to live with it.

I stepped back to the past again.

Back then, I'd walked towards Colm. My gorgeous Colm. Now, he walked beside me, his hand on my back, guiding, supporting me.

Back then, I saw flowers, and light and love. I saw promise. Commitment. Belonging. Delight. Contentment. Lust. Excitement. The realization of dreams. An incredible future.

I saw happy ever after.

Now I knew there was no such thing.

Fifteen years ago, I walked up the aisle in white.

This time, I was wearing black.

The service passed in a blur of platitudes, of empty words that proclaimed what an honourable man Jeff Williams was, a wonderful husband, a beloved father. He was none of those things.

Only when the coffin was slowly lifted and removed by the church pallbearers did a sob escape me. Not for his loss, but for the waste of a life and the pain he left behind. My mother, no matter how unfathomable their relationship, had been cast adrift without her soulmate. My friend, inconsolable, her best years wasted on a man who didn't deserve a minute of her time.

I cried for the father I never had, for the memories I'd never cherish.

I said goodbye to a man who had never loved me. Now all that mattered was keeping a man who did.

As the last of the mourners left, I placed my hand on Colm's arm.

'Can we wait a moment?' I asked.

'Of course.'

The rain was drizzling, but I didn't care. I needed to walk. I took his hand and he offered no resistance, staying by my side in silence as I wandered across the grounds, eventually settling on a bench, protected from the rain by the huge oak tree that stood over it.

We sat in silence, the first time in days that we hadn't been surrounded by people.

'Shauna, I'm sorry.'

'For what?'

'Everything.'

I turned to him, his tired eyes the windows to a heavy heart.

For a second, I wondered if he was going to tell me about Jess, but no. I'd seen it in his eyes that night. He had the courage to live with his illness and he had the courage to protect us from what happened with Jess.

Neither of us was blameless in how our lives had come to that point or this one. It was time to let go of the fighting and the resentments and the pain.

'Colm, don't.' I paused, so much to say, but no clear idea how to say it. 'I'm so sorry too. I don't know what happened to us. I think we got lost. But I don't care any more about what you've done, or what I've done, or where we went wrong or who should have done what. Nothing matters. All that matters is now. Today.'

After the longest time, he spoke, his voice low and thick with unfamiliar emotion. 'You know, since they told me I was dying, I've thought so many times that I want to be given the chance to live my life again.'

My heart stopped, terrified that this was going to be an admission of regret.

'But every time I imagine how that would be, no matter how many times I could press rewind, I realized that every time, I'd want to do it with you.'

It was all we needed. For however long was left, we had this and we had our family.

Nothing else mattered.

I stroked his hair, traced a line across his brow, down the bridge of his nose, ending with my fingertips on his lips. 'I love you, Colm O'Flynn,' I whispered. 'You're everything.'

He kissed me, his touch leaving a memory that would last until there was no more breath in either of us.

'You're more,' he said.

46

2016

Until Death Do Us Part

'Mummy, look what I can do. Look!' Beth squealed, as she glided past me, one foot on her scooter, the other sticking out to the side in a feat of balance any seven-year-old ballerina would be proud of.

'Do you think Daddy can see me?'

'I'm sure he can, darling.'

She turned the scooter around and flew past me again. 'Look, Daddy, look!' she trilled to the sky.

There was no sadness there. Just a little girl, on a scooter, gliding up and down a path in a deserted cemetery, her mum, sitting on a bench, laughing as she watched.

I pulled my coat tighter around my neck to stop the December wind biting. If Colm were here, he'd have been laughing too. Then he'd have swept Beth over his shoulder, picked up her scooter, and demanded that we all went for ice cream, even in winter.

I'd heard it said that after a loved one dies, you could forget their face, or their voice, but that hadn't happened. Colm was still so vivid, so present in our lives. He was everywhere, in everything, especially his wild, crazy, mischievous daughter.

God help us.

'Mummy, there's Auntie Lu!'

Lulu and Dan both opened their arms as she ran to them. No one who saw them could ever have guessed the turbulent path they'd travelled to get here. Somehow Colm's death had glued them back together, made Lulu realise how precious their lives were. She swore she'd never let Dan go again. I believed her.

Crouched down now, they enfolded Beth in a team hug, before Dan picked her up, swung her around. Just like Colm would have done. That made me smile again.

Lulu joined me on the bench. We'd had it placed there a few weeks after Colm died, so we could sit, just be with him.

'You remembered.'

She leant over, hugged me. 'Of course we did.'

I grinned. 'Be honest.'

'Okay, so Dan remembered,' she conceded ruefully. 'But I would have too. Just got a bit of a hangover so it's taking a while for information to process this morning.'

Of course. Rosie's party last night.

'How did it go?'

'It was quiet. She asked me to thank you for the card. We drank too much. She cried.'

I didn't respond. What was there to say? I was glad that Rosie had decided to lease out the café and go travelling for a year, pleased that she was moving on with her life. Our friendship had been wounded, but not fatally. We still talked occasionally, staying on neutral ground, trying to build a new foundation for a relationship based on truth this time.

I'd thought about going to say goodbye, but in the end I'd stayed home. There had been too many goodbyes lately.

Lulu slipped her arm through mine and rested her head on my shoulder, as we watched Dan running up and down, chasing a delighted Beth.

'So what are you doing for the rest of the day?'

'Jess and the boys are coming over for lunch.'

Today was a special day, but visits from Jess and the boys weren't an unusual event. We usually saw them every second weekend, keeping up the schedule that had bonded her boys to our lives for so long. Beth would hang on her brothers' every words, utterly devoted to them, while Jess and I would cook and chat. After the kids had gone off to bed or to do whatever it was that teenagers did online, we would sit up, talk nonsense, watch a movie, drink wine. We'd even gone to Ireland together, taken the kids to visit Colm's family and had a week of reminiscing filled with tears and laughter. It probably shouldn't have been a surprise that we were so alike, because after all, Colm had loved us both.

'Do you want to join us?' I asked Lulu.

'Depends on the hangover. But I'll pop up and say hello.'

Another lovely thing had happened over the last few months. I'd sold our home, and moved into one of the flats up above Lulu and Dan in the building they owned on Richmond Green. An uplift in the market and a decent offer had turned around the negative equity on our house, and given me enough to make a dent in the credit card bills we'd run up during Colm's last year. Work was so busy that I'd soon have them cleared. Would I have done it again, allowed us to sink into debt, indulged his desire to travel and make the most of every minute?

Without a shadow of a doubt.

'Honey, it's time to go.'

Beth responded to my call by bounding over, an exhausted Dan following behind. Standing now, I hugged him, grateful that he continued to be such a great friend.

'Mummy, the flowers. Can I do it?'

'Sure.'

Beth picked up the three sunflowers that had been beside me on the bench, and laid them on the grass in front of the granite headstone that bore her father's name. One for Colm, one for Annie, and one for Daisy, the half-sister that she'd never known.

For the millionth time, I read the words carved on the stone in front of me.

COLM O'FLYNN

1.12.73 – 1.9.16

A WONDERFUL SON, BROTHER, HUSBAND, FATHER.

LOVED UNTIL THE END OF TIME.

I smiled, my words to him unspoken.

Goodbye, my love. Happy birthday.

THE END